A CRAFT OF STARLIGHT

A Craft of Starlight

BOOK ONE

LAYLA RAZ HANSON

For you, because you persevered.

Before

It is my tenth birthday and the first day of my exile.

My uncle deposits me at a desolate cabin in the Barren Forest. The bandaged wounds across my back burn from the cold, but I keep my expression blank.

Someone will bring supplies, my uncle tells me.

Not him. He won't be back. I can see it in his eyes.

"May the Source have mercy on you," he says.

I examine these shabby walls that are my new home, so different from the manor house on the southern edge of Alos.

Then my uncle, the only family I have left, leaves with only a simple *goodbye*.

There is little else to say.

After he is gone, I kneel in the snow, the ice stinging my skin, and I make a vow.

A vow that eleven years later will result in death.

Ice

1

A SMALL *THUMP* on the porch brings me back from my dream.

My eyes open and I rise, pulling back the blankets as I go to the door. That *thump* is new, and I feel the first glimmer of intrigue that I have felt in…I am not sure how long. Perhaps the entirety of the interminable years I've spent in my exile.

I open the door. My usual pack is there, filled with food and supplies to keep me alive.

I kneel down to examine it. My magic is inept. I only had three years of training before I was sent to my exile, though most of those memories are gone. All that's left are dull remembrances of the hushed, uneasy conversations I wasn't meant to hear. No one had been able to figure out what my gifts were, what kind of Crafter I was to become – one of the stormbringers, or the wind whisperers, or even an earth-speaker, though the idea had bored me as a child. Now my blood aches for the magic so badly, I would gratefully accept any gift.

I can still feel, somehow, that the essence of the pack is different from usual. As though the giver has changed.

I hold out my hand, willing the magic to come and tell me what I don't know, but all I feel is a dull ache, a throb in my veins. I know from previous attempts that if I strain myself, that dull ache will turn into a splintering pain that feels as though my bones are shattering. I drop my hand.

Inside the pack is a soft sweater, rolled up. Balanced on top is a cloth-wrapped pastry, slightly warm.

How is that possible?

I unwrap the cloth. A light, flaky crust surrounds what looks like sugared peaches. Something tumbles from the sweater, clattering against the porch, and I bend down to pick it up.

A knife. It's small, slim, with a leather handle, and a piece of parchment wrapped around the blade. I pull it off, noticing a fine scrawl.

I like to be thrown, it says.

2

THE SNOWFALL HAS increased recently, and my thighs burn as I clamber through the snow. I trudge over to the black, gnarled tree. Despite its dead appearance, it spirals into the sky, towering above me. I pick up the blade from the snow, the ice burning my fingertips.

I have not yet managed to sink the knife into the bark, but I've sliced my hands so many times, I've lost count. Scars and dried blood litter my palms.

I return to my starting point, feeling the balance of the blade in my hand, and I pull back my arm, preparing to throw.

Blood, seeping into stone—

I throw. The blade bounces off the tree and lands in the snow. I retrieve it.

The small, delicate snap *as my sister, Zassa, crumples to the earth—*

The second throw scrapes against the trunk, barely leaving a scratch, before it tumbles to the ground.

They're gone, my uncle tells me. You did this, Luze.

Saelis stands nearby, face pinched with worry, but says nothing.

My fault.

I throw and the blade nicks my palm. I barely feel the blood trickling down my fingers as I stare at the knife: quivering where it rests, solidly embedded in the tree.

"I see you've made progress."

I freeze. Sometimes the dreams bleed into my waking life, becoming little more than hallucinations, but this voice…it sounds real. It *feels* real, like a caress against my skin.

I turn. Slowly. There is a male standing only ten yards from me.

Behind him, the dome of silver-white magic that keeps me trapped shimmers faintly. It's beautiful—a gilded cage. I hate it.

I study the male. He is fair, like Zassa was. His hair gleams golden in what little light the forest provides. He looks tidy. I'd nearly forgotten what that word meant. I stopped bathing regularly long ago, and only recently cut my hair, using the throwing knife to hack through the tresses.

It hangs down my back now, matted, bound in a dark braid.

He steps forward, and I watch the movement. "Do you remember me?" He sounds hesitant. "You would have known me as Clydon. Lord Haverly's son."

I just stare at him. Waiting.

He takes another step forward. "My father…he knew your mother. He passed away recently. My father, I mean. I suppose that means I'm Lord Haverly now." He lets out a small laugh as though the idea is ridiculous, but his smile fades all too quickly, and his face tightens.

Something stirs in my chest. "I'm sorry."

He blinks a little and suddenly he's staring at me, too.

"Your eyes," he says. "They're…"

He trails off, not bothering to finish his sentence. It triggers a dim melody of memories—the reactions I'd gotten as a child. Why my mother had tucked me away in the manor house in the southernmost part of Hatal, away from court.

"You've taught yourself well," he says, his eyes flickering over to the knife embedded in the tree. I don't look. I can't tear my gaze away from the first person I've seen in…How many years have passed now? I try to calculate it, the number of cycles, but it all blurs together.

He seems unnerved by my silence, and I can see he's struggling, deciding whether to leave or continue to attempt conversation. I realize I can't bear for him to leave. Not yet.

I step towards him. "Would you…" I hesitate, reaching up to touch my mother's necklace. "Would you like to come inside? For…for tea?"

His face breaks into a smile, and it's like seeing the sun emerge. I stare at it, feeling hungry for something I cannot name.

"Yes," he says. "I would like that very much."

3

CLYDON BEGINS TO visit every three moon cycles, though only for a few days. He sleeps on a makeshift bed I create for him, his only chance to rest before his return travel. Occasionally, he's late by a moon cycle or two, and I find myself pacing the cabin, unable to breathe or think or feel anything until he returns.

Now, we sit at the small table in the cabin, each drinking a mug of woodsbark tea, one of the only gifts of the Barren Forest. The tea is nutrient-rich, smoky in flavor, and will keep even the sickliest person alive.

"It was your uncle," Clydon says. "He had been sending lone servants to deliver the supplies. They could hardly withstand the journey with only Lower magic. One nearly died and it felt dishonorable to allow that to continue. I volunteered."

This does not surprise me. My uncle was born only minutes before my mother, losing the Crown only by his inherent maleness. Even when I was younger, I could see how our matriarchy as Crafters frustrated him. A privileged creature made to feel lesser will always turn to those he considers inferior to find his power; it does not surprise me that my uncle would instruct Lower Crafters to sacrifice themselves for what he considered a tedious job.

"Luze," Clydon says, and I look up from my mug, "your nineteenth birthday…it's soon."

I care nothing for my birthdays, even my nineteenth, which marks the day that time will begin to stand still for me, the aging process to be so slow as to be indiscernible.

He has not touched me. He has not touched me, and I do not know why.

It exhausts me, but I bathe every week now. I haul water from the creek that runs behind the cabin, filling the small tub that I drag in front of the fire. I scrub everywhere, all of the places I'd forgotten were mine. My toes and the insides of my thighs and the soft spot at the base of the skull.

Still, he does not touch me.

All I want is a hand on mine, or perhaps, if I were very lucky: arms wrapped around my body. Anything to be touched.

"Luze?" Clydon says. His hand twitches slightly, as though he is going to reach out, but he doesn't. "Are you…well?"

It is a stupid question, and he knows it. His face flushes.

We sit for another moment, and all I can think is *touch me*.

But he doesn't, and we drink our tea.

❧

Clydon carries a sword. It doesn't surprise me. All male High Crafters go through rigorous training. Aside from the Wards, they are our only defense against the Galdrion and the Strin, should either manage to invade. The idea of the enemy Althearan army and the shadow-creatures bordering our land both fill me with fear. Even alone out here, as I am, I fear for my kingdom. It's what I was born to do.

I ask him about his sword one day, and I see the surprise on his face. Female Crafters rule, lead, and hold the most powerful magic, but we do not fight.

He lets me hold the sword, and I think I glimpse a look of amusement on his face. I look like a child. I am weak, frail. Clydon's visits are the only things holding my bones together.

The sword is heavy, made of a dark blue metal that gleams even in the dim light of the Barren Forest.

"Belon metal," he tells me. "Infused with earth-magic. It's poisonous to the Strin."

It looks awkward in my hand, but I wonder what it would be like to wield such a weapon. To feel powerful.

"Can you teach me?" I ask him.

Teach me. I'm reminded of Zassa's impatience. To learn. To grow, and to change.

Someday, I'd told her. Except there was not always a some-day ahead.

Clydon looks nervous. "Teach you to—fight?"

What I am asking him is risky. If anyone found out…

There is a pause, and I know he will refuse.

"Yes," he says.

4

"Eyes *up*."

I jerk my chin up. I never knew this side of Clydon existed. Until we started training, that is.

He whacks me with the flat side of his sword, and I grit my teeth at the reverberating pain that echoes through my ribcage.

"You're weak," he says. "Why haven't you been eating?"

Because you weren't here last month, I think. He had been late, yet again. I had paced the magical boundary for days, my shoulder brushing against the immovable white light until I had finally collapsed in the snow, dragging myself back to the cabin.

I say none of this, lifting my sword in response. It's a Zashet. It's slightly shorter than a traditional blade but razor-sharp, with a clipped edge on the tip. It's made with Belon metal, a cold, gleaming blue.

Clydon lunges without warning and I lift my sword. The metal clangs and the scent of salt fills the air.

I am weak, though—Clydon is right—and I twist away, narrowly avoiding the cut of his blade.

"Wait," I gasp, as he lifts his sword again. "I need a moment to—"

He slices anyway and I barely make it in time. My sword meets his before I duck, rolling out of the way. I lay on my back, breathing heavily.

"There are no moments in battle," Clydon says. He circles me, flips the blade in his hand, clearly at-ease, and I marvel at it. "Your enemies will not allow you time to catch your breath or build your strength, Luze."

I let out something halfway between a laugh and a gasp. "What enemies, Clydon?" I sit up, shaking the snow from my hair. "I'm alone. There's no one out here but me."

He kneels down, his face inches from mine. I feel a shiver run through me that has nothing to do with the cold.

"*I'm* here," he says. He reaches out, fingertips cradling my jaw.

I go very, very still.

"Thank you," I say.

His fingers tighten on my jaw. "For what?"

For touching me. I swallow. "For being here."

And then he kisses me.

Clydon tells me that the southern kingdom has become a threat again.

The continent is split into two kingdoms. Our side, in the north—Alos—is ruled by Crafters and magic. Altheara is the mortal side, in the south.

Saelis, my tutor, had explained it to me: during the terrors of the Thousand Year War between Alos and Altheara, Altheara had developed a military known as the Galdrion. They were formidable. By the time the war ended, Alos' reluctant offer of a truce came not from mercy, but from fear. For the first time in many eons, Crafters faced a true threat. Our lands were separated by a massive wall with only a single gateway, ruled by the most ancient of magic—the kind that had a mind of its own. No one had crossed either side in over a hundred years, and only rarely were diplomatic messages traded across the lands.

"The Althearans sent a letter to our council," Clydon says. "The Althearan prince is set to ascend the throne soon. There's fear that a new ruler will bring war. Apparently, the prince wrote the letter himself and there was a certain… tone."

"A tone?" I ask. I try to hide my skepticism.

Clydon's expression flickers. "You know little of ruling, Luze. You have been away for too long. War does not always begin with the blast of cannons."

I feel my cheeks flush. He's right. What do I know?

Clydon flicks his fingers, and a small flame appears in his palm. One of his gifts, he told me. I know he can summon more, but the bubble—the boundary—evaporates almost all magic. Clydon can still summon some because he knows his magic so intimately. I, however, know nothing of mine.

Clydon clenches his hand, and when he opens it again, the flame is gone. "We have magic on our side. But unlike Altheara, we're not barbarians. We won't force females into battle. Which means our numbers are low. Too low."

"Perhaps at least allowing the Lowers to train?" I ask.

A look of distaste crosses his face. "Allow them to train alongside our nobility? What use would their magic be?"

"I have no useful magic." I keep my tone even. "And you've trained me."

"That's different," Clydon says.

I want to ask how, but I stay quiet.

"Let's not talk about this," he says, but I know what he

means and within minutes we're on the bed. It's always fast, his fingers intertwining with mine, the sound of his breath filling my ear.

After, I drink from the bottle of tonic he gives me. It prevents pregnancy; this much I know. It always makes me feel dull-witted and queasy, though. I wonder how our Healers have not invented something better, but I had only been ten when I was sent to this cabin, so my knowledge of contraceptives is hardly extensive.

"I should go," Clydon says. I watch him rise, tugging his clothes back on. Already, I can feel the ice seeping back in the absence of his touch. The heat he brings never seems to last.

He turns, giving me a long look. He never asks about the punishment that was done to me, the way my mind had been toyed with by the Healers. He never asks about the thick scars that ripple across my back either, though I've felt his eyes trace over them more than once. I can sense his pity, but he never tries to touch them, for which I am grateful. Even the slightest bit of contact fills me with a wave of revulsion. The one place I never want to be touched.

Finally, Clydon opens the door to leave. "I'll be back next month, Luze. Make sure you finish your tonic."

I nod, and then he is gone.

5

Two years later.

I pick up my Zashet, flipping it in my hand with ease. This one is newer, made from a shimmery, silver-white metal. A gift for my twenty-first birthday, from Clydon. To match my eyes, he said, though the sword doesn't glow quite as brightly.

It has been eleven years since the beginning of my exile, and for the first time, I begin to feel acceptance. This is my life now. If not for Clydon, I would have broken or perished or taken my own life, but with him, I can find contentment. I still feel the loss of my life before, and I feel the loss of my duty as heir to Alos, but I can move on. I can survive.

These are the things I try to convince myself of.

Clydon had brought me a small mirror on his last visit. I hadn't seen my own reflection since I was ten, and it had been unsettling to look into that mirror, to see how my face had thinned, to see how pale my skin had gotten. My eyes were the only thing that had been familiar. From a distance, they could be called grey, but as one stepped closer, they glowed a bright, shimmery silver. It was unnerving, even among Crafters. I envied the pale blue of Clydon's eyes.

I turn as I hear a sound at the edge of the boundary, and the corners of my mouth curve. I only smile for Clydon.

That smile fades when I see who accompanies him.

"Clydon," I say. "And…Uncle Eskar."

They dismount, leaving their horses outside the boundary. The bubble parts for them like silk, and I feel a stab of envy.

"Luzeandra," my uncle says. His gaze lands on the sword I hold, but he doesn't comment. "Shall we?" He gestures towards the cabin.

I set the Zashet aside. We go inside and sit at the small table. Clydon stares down, refusing to look at me.

"What's this about?" I ask.

A peculiar smile appears on Eskar's face. "You're free, Luzeandra. You've been pardoned by the council." He pulls a folded letter from his pocket, placing it on the table between us. I see the wax seal of the council stamped across—an official edict.

I feel a blossom of hope burst in my chest, and I try not to let it take root. "But my exile is permanent," I say. "It's only been eleven years. Surely…"

I trail off, wondering why I am arguing against my own release.

"There are extenuating circumstances," Eskar says.

Ah. I feel a flicker of distrust. "What circumstances?"

"This and that." His face gives nothing away. "Why ask questions? You're free, Luzeandra."

I glance at Clydon, but he is staring at the table. "Truly?" I ask.

"Truly." Eskar leans forward, places his palms on the table.

I stare at him, but I detect no falsehoods in his face. I reach forward, placing my hands across his. "Thank you."

He pulls his hands away. "There is, of course, the matter of the Crown."

I notice Clydon wince slightly. "What of it?" I ask.

My uncle leans back again. "I have served as the interim Crown, as I'm sure you know. Unfortunately, your lineage is rather rare, as it is. After the, ah, *incident* you caused, it's become nearly extinct. Aside from you and I."

I still. What is he suggesting?

"However, it would require many laws to change should I be the one to produce an heir," Eskar continues. "It could be done, but as you know, Crafters live by tradition, and our people would be rather scandalized by the concept of changing our laws. I find the idea of modifying all of those pesky little rule books rather tedious and boring." He yawns.

I sit back in my chair. "Stop trifling, Eskar. What is it you want of me? To become some sort of broodmare and produce an heir?"

Eskar chuckles. "Goodness. I see why Clydon enjoys you. I'm surprised eleven years in this dreaded place hasn't dampened your spirits more." He glances out the window, where snow has begun to fall. "No, Luzeandra. If you were Crown, you would certainly need to produce heirs, but there remains the question *if* you can become the Crown."

I sit up straight, my hands tightening in my lap. "You mean, not merely releasing me from my exile, but allowing me to resume my position as heir?"

He studies his hands. "Yet, the question remains: are you worthy of it, Luzeandra? We've never had a firstborn daughter guilty of murder. Certainly not one who murdered the previous Crown. Your own mother and sister, to boot."

I take a breath. "I understand I would have to re-earn the trust of our people, but—"

"No," my uncle interrupts. "You will not. Because you are not fit to rule."

My gut twists.

"However, Altheara has become a threat once more," my uncle says. "Their prince is plotting something."

My brows pinch. "How could you know such a thing?"

My uncle sighs. "Really, Luzeandra, are you so out of touch? Has Clydon told you nothing of our lands, of our enemies? If the Thousand Year War were not enough, that insipid little prince still angers over our refusal to aid them during their land's sickness. His letter to our council made that clear."

I remember this story, though only vaguely. The Althearan lands had fallen to some sort of sickness. It had killed their king—the prince's father, I presumed—though the queen survived. I had thought little of it, and I knew no other details.

My uncle snorts. "The prince's entitlement is amusing. As though an Althearan wouldn't watch a Crafter burn before their very eyes, even holding a fountain of water."

"What would the prince have to gain from war?" I ask.

"Magic. The mortals have always coveted our magic. They would like nothing more than to find a way to extract it; use it for their own purposes. Which is why you will put an end to their plans, Luzeandra."

Dread pins me to my chair. "How?" I ask.

"You will invade their kingdom," my uncle says. "You will learn their secrets—why the Galdrion are so formidable, why their kingdom has thrived despite the lack of magic. And then…you will kill their prince."

I stare at him, my stomach still roiling. I can think of nothing to say, other than, "How?"

My uncle smiles. "By marrying him."

6

I FEEL THE breath whisper across my lips, too fast, and I wonder if I will faint.

"You will marry Prince Adriel, and then you will kill him," my uncle says. "Only then may you return to Alos. When you do—if you have succeeded—I will step down. You will become Crown, as is your birthright."

There are too many questions, but the one that tumbles out is: "And how would I convince the Althearan prince to marry me?"

My uncle waves a hand. "He's already agreed. For as much as that prince was a little snot in his letter informing us of his ascension to their throne, I saw an opportunity. He would not have informed us if he did not desire something. A long-lived feud finally put to rest—it's rather poetic, isn't it? A feat of diplomacy I'm certain your mother wouldn't have been able to manage."

My fists clench, and I hide them in my lap. "And what happens once I've murdered the Althearan prince, angering their entire kingdom and inciting a war that you were attempting to avoid in the first place?"

My uncle's lips thin. "Don't be obstinate, Luzeandra. The

Althearans are already our enemies. The murder of their only heir will send the kingdom into a tailspin. It will weaken them, reinforcing our power. The information you provide upon your return will also be invaluable."

And what if I don't return? I think. There will be ample opportunities for the Althearans to kill me for any number of reasons.

I have seen through my uncle quickly, however. If I die, he will have unfettered access to the Alosian Crown. Laws do not change here, but if there is truly no other option, they will have to. Perhaps my uncle will become the first true male Crown.

And if I succeed…will he still plot to use me in some other way or get rid of me entirely?

"Why not someone else?" I ask. "Why me?"

Eskar shrugs. "I have my reasons. The most obvious of which is that you are the only Alosian with enough power for a diplomatic marriage to make sense, and the only Alosian insignificant enough that can be risked to go to such a dangerous place."

The word *insignificant* stings. "Why not merely send an assassin? Someone trained to kill?"

Eskar gestures to the shelves on the far side of the cabin, where books are stacked. They come with the packs: history, language, philosophy. Whoever was in charge of keeping alive had also decided my education was important, even if self-taught. "You must know, Luzeandra, even with your remedial studies, that the gateway between Alos and Altheara has a mind of its own. It will not allow either side to cross unless both parties agree."

His lips are thin, and I realize: he's already tried to send someone. More than one, perhaps. I find it gives me a bitter sort of satisfaction that even my uncle, as conniving as he can be, has been defeated by a wall.

"How am I expected to do this?" I ask.

"You'll travel to their kingdom, where you'll enjoy an engagement with the prince. I've granted permission for an entourage from Altheara to come get you. I would have preferred to send you to the wall with a retinue of Crafters, but the Althearan prince required his people fetch you. Rather insistent, that one."

Clydon makes a small sound. I look at him, but he doesn't meet my gaze. I turn back to my uncle. "And if I agree to this..."

"If you survive and return to Alos, then I will honor our agreement," my uncle says. "I will step down, and you will become Crown."

I want to agree. With one simple word—*yes*—I could be free of this exile.

Yet, this plan is an immoral scheme. I have no love lost for mortals. If this were a battle, I would kill without remorse, but to sneak into their lands under the guise of diplomacy...

What would my mother think of me?

"Luze," Clydon says, surprising me. "I know this feels unjust." He reaches out, clasping my hand. I glance at my uncle, wondering how he will react, but he simply watches us. "As Alosians, we've been raised to understand honor," Clydon continues. "You have to understand—the Althearans know little of such things. We cannot trust these people."

"You would have me kill someone, Clydon?" I search his face. "Not in defense of myself, not in a battle of any kind—but murder? An assassination?"

Clydon's expression is pained. "If it means keeping Alos safe, then yes."

I pull my hand away. "What if the marriage agreement wasn't a ruse? What if by marrying the prince, I can create true peace between our lands?"

I keep my eyes on my uncle. I don't want to see how Clydon reacts to my words.

My uncle looks mildly impressed. "What a surprise, Luzeandra. You would allow yourself to be stripped of your birthright, to leave the lands of your people, perhaps forever?"

I wonder why this surprises him. Is it any different than the exile I was in? But all I say is, "Yes."

"An interesting thought. And yet, I fear you would simply be used as a pawn." His eyes rake across my skull, as though he can see through it. "We all know your mind is not resistant to meddling."

I suck in a breath at the reminder of what has been done to me, the way that this imprisonment had not been my only punishment—nor the worst.

"This is the only way, Luze," Clydon says, his voice low and urgent. "This is what you were born for. To protect Alos. Your mother would have done the same."

Is he right? My mother had been unyielding and fierce, but never cruel.

"Just this one thing, Luze." Clydon's voice is soft. He reaches across the table, touching my hand again. "Just this one thing, and you won't be alone anymore. You'll be pardoned by the council. You'll be free. *We'll* be free, and Alos will be safe."

My heart feels like it's splitting in half. "Fine," I say. "I'll do it."

Clydon looks relieved. He smiles, even as he pulls his hand back.

"Excellent," my uncle says. "You should know, Luzeandra,

that the next Tide is in three moon cycles. You will need to return by then should you wish to ascend."

The Tide of Crowns…the only time for a new ruler to permanently and formally ascend, is every seven years. If I miss this one, I will have to wait for the next one—in seven years. I have not kept track of such things; why would I? Yet the timing feels too convenient, and I wonder yet again what my uncle is plotting.

My uncle pulls something from his pocket, sliding it across the table to me. A silver ring. "I'll also need you to make an Oath, of course."

I freeze. "An Oath?"

My uncle tuts. "Come now, Luzeandra. You can hardly expect I would enter such an agreement without a guarantee."

I pick up the ring, its metal warm beneath my fingers.

"This one uses fire magic," my uncle says, as if reading my thoughts. "To bind the Oath into the ring."

I glance at Clydon, wondering if he's the one who Crafted it. I have nothing left to lose, so I slide the ring onto my finger, watching as it glimmers in the light.

"Go on," my uncle says, sounding impatient.

A chill runs over my neck, but I ignore it.

"I, Luzeandra Vyzrais, firstborn daughter of the Crown of Alos, Bind myself to the following Oath." I swallow, feeling weakness seep into my blood. "I will travel to the mortal lands of Altheara, under the guise of marriage. I will court the Althearan prince, and learn all that I may of their secrets, about the Galdrion, and the Althearan kingdom. And then…I will kill the Althearan prince." As I speak, the ring burns hot before cooling once more.

"Very good," my uncle says. "I'm sure you know what happens if you don't fulfill an Oath."

"I know." My voice is thin.

My uncle stands. "I'm sure I don't need to remind you that it would be unwise to inform the Althearans of your unique situation. They believe your residence here"—he glances around the cabin—"is part of an Alosian pre-marital ritual. They've been informed of little else. I will allow you to choose what lies and truths you wish to share, but I hope you are wise, Luzeandra, or else…"

He doesn't need to finish his sentence. It is not merely morals and character on the line; my life is as risk. My gut churns. I am no spy or assassin; I have no idea how to weave a web of lies.

My uncle pulls out a timekeeper, checking it before he speaks again. "Be sure not to trifle, Luzeandra. Though you were never the frivolous one, were you? I suppose that was your sister. Such a silly, inane child."

My vision goes white, my breath catching at his words, but I am unable to sort through my warring emotions. I simply sit there, gripping my hands in my lap.

My uncle looks bored at my lack of response. "The Althearans will be here in a fortnight. I'll send servants to attend to you before they arrive." He turns to leave. "Come, Clydon."

Clydon says nothing as he gets up, turning away. I swallow hard, the pain lancing through my chest.

My uncle pauses at the threshold, and I think of all those years before, when he brought me here and left me to rot. "Goodbye, Luzeandra. May the Source have mercy on you."

I say nothing as the door closes behind them.

The ice settles in completely.

7

Alosian servants arrive the night before the Althearans are due.

Two of them are females, accompanied by a sour-looking male Crafter—one of the nobility, maybe another lord—but he refuses to step beyond the boundary, waiting with the horses at the edge.

They help me bathe, one of them working through the twisted gnarls of my hair. By the time they're done with me, I smell like flowers, my skin is raw, and I've lost more hair from my body than could ever possibly be necessary. Were these the current customs of Alos, or had I simply never gotten a chance to experience them before my exile?

They give me two satchels. One is filled with silky, expensive gowns. The other has supplies for my journey to Altheara, including a soft pair of breeches, boots, and a thick sweater.

When I awaken the next morning, I feel heavy, even as my stomach burns with anxiety.

Freedom, I remind myself. And Clydon.

I tug my nightgown off, pulling the new clothes on, before slipping on the boots. They hug my leg nearly all the way to my knee. Something pokes my foot and I pull the boot off, turning it upside down.

A small knife tumbles out. A throwing knife.

I grab the other boot, shaking it, and another knife falls out. I examine the boots more closely, noticing a small, hidden sheath on the inside—one for each blade.

Clydon. I'm sure of it. *I'll find you,* I promise him silently. *I will come back, for you.*

I yank the boots on again, sliding the knives into place. I quickly braid my hair—it now hangs down my back, long and silky—before I gather up my traveling satchel. As I do, I glance out the back window of the cabin, which is when I notice the bubble has disappeared.

Is it really—can I—

I nearly sprint to the window, pressing my hand against the glass.

It's—gone.

I want to scream and laugh and cry, all at once. Am I really…free?

Part of me doesn't believe it. I run across the room, wrenching open the door to the cabin, nearly stumbling down the steps in my haste, when I stop in my tracks. The satchel I'm carrying falls to the ground beside me.

Four males on horseback are before me.

The one in front dismounts his horse, the movement exceedingly graceful for a mortal. The others follow suit. The first male steps forward, coming to a stop a few yards away.

"Luzeandra Vyzrais?" he says, his voice clear.

I study the handsome planes of his face, the fine cheekbones, the hair that reminds me of woodsbark tea—a dark brown color, curling against the nape of his neck.

The male in front cocks his head. "Are you not Lady Vyzrais?"

I flinch at the title. *Lady Vyzrais.* I have not heard that in many, many years. I lift my chin. "I am."

Something shifts in his expression as he looks at me. "Were you not expecting us?"

I probably looked flustered, wisps of hair falling into my eyes. I can feel that my cheeks are flushed, too. I stand taller, ignoring the uneasy tension in the air. "I was expecting you. More, actually."

"Unnecessary," another male says. He's more roguish-looking than the first, with midnight-black hair. He seems the most relaxed of us all. "Four was more than enough. Though we did lose our spare horse in this gods-forsaken forest. Simulas himself would dread coming here."

I keep silent. I hardly care for their hardships, but I am surprised to hear they still honor the Old Gods. Even Simulas, God of War.

The male in front steps forward. "I'm Thysol—Thyo."

I try out the syllables silently. *Thee-o.* "You all work for the prince?"

"We do," Thysol says. "I'm Prince Adriel's Atemox. His Hunter, more specifically."

I cross my arms. "His Atemox?"

Another one of the men speaks. "The highest ranking of the Galdrion." His skin is the darkest I've ever seen, but his eyes are a light blue, like Clydon's.

So, they're all part of the Galdrion. Just my luck. I had assumed the Althearans would send advisors or attendants, which I now realize had been idiotic. They would have never survived the trek. Not with the abundance of Strin that lay deep to the south, close to the wall.

It's strange, however, to see these Althearans in the flesh. They look…refined. Not the sweaty, barbaric males I'd envisioned. Somehow, this is more unnerving.

There is a pause where no one seems to know quite what to do.

"If you're ready, we should leave," Thyo says. "We have a long journey." He gestures towards his mount. "You can ride my horse for now. It's been requested that we not delay our journey, but we'll take a detour into Hatal for supplies on our way back and acquire another mount."

Hatal, the southern province of Alos that skirts the edge of the Barren Forest, the last province before the wall; what had once been home. Clydon had spoken of it often, and all I'd wanted was to be free to go with him. The only happy years of my life were spent there in my childhood. Which, of course, means I remember none of it.

I sense an undercurrent to what Thyo has said, however, and I know these males have most likely been ordered not to visit any of the provinces unless absolutely necessary. Althearans are not welcome on our land, as we are not on theirs.

I ignore the thoughts churning in my head, striding over to Thyo. "I won't take your horse from you. I'll walk."

A stunned expression crosses his face. "Your eyes," he says.

I look away. "It's nothing."

"They glow like a shined blade," the midnight-haired man says. "That hardly seems like *nothing*."

"Demelan," Thyo says. "Enough."

Demelan mutters something under his breath that I can't decipher.

"I'll walk." My legs are strong. I'm not sure how far Hatal is—halfway to Altheara, perhaps—but I can do it.

Thyo frowns. "*I'll* walk. You'll ride. I won't have you trudging through the forest."

"I'll walk," I repeat, my tone cool. I'm not sure why I'm arguing. Why do I care if he hikes through the snow and suffers?

Thyo studies me for a moment. Up close, I can see how dark his eyes are. If mine glow with light, his are made of shadows.

"No," he says. Just like that—*no*.

I stare at him. "What do you mean, *no*? You have no authority over me."

His face is calm. "As the prince's Hunter, it's my responsibility to get you across the wall to Altheara. Preferably in good health. You'll ride."

It occurs to me that I'm feeling a foreign sensation—a rising of heat under my skin, my cheeks flushing; something that makes me want to throw a knife. Anger. Am I feeling… angry? The feeling unnerves me so much that the sensation quickly disappears.

I gesture toward his horse. "Can your mount carry two?"

"She can," Thyo says. I don't doubt it. His horse is huge. Not overly tall, but broad and muscular, with a glossy coat that shines copper.

I walk over to the side of the horse. I haven't been on one in years, but I'm sure it will come back to me. "We can ride together."

He looks surprised. "You would be comfortable with that?"

"No," I say evenly. "But it's faster this way."

The possibility of physical contact with one of these Althearans repulses me, but I keep my gaze steady.

"You're right," Thyo says. "It is faster." Still, he hesitates before stepping forward. Realizing he's going to try to assist me, I quickly hook my foot in the stirrup and pull myself into the saddle. The male with the black hair—Demelan—snorts.

Thyo casts him a look. "You and Gideon take the lead. Aslen will follow."

Demelan nods, his face serious again. He grabs the satchel I left on the ground, attaching it to his saddle.

I glance back. The fourth figure, the one I had assumed was another male, is in fact a female. The hood of her cloak falls away as she mounts, revealing rich, auburn hair. It's bound in a tight braid, rolled up and pinned at the base of her skull.

She looks strong. There's a thin scar running across her face and down her neck which tells me she's survived at least one opponent. A quiver of gold-tipped arrows is strapped to her back, and a massive bow is hooked to her saddle. Despite my own training, it shocks me to see a female with weapons, one who looks as though she knows how to use them.

Her eyes are darker than even Thyo's—I can't discern the pupil from the iris.

Her expression is cold. Unfriendly.

I turn away, feeling nothing. I am sure I hate her as much as she hates me.

Thysol mounts behind me, and though I am stiff, holding myself to the front of the saddle, I can feel his warmth.

"Ready?" he asks quietly. I nod, staring straight ahead as he picks up the reins. Demelan and Gideon ride ahead of us. The female—Aslen, Thyo called her—takes up the rear.

And we begin our journey.

8

A few hours in, and I am frozen to the bone.

I suspect my discomfort is made worse by the fact that I've been holding myself stiff for the past few hours, clinging to the front of the saddle, determined to keep a gap between me and Thyo. I suppress a sigh as I think of the long days ahead.

"Are you cold?" Thyo asks. His voice startles me. We haven't spoken since we began our journey. Up ahead, Gideon and Demelan have been talking and laughing. Their voices are quiet, though, and I've been catching only the faintest pieces of conversation. Mostly, I've been staring off into the forest, thinking of Clydon.

"No," I lie. Behind us, I can feel Aslen's silent presence. I feel her stare, too. Like a blade against my neck.

Thyo says nothing else.

It's a few hours later when I begin to notice a change in the light. The snow that coated the ground in a thick powder has faded, leaving behind only damp earth, though the air is still frigid. I notice the trees changing, too. There are leaves on these trees, and moss clings to the trunks. I stare down at the ground, seeing if I can recognize the plants littering the forest floor. There's so much *green*.

And then, suddenly, I am blinded.

There is so much brightness, everywhere, and it almost burns in its intensity. My hands fly up to my face, covering my eyes, a stabbing pain spiking through my head.

"Lady Vyzrais?" I feel Thyo pull our horse to a stop. "What's wrong?"

I'm unable to speak. The heat, the brightness, it's almost unbearable, and I swallow back bile.

I feel the horse moving beneath us again, and then the coolness of shadows once more. Slowly, I open my eyes. We're back in the forest, a few yards from the edge of the tree line.

"Are we making camp?" Demelan calls. Thyo ignores him.

I release a shaky breath. In front of me is a road, or at least some version of one. Golden light rains down. Sunlight.

Thyo speaks again. "Lady Vyzrais, if you're unwell, we can—"

"I'm fine," I snap. As if I need the pity of an Althearan.

Before he can respond, I dismount. My nerves feel frayed.

"We'll make camp here," Thyo calls to the others. I glance behind me to see him dismount. I turn away, staring at the break in the forest again. The light seems slightly softer now, a warm orange rather than a blinding gold.

Almost as if in a trance, I walk to the edge. I am still shaded by the trees, but if I reach out my arm, my hand, then...

A pale warmth filters over my skin, and this time it's less intense now that I know what to expect. A comforting bath, rather than boiling water. I take another step, allowing the light to soak over my arm, my chest, and finally...my face.

My chest tightens, almost painfully. The first sunlight I've seen in eleven years.

I open my eyes, keeping my gaze down while I continue

to adjust, and I notice a spot of color on the ground. I bend down, reaching out.

A flower.

Its petals feel like velvet, the color a bright orange, like the flower has swallowed the sun and lived to tell the tale.

"Lady Vyzrais?" I hear Demelan's voice, and I turn, standing again. He holds what looks like a blanket or perhaps a towel. "Would you like to—"

He stops talking abruptly, his eyes widening. I reach up, feeling the dampness that has trickled down my cheeks, and I quickly wipe it away.

Keep it together, I order myself. It's only been a few hours and I'm already falling apart in front of these Althearans. "What is it?" I ask, my tone cool.

Demelan clears his throat. "We'll set up a tent for you. I can show you where the creek is if you'd like to wash up before dinner."

I nod, not trusting myself to speak.

Demelan shows me where the creek is, not far from our camp but with enough distance so that I have some privacy. When I return, Demelan is attending to the horses, Gideon and Thyo are still making camp, and Aslen is inspecting one of her arrows, but I somehow feel as though she's watching everything. Watching me.

I sit as far away from the others as possible during dinner. Gideon and Demelan keep up a near constant stream of conversation, mostly jokes I don't understand. Eventually, Aslen moves closer to the fire to join them, rolling her eyes every now and then.

It surprises me when Thyo comes to sit beside me, stretching out his long legs, and I stiffen, wondering if I will be forced to make conversation. Doesn't he know I want to be left alone? But he says nothing, and after a while, I relax.

Eventually, I rise as the flames begin to dwindle. From what I've ascertained, one of them will always be awake for guard duty, and they will trade shifts.

"I think I'll retire now," I say to no one in particular. Only Thyo seems to hear me.

"We have a long journey ahead of us," he says. "Sleep well."

It sounds less like a sentiment and more like a warning.

❧

"Luze!" my mother cries. "Luze, take your sister and—"

But it is too late, and they are here.

I am yanked backwards, claws raking across my back, deep enough that they drag across the bones of my ribs, and I scream, my vision flashing white.

Zassa, Zassa, Zassa—

All I can think is: I had so much I wanted to show you.

Something slaps me across the face, hard, and I throw my hands up protectively.

"Aslen!" a voice says, and the voice is so dark and commanding I am filled with fear, something beyond the panic I am already experiencing.

Something grips my shoulders. Hands. "Luzeandra?" The hands shake me slightly. "Lady Vyzrais, wake up."

I blink open my eyes, the blurred line between nightmares and reality becoming clearer and then—

I stare into dark eyes, lit only by fading firelight. I look past, to the sky. A new moon.

I sit up slowly. Every part of my body hurts.

To my left, Gideon and Demelan are standing, looking

distinctly ruffled. Demelan has his sword drawn. Ahead of me is the fire, the embers still softly glowing. Aslen stands by it, her arms crossed. She looks furious.

Thyo is kneeling before me. Kneeling in front of where I sit in the dirt, I realize. Somehow, I'm outside of my tent.

"Luzeandra," he says, and the name sounds oddly familiar falling from his lips. "You were having a nightmare."

It all comes rushing back at once. Where I am. Who I'm with. Everything that's happened in the last day.

I can see they're all waiting for some sort of explanation, but I feel confused, shaky. Not that I have any intention of letting them see that. I sit up straighter, brushing my hair from my eyes. "It was nothing," I say curtly.

"There she goes again," Demelan says. He sheaths his sword, his face grumpy as he reaches up to rub at his eyes. "More of those *nothings*."

Thyo stands, turning to Demelan. I can't see Thyo's face, but Demelan blanches.

"We all thought you were being murdered," Aslen says. "One day of travel, one day without servants attending to your every need, and suddenly the delicate Alosian lady can't handle herself? You're not coming to Altheara to be some useless damsel. The prince doesn't need a weakling to coddle."

"*Enough,*" Thyo says.

His voice sends an uneasy shiver through me, but Aslen seems unintimidated by Thyo. She gives me one last contemptuous look before turning on her heel and striding into the dark forest. I have no idea where she's going, but I don't care.

Thyo reaches out a hand to help me up, but I yank my arm away. "I don't require your assistance." My voice is cold.

Thyo's proffered hand sends a wave of revulsion through me. I refuse to accept help from any of these Althearans.

His eyes narrow. "You should try to rest. We're leaving in a few hours, once the sun is up."

I go back into my tent, not looking at any of them. I wonder how I ended up outside of it. I assume I was dragged out. Unless I was sleepwalking. I shudder, dropping my head into my arms.

Try to rest, Thyo had said. I smile humorlessly.

And sit, staring at the walls of the tent until the sun rises.

9

THE NEXT FEW days are miserable.

They follow the same pattern as before: we ride for hours at a time, stopping for breaks and for a short lunch, before continuing on. Eventually, we find a place to make camp for the night.

My spine aches constantly, particularly in my low back, due to how stiffly I sit in the saddle, making sure I keep space between me and Thyo. After the first night—after the nightmare—I feel even more unable to relax.

"We're about a half-day's ride from Hatal," Demelan calls back to us. He points to a massive boulder on the side of the path, like it's a signpost.

"We'll make camp tonight, and plan on arriving mid-day tomorrow," Thyo says, loud enough for everyone to hear. I'm gripping the pommel of the saddle so tightly my fingers are numb, but despite the space I'm keeping between my back and Thyo's chest, I can feel the vibrations when he speaks. I find it strangely soothing, which annoys me.

"We'll have some time in Hatal," Thyo says. His voice is quieter now, and I know he's speaking only to me. "Enough to acquire a horse for you and perhaps allow you to rest. I know the travel has been long."

This is the most he's spoken to me since the first day, and I open my mouth to respond, before slowly closing it. Instead, I simply nod.

If it weren't for my Crafter senses, I wouldn't have heard it. Behind me, Thyo releases the smallest of sighs, and it nearly sounds…frustrated.

But I must be mistaken.

⚘

A few hours later, we stop when the sun is beginning to set.

I decide to go to the creek before dinner. I kneel down at the edge, splashing the cold water on my face. Just one more day, I tell myself. Then we'll be in Hatal. Even better, I'll have my own horse for the rest of the journey.

I dip my hand in the water, feeling the current rushing through my fingertips. I've felt no change the past few days, aside from the weariness and pain of our travel. Part of me hoped that as soon as I escaped my exile, magic would come rushing in and my gifts would come to claim me. But I feel no different.

I concentrate, using what little knowledge I have: still the mind, clear any emotion, feel the subtle vibration that connects you to the element, almost as though it is an added limb. I try to invite the water to form, to mold into a shape, any shape, even just a sphere. The Source has a mind of its own, but its magic can be controlled with enough focus. The less emotion, the better.

None of these things come to me easily.

"Please," I murmur, staring at the water rushing by. Nothing happens.

I stand to leave, trying to stifle the crushing disappointment, when an icy burst of wind whips the forest around me, accompanied by a bright, shimmering light.

The creek glows as thousands of droplets float above it, like diamonds have rained down to meet the water. Light prisms off the droplets, reflecting onto the trees and leaves surrounding us.

I stumble back, falling to the ground. A breeze rushes past me, scattering the droplets back into the water, and I catch a scent—a scent of pure magic, and something else. Something that smells…powerful. Potently so.

Whatever magic this is, I've never experienced it before. And I'm certain it couldn't have come from me. I feel no humming in my skin, no quickening in my veins.

"What are you doing?"

I turn, still sprawled on the ground. Aslen is standing a few yards away, her hand resting on her bow.

I'm still too stunned to come up with a good excuse. "Nothing."

"As always." Aslen goes to the creek, filling a canteen. "You might try being a bit more creative with your lies. Unless you lack the intelligence. Which, for an Alosian, wouldn't be surprising."

I push myself to my feet. "Says the Althearan who knows little more than how to torture and kill."

She grins. "And well, might I add."

I feel the disgust on my face, and I turn to leave, but she blocks my way.

"Move." My voice is ice-cold.

She cocks her head. "Or what?"

My fingers itch to reach for my throwing knives, but I do nothing.

"I thought so," she says. "Nothing more than a pretty face. Just like the rest of your kind."

I cannot retaliate. The consequences aren't worth it. And yet…

I step around her, wondering if she'll try to stop me again, but she doesn't move.

"You're unworthy of our prince," she calls after me. "Remember that this alliance is fragile—as are you."

I stiffen, even as I keep walking. Is she threatening me?

I am not sure I want to know the answer.

⁂

At dinner that night, I sit on the outskirts of the circle for dinner, pulling food from my satchel. My supply is slowly dwindling, but I quietly refuse to take food from the Althearans. At one point I look up to see Thyo watching me, his brow pinched slightly, as though trying to solve a problem. I quickly look away.

"And then," Demelan says, "I told Rolond that every *alchea* jumps off the top of Etalus, that it's tradition, and if you can believe it, he fell for it. I had to stop the fool at the top of the staircase." He dissolves into peals of laughter.

"You idiot," Aslen says, though I can see a hint of a smile on her face. "You could have killed him, and then where would you be? Shipped off to one of the isles, that's where."

Demelan looks indignant. "I'd survive any of the isles. With my irresistible charm and outstanding swordsmanship, I could start my own kingdom."

Gideon snorts but doesn't comment.

"Sure," Aslen says. "Remind me to tell that joke to Cyrian when we get back."

Demelan reaches out, poking her in the ribs, and she slaps his hand away.

I suddenly hear myself speaking. "What's Etalus?"

Silence falls over the group. I clamp my lips shut, wishing I could take the words back. I'm not sure why I spoke. I have no wish to know these people.

Demelan recovers first. "Etalus is one of the great towers of the Old Kingdom. Before the Thousand Year War. It's nothing more than a relic now."

"The tower is built into the edge of a deep river," Gideon adds. He glances at Thyo. "It isn't tradition, exactly, to jump off at the midway point once you've reached your fifth year of being *alchea*, but…"

"But somehow they all do," Thyo says. "Despite the reminders from their fellow initiates of the consequences, I'm sure."

Aslen snorts.

I clear my throat. "And the *alchea*, is that part of the Galdrion?"

"Lowest ranking," Demelan says. "Initiate."

"The word means 'equal' in the old dialect," Gideon says. "The idea being that every new recruit is full of equal potential, that you only need prove yourself."

"And that you recognize you've become both man and warrior, in equal halves," Thyo says.

"Or woman," Aslen interjects.

"Is it not that way for Alos?" Gideon asks.

I cross my arms. "No. Nobility must be born, according to our laws. You cannot ascend in position unless you're born to it."

"What happens if one of the non-nobility marries nobility? Do they inherit the title?" Demelan asks.

"One of the Lowers," I correct him. "Their magic is weaker. Relationships between High Crafters and Lowers are forbidden, to keep the magic purer. But there's only one Crown and any child born of her is an heir. Any female children, at least. Males are ineligible."

Demelan looks indignant. "That hardly seems fair. Shouldn't the title go to the firstborn child, regardless of sex? Or perhaps the worthiest, regardless of age?"

My lips press together. "The strongest magic is carried through the female bloodline."

"Still," Demelan says. "Do you have any brothers or sisters? Perhaps they think differently."

Breathe, Luze. "No," I say tightly. "I have no siblings."

"And you?" Gideon asks. "You mentioned the female bloodline carries more magic. What is yours?"

I look at the fire, my expression blank. "Crafters have access to the four elements. Water, air, flame, and earth. Most High Crafters are gifted with two elements. A few of us have been famous for having control of three elements, but it's rare."

And I will be famous for having zero, I think. I wonder if they've noticed I've managed to avoid saying anything about *my* magic.

There's a pause, and then Gideon speaks. "This talk of magic certainly beats your Etalus story, Dem." He reaches out, giving Demelan a shove, and I feel a wave of relief.

"A bit of water and rain hardly compares to Roland nearly jumping from the *top* of Etalus," Demelan says. He glances at me. "No offense."

Aslen crosses her arms. "You know, I'm sure we wouldn't mind a demonstration. Just a little show for entertainment, of course."

I stiffen, but Thyo speaks. "This isn't the time," he says.

He sounds weary, as if she's a wolf on a leash and he's unable to keep her tethered.

He and Aslen stare at each other for a moment. Demelan rubs his neck, and Gideon inspects a thread on his sleeve. Finally, Aslen looks away.

"Fine," she says. She stands. "Gideon, wake me when it's my turn to guard. And keep the fire going this time." She starts to head towards their tent a few feet away.

Which is when I hear it.

"Wait," I say, pushing myself to my feet, "there's something—"

It bursts into the far end of camp, moving incredibly fast despite its stubby little legs.

An Alosian boar. I'd heard of hunts for them as a child. They weren't exactly uncommon, but the boars tended to keep to themselves, and they loved the woodsbark native to the Barren Forest, so they weren't usually an issue closer to the provinces.

Except in situations like these.

It turns, squealing, its focus immediately on Aslen, as though sensing a worthy opponent.

Demelan and Gideon surge to their feet, and the boar stops, momentarily confused. I realize that Thyo—who reacted as quickly as I did—has drawn his sword. Aslen takes a step to where her bow is leaning against a boulder by the fire, and the boar charges. She moves with an uncanny level of speed, side-stepping the boar and rolling out of the way. It's a near miss.

And now I'm about to be trampled.

Thyo pushes me out of the way, his sword swinging at the same time, moving so fast I'm nearly blinded, but the boar lets out a hideous squeal of rage, skidding to a halt a few yards past us.

Its tusk, I realize. Thyo had managed to push us out of the way and slice off one of its tusks, faster than a mortal should be able to move. Unfortunately, the boar looks interested in returning the violence.

Aslen, who now has her bow, lets an arrow fly. Demelan and Gideon stand there, swords at the ready, but their faces are calm. Too calm. They have too much faith in Aslen.

The arrow hits the boar's flank. The arrow embeds itself deeply and the boar squeals, stumbling to the ground, clearly enraged, but it won't stay down for long. It's roughly the size of a small pony. Aslen lets another arrow fly, and it pierces the boar's shoulder, but this time it barely falters.

My handle scrabbles towards the sheath of my boot for one of my knives, but Thyo wraps an arm around my waist, pulling me back.

"Stay away," he orders. "Aslen will kill it."

I try to yank myself from his grasp. "Don't touch me, you—"

I'm not sure exactly what word I'm going to call him, but it doesn't matter, because I suddenly see the blood pouring from the boar's wound.

Everything stops.

Nausea wells in my stomach. Everything fades, becoming blurry. Suddenly, I am no longer in the forest. I am somewhere else entirely, a place haunted by screams and blood and the lifeless bodies of my mother and sister.

"Luze—take her—take Zassa and run—"

Blood. So much blood.

As if sensing weakness, the boar turns to look at me, malice glinting in its beady little eyeballs.

"Luze." Thyo is there, his tone urgent. "Luze, you need to—"

His voice sounds as though it's coming from a tunnel. He reaches out, grasping my arm.

I feel a horrible crawling sensation climbing up my skin. Perhaps it's terror.

It's eye, I think. *Someone has to stab it in the eye.*

Which is when the boar charges at me.

I hear yelling—Demelan, maybe—and I see Aslen draw her bow again, all of it seeming to happen slowly as I kneel there, paralyzed, torn between the present and the past—

And then I am pulled away, narrowly avoiding being trampled, as a knife sails past me and pierces the boar in its left eye. The beast lets out a horrific bellow, almost a scream.

And then, slowly…it falls to the ground.

Demelan lets loose a string of curses. Aslen doesn't say anything, staring at the boar with an expression I can't read.

My pulse is thundering, and it propels me to my feet. Slowly, I step to where the boar lies, unmoving. I hear someone begin to protest, but I put my hand on its belly. No heartbeat.

I want to retch, but a wave of grief crashes over me, almost making me drop to my knees again. "Go in Source, friend," I murmur, brushing my hand over its wiry fur. I close my eyes, a different vision filling my mind: in the manor house from so long ago, brushing the blonde strands of my sister's hair away from her eyes.

"An Alosian boar," I say, almost to myself. "They're native to our lands."

Aslen stalks toward me. "Are you out of your mind? What were you *thinking?*"

My lips feel numb. "I don't understand."

"You just stood there," Aslen says. "You could have died."

"Aslen—" Demelan says, stepping forward, but she waves him off.

Aslen yanks me up, and I trip slightly, my knees still weak. "Are you really that stupid and incompetent?"

My back feels sticky, and a bead of sweat is making its way down my cheek. I pull my arm away, but I don't have words. I'm not going to tell her I was caught between worlds, that I had been trapped in a memory much, much worse than this one will be.

"If Thyo hadn't stabbed it in the eye, you would be dead right now," Aslen says.

I suddenly notice Thyo hasn't said anything. He's not even looking at us; instead, he's facing the forest. His hands are clenched.

"You knew," I say to him. "How did you know?"

He turns just slightly, though his face is still in shadows. "Know what?"

I struggle for words. "One of the only ways they can be killed is through the eye. Only a Crafter would know that. How did you know?"

"Does it matter?" Aslen snaps. "Just thank whatever gods you pray to that he did. No thanks to you."

"It was charging her," Gideon says. "It happens, Aslen. We've seen what instincts can do, the way some of our own initiates freeze."

I notice my breath feels thin, as though the air can't reach my head.

"Still," Demelan says. He's watching me carefully. "Perhaps we ought to prepare you for any future incidents, Lady Vyzrais. Being untrained on this continent can be a death sentence."

"Great idea, Dem," Aslen says sarcastically. "Give the idiot Alosian a sword. She's useless. She'd probably stab herself on accident and then we'd have one more thing to take care of."

My temper, unrecognizable to me, snaps. Without

thinking, I step forward, giving her a hard shove. Her eyes widen in shock even as she stumbles, and quicker than my eyes can track, she pulls an arrow from her quiver, thrusting it under my chin.

Demelan sucks in a breath, and I freeze, feeling the sharp tip of the arrow's point cutting into my neck.

"I knew this agreement was a bad idea," Aslen says, her voice almost a hiss. "There is nothing, *nothing* some stupid Alosian twit has to offer us."

"Better a twit than a barbarian." I gasp, feeling the point cut into my skin as I speak.

Aslen twists the arrow slightly. "You—"

"*Enough.*"

We all freeze.

I can't see Thyo's face—I'm afraid to move in case Aslen truly impales me—but his voice cuts through the night. "That is enough, Aslen. Continue, and I will ban you from the Galdrion."

Silence falls over us all. I don't think I'm the only one shocked by his words.

Aslen is staring at Thyo, her expression unreadable. Gideon looks between the two of them, as if he might need to intervene. Demelan seems to be the only one watching me, a slight frown on his face.

Finally, Aslen steps away. She tosses the arrow aside, and without another word, stalks away.

I stare at the arrow, thinking about stepping on it and snapping the wooden shaft. Small white stars appear in front of me, and I try to wave them away, noticing my fingertips feel numb. I frown. I can feel something cool trailing down my neck, and I reach up. A large drop of blood moistens my finger. My vision spins.

"Lady Vyzrais," Demelan says. He steps towards me, his hand outstretched. "Are you—"

I don't hear the rest of what Demelan says, because the white stars become a black sky, and I fall into the dark.

10

I awaken in soft sheets.

I take in my surroundings. I'm in a large bed. Silks the color of fresh wheat are draped across it.

I flinch when I realize I am not alone. Thyo stands by balcony doors, his back to me. The balcony doors are thrown open, with gauzy curtains fluttering in the breeze. I can hear the faint sounds of a fountain.

I must make a sound, because he turns. "You're awake," he says.

"What happened?" My voice is hoarse.

"You collapsed after the boar attack," Thyo says. "And then you were…confused, when you came to."

I wince. *Confused* sounds like a polite placeholder for *delirious*. I don't think he's lying, either. Bits and flashes are coming back to me in pieces. I reach up, brushing my neck. I can feel a small scab there.

Thyo clears his throat. "It's understandable, of course."

I ignore his weak attempt at consolation. "Where are we?"

"Hatal," he says. "At the Star Rose Inn. We arrived early this afternoon."

Shock freezes me for a moment. We're here. In Hatal. The province of my childhood.

Slowly, I sit up. "Where are the others?"

"In another room," Thyo says. "I assumed you would prefer to be alone."

I take a deep breath. The air feels different somehow, more alive. It must be the magic within the province, so much more abundant than the Barren Forest.

There's a pause, and then: "I'm sorry," Thyo says. "Our job is to protect you. I wouldn't expect you to know how to fight off a wild boar."

I stay silent, unsure of how to respond.

Thyo sighs. "As for Aslen, she is…complicated. I hope you understand that her nature comes from a place of loyalty to her kingdom. To the Galdrion. And that loyalty will extend to you. Eventually."

I don't respond to this, either. Clearly, he's delusional. The small wound under my jaw is minor, but I'm certain Aslen had been only moments away from thrusting that arrow into my neck.

There's a brief silence, not exactly awkward, but not comfortable, either. "How long will we stay here?" I ask.

"Just for the night," he says. "The orders of your council were clear. We're not to stop unless necessary. Your kingdom distrusts Althearans, after all."

I let out a dark laugh. "I wonder why." My hand floats up to my neck pointedly. "You can hardly blame us for our caution, considering the history of your people. It seems little has changed."

He pauses. "Many unsavory acts were committed during the war. From both sides."

My voice is cold. "Is that what you would call capturing

and torturing Crafters to try to drain their magic? An 'unsavory act'?"

Thyo's voice is equally cool. "I would say that I hope you have not blindly trusted what has been written in your history books."

I don't respond, though my pulse pounds with anger.

"Demelan found a horse for you," Thyo says, breaking the tension. "So we won't have to share one any longer."

For some reason, this comment irritates me even more. "Thank you," I say frostily.

He nods. "Dinner is in an hour, if you'd like to join us downstairs. If not, I'll request something be sent up. And Luze, I'm sure I don't need to remind you that it would be to both your benefit and ours that you do not reveal you're traveling with Althearans."

Usually, mortals are smaller, weaker, and plainer, but the ones I am traveling with are strong and healthy enough that no Crafter will suspect them. Unless I say something. It would most likely get them killed.

Thyo leaves, and I rise, slowly crossing the room. I warily step onto the balcony.

The city is filled with low buildings, no more than three stories. The elegant, romantic structures hint at a province that has seen riches for a long time. Rolling hills surround the city on all sides, flowers and trees blossoming on the curves. In the distance I see mountains.

In front of me is a large square. In the center is a massive sculpture of a tree, its glass branches twisting into the sky like spires. I shudder. It reminds me too much of the trees of the Barren Forest. I quickly look away.

There seems to be some sort of market in the square. There are stalls for everything: exotic fruits, delicate glass sculptures, fresh breads, even a marketeer selling hundreds of spices. I catch a whiff of lemon, anise, fennel, pollen…

It's slightly chaotic, filled with Crafters perusing the items of the market, haggling with vendors, tugging their children out of the way. Cacophonies of voices and laughter roll over one another, and I feel a small twist of anxiety. I haven't been around this many people in so long.

Most males are wearing simple pants and boots. Almost none have a jacket cinched over their shirt; it's too hot here. They wear bold shades, however: rich bronze, deep red, midnight blue. The females wear colors that are just as vibrant: amethyst, bright orange, crimson. Some wear veils, a sign of being married or joined with another, though the custom is usually only seen in Hatal, where such traditions still exist.

So much color. I'd forgotten that.

Someone glances up at the balcony, and I step away into the shadows, my nerves frayed.

I can't help but wonder if Clydon might be here. Thyo had said the council had granted the Althearans permission to stop in Hatal; surely Clydon knows this. Perhaps even now he is nearby, waiting for the chance to find me. If I could just see him one last time…

I think about Thyo's offer for me to join dinner. The idea fills me with trepidation; it would be easier for me to eat in my rooms, alone. Yet…my job is to gather information on Altheara, and I can't do that very well if I huddle in my rooms alone. And perhaps I can use the opportunity to sneak away, to look for Clydon.

So, I steel myself and prepare to go dine with my enemies.

11

I CROSS THE room of the inn's tavern, hoping my expression is calm and confident. I'm wearing a dress I found in one of my satchels. It's modest by Crafter standards, a pale, cream-colored fabric that shimmers, but it's certainly an upgrade from my travel-worn breeches and sweater.

Demelan raises a brow as I approach their table, his expression appreciative. He stands up, playfully sweeping into a bow. "My lady," he says.

His friendliness unnerves me. He's the only one who makes me question whether or not he is my enemy.

Aslen rolls her eyes at Demelan. She stands. "I'm going to see what's taking that infernal waitress so long," she says. She brushes past me without looking.

I sit across from Thyo. He's studying me, his expression unreadable. My stomach tightens; I'm not sure if its nerves or irritation. I lift my chin. "Have I met the Hunter's strict code of conduct?"

I think Thyo's mouth twitches in what could be a smile, but it disappears just as quickly. "You'll do."

Somehow strangely relieved and yet disappointed, I resist

the urge to scowl. Gideon, who's sitting next to me, pours me a cup of wine from a pitcher, and I accept it. I take a long drink of wine, my awkwardness growing. So many people; so much noise. The tavern is full tonight, and Crafters are known for their revelry. Across the room, Aslen's bright hair catches my eye as she stands at the bar, looking annoyed.

"What rank is she?" I ask Thyo.

"Aslen is...newly promoted. And eager to prove her worth."

"Is she an Atemox?" I try to sound curious, rather than eager. "A Hunter, like you?"

I can feel Demelan and Gideon listening intently, but I keep my eyes on Thyo.

"There's only one Hunter," Thyo says. "Except in rare cases. The ranking of Atemox is someone who's ranked to Fourth Order, but the Hunter—the prince's personal Atemox—is a unique position within that Order."

"What are the rankings?" I ask.

"There are the *alchea*, our initiates," he says. "Then our First Order, *axelec*. Our thinkers. Those who may not be skilled in combat, but who excel in strategy, in military structure and organization."

"Axelec," I repeat, wishing I could write it down. I take a sip of wine, trying to appear casual. "And then Second Order, I assume?"

"Adnexas," he says. "Soldiers who excel in combat, who live to wield a weapon, but care little for how they use it; they have no interest in planning and strategy. Demelan is an excellent example."

Demelan makes a sound of indignation. "I'm an excellent strategist. I just don't see the need for it."

"True," Gideon says. "Which is why you're Third Order. If

you were really as dumb as you seem, they would've kept you in the barracks permanently."

There's a *thunk* and Gideon winces. My guess is Demelan has kicked him under the table.

A surprised laugh escapes me. "So, Third Order is…?"

"Adolex," Thyo says. "A captain. Someone with the ability to give direction. It's surprisingly difficult to find those suited to roles of leadership; they have to be someone others are willing to follow."

Demelan puffs his chest a little, looking pleased. Gideon snorts.

"But rank is rank," I say. "If a person is granted a position of leadership, surely others will abide their orders?"

"Not always," Gideon says. "Most men and women are unwilling to die for someone they can't trust to give them their best chance of survival. I'm still not sure why Thyo promoted Demelan, seeing as he's almost gotten us all killed more than once."

They all laugh, but something about this statement catches my attention. "You hold that much power in the Galdrion?" I ask Thyo. "To appoint people?"

Their smiles fade. "Not really," Thyo says. "I just happen to have a high enough ranking to offer advice. It's only rarely taken." He smiles, but it looks forced.

I study him for a moment, pondering why he's downplaying his role in the Galdrion. He looks back, his gaze steady. It's only when Gideon coughs that I realize Thyo and I are staring at each other.

I quickly take a gulp of wine. "So, tell me about this Prince Adriel. Is he handsome?"

They all freeze. I realize the wine has probably made my tongue too loose but seeing them unnerved is entertaining.

Thyo clears his throat. "Is that important?"

I lean back. "Not particularly. Though being attractive might help if he has the personality of a miserable old toad. Does he?"

Demelan chokes on his wine, spilling some onto the table. Gideon gives him a look, grabbing a cloth to mop it up.

Thyo's gaze narrows. "I wouldn't say so."

"I suppose you're not the most objective judge of such a thing," I say. "Seeing as you're his Hunter."

"He wanted to come meet you himself," Demelan says. "Though everyone warned him it was a foolhardy idea. Having the only heir to Altheara in Alos would be too great a risk, though the prince disagreed. So, I suppose you could say the prince is brave."

I raise a brow. "Except he didn't come. He sent his personal guard, instead. Not very brave, is it?"

I'm not sure why, but I look at Thyo as I say this, almost as a challenge.

"True," Gideon says. "But perhaps it's the thought that counts."

I open my mouth to ask another question, but Aslen returns. "That waitress ought to join the Galdrion," she huffs, sliding into a chair. "Every time I think I've cornered her she slips right through my fingers."

I snort a little as I try to take another sip of wine before I realize my cup is empty. Demelan leans forward, pouring more for me from the pitcher.

Aslen watches this with a frown. "How many of those have you had to drink?"

I flush defensively. "Only one."

Aslen turns to Demelan. "Are you trying to get her drunk? You do realize she hasn't eaten."

"I'm doing nothing of the sort!" Demelan protests. "It's been a long journey, Aslen. We all deserve a night of relaxation."

She leans back in her chair, crossing her arms. "Not all of us are pigs, Demelan. You could probably swallow that entire pitcher and be fine come morning. We" —she gestures between me and her—"cannot."

I'm taken aback at being grouped with her. I'm not the only one.

"Who is 'we' Aslen?" Gideon asks, looking amused.

"Women," she says. "Particularly those with their dignity intact."

"Female," I say.

They all turn to me, and I immediately wish I hadn't spoken.

"What?" Aslen says.

"Females. Not women."

They're all still staring, and I trip over my words to explain—why do I care about explaining?—the wine making my tongue feel heavy. "Crafters don't consider themselves to be mortals. It would be like calling a fish a woman."

"A fish," Aslen repeats flatly.

It's a bad example, but I don't tell them the truth: the real reason Crafters hold so much disdain for the word *woman* or *man* is because they believe themselves to be far superior to Althearans. I also don't tell them that I agree.

"You certainly *look* like a woman," Demelan says, smiling at me as he leans forward. Aslen gives him a sour look. He leans back.

I take another sip of wine.

Thankfully, the waitress arrives bearing a tray filled with food. There's a plate of soft, flaky bread and bowls of stew that smells of lentils and spices. I set my cup of wine aside and busy myself with eating. The others resume their conversation. They discuss things I have no understanding of—some place called Dolaon, and something about the upcoming exams for those graduating the Galdrion. I focus on my food instead, keeping my eyes down.

I've almost finished my bowl when there's a loud cheer from the opposite side of the room. I twist in my seat. From the looks of it, a card game has just been won. One of the participants rises. His back is to me but that fair hair, something about the way he moves…

It can't be. Can it?

I feel as though my heart has stopped, then suddenly restarted. I stand abruptly, my chair nearly toppling over. "Pardon me," I say, not bothering to look at the others' reactions. I weave past a table, ramming my hip into the corner, but I ignore the pain, my eyes still on the fair-haired man by the entrance. My heart thrums wildly. It's Clydon, I *know* it's him, and he'll be able to tell me more, to help me and reassure me and—

"You." I'm stopped by a large, hot hand gripping my arm. I look up at its owner, a broad-shouldered male. Most likely a High Crafter, if his richly embroidered jacket is anything to go by. He's handsome, in a bland sort of way. And drunk, judging by the stench on his skin.

"Yes?" I say. My eyes dart around him, trying to find Clydon in the crowd again.

The male Crafter smiles at me, though it's more of a leer. "I haven't seen you here before. Visiting from another province, are you?"

I try to pull my arm out of his grip, but he's strong, in the way all male Crafters are. I give him the politest smile I can muster, ignoring his question. "If you don't mind, I need to meet a friend," I say, glancing at the entrance. I see the briefest flash of blond hair, and my pulse quickens with joy.

The male Crafter continues as if I haven't spoken. "Come. Have a drink with me. Are you staying in rooms at the inn?" The suggestion in his voice is clear.

He cannot be serious. "No," I say. I give my arm another yank, and this time I pull free, surprising us both. "If you'll excuse me—"

I step around him, heading towards the entrance, my eyes roving the crowd once more.

"Wait," the male says from behind me, and I feel his heat a second before his hand lands on my skin. Four fingers, skimming the curve of my spine. Four fingers, tracing the scars hidden beneath the fabric of my gown. Four fingers—

Like a claw.

I move without thinking, twisting from his touch as I turn, grabbing his hand, yanking it sharply—like Clydon taught me—and pinning it behind his back. Within a second, the male is on his knees, his face contorted in pain.

"Unhand me at once!" he cries, though he's panting, most likely from the considerable discomfort he's experiencing. "I am a *lord,* and I will not be treated to such—"

"Quiet," I tell him, and strangely, he falls silent, his face blanching as he tries to peer up at me. One small move, and I could break his arm.

"*Luze,*" a voice says, and I look up. Aslen is standing only a few feet away, a dagger in her hands, slightly out of breath, like she's had to push through the crowd to get here. Thyo is right behind her—he looks like he wants to be in front of her, actually—but her body is blocking him from coming any closer.

I look down at the male Crafter on the ground. Something

sour reaches my nostrils: his scent of fear, washing over me. I release his arm and he falls to the floor, sputtering.

"It is against our laws to touch a female without her permission," I say. "You would do well to remember that. Or next time, I'll rip the hand from your arm and feed it to you."

Shockingly, I haven't made quite as big of a spectacle as one would think, probably due to the level of drunkenness in the room. Only a few people nearest to us have frozen, watching the debacle. One or two male High Crafters are standing, hands on weapons, as though considering intervening. I meet their gazes, and both hesitate.

I look down again. I feel as though I am not quite in my body. Or perhaps as though I am both in my body, and just outside of it, watching.

The male Crafter stares up at me, his mouth gaping, but I feel nothing, the numbness settling over me as I turn and walk away.

12

It's EARLY WHEN I slip out of my room the next morning. I walk down the hall quietly, wondering if any of my entourage are awake. I cringe involuntarily, thinking of the incident last night. The way I had lost control, and so visibly…

The violence that had risen within me in that moment had frightened me. After leaving the dining hall, I had escaped to my room, locking the door. No one had knocked or attempted to enter. I could only hope I wouldn't be questioned about what had happened, because I have no answers. Nothing I can tell an Althearan, at least.

Just as the sun is fully emerging, I manage to find what I'm looking for: a metalsmith shop, tucked away into one of the alleys.

The metalsmith does not seem to be an early riser, judging by the way he stumbles slightly as he opens the door.

He peers at me with half-lidded eyes. "Yes?"

I decide bluntness is in order. "I'm in need of a sword."

He snorts. He almost looks old, his forehead wrinkled as though he frowns a great deal. "My weapons are not for decoration. Perhaps you should purchase a vase if you're looking to adorn your fireplace."

I grit my teeth. "It isn't for decoration. A Zashet would be preferable. Belon metal. Do you have one?"

He looks more awake now, probably due to his irritation. "Perhaps, lady, you should check with your husband before making such requests."

I had chosen to wear a veil today—in Hatal, it's a sign of being partnered—in a meager attempt to make myself less noticeable. Unfortunately, it seems to be having the opposite effect on the metalsmith.

I try to mask my impatience. "My husband hardly cares whether or not I wield a weapon. Do you have the sword or not?"

"No," he says shortly. "And if your husband is so comfortable with his wife wielding a blade, I suggest, lady, that you seek a separation decree from court." And with that, he shuts the door in my face.

I consider pounding on the door, but instead I turn to leave. I would have felt more secure with a sword, but at least I have my throwing knives.

It's still early, but more people trickle down the street as I walk through the city. It seems to be mostly Lower Crafters and business owners. I imagine High Crafters are sleeping off the revelry of the night before. I step around a female wearing a green dress as I look for my next destination: an apothecary.

It doesn't take me long before I find one. Scents overwhelm me as I step through the doorway—lovage, feverfew, nettle, alcohol, distilling sugars. There's a female behind the counter, her hair twisted into a thick knot, but she's chatting with another patron. I walk over to one of the shelves lining the wall and scan the labels.

Azuria lexeria, for headaches. Namaris rose, for quickening the blood. Midnight Bluethorn, for unwanted fertility.

I nearly continue with my search—I'm looking for the only poison I know of, Blackvine—but the Bluethorn catches my eye. It's in a familiar blue bottle. There's a small note under the label, and I lean closer to read it:

For use in only the most necessary cases. A potent abortive tonic. Side effects include mood fluctuations, fever, nausea, and suppression of magic.

That can't be. That small blue bottle, which looks exactly like the one I've been taking for years, the one Clydon had been giving me—had he known? This is clearly not merely a contraceptive tonic; it's much more powerful.

"Looking for something?" I jump at the sound of a voice behind me. It's a female with long, honey-colored hair. Gold pencil rims her lashes.

I realize she's waiting for me to respond. "I'm not exactly sure what I'm looking for," I say. "I'm not an expert with herbs."

What I'm looking for the only poison I know of, Blackvine, but I think it would be unwise to reveal that.

"You're not considering the Bluethorn, are you?" She gestures to the bottles behind me. "Nasty stuff. I had to take it once. One of my lovers conveniently forgot to take his tonic and I was afraid the Source would finally decide to damn me." She sighs, as though it's completely normal to share such sordid tales with a stranger. "I would rather be barren than have that dull-witted male be the father of my child."

I'm amused, despite myself. "I take it he's no longer your lover?"

She smiles wickedly. "Oh, hardly. Towan's mind may be dull, but his mouth—and other parts—are not. Of course, after a month of fever and feeling rather dull-witted myself, I thought about chopping off some of those parts."

"The Bluethorn?" I ask. "It made you so ill?"

"Velinda warned me it would"—she gestures towards the shopkeeper— "but I had no idea it would suppress my magic so harshly. It's a mild poison, you see. A dose, and you'll be fine. But take it for two months or more, or in an excessive dose, to ensure effectiveness…" she shudders. "I've never felt so much like a *mortal.*"

My heart drops. "But surely, someone would need it if they had a great fear of bringing a child into this world, into less than favorable circumstances—"

"Hardly. There are tonics for males that are equally as effective. Like the one Towan was supposed to take." She scowls. "Of course, they can cause mild symptoms, so the particularly arrogant males simply decide not to take it. Never mind that a tonic such as Bluethorn turns us into weaklings. Then again, perhaps that's what they want." She shoots a sour look at the bottle on the shelf.

It must be a different tonic Clydon was giving me, I tell myself. I must be mistaken.

The female steps away, examining an amber bottle labeled *Cerdalean helaris.* She's clearly a High Crafter, judging by her gown and jewels.

"I'm Lady Ozare," I tell her, not daring to use my real name. "From the north."

She looks up from the bottle. "I'm Maeven. Maeven Haverly, but you needn't bother with any 'Lady Haverly' nonsense." She rolls her eyes. "The rules of court are such a bore, don't you think?"

For this to have practically fallen into my lap…. "Haverly? A relation to Lord Clydon Haverly?"

Her eyes light up. "You know Clydon?"

"Distantly," I lie. "I met him once at court. In the capital. He mentioned he visits Hatal frequently?"

"Oh, yes," she says. "In fact, he lives here. He journeys to Almaru for court matters."

My stomach clenches. "Lives here?"

"He has the most wonderful townhouse," she says. "My apartment is nice enough, but when I'm feeling particularly grand, I like to—"

"Is he in Hatal now?" I interrupt.

She nods. "He's been here for…oh, a few days or so? Which means he'll be leaving soon, which is a shame because—"

"Perhaps I could visit," I say. My heart pounds, and I try to control my expression. "To say hello. He was so kind when I was at court."

Maeven seems thrilled by the idea. "How lovely! And if I bring a guest, Jozelin will be forced to offer us those cream cakes she thinks I don't know she hides away."

I'm entirely uninterested in the antics of the Clydon's cook, but I force myself to smile as Maeven links arms with me, chatting excitedly. I can return for the Blackvine later.

"So," Maeven says, as we wind our way through the market, "your veil seems to indicate you're betrothed, and yet you certainly don't seem dour enough to have trapped yourself with a husband."

My free hand flutters up to my veil, and hesitantly, I tug it away. "It's my eyes," I admit. "They're unusual. I have to confess I'm not entirely comfortable with the attention."

Maeven's own eyes widen slightly as she examines my face. "How exotic," she says. "I've never seen such a thing before. Perhaps an influence of your magic? What elements do you possess?"

"Earth," I lie. "And…water."

She makes a humming sound. "How lovely. I only have one." As if in response to her words, a strong wind blows by us. A passing Crafter shoots us a dirty look, clutching at her veil. Maeven grins. "Though I have to admit, I *am* a particularly powerful air user."

We take a side street that features the largest townhomes I've seen yet. Maeven pulls me along until we're in front of one the color of pale ocher. White roses climb the front of the house, framing the windows.

"Marvelous, isn't it?" Maeven says. She gestures for me to follow as she knocks. A female answers the door, her plain dress indicating she's a Lower. As we enter the foyer, Maeven greets her with familiarity that the female does not seem to return.

"We'll be in the parlor," Maeven announces. "Bring some of those cream cakes Jozelin likes to hide and some tea, please."

The female dips her head and leaves. Maeven guides me to a small sitting room off the hall. It's decorated with rich tapestries and carpets; delicate vases and figurines scattered throughout the room. Maeven goes to one of the couches, draping herself across it like a cat. I go to the fireplace, examining the painting that sits above it. It depicts a woman in a field of flowers. Far more feminine than anything I would expect from Clydon.

"I chose it," Maeven says, watching me. "Clydon has no taste whatsoever. I think he would live in barracks if he could. If his position didn't require"—she gestures around the room— "this. All he cares about is coin for his card games, anyway."

"It's lovely," I say quietly. And so different from my cabin in the Barren Forest. Was Clydon living here in this opulence, all this time?

I sit in one of the plush chairs across from Maeven as the female Lower returns, bearing a tray filled with little cakes and a set for tea. I wonder if my absence has been noted yet and if the Althearans are looking for me. I hope not. For this, I will delay my return, even if I'm caught.

"Excellent." Maeven sits up, eyeing the cakes as the servant sets them on the table between us. "I'm starving." She puts a cake on a plate, licking a bit of frosting from her finger. "Mmhm. Delicious." She smiles slyly. "Some things are more enjoyable when they're a secret, don't you think?"

"I suppose," I say, though I have no idea what she means.

The servant exits wordlessly, and as soon as she does, Maeven's smile disappears. She drops the cake back on the plate.

"Now," she says. "Why are you really here, Lady Vyzrais?"

13

I freeze. "I'm not—"

"Don't bother," she says. She pours herself tea, adding an excessive amount of sugar. "I told you I'm a powerful air user. The most powerful one to ever exist, at least in this age. Do you know what that means?"

"The stories of the old legends said air was instinct," I say slowly. "But that was the old days, when our people believed emotions fed power. We know better now."

Her eyes are hard, nothing like the mischief from earlier. "And yet, here I am. I know when I am being lied to, Lady Vyzrais."

My hand instinctively floats up to grasp the blood pendant I wear, my only token of comfort. "You have to understand, there are certain diplomatic—"

She cuts me off. "Please don't bore me with court chatter. I've had my fill of it for too many years. Especially now that Clydon resides on the council."

"Clydon isn't on the council. He would never serve the current Crown."

She gives me a pitying look. "And yet, you would know

that he *does* sit on the council if you'd truly met him at court, like you said."

I grimace, caught in my fib. "Is this even his home?"

"Of course," she says. "Though he won't be back from court for quite some time. He left late last night, after his weekly game at the Star Rose."

I cross my arms, even as the disappointment threatens to crush me. Clydon had been here. And I had missed him. "According to you, you can simply flutter your fingers and know whatever it is you wish to. Why ask me anything?"

Her mouth thins. "My instincts are stronger than most, but it does not make me a mind reader."

"And yet, you know I am Luzeandra Vyzrais." There's no point in trying to hide it.

"I made it my business to know of the rumors. The silver-eyed daughter of the Crown." She studies me intently. "Forgive my bluntness, Lady Vyzrais, but I must ask: do you know what is said about you? In the capital, and beyond?"

Maeven doesn't wait for a response. "Your uncle Eskar says that you are a traitor. He furthers the tale that you murdered your mother and sister in cold blood. That not only did you summon the Strin to do your bidding, but that you have some form of control over them."

I gape at her. "My uncle—Eskar—he would not say such things."

"He doesn't. Not directly. The rumors seem to appear out of thin air, as though from the Source itself. They fill the heart of the capital. Here, in Hatal, the people do not care for such things. They remember your mother, and there is still room in their hearts for her daughter, the rightful Crown. The true High Lady of Alos. But in Almaru? You will have a great challenge ahead, should you wish to take back the Crown. The capital province has no love lost for you, Lady Vyzrais."

Panic fills my veins. "How can you know any of this?"

She smiles. "Because I work for Eskar."

I go still. If this is a trap—

"Come now, don't get flighty on me," Maeven says. "My position grants me certain privileges, but my loyalty does not lie with Eskar. It resides with the true heir. You."

"But you don't even know me," I sputter. "How can you possibly—"

"You ask the wrong questions. You need only know that there are those loyal to you when the time comes."

I pause. "Is—is Clydon—?"

Contempt fills her face. "Clydon is weak, and a fool."

The room seems to be spinning a bit. Maeven watches me carefully.

"Don't tell me you actually care for him?" she says. "Eskar would rejoice if he knew how well that little plan had worked out."

"Plan?" My mouth tastes sour.

"It was intrigue, at first. Lowers were dying trying to traverse the Barren Forest. Clydon volunteered. He was eager to claim a place high in court. But as time went on, as your uncle continued to interrogate Clydon about you—I think Eskar was half-hoping you would go mad—it was clear enough that you would be driven to any kind of comfort, given the chance."

"No." I shake my head. "No. Clydon wouldn't do that. He cares for me."

"Does he?" Her face is impassive.

Anger floods my veins. She's wrong; she does not know him as I do. "Why should I trust you? You could be feeding me a web of lies, trying to distract me, make me fail."

"You can trust me," she says, "because there is no one who would like to see Eskar fall more than me." She rises, going to the fireplace. Her hands are clenched. "My father and Clydon's father—my uncle—were investigating the spreading of the Barren Forest." She gestures toward the window, towards the lands that lay beyond Hatal. "The forest curves around the city, ever encroaching. The Strin multiply, and the council simply sit in their polished thrones, hoarding magic for themselves. My father and uncle took it upon themselves to try to help, to keep the province safe. They died on that journey, murdered by the Strin. Because Eskar and his feeble council did nothing and refused them aid."

I remember my first meeting with Clydon. He had mentioned his father's passing.

Maeven drifts back to her seat on the couch. "I am very little older than you. I was young and naïve. Eskar offered me a position at court—one more important than my name already granted me. I did not realize it would constitute sharing the bed of anyone he told me to."

I feel a wave of sickness. "I'm sorry."

Maeven shrugs, looking away. "I made the best of it. They weren't all terrible. I found a lord—and more than one lady—willing to train me. In weapons, politics, court matters. All in return for favors."

Her mouth twists on the word *favors*. I remain silent, intimidated by the bitterness in her voice.

There's a long moment before Maeven speaks again. "Do you love him?"

I hesitate. "I care for him. Even if what you say is true, I know Clydon cares for me, too." I think back of the years we shared together. Not all of it could have been a lie.

Maeven studies me again. "Did you bed him?"

I feel a flush rise to my cheeks. "That's hardly your concern."

There's something calculating in her gaze. "I would think nothing of it if you had. You were a young female, sent to live with nothing more than the trees. I would have bedded the first male I'd seen. Even if he looked like a troll from the old legends."

I cannot bring myself to laugh. I take a deep breath instead. "Clydon gave me a tonic that I believe to be Bluethorn. Did you know?"

Maeven taps a finger against her lips, considering me. "No. If he'd created another heir, Eskar would have his head. But I did not know he would give you something so poisonous as the Bluethorn. If he gave it to you, he chose to do so himself. Or perhaps upon the advice of your uncle, to truly strip away your magic. What little you might have had in that Source-forsaken forest, at least."

I don't want to believe her, but honesty rings clear in every word.

"Your magic would appear again, given time," Maeven says. "I imagine your gifts are already beginning to awaken."

I stay silent. Even to Maeven I cannot reveal the truth: that I have no magic.

"I know what was done to you, you know," Maeven says softly.

I look at her sharply. "You know nothing of what I've survived."

"You're right," she says. "But the way the Healers ripped those memories from you… Very few people would have been strong enough to survive that."

I look away. "It's not important. Not anymore."

She pauses. "When you cross the wall to Altheara, your magic will not. The boundary wall hoards magic into Alos.

Your lineage will only carry you so far. You will not have magic, and you will not be ageless in the same way. The Althearans know this. They would never let you marry one of their own believing you to be a powerful, eternal ruler. To be honest, I expect they want you merely as a broodmare: create heirs, then find a way to kill you off."

My mouth is dry. "Then you know. About the Althearan prince, and—"

The door to the parlor bangs open and a female enters, cutting me off. Her red hair in an intricate knot atop her head, a crimson gown flowing down her body. She does not look friendly.

"Maeven," the female says. "I believe I told you to *stay away* when Clydon is not here."

"Isn't Clydon here, Jozelin?" Maeven says breezily. "Lady Ozare and I were just having a bit of tea while we wait for him."

Jozelin looks as though she's swallowed a mouthful of mud. She's beautiful, but the anger on her face clouds it. "Clydon left for Almaru last night, as you well know."

"Oh, dear," Maeven says, fluttering a hand. "I must have forgotten. I get so confused about these matters of court. May I see Melyssa, at least?"

There's something pointed in her tone. I stare at her, but she keeps her gaze on Jozelin.

Jozelin narrows her eyes, opening her mouth to respond— to say something ugly, I'm sure—when a young girl appears from behind her, maybe six years old.

"Mae!" the girl cries, running into the room and throwing herself into Maeven's lap. Jozelin looks furious, but Maeven picks the girl up, squeezing her tightly.

I study the girl. Fair hair—almost the same shade as Maeven's—and pale blue eyes.

"Where are my manners?" Maeven says. "Lady Ozare, this is Jozelin—Lady Haverly, that is—and Melyssa."

I stop breathing. She can't mean…

Maeven's face is smooth, polite, but there's pity in her eyes as she says her next words:

"Clydon's wife—and daughter."

Flame

14

ALL THIS TIME and I had been nothing more than a secret and a lie.

Six years. That's when Melyssa had been born. Melyssa, Clydon's offspring. His child.

His daughter, as I had once been someone's daughter.

I ease through the side entrance to the Star Rose. Only a few hours have passed since I left my rooms. Part of me recognizes I have been gone for far too long, that my absence may have been noted, but any sense of panic feels dulled by despair.

I had known Clydon was older, though he had never given specifics. It had never bothered me. Crafters viewed age the way others might view hair color. It was meaningless when you had such an extended lifespan. If you outlived your partner, there would be immense pain, yes, but when you had so many years to live, you could heal and love again.

I had never stopped to think of the implications. Unlike before my exile, time had become agonizingly meaningful to me. I had counted and felt every second while in the Barren Forest. Clearly, Clydon had not. And his wife, his partner, as unpleasant as she was…had she known? The thought makes me feel unclean, to think that I have been a pawn in Clydon's betrayal.

I enter my rooms and slump onto the bed. Something feels as though it has cracked open inside of me. As if all those years, Clydon had not been helping me to heal, but had simply been masking wounds that continued to fester under his attention. Perhaps my time in the Barren Forest was simply the Source's plan to prepare me for my fate. Perhaps I am not meant to be with others, in rooms full of laughter and stories and history. Perhaps I am meant to be alone.

I push myself to my feet, unable to stand the thoughts in my head, which is when someone knocks on my door. Aslen strides in the room.

"You're late," she announces. "I've been waiting for you downstairs for gods know how long. We're leaving today, in case you'd forgotten. What were you doing, lounging in the bath?" She makes a sound of annoyance, grabbing a pair of breeches off a chair and tossing them at me. "You haven't even finished packing." She looks me up and down. "And if you wear that dress, you're going to freeze to death before we even get to Altheara. Of course, I suppose that would make my life a lot easier."

I go into the bathing chambers, yanking off my dress and putting on my riding clothes. *Breathe.* I have to breathe. I can't let Aslen or the others know someone is wrong. I compose myself, trying to arrange my features into what I hope is a relaxed expression.

When I come out, Aslen is crumpling a dress into a ball and stuffing it into the carrying satchel. "Did someone teach you that technique for packing, or does it come naturally?" I ask bitingly.

"Not as naturally as some things. I'm quite good at removing fingers when the situation calls for it, for example."

I make a sound of disgust.

She jostles the satchel, roughly yanking it closed. "It's interesting, you know. You certainly knew how to handle that Crafter lord. For all of your ineptitude, I wouldn't think of you as much of a fighter. Especially after the performance with the boar."

I busy myself with the dress I'm holding, fussing with the way I've folded it. I shove the dress into the satchel, snapping it closed. "*My performance with the boar*...would that be the same night you tried to slit my throat with an arrow?"

"Exactly."

I shrug. "I'm not used to fighting boars."

"But you are used to fighting men?" She sounds skeptical.

A feeling of bitterness wells inside of me. "If I have to."

"Hmm." There's a brief pause, and then: "Well, for future reference, wild pigs aren't really that different from men most of the time." She heaves a satchel over her shoulder.

We walk to the stables without speaking. At least she's distracted me from Clydon's betrayal. I can feel the edges of my despair lingering, but it's easier to shove aside.

We reach the stables, and everyone seems busy, readying the horses and packing supplies. I feel another wave of relief that my absence wasn't noticed.

Demelan walks over to me, leading a dark, leggy gelding. He hands me the reins. "For you," he says.

In all the chaos of the past day, I'd forgotten the promise that they would acquire a horse for me. I take the reins, smoothing a hand across the inky blackness of the horse's neck. He turns, his whiskers nuzzling my arm.

"His name is Arturon," Demelan says. "Still a bit green—he got a late start, and he's only five—but a good temperament. Good legs, too. A little long in the back, but he's got a powerful hind to make up for it."

I stroke a hand down Arturon's nose. "You know horses?"

"My father is a horsemaster. I helped him around the stables as a child. Before I joined the Galdrion, of course."

"Would you have rather become a horsemaster yourself?" I ask.

He keeps his eyes on Arturon. "All children who are eligible are required to join the Galdrion once they become of age."

It's not really an answer, I notice.

The others are already mounted, waiting for us. I have to use a wooden block to mount Arturon—he's tall, over seventeen hands—but I'm surprised to find it feels natural, as though my muscles have finally remembered how. Arturon stands perfectly still while I adjust my stirrups and settle more fully into the saddle. It feels odd to be in it alone.

I assume they've planned for this part of our journey, because they fall into a formation quickly. Aslen falls back with Demelan, taking the rear. Thyo rides in front, leading us, and Gideon sets his horse's pace to match Arturon, riding abreast of me.

We follow a winding path that leads south from the stables. From what I can tell, it will take us past the large, shimmering lake, along a road that travels past the grand homes on the outskirts of Hatal.

Behind us, I can hear Demelan and Aslen talking—mostly insulting each other—and up ahead, Thyo is watchful, constantly scanning our surroundings.

We pass one of the first manor houses. It's painted a soft white, with a garden nestled to the side. The color makes me think of the flowers I'd noticed growing on Clydon's house. I wonder if he'd chosen that house before or after he'd met his wife; if the house was to her taste, or to his.

"Are you well, Lady Vyzrais?"

I turn to Gideon, pulled out of my thoughts. "I'm fine," I say. I shift in the saddle. "I haven't ridden as much recently. I suppose I'm out of practice."

"It won't be much longer now." He glances at the road ahead. "I have to admit, I'm eager for our arrival in Altheara."

Unlike the others, there's something almost gentle about Gideon. "What do you enjoy most about Altheara?" I ask tentatively.

He smiles. "My husband, Cyrian."

"You're married?" I don't know why this surprises me. "For how long?"

"Nearly a year. I would have married him the day I met him, but Cyrian wanted to wait until he finished his training. He entered the Galdrion a few years after me."

His words prick my curiosity. "What is training for the Galdrion like?"

An expression crosses Gideon's face that I can't discern. "It's…unusual. To be taken from your family at such a young age, to devote yourself to the Galdrion and see them so rarely…The training itself is meant to push you beyond what you believe your capabilities to be. My husband likes to say that the training method of the Galdrion is to make you suffer in such a way that the thought of war is a relief."

His tone is light, but I wonder how much truth actually lies in his words.

We pass a pale green manor, this one bigger than the last. "It must be nice," I say. "To have a partner. Someone you can trust."

"It is," Gideon says. "But it also means you have one more person whose fate you worry about. It's not only your own life that matters anymore."

"I suppose I won't have to worry about that," I say. "Since this is merely a diplomatic agreement."

"You never know." Gideon looks straight ahead. "You may find you have more in common with the prince than you suspect."

I ponder our conversation. If someone were with me—say, Clydon, at least up until today—I would be struggling even more with the task ahead of me, but I find the idea of that happening with the Althearan prince highly unlikely.

I'm so lost in thought that I fail to notice the large, honey-colored manor in our path until fills my view. I pull Arturon to a stop.

The manor is large and yet somehow quaint. Lilac and lavender spill unbidden across the arched entryway, and Weeping trees frame the walkway, their vines drooping. My eyes are immediately drawn to the left wing that spirals to a turret, to the circular room I know is housed within. It holds a library, one with stained glass windows that depict all kinds of fantastic beasts. And yet, it looks unkempt, as though it hasn't seen inhabitants in many years. Eleven, to be exact.

I've dismounted before I realize what I'm doing, walking up the path that leads to the entrance of the manor.

"Lady Vyzrais," Gideon calls, but I barely hear him.

"Why are we stopping?" Aslen says. She sounds annoyed.

The weather is less serene this close to the boundary, and the wind whips stray hairs around my face. My heart seems to both swell and constrict as I stare at the manor.

Dimly, I register that Thyo has joined me.

"The kitchen is right through there," I say, pointing. I'm not even sure if I'm speaking to him, or myself. "There's a table, that sits in one corner. For servants taking a break, I suppose, but it's most often used by anyone wanting to visit the kitchen, perhaps to steal a bit of food. It has a crack in it, from a language book being thrown across the room."

A memory comes to me, though it makes my head ache: the seven ancient languages Saelis had sworn I would learn. I had sworn back at him with equal vehemence, eventually chucking the book across the room—aiming for his head— but it had missed, of course. Saelis was not only a scholar, but a warrior. One that had fought during the Thousand Year War, and one that was hardly intimidated by the tantrums of a young girl, even if that language book had been the size of a tombstone.

"You lived here?" Thyo asks.

"As a child," I say. "I lived here with my mother…and my sister."

He shifts slightly, the only sign of his surprise. "The night of the boar attack, you told Demelan you didn't have any siblings."

"I don't." My voice is quiet. "Not anymore."

I wait for him to ask more questions, perhaps offer platitudes or apologies. A sense of relief washes over me when he does neither.

There's a long moment before he says, "I lost my father many years ago. A sickness spread through our lands, and he took ill. The sickness claimed him within days."

I know exactly what he's referring to: the outbreak of illness in Altheara years ago that Alos had refused to aid. The story had been insignificant to me. This is what happened to mortals. They were weak. They became sick and died. Why would we offer our valuable medicines and Healers to those who had only ever been our enemies?

I risk a glance towards him. "Do you still miss your father?"

His eyes are on the house, tracing the graceful arches. "I find it lessens when I'm preoccupied—focused on what's needed, on fulfilling the duties I have, on making sure such an illness never happens again. I very seldom have the luxury to do what I want, due to my rank."

I'm surprised by such an open, honest answer, and I speak without thinking. "That sounds lonely."

Thyo's face is difficult to read. "Don't you find your position to be the same?"

"Not until I was older. I never knew what it was to be alone."

"And now?"

"I suppose I've realized it's sometimes far lonelier to be with those who do not see you as you are, than to be truly alone."

Why am I telling him this? I feel too unsteady from my earlier encounter with Maeven, from my encounter with the male lord last night, and now this, this reminder of everything that I have lost.

Thyo speaks again. "When that Crafter lord touched you last night…what happened?"

Those fingers brushing across my spine, across the scars hidden beneath the laces of my dress…

Maybe if I understood the workings of my wounded mind, or maybe if Thyo weren't an Althearan, I would have told him. Instead, I fight for nonchalance. "He made the boar we encountered look genteel. I hardly think I needed a reason beyond that. I simply reacted on instinct."

"We tried to get there sooner, but the crowd…I saw him grab you. I was considering slicing his arm off. I was rather eager to see you pull it out of its socket, actually."

A surprised laugh escapes me. There's something between us, not friendly, but not exactly hostile, either. It unnerves me.

I look back at the house. "We should go," I say. There's nothing left for me here.

Demelan and Gideon are relaxed waiting for us, but Aslen wears an expression of impatience. Her mare seems equally as frustrated, stepping uneasily and tossing its head against the reins, as though Aslen's mood has channeled down the leathers.

I realize how problematic my decision to dismount was as I stand before Arturon. The saddle seems to tower above me. I'd been able to mount Odreya myself, but this horse… I could launch myself at the saddle and try to jump up, but I grimace as I realize how foolish I'll look.

"Here," Thyo says, noticing my dilemma. He stands by Arturon's shoulder, his hands slightly cupped. I stare at him in confusion.

"Your leg," he says, smiling slightly at my expression. "I can help lift you."

I move to stand in front of him uncertainly. Arturon is so tall, we're shielded from the others.

"What do I do?" What he's suggesting seems unbelievably complicated. What if I get stuck, flailing into both Arturon *and* him?

Thyo leans down, his hand skimming behind my knee. "Bend your leg here."

I do as he says. His hands cup my knee and shin.

"I'll help lift as you jump," he says. "Use the pommel—the front of the saddle—for balance as you swing your leg over."

I can already see the numerous ways this could go wrong, but I reach up, my hands gripping the saddle, and with a nod from Thyo and a slight hop, I use the support of his hands to mount.

He's strong, lifting me with ease, and the movement is surprisingly graceful. I can't help the small smile that forms as I settle into the saddle. His hand lingers on my leg.

"Thank you," I say. "That was much more dignified than what I had planned."

He pulls his hands away, his fingertips grazing the back of my calf through my breeches. My chest tightens, though I'm not sure why.

There's the squeal of a horse behind me and I turn. From what I can tell, Aslen's horse has just bitten Demelan's. Neither he nor his horse look happy about it.

"Learn to control your beast of a horse, Aslen," Demelan snaps. Gone is his usual blithe mood.

Aslen's mare flattens her ears, yanking towards Demelan's horse, and he quickly maneuvers out of the way. Aslen barely tightens her reins.

"Perhaps she wouldn't have been able to bite him if your horse didn't have such a fat rump," Aslen says. "Maybe you should feed him less."

"Or perhaps Vhetta's a she-demon, just like her rider," Demelan retorts.

"Aslen," Thyo calls. "Switch out with Gideon."

Her mouth flattens. "But—"

"Now." Thyo's tone brooks no argument.

I'm amused until I realized she'll be riding next to me.

Aslen heaves a sigh, walking her horse forward so it's astride from me and Arturon.

I pat Arturon's neck. "Don't worry," I say to him, loud enough for Aslen to hear. "I won't let her demonic horse eat you."

Aslen narrows her eyes, opening her mouth to retort, but Thyo calls for us to move onward and we do.

Hours pass, and I'm not certain, but I think we're skirting the Barren Forest. The temperature has dropped, and the plants here look slightly lifeless. I shudder as I stare out into the forest, noticing the waxy bark of the trees and the color-less leaves. It's so close to the city. If the sickness of the Barren Forest reaches the Wards…

I feel it when we cross the Wards bordering Hatal. It's barely visible; I'm sure the Althearans can't see it. Just a dim glimmer in the air, but I feel the change in magic as soon as we cross.

We stop and make camp as soon as the sun begins to set. I tend to Arturon, loosening his girth, when a hand on the saddle flap stops me. I look up.

"Don't untack him," Gideon says, his face unusually grave. "Only loosen the girth. You can remove his bit too, if you'd like, but the leave the bridle on. If something happens, and we should need to flee…"

He trails off, but I can read the rest on his face. I swallow against the fear creeping up my throat. "I understand."

I have spent the last eleven years suppressing any thought of the Strin. Now we could encounter one at any moment. The thought fills me with a flash of terror.

Gideon leaves to go help Aslen with the tents. I unhook the bit from the bridle, carefully sliding it out of Arturon's mouth, before digging out some grain from my satchel for him.

Left with nothing to do, I feel restless. Every time I stop moving my thoughts drift to Clydon and I have absolutely no desire to think of him.

I decide to go to the creek to wash. It's a short walk. I cross through the line of trees that border the creek's edge, hearing the water splash.

Which is why I come across Thyo, standing at the creek's edge. Shirtless.

I stop abruptly. His back is to me, and water droplets run

down from his neck where he's splashed water on himself, despite the cold.

I must make a small sound, because he suddenly turns. I can't help it: my gaze drops to his abdomen, which happens to be more chiseled than I would expect from a mortal.

"Hello," he says, breaking the silence.

I suddenly realize I'm staring, and I jerk my gaze away. Thyo doesn't seem bothered. He grabs his shirt from a nearby rock and pulling it on.

"Sorry," I say. "I was just…"

My mind goes blank. What am I saying?

Luckily, Aslen arrives, emerging from the treeline behind me. Thyo grabs his jacket, tugging it on. He gives me a small smile as he leaves, and I feel my cheeks flush.

Aslen has stripped her jacket off, her shirt following. Her body is nearly as sculpted as Thyo's, shockingly muscular for a female. Shirtless, wearing only a band around her breasts as an undergarment, her strength is apparent. Her waist is thick, her torso surprisingly chiseled, with muscles rippling down her bare arms.

More interesting is the scar that I now realize extends not only along her cheek and jaw, but down her shoulder and left breast, before it disappears in her bindings. I wonder what could have caused it.

"Done gawking?" Aslen says. Her teeth are gritted, but she seems resigned, as though she's used to this reaction.

"You know, I can't go anywhere without you showing up," I say. "Why is that?"

She pulls her shirt back on. "My job is to make sure you don't die."

I make a face. "And I can't be expected to manage more than a minute alone?"

"Even if you could, I would still follow you," she says. "Thyo would have my head if I didn't."

I don't quite believe her. For one, I can't quite imagine Thyo having that kind of wrath. He's intimidating, but not exactly rageful. For another, I can't see Aslen taking orders she didn't at least somewhat agree with. She's too pigheaded.

"Don't worry," she says. "I still don't like you. I just don't want to get demoted if you die."

I roll my eyes. "Good to know."

She stands, pulling her clothes back on. "I'll give you some privacy to wash up." Her tone suggests this is a frivolous notion. "And be quick about it. I'm hungry." She disappears into the trees.

I pull my sweater off, leaving only my thin, silky half-shirt. Already, I can smell the sourness of sweat on my skin, and it's been barely a day of travel since Hatal. I kneel at the edge of the creek, splashing water on my face and swallowing a few mouthfuls. I rock back on my heels, watching the water rush by, when I smell *it*.

It's the same scent as that day by the creek with the light-filled water droplets. That day already feels like eons ago, but I remember it clear—this is the same. Something potent and powerful.

I straighten abruptly. My eyes scan the shore. "Hello?" I call uneasily. I strain my ears, but I hear nothing.

The wind shifts again, and I lose the scent, but I can still feel the same presence, something powerful enough to make my skin tingle.

Aslen comes striding back to the creek, muttering under her breath. "I'm not a dog, you know."

I only half pay attention to her. The other half is focused on straining my nose and ears to see if that foreign, powerful presence is still nearby.

"So?" Aslen says impatiently. "What is it?"

I grab my jacket, wrapping it in my arms securely. I can tell that whatever presence was here has disappeared. Even without the lack of scent, my skin is no longer prickling.

"Nothing," I say. "I just thought I heard something."

"Whatever," she says. "Time's up. Let's go."

Dinner that night is subdued. It feels odd for the others to be so muted. Somewhere along our journey, I'd gotten used to the jokes and laughter.

Thyo sits closer than usual, barely a foot of space between us. I feel an urge to edge closer, even as I want to run away. I look down at my hands, absentmindedly tracing the scars there, lost in thought.

Aslen and Demelan are sharing conversation in low tones—nearly undecipherable from across the fire, even to me—when Thyo reaches out. His fingers are light on my wrist as he angles my hand. "Your hands are scarred."

"Yes," I say warily.

"From a blade?"

"Females handling weapons is looked down upon in Alos," I say. "But I wanted to learn whatever I could, so I tried to teach myself. I suppose I wasn't very good at it.

A single cut would have healed on its own with proper care. Many cuts, even. But not this many.

His fingers still touch my wrist. "In Altheara, both men and women are expected to learn how to handle weapons."

My pulse has quickened. I hope he can't feel it. "Does every child join the Galdrion?"

"Yes, for the most part. Once they come of age, at nine."

This surprises me. "That seems rather…extreme."

"And yet you sought out weapons training, despite it being looked down upon by your kingdom."

"Yes, but…" I struggle to formulate my thoughts. "I *chose*. I wanted to learn. To force someone seems…precarious."

"And yet, sometimes we sacrifice our morals for the greater good. Wouldn't you do the same for Alos?"

I open my mouth to contradict him, to say that I would never yield my morality in such a way, but I stop. The Oath ring glinting on my finger signifies that I am willing to do such a thing.

I stand abruptly. "I'm rather tired. I think I'll go to bed."

Thyo looks relaxed, as though nothing is amiss. "One of us will be on guard throughout the night. You'll be safe."

My heart hammering, I go to my tent, ducking between the flaps. I grasp my wrist, where Thyo had touched me. These people are my enemies, I remind myself. Thyo is my enemy. They all are.

So why does my tent suddenly feel less like a refuge and more like a prison?

15

THE NEXT DAY of travel is unpleasant.

I'm unnerved by the fact that we haven't had any encounters with the Strin. It seems unusual, even impossible, that we've traveled this far and haven't had a brush with one. It makes me more nervous, my stomach roiling as we ride without conversation, hoping not to attract one with sound. I feel as though I'm constantly holding my breath, waiting for the chaos and terror to ensue. Part of me wishes we would simply be attacked so I could stop anticipating it, which is ridiculous.

The other source of my unease was closer than I would have liked. Riding in front of me, to be precise. Just a few more days of travel, of being forced to be in his presence, of being forced to feel the conflicted feelings I'm having. Surely, I can avoid Thyo once we reach Altheara.

Then again, Thyo is the prince's right hand. *Will* he be avoidable?

These are the thoughts that preoccupy me as we near the end of our travels. We'll reach the wall tomorrow, but we have to stop for one more night. It's nearly dark by the time we make camp, and I watch as Demelan and Thyo tend to the horses. I had taken care of Arturon as soon as I'd dismounted, but I watch as Thyo steps over, giving him a pat and murmuring something that I can't hear. Arturon nuzzles Thyo's jacket as he does, and Thyo smiles slightly, giving him another pat.

Before I can turn away, Thyo glances up, meeting my eyes, a rare smile on his face. Something flutters low in my gut, and I quickly look away.

Stop it, I scold myself. I'm not exactly sure what I'm feeling, but I know it's nothing I want. I'd had fluttering feelings for Clydon, too, and look at where that had gotten me.

I cross the camp, heading into the trees. I walk far enough beyond the boundaries of camp to be out of sight and sound. Probably unwise, but I'm sure Aslen will show up any minute and drag me back.

I sense, rather than hear, as Aslen approaches. "Took you long enou—"

The words die on my lips. Thyo is standing there.

"It isn't safe out here," he says. "We should go back."

My immediate instinct is to flee, so I don't argue. "Fine." As I move to pass him, he reaches out, stopping me.

"You're avoiding me," he says.

"I'm not avoiding you." He's right. I am.

"Was it something I did?" he asks. His hand is still on my arm.

"No," I say. "No, it's just…" I clear my throat. "I've been preoccupied."

"With?"

All I can feel is his hand on me, the nerves that it brings. "Everything."

Thyo's quiet for a moment. "I see."

"You do?" I ask, unnerved.

"What is it you're afraid of, Luze?"

Luze. Not Lady Vyzrais.

I am caught in the moment, and I speak without thinking. "I'm afraid of what's ahead."

He's watching me, too. "And what is it you're hoping for?"

My smile is grim. "Someone not intent on torturing me or beheading me would be a start."

His brows tighten. "You really think so little of Althearans?"

"I'm sure it's equal to whatever esteem you hold for Alosians."

"Actually, my opinion of Alosians has changed recently."

I feel it again: that creeping sense of treacherous intimacy. "We should go back," I say.

"If that's what you want."

Neither of us moves.

He shifts a little. "What do you want, Luze?" He almost sounds frustrated.

"I'm not sure it matters what I want." I hate how sad I sound.

Thyo's brow furrows. Slowly—so slowly—his hand reaches up, just barely brushing my jaw. "It matters to me," he says softly.

My breath catches. We're completely alone right now.

"Why?" I ask, my voice barely a whisper. "Why would you care?"

I swear his eyes darken, shadows swirling in their depths. "I think you know."

His lips are barely a breath away from mine. I could just lean in, rising slightly to meet—

What am I doing? I jerk away from Thyo's hand.

"What is it?" he asks, startled.

I step back, running my hands over my hair, flustered. "I just—I can't do this."

"Can't?" he says softly. "Or won't?"

Something feels stuck in my throat. "I'm sorry. I just… I can't."

"Good," he says. He steps away.

"*Good?*" My brow pinches. "Why—"

"Loyalty is highly valued by the prince," he says, cutting me off. "It's one of the values instilled in the Galdrion. In the entire kingdom. What I said was true: my opinion of Alos has changed. But I have to be careful. I have little trust in Alosian honor. I wasn't going to cross the wall without knowing your character."

I'm still dazed, but I string his words together, deciphering their meaning. Suddenly, it clicks. "Was that some kind of test?"

His expression flickers. "I wanted to know whether I could trust you. And if you were playing a game…I wanted to see how far you would go."

Anger is slowly clearing my head. "And how far were *you* going to let it go?"

"As far as I needed to."

My temper snaps, hard and fast, fueled by embarrassment. "You bastard."

His lips press together. "I didn't get to where I am by blindly trusting, Luze."

My instinct is to flee, to pretend this never happened. This ugly, twisting feeling inside of me, that I have been fooled—isn't this just a smaller, less significant wound comparable to what Clydon had done?

But my temper simmers, and the trapped anger of so many years makes me impulsive, makes me want to find some small way to release.

I shift closer to Thyo, tilting my head. "Are you sure testing me was the only reason?"

"Yes," he says. There's a slight stiffness to him that strikes me as uncertainty.

I touch his chest, just barely grazing him with my fingertips. "You asked me what I want, Thyo. But what do you want?"

His expression doesn't change, but I can feel his heartbeat quicken underneath my hand. "I want a trustworthy alliance," he says. "One that will serve Altheara, as I serve it."

"And that's all?" My fingertips begin to trail down.

He catches my wrist. "What are you doing?" His voice is hard.

I look up at him. "You have your tests, and I have mine."

"And what exactly are you looking for?"

I purse my lips "You said Prince Adriel ordered you to ensure my character, but I wonder if that's true. Perhaps you just desire me. It doesn't matter, though. I'm not interested."

I am playing a role that I have no experience with, but by the way Thyo has frozen, I know I've hit a mark. "That's not what it seemed like a minute ago," he says.

"I was caught off-guard," I say, keeping an innocent expression. "I was trying to be polite. I don't have even the slightest interest in you."

We stare at each other, neither of us moving.

"So you wouldn't like me to touch you?" he asks. "Like I was?" His hand rises to cup my chin, his thumb gently pressing against my jaw. "Like this?"

"You could," I say. "But it's meaningless to me."

"And you wouldn't like me to kiss you?"

I raise my face to his. "It would be like kissing a rock."

"A rock?"

"Or a tree."

We watch each other, neither of us moving. I swear his eyes darken, shadows swirling in their depths. He shifts toward me just slightly, his lips inches away.

Which is when I hit him.

I swing my elbow, and it lands across his cheekbone with a loud *crack*. He's already off balance from leaning towards me and the hit stuns him, judging by the way his eyes widen. Before he can react, I spin, shoving him hard, one hand yanking a throwing knife from my boot. Only a heartbeat passes, and Thyo is pressed against the tree, my knife at his throat.

"Are you out of your mind?" My earlier timidity is wiped clean. "You really thought I'd fall for that? Just another one of your petty tests?"

"The knife isn't necessary, you know," he says. He doesn't seem concerned about the weapon at his neck. "If you don't want me to kiss you, I won't kiss you."

I snort. "Have you forgotten I have a blade to your throat? I don't need your assurances."

"You won't use it."

Some part of me recognizes that he's probably right, that I won't actually cut his throat right here and now, but another part is surprised by how natural it feels for me to hold a blade to a male's throat. A part of me seems to sing for it, actually.

I twist the blade slightly. "Perhaps I'm only warming up."

"I would say so," he says. His suggestion is clear.

My eyes narrow, my grip on the knife slackening. "You—"

I realize my mistake too late.

Thyo moves with lightning speed, his hand grabbing my wrist and twisting it painfully, hard enough that I cry out and my fingers are forced to drop the knife. Almost simultaneously, his leg swings up, hitting the back of my ankles, and I crash to the floor of the forest, my breath coming out in a gasp. He kneels beside me, his hands pinning my wrists to the ground.

"Much better," he says. He gives me an appraising look. "You're stronger than you look."

I assume he's referring to the wrists I'm attempting to pull from his grip. I curse internally, even as I give him a cool smile. "You would pin a lady to the dirt?"

"I've trained with women since I was nine," he says dryly. "I have no qualms about pinning you to the ground."

I don't even have chivalry to rely on, then.

I think through my options. I have only my two throwing knives, one of which has been tossed to the ground, out of sight. I know some hand-to-hand fighting maneuvers, but judging by my current predicament, so does Thyo.

An idea comes to mind. I look up at him through my lashes, relaxing my wrists. "You can let go of me."

"I don't think so," he says. "The murderous look hasn't quite left your eye."

I take a breath as I look past him, staring at the night sky. "I'm disappointed you think so little of me, Thyo." I do my best to sound pitiful.

It seems to work. Thyo's grip on my wrists relaxes. "Luze—"

A mistake, just like the one I had made. I take my chance, rolling over and driving my knee into his gut, hard. His breath comes out in a gasp—too bad I hadn't been able to aim lower—and I hook my leg over, shoving him to his back, my other hand slipping into my boot and pulling out my second knife as I straddle him, shifting the blade to his throat again.

I keep the knife carefully angled. "Now, tell me—"

"I would drop that knife, if I were you."

Aslen is standing perhaps thirty feet away, as though she'd witnessed our grappling and had maneuvered for the best spot to aim with one of her arrows.

One of which is currently notched and pointed at me.

16

I keep still. "You finally showed up."

"Just in time, it appears," Aslen says. "I'm not going to ask again. Drop the knife."

My eyes narrow, but slowly, I pull the knife away from Thyo's throat, tossing it aside.

"Now get off of him."

Slowly, I maneuver out of my straddle, easing one leg over Thyo's hip, but I stay on the ground, kneeling. Thyo sits up, brushing leaves off his clothing.

"Believe it or not, your timing was rather poor," he says to Aslen.

She arches a brow. "Would you have liked me to wait until she'd actually stabbed you?"

My lips tighten. "*She* is right here."

They both ignore me.

Slowly, I let my hand drift, my fingers grazing across the ground for one of my knives, but I touch only leaves and ice. Where did the damn things go, the other side of the forest?

Aslen turns to Thyo, tucking her arrow back into its quiver.

"Next time, you don't make me wait behind. I don't care what little trysts you want to have in the forest."

Thyo plucks another leaf from his jacket. "I was enjoying myself, actually."

"I'm sure you were." Her expression is full of distaste. "Interesting that whatever you did resulted in a knife to the throat. You ought to work on your technique."

He makes a face at her, and it's like a mask slipping off. The interaction between them is strange. I have the sickening feeling that I am part of some plot or joke.

I can feel my face flushing from the warring emotions. "Were you all having a good laugh behind my back? Was this planned from the beginning?"

Aslen sighs. "Don't be ridiculous."

"Do not condescend to me," I snap.

Thyo steps toward me, reaching out as if to soothe. "Luze—"

I step away. "*Don't* touch me."

If only I could tell them how poor their timing is. Only days ago, I'd discovered Clydon, the one person left in the world I thought I could trust, had never loved me. I'd thought I was controlling how I felt about it. Only now I realize those emotions have merely been trapped, waiting to emerge.

"Luze," Thyo says. "Let's just—"

Maybe it's the pity on his face—hadn't Clydon always looked at me with the same pity? Or maybe it's that I'm simply furious at my uncle, at this marriage plot, at Althearans for existing, at everyone and everything.

Thyo is reaching for me again, and I rip my arm away before he can touch it. "I said *no*."

My voice has become loud. Too loud. As are Thyo's and Aslen's. In the midst of this argument, we've gotten careless.

I know this as soon as I hear the low, hissing growl of a Strin coming from behind me.

I spin, my hand moving instinctively to my boot, ready to grasp one of my blades. I'll actually *do* something, not like with the boar—

Until two things happen at once.

One, I remember my blades are still scattered somewhere on the forest floor.

Two, I actually see the Strin that's staring me down from mere feet away.

"Luze." Thyo's voice is filled with a sharp quality. *Fear.* "Luze, step away. Slowly."

His words seem to be coming through a tunnel, as though I'm floating from a distance. All I can feel of my body is my stomach heaving and acid coating my tongue as terror rolls over me in waves.

The Strin.

It's exactly like from my nightmares—from my memories.

I stare up at it—at this *thing,* dark as midnight, with its shiny, slicked skin, scabbed and pulled taut, as though the webbing of its tissue is not enough to contain everything underneath. It towers above me, nearly twice my height, and its face—I can't bring myself to look above the razored teeth that drip with milky-grey slime. To the white, soulless eyes I know lie above those fangs.

Something between a gasp and a sob breaks from me, the fear so overpowering I'm rooted to the spot. All I can see is my mother, ripped open by those teeth and my sister's lifeless body painted red on the floor.

The terror and anger and shame flares insides of me, deep and fiery, completely uncontrollable. Heat rushes to my palms.

The moon seems to have brightened in the sky, illuminating the forest.

Not the moon—my hands. There are shimmering, silver threads of light dancing on my palms. I stare at my hands, at the radiant threads emanating from them, winding their way across my fingers.

I have…magic? I can feel the current of energy running beneath my skin, as though a current of lightning has worked its way into my veins. A loud humming sound fills the air.

I have magic.

Then a sharp bolt of fear works its way through me. What *is* this? Not flame, nor air or water, and certainly not earth. Something else entirely.

Something wrong.

"What in Sehenna," Aslen breathes from behind me.

There's no time to ponder what has just emerged from me, because the Strin, seemingly mesmerized by what has just occurred, has regained its instincts. It opens its mouth in a bone-rattling hiss, and I stumble back.

"Thyo." Aslen's voice is urgent. "Thyo, I thought you were shielding us—"

Her words make no sense, but they draw the Strin's attention. I hear the sound of a bow being drawn.

And with a deep, slithering growl, the Strin crouches, almost until it's on all fours, and I know exactly what comes next.

"Run." The word tears from me. "*Run!*"

I turn, sprinting, and Thyo is there, gripping my arm and dragging me along but I know we have no hope. I have no weapons and neither does Thyo, and we cannot outrun the Strin. There's only Aslen, her eyes wide but fierce as she releases one arrow and then another.

Her aim is true and the Strin shrieks, a rattling cry that echoes around the forest, like nails raking across metal, and it's all I can do to keep running and not clap my hands over my ears.

"Faster." We're out of the clearing and Thyo is half-dragging me. I'm not sure where we're going, only that we're deeper in the forest, the blind panic making me lose any sense of direction. "*Faster.*"

Every sense is straining, trying to hear the pursuit I know must be behind us, the hot breath I will feel right before the Strin sinks its teeth into my spine, when I hear an ear-shattering scream.

"Aslen!" I stop, yanking my arm out of Thyo's grasp.

"Luze—" Thyo grabs my wrist again, trying to pull me along, but I resist.

"We can't leave her!" My voice is shrill. "We can't—we have to go back—"

Thyo's face is hard, unforgiving. "Luze, we can't go back."

I jerk my arm away again, pulling back so he can't reach me. "It wants *me*. It was me it was coming for, for my magic—"

"Luze, *it will kill you!*" He's suddenly shouting at me.

It cuts through me: how clearly I can hear the fear in his voice, the terror that he cannot protect me.

I try to just *think,* to figure what to do—

Zassa. I think of Zassa. What if I had been able to save her?

Thyo sees the resolve as soon as I make the decision. His eyes widen, and he reaches for me, his fingers almost touching me—

But I'm gone, running back the way we came.

I hear another scream, filled with agony, and I push my legs harder, faster, the forest blurring around me.

Aslen can't die. She *won't.*

I smell the blood before I see it, a heavy, metallic scent that coats my nostrils. The scene I emerge on is even worse.

Aslen is on the ground, the Strin standing over her. It reaches down, one claw stroking her abdomen, at the open wound there. There's a gelatin-like consistency to it, as though it is not merely blood, but soft, wet tissue, too.

The Strin lifts the claw from Aslen, now coated in her blood, and its tongue flicks out. Tasting it.

Bile washes up my throat, but I force it back down. I step into the clearing.

"You." My voice is weak, shaky, but I force myself to take another step.

The Strin jerks its head, looking at me with those white, pupil-less eyes.

"That's right." I take another step, and it tracks the movement. "You want me, don't you? Not her. Me. My magic."

At the word *magic* the Strin hisses again, sharper this time, that sound of metal screeching on stone, and my ears throb painfully.

My throat closes. Aslen hasn't moved.

Please. Don't let her die.

A cold breeze rustles through the trees, helping me focus.

Be brave. I'm not sure if the voice is from my head or the wind or the Source itself—but it's all I have and it strengthens me. I force myself to look directly into the Strin's eyes.

"If you want me, come and get me," I say.

And for the second time, I run.

This time, there's no quiet terror that something *might* be pursuing me.

This time, the terror is real.

I barely make it out of the clearing before I hear the Strin close behind me, a disturbing, cracking sound as it runs, as though its bones are breaking with every step.

Close. Too close.

I push my legs to their breaking point, my body screaming for air, for rest, but I simply run faster, the forest a dark blur around me.

Which is when I slip on something—a patch of ice, a root, I don't know—and my foot twists unnaturally beneath me. I'm going too fast to control the movement and with a sickening *crack* my ankle breaks.

A scream of agony rips from me as I fall to the ground. White-hot pain climbs up my right leg, and my body arches involuntarily, the pain crippling me.

I can hear the rattling sound of the Strin behind me, and panic overtakes me. I roll onto my knees, trying to stand as my ankle burns with pain. Acid washes up my throat and I retch, but my fingers scrabble at the ground, still trying to push me to my feet, to go, to *run*—

I start to push myself up, my leg hanging limply behind me, when I feel the claws close around me.

My scream is from fear this time, a fear so bright is overshadows the pain. There's a clicking sound of teeth behind my ear, the claws that threaten to pierce my ribs tightening, and I desperately try to pull myself away. The smell of its skin fills my nostrils, a stench of rotten meat and rancid oil. My fingers bite into the ground for purchase but the ground is cold, too hard, and I feel my nails rip.

It becomes clear to me: I am going to die.

"*Please*," I gasp. I'm not sure who I'm speaking to, or for what: for life, for death, for an escape.

The claws grasping my side contract, cutting into flesh, and I scream, waiting for them to slice all the way through me, when they suddenly tear away, and there's a sharp screeching sound, and this time I *do* clap my hands over my ears, collapsing on the forest floor as I await the final blow I know is coming.

Except it doesn't.

There's a sharp crack, a ripping sound, then another, a second screech and then—

Silence.

I stay curled up on the ground, my eyes squeezed shut and my palms still over my ears. Warmth floods my side, and a small part of me wonders at that sensation when it's so cold everywhere else.

Something touches me and my body jerks violently, but this touch—there are no claws.

It's a hand, the skin hotter than I'm used to. I feel my sweater pushed up, cold air touching my abdomen.

"Fuck." The voice shocks me, even in my daze, but I can't bring myself to move. And then: "Luze. Can you hear me?"

I try to open my eyes, but my eyelids feel heavy, as though the muscles around them are too weak for the task. "Thyo," I mumble. I reach out, groping blindly, for something. I don't know what. "You came back for me. And Aslen. Is Aslen—"

The voice curses again. "Stop moving. It's making you bleed faster." The voice is deep—male. I wonder why it sounds different. Familiar, and yet not.

Some small part of my mind realizes that the warmth flooding my side is the same warmth as my ankle. Bleeding. I must be bleeding. A hysterical burble escapes my wet lips, the flavor of salt coating my tongue. Hands skim over me, moving efficiently, confidently.

"This is going to hurt," the voice warns. Hands settle over my ribs, followed by a burning, radiating pain that makes me gasp. "Good. That was the easy part." I want to laugh, but I suddenly feel as though I'm floating away from my body.

The hands move down to my ankle, the touch impossibly gentle, and yet I want to scream to leave it alone, to not touch it.

"Luzeandra." The voice is close to my ear again. "The bone broke through the skin. This is going to hurt. Badly."

Then just do it already, you bastard.

The voice lets out a sigh of exasperation, and I realize I've spoken out loud.

The hands move down to my ankle again, and the part of me hanging on by a thread sends out a prayer to the Source, because I know, I *know* how much this is going to hurt—

And it does.

I feel my skin split, ripping apart even more than it already has, and a white-hot pain as though a thousand needles have been shoved into me and then thank the Source there's nothing but a deep, blissful abyss of unconsciousness as I pass out.

Unfortunately, I come to only moments later. The hands are still on me, but the pain has receded. A deep, aching soreness, but no agony.

The hands pause over my ribs, and there's another burning sensation, but this time it's not altogether unpleasant, just hot. I have the sensation of blood rushing behind my skin, the heat reaching its apex, and then the hands leave my body.

The voice murmurs something to me, something that makes me want to open my eyes—

There's a whisper of wind, and my eyes finally open.

There's no one there.

17

I'd forgotten about the shaking.

It's uncontrollable, the shivering. It reminds me of before, at the manor house after the attack of my family, how I was unable to stop shaking. On and on and it went, until I'd simply accepted I'd be rattling around in my body for the rest of my life. Of course, I hadn't; the trembling had stopped after a few hours.

I sit in the spot where the voice left me, tremors rolling through my body. I'll have to get up at some point—to try to find the camp, to find the others, if they're still alive—but I know if I try to stand right now, I'll simply fall back down.

I'm not sure how long it is I'm sitting there before I hear the rustling sound of the forest floor being disturbed. My body tenses, and I prepare myself to run—

—and then Arturon emerges from the darkness.

I blink, wondering if I'm hallucinating, but he ambles over, his head coming down to nuzzle me. His lips nibble at my hair and a surprised laugh bursts from me.

"How did you find me?" I murmur, reaching up to pet his nose. "Now that I think about it, *why* did you find me?"

I've never had a horse seek me out like a bloodhound. The horses I'd ridden as a child were far happier to ignore people, spending their days in a pasture, filling their bellies with sun-warmed grass.

A far-off screech reaches my ears and I flinch, though from the sound it's not a Strin. I push myself to my feet, using Arturon for support. He waits patiently as I do.

I gingerly test my weight on my ankle. It's tender, but I can stand on it. I lead Arturon to a rock, using it to mount. I'm about to squeeze him to go forward, but he begins walking before I can.

"Right." I let my right leg hang loose, gingerly stretching my ankle. "I guess you'll just lead the way, then."

A sickening smell suddenly overwhelms us.

Eyes watering, trying not to gag, I squint, trying to see through the darkness—even my Crafter eyes can only see so well—when a jagged, distorted shape appears in our path.

I bite back a scream, ready to wheel Arturon around and gallop away before I realize the figure isn't moving.

It's a Strin—a dead one. The same one who attacked us earlier. In pieces.

It's been torn apart, limbs ripped from body, head from trunk. It's milky-white blood drips, a sour smell emanating from it. Strin are nearly impossible to kill, but this one was, clearly. Whatever creature did this must be equally as blood-thirsty and terrifying, to have inflicted such violence. The question is—who? And where are they now?

I think of the hands that healed me. It must have been the same being who had killed the Strin, and yet, I can't believe those warm, gentle hands that had glided over my body could also create this kind of carnage.

I sit on Arturon, staring for a long moment, before I'm

finally able to convince myself the Strin isn't about to reas-semble itself and attack. Uneasily, I urge Arturon around the body and we continue forward.

After a while, I begin to smell something acrid and charred—smoke. Fire.

The camp.

It's too dark to go faster than we already are. I ride with my heart in my throat, wondering what I'll find when I get there. After what feels like an eternity, I see light through the trees.

Thyo is standing at the edge of the clearing, his face ter-rifying as he stares into the darkness. Demelan is at his side, his face terse as he speaks in a low tone, too low for me to hear the words. One hand is on Thyo's arm, as though he's about to restrain him, or already has.

A flash of movement by the fire catches my attention. Gideon is kneeling on the ground, tending to someone.

Aslen.

I urge Arturon forward, dropping from the saddle without another thought for my ankle. Gideon looks up in surprise as I kneel next to him.

Aslen's eyes are closed, her breath rattling faintly. The wound is disgusting, the edges of it already turning a greyish-green tone. The cut is deep, but the bleeding is slow. More of an ooze than a flow.

I feel a hand on my shoulder, and I look up.

"Luze." Thyo's face is white. "How did you—"

I move my arm from under his grasp. "How much blood has she lost?"

Gideon is blunt. "Too much. She'll die soon if I can't stop the bleeding. Even if I could, it seems to be infected, and I've never seen anything this rapid."

"You cleaned it already?"

He nods. I return my attention to the wound. Gingerly, I reach out, touching the edges. The skin there is hot and swollen.

I feel surprisingly clear-headed. I'm not sure if I've recovered from the shock, or if whatever was done to heal me out in the forest is still affecting me.

"Boil water," I say to Gideon. "I need any supplies you have."

Gideon's expression is grave. "Of course."

I turn to Demelan. "There's a small leather pouch in my tent, with stitching on the side. Please bring it to me."

Demelan's eyes widen in surprise, but he does as I ask. I look at Thyo. "I need you to hold her steady, in case she wakes up."

He moves without question, situating himself by Aslen's head.

It seems like only seconds before Gideon and Demelan return. Gideon deposits a small bag of supplies next to me, before situating a metal canteen on the spit hanging over the fire. Demelan hands me the pouch I'd requested.

I unscrew the lid of the canteen before it gets too hot, shaking out the contents of the pouch and adding them to it. Next, I dig through the supplies Gideon has given me. It's fairly basic. There's nothing here that will help me until I can stop the bleeding.

Some of my shakiness is returning. My head pounds as I try to recall what my childhood tutor, Saelis, had taught me about staunching blood flow.

"You can pack it with clean linen to stop the immediate flow," he'd told me. *"You can also apply a salve of Silverweed. Wounds that are deep enough will have to be stitched, but you'll need to make sure there's no internal injury before you do."*

I stare at the wound. Beyond the skin, Aslen's abdomen is…damaged. Merely stitching the skin will not be enough. Of course, the easiest way to aid healing is to use a water or earth element. The Healers of Toluz almost always had both.

And I have neither.

Think, Luze. Think.

I glance at Aslen's face, at the bone-white color of her skin, the way her breath has begun to rattle faintly, and my pulse races. She has little time, if any. I have to do something. Now.

"What is it?" Thyo asks. "What's wrong?"

"It won't be enough. These supplies—they can't help her. I don't have what I need."

I can feel myself beginning to panic, that I'm going to watch Aslen die, that there's nothing I can do, yet again.

"Magic," Thyo says. I sense Gideon and Demelan go still. "You're a Crafter. You can use magic."

"Toluzian Healers use certain elements," I say desperately. "They train for years, and they have natural abilities. I don't have that kind of power."

"Yes, you do." Thyo's voice is soft, but insistent. "I saw it, Luze. When the Strin showed up. Whatever that was, it was power."

I can't tell him—how do I explain I don't truly have magic? Not anything real, at least.

"Please," he says. "Please try."

I squeeze my eyes shut. The light winding around my hands earlier, even if only for a second, proves I have at least a small fragment of power. It's a last, desperate bid based on nothing more than hope, but it's all I have.

I open my eyes. "Take the canteen off the fire to cool," I tell Gideon. "I'll need it." I place my hands by Aslen's wound, the gesture uncertain. I notice Gideon has drifted to Aslen's feet. Demelan is still standing, his expression distressed and queasy.

I take a breath, closing my eyes again. I need to ignore my audience if I'm going to have even a slight chance of accomplishing what I want.

Magic in Alos is taught depending on the strengths of the child—what elements they possess, whether they're a Lower or High Crafter—but sometimes discerning gifts can take time. All Crafter children are taught to harness the essence of magic, the Aether that flows from the Source. The child is taught to control their emotions, which are a distraction. It takes years of focus and control, learning to become empty from within. Something that has never come easily to me.

I think of the time I'd broken a finger as a child. I'd been playing in the library with Zassa, and my finger had gotten hooked between a rolling ladder and the bookshelf. Such a minor injury, but a Toluzian healer had been called in. Anything for the future heir.

I try to remember what it had felt like as the Healer had worked. The cooling feeling of the water element as it soothed the pain and inflammation. The tugging sensation as the Healer's earth element had knit my bone back together.

I try to force the magic from me. I can do it. I know I can. Because if I can't...

I shove the fear away. My hands ache as I *will* the magic to come from me in the same way, to flow from my fingertips, to *fix this*—

A beat passes. Then two.

Nothing happens.

I open my eyes, examining the wound again, but it looks exactly the same.

"Did it work?" Demelan asks. He still looks sick. "Is she healing?"

"I don't have enough control over my magic," I say. "I don't—I can't help her. I'm sorry."

"Try again." Thyo's voice is quiet. "Please."

There is pain in his eyes. It doesn't escape my notice that his hands cradle Aslen's head like it's that of a child's.

I take another breath, closing my eyes again, trying to let the world go quiet as I sink into a memory—this one much more recent.

I think of the hands on me, the voice that had saved me out in the forest. The sensation of blood heating, spreading, flowing, cooling under my skin. The shimmer of magic that had spread across my wounds, the healing that had left only a faint, tingling imprint behind.

I feel it, then—a warm, golden thread. Something strong, unyielding. Almost…devout, though the thought confuses me. I ignore it, following the feeling, grazing the edges of the magic as though it is a limb. I feel it tug at my chest, a palpable glow that curves through me.

There. At the end of the thread is something stronger, but my hold on it is fragile. I try to coax more magic from it, trying to allow it to skim my veins, to flow easily to where Aslen's skin burns beneath my hands. I feel the golden thread tug back slightly, almost like a hand caressing me, the magic on the other side exploring my own.

There you are. The magic can't hear me, of course—it's only magic—but it feels like something I've known for a very, very long time. I feel, rather than see, the gold twist slightly, meeting silver, and—

I gasp, my hands leaving Aslen's abdomen to clutch my own. With a *snap* I feel the golden thread disappear completely.

"Luze?" Thyo's voice is worried. "Luze? What's wrong?"

"I'm fine." I straighten, still recoiling from the sensation I'd felt. As though a hook had been inserted into my belly and then yanked out again. "Aslen—is she—?"

"She's healing." Gideon is the one who answers, his voice filled with quiet awe.

The skin near the wound is now bright red, but it's not a sickly, inflamed red. This looks like a healthy flush, as though all of the blood has rushed to the injury to heal it. My magic has only gone so far, however. Aslen has stopped bleeding, but the wound hasn't closed.

I feel a small spurt of hope. "Gideon, the canteen." He hands it to me immediately, and I swirl the contents around before slowly pouring half of it over the wound.

Aslen lets out a faint groan, which makes me nearly collapse in relief. I hold the canteen up to her lips, letting a small dribble trickle out, trying to hold the canteen steady even as my hands shake.

"What is that?" Demelan has stepped closer, his face less green now.

"Woodsbark." I watch as Aslen swallows. "It can help heal any remaining infection. And it will help with the blood loss." I hand the bottle to Thyo. "Keep giving this to her. She needs to drink the rest of it."

I take a breath, trying to compose myself, to not let the others see the way I want to collapse right now. "The wound will still have to be sutured for it to heal properly."

Gideon rummages through the medicine bag, pulling out a small suturing kit. "I can do it," he says. "We've all had basic training. Unless you'd like to."

I wave him off, still trying to act normal. "No, you do it."

I remember vividly how to stitch a wound. It's probably

one of my clearest memories from my childhood, purely because of how much I hated it. I have no issue with allowing Gideon to handle that particular task.

Also, I am feeling more exhausted than ever. All I want is to escape to my tent.

Demelan is still standing there, watching Gideon prepare the suture, his face pale again. He looks nearly as sick as I feel.

"Demelan, maybe you could…" I wrack my brains, trying to think of a task. "Guard. I would feel comforted, knowing you were looking out." I wonder if I've gone too far by being so direct, nearly ordering him.

Fortunately, relief washes over his face. "Of course." He heads off to pace the perimeter of the camp.

"Very diplomatic," Thyo says quietly. "Instead of telling him he was making you nervous with the way he was about to faint."

I look at him, startled. "He faints?"

"Demelan has always hated blood," he says. "And needles. An interesting personality trait for a war captain."

"How in the world would he manage to make it through battle?"

"He doesn't seem to notice when he's in the midst of it. I've seen him behead someone without flinching. I've also seen him pass out while receiving stitches."

What he's said shouldn't be amusing, but a small laugh escapes me. The sound wakes Aslen, her eyelids fluttering.

"Aslen." I lean forward, but her eyes have closed again. "Can you hear me?"

There's a long moment of silence, and then: "Of course I can. Do either of you ever shut up?"

Thyo's face cracks into a smile, and he bends down to press

a kiss to her forehead. Aslen's eyes fly open, staring up at us. Her face is still frighteningly pale, but her eyes look alert.

"Aslen," Gideon says softly, kneeling by her. "I have to stitch the wound."

Her lips press together. "Have at it, then."

I glance at Thyo, but he doesn't look surprised by her blunt attitude. I suppose I shouldn't be, either. I stand. I have no desire to watch this. "Let me know if you need anything," I say to Gideon, and he nods. I hear Thyo say something to Gideon, his voice quiet, but I ignore them. I'm halfway across the camp when I hear Thyo's voice behind me.

"Luze."

I face him. I'm so tired I'm unsure how I'm still standing.

"I'm sorry," he says. "I should have never put you in danger. It was foolish. Stupid and reckless. I should have brought you back to camp immediately. And…" He clears his throat, his gaze searching my face. "I need to talk to you."

It comes back to me in a rush—everything that happened before the Strin. The almost kiss. The way we'd fought.

"Now?" I ask.

"It's important," he says. "There are things…well, there are things I should have told you earlier, but didn't. I had my reasons, but there is something you should know about me."

I frown. "Such as?"

"Something that may affect our interactions from now on," he says evasively. He clears his throat. "I wouldn't want you to—"

I cut him off. "What? Jeopardize our alliance, betray our agreement? Waste time playing senseless mind games?"

He hesitates. "No. I just…"

I feel another wave of fatigue, strong enough to pull me over. "This is a conversation best left for morning."

He seems like he's about to argue, and then he stops. "You're right. Perhaps we should speak another time. I only wanted you to know you can rest tonight. You'll be safe. We won't encounter any more Strin."

He can't possibly know that, but I'm too tired to argue. "Fine."

"And Luze?"

I turn back again. "What?"

He looks strangely young. "Thank you. For saving her."

"I didn't do it for you."

Perhaps if this were a different time, in a different place, under different circumstances...

Finally, he nods. "We'll speak in the morning. Goodnight, Luze."

As I walk away, my exhaustion reaches a peak. A haziness comes over me, a fog that makes me fight to keep my eyes open. Shadows flicker in my vision.

I reach my tent, desperate to get to my sleeping mat, and I pull back the flap—

I blink, and the shadows descend.

18

I am somewhere between sleep and death. This is not merely unconsciousness; this is an inky, liquid blackness that coats everything and keeps me under its spell.

I don't resist. Something about it soothes me. It carries me to a memory; one I'd nearly forgotten. One that had been taken from me.

Zassa and I lay in the grove behind the manor house, the sky shimmering with stars above us.

"There," I tell her, pointing. "Ahmela, the Old Goddess of the Othos."

Zassa stares up at the smattering of stars that resemble the curve of a hand, three dots rising above her cupped palm. "Tell me the story of the Othos again," she says.

I smile. I've told her this story many, many times.

"Before Alos, before Crafters, even before the Old Gods, there was only the Source," I say. "Once the Source was born, it was created to create, and as such, it birthed many."

"The Othos," I continue. "Those with the golden eyes, the true immortals, with the abilities of seven elements—the earthly elements, of Flame, Wind, Water, and Earth, and the Source-gifted

elements of the ancient times: Light, Shadow, and Blood. Though the Othos are now extinct, the Old Stories tell us there were no creatures fiercer on a battlefield. But the Source decided to birth another creature on a hidden isle, unbeknownst to the Othos: the Wytches."

Zassa has torn her gaze away from the night sky, and she's curled up next to me now.

"The Wytches were unlike the Othos in almost every way," I continue. "They were born into mortal bodies that lasted only decades, perhaps a century, if the Wytch was lucky."

"The Source had granted them some magical abilities, and as such, they were not true mortals. Perhaps fire came more easily to them on a cold night, or a Wytch might have a gift with the flora, to grow and gather more food for the community. They were slightly stronger than normal mortals, slightly less prone to sickness. Some say the more powerful Wytches even had unusually strong intuition—to know when a storm was coming, or which crops were destined to fail."

"Centuries passed, and the Othos and Wytches did not encounter each other. One year, a daughter of the Crone was born—the most powerful Wytch in the community. Her name was said to be Rilleah, with hair the color of the midnight sky and skin so dark it glowed as if kissed by Ahmela herself. Rilleah was different from the other Wytches. Her blood sang for adventure. One night, Rilleah snuck away, traveling to the Land of the Gods—what we now call the West Continent."

"Rilleah traveled for many weeks, looking for something she could not name. She knew only that she hungered for something her soul called to, and that she must find it. She was so hungry for this nameless thing that she often forgot to eat or drink or sleep, traveling at a pace faster than a mighty Alosian boar." I throw this part in for Zassa's benefit, and I'm pleased to hear her giggle.

"Silly," she says. "Alosian boars are too fat to be fast."

"That's what you think," I counter. "Until they spear your guts with one of their sharp tusks." I poke her in the stomach for emphasis, and she bursts into laughter.

"Go on!" she tells me. "What happened to Rilleah?"

"Rilleah was exhausted after traversing the lands for so long. Magic was stronger on these lands, but even so—she was far from home, and home, with her coven, is where a Wytch is most power-ful. Finally, Rilleah could not withstand the wildness of the Old Gods and their lands. She collapsed, soon to die."

Zassa sucks in a sharp breath, and I bite down my laugh. "Little did Rilleah know, she was in the Northern Kingdom—what was the true land of the Othos, in the northernmost part of the West Continent, north only to Alos. Rilleah was discovered by one Othos in particular, a young male named Cariel. He scented Rilleah, and curious of her peculiar Wytch smell, he sought her out. Cariel was young, but he saw something in Rilleah that called his most powerful magic to him. Only in his true form could Cariel have saved Rilleah, for his immortal form was even faster than that body which resembles Crafters and mortals. Aside from their golden eyes, of course. Cariel brought Rilleah to his ruler and begged the queen to save her. Seeing the truth of the young male's attachment, that he had somehow found his Source-given partner, she agreed, and healed Rilleah using her immense gifts."

"I think that part is silly, like the boar," Zassa interrupts. "There can't only be one person the Source tells us to fall in love with. What if they die, or live in a different kingdom?"

My stomach tightens. I will have no love at all; my life will be filled only with consorts and duty. "If the Source fates it, then that person will not die before you meet them. And if they live in a different kingdom, somehow, you will find yourself there."

I continue, "When Rilleah awoke and saw the golden eyes of

Cariel, she knew she had met the one the Source had fated her to be with. They were mated and joined—as they did in the Old Ways, before mating became marriage—and lived happily for many, many years."

"And lived forever?" Zassa asks.

I stare up at the stars. I always hate this part of the story. I want to remember Rilleah and Cariel as two fated lovers who never parted. But that is not how the tale ends.

"One day, another Wytch arrived in the Northern Kingdom," I say. "Ilestra was different from the other Wytches. Like Rilleah, she craved adventure. However, she also craved something much more dangerous: power."

"Ilestra tracked Rilleah to the Northern Kingdom. Rilleah was overjoyed to see her sister Wytch, whom she had not seen in decades, though Rilleah and Ilestra had grown up together. Ilestra had aged and was a matron of thirty-some years; Rilleah had not aged since mating with Cariel."

"Ilestra was filled with envy when she saw Rilleah's youthful face and her power, which had only grown since living with the Othos. Ilestra concocted a plan: she would steal the Othos' magic."

"No!" Zassa exclaims, as though she has not heard this story many times.

"Yes," I say. "Ilestra was powerful in her own right, and deeply connected to the magic of the earth. She trapped Cariel one night. She used her gifts, channeling the power of Cariel into herself, except..."

"Except?" Zassa says impatiently.

"Except Ilestra did not know that such a power would destroy her body if she truly tried to contain it all. She took one element and would have taken more—and died, with the elements lost forever—had Rilleah not, sensed her mate's pain and rage and sought him. She was unable to slay Ilestra—there are few kinds

of love as deep as a Wytch's love for her sister—but she banished her from the Northern Kingdom."

"She should have killed her," Zassa says. I say nothing, though I secretly agree.

"Ilestra suffered her own fate, meted out by the Source. She had stolen power—and it was power she had. Wytches are intimately linked, and the element she took from Cariel rippled across the coven. But it was not wise, that magic that she stole. It was a gift of the Old Gods, too powerful for the Wytches bodies, and it warped their minds. Where once they had been content and peaceful folk, they now became violent and greedy. Wars broke out; blood was shed. Eventually, their own violence drove them extinct."

"Sad," Zassa murmurs. I am not sure I agree with her; I get chills when I think of the Wytches. "What happened to Rilleah?"

My heart sinks, but I continue. "Rilleah had saved her mate, and she and Cariel were still deeply in love—forever bound. But the First Queen was enraged at what had happened, and she blamed Rilleah."

"That's not fair!" Zassa protests. "It wasn't Rilleah's fault."

"True," I say. "But the First Queen needed to punish someone, and Rilleah was the only one not of her own—the only outsider. And when Ilestra stole Cariel's magic, she stole it from all Othos— so interconnected were they, like the Wytches. Never again would an Othos be born with power over the element she had stolen. The First Queen would not live without vengeance."

"What did she do?" Zassa asks.

"She banished Rilleah from the Northern Kingdom. No matter how hard Rilleah tried, she would never be able to find the Othos again. They were lost to her forever."

"But what about Cariel?" Zassa says. "Did he go with her?"

My eyes are stinging a bit. Silly, as Zassa would say. "No. The

First Queen used her magic to do the opposite to Cariel—while Rilleah could never return, Cariel could never leave the Northern Kingdom. They would never see each other again. Rilleah wandered, brokenhearted, close to killing herself every day—for the pain of separation from her beloved was so great, so overwhelming, she could hardly breathe. Until she realized she was carrying his child."

"A baby!" Zassa gasps.

"Rilleah realized she would never see her beloved again in this life, but she would have his child, and that was reason to live. She discovered mortals living in the lands southern to the Othos, and she stayed with them. Eventually, she gave birth to a beautiful, strong daughter, and though her heart still ached for Cariel, she found that her love for her daughter—Faela—was beyond anything she had ever known."

"Eventually, Rilleah found a mortal man who was kind and eased the pain in her heart. Rilleah was perhaps not happy—but she loved and was loved. She had more children with her mortal husband and lived a long life—longer than that of a mortal, but not truly immortal, either. She might have lived longer, but one day, she received news of Cariel's passing. In his despair, he was unable to endure the separation from his mate, and he fought in a battle after he had weakened himself—intending to lose and be killed."

"I hate this part," Zassa grumbles.

"When Rilleah heard that Cariel had slipped into the hands of the Source, she poisoned herself with Blackvine—slipping into a deep, irreversible sleep. She knew she would see Cariel in death, and she wanted nothing more than to be with him again."

"What about her kids?" Zassa asks.

"Rilleah's children created a new magic the Source could have never imagined—or perhaps had fated to emerge in the kingdom.

Rilleah's first daughter, Faela, was the most powerful. That is why the Crown is given to the firstborn daughter, and why Crafters believe females carry the magic so strongly. However, even Rilleah's other children were powerful; they had access to the four earthly elements, and their lifespans were long—nearly immortal, if they did not succumb to sickness, or fall in battle. Some lived to only five hundred years, but others lived for nameless lengths of time. Some say the lifespan of a Crafter is tied to their magic. Others say it depends on the star under which a Crafter is born, or the will of the Source."

"But some of Rilleah's other kids weren't as powerful," Zassa says. "And that's why Saelis says we have Lower Crafters. Because their magic wasn't as strong."

"And, of course, some of Rilleah's children married and had children with mortals, which weakened the magic. Faela took only one consort—her half-brother, Kvez—in order to keep magic strong in her bloodline."

"Gross," Zassa says.

I agree. And yet, the things the daughters of the Crown do for duty…

I find the constellation of Ahmela again. If the Old Gods ever truly existed, I wonder what they had seen. If they had watched or helped fate shape the generations of Rilleah's bloodline. If the gods had not faded, would they be watching me?

"Luze," Zassa says. She pushes herself up to a seat, looking at me with a frown. "You didn't finish the story."

"Of course, I did," I say. "You know the rest of the story—generation upon generation was born, until war broke out between mortals and Crafters. Crafters were outnumbered but won because of our magic. The Thousand Year War was not long ago, Zassa. Never forget battle may be on the horizon."

She rolls her eyes at me. Such attitude already, at such a young age. "I know," she says. "But what happened to the Wytches?"

I push myself up to a seat, too. "The Wytches died out, just like the Othos," I say. "You know that."

"Yes," Zassa says, although her face looks pinched. "But how does anyone really know what happened to the Wytches and the Othos? Maybe they're just hiding, watching us."

Why is she asking me such questions? Perhaps I ought not tell her stories so close to bedtime. Mother will scold me if she hears Zassa has had a nightmare. Then again, I rarely see my mother long enough for her to scold me. Saelis, however…

"Enough storytelling," I say. "We ought to go to bed. Saelis won't be happy if he catches us again."

Zassa rises willingly enough, taking the hand I offer, but she's still frowning.

"What is it?" I ask her.

She chews on her lip. "The element Ilestra stole, the one the Wytches took—which one was it?"

I feel chilled despite the warm night air. "Shadow," I say finally. "The Wytches stole shadow."

19

THE FEELING OF falling doesn't wake me, but my head cracking against the ice of the forest floor does.

It feels like a dagger being driven into my temple. Stars burst across my vision.

"What in *gods*—" That sounds like Aslen, but there's a skittering sound and then the sound of a horse squealing and I squint, trying to clear my vision, but it's absolute chaos. There's a flash of red—Odreya—and I hear another squealing sound, turning in time to see Demelan's horse, eyes wild, trying to bolt, as it's attacked by a bird.

Correction: a bird monster.

It's one of the *iikampi,* a massive hawk-like creature with razor-sharp talons and a penchant for aggression, particularly the females, which are recognizable for their red-tipped feathers.

Even in my disoriented state, I notice this *iikampi* has particularly bright crimson wings.

Gideon is yelling, his sword out, and I catch a glimpse of Aslen, her bow drawn, as the bird-creature dives down for another attack.

My body seems to move of its own accord, rolling away. I'm on my feet, my vision swimming, but at least I'm up.

I had been asleep in my tent only a moment ago—hadn't I? Except I see no tent.

Thyo is shouting something, and I look up and see his eyes are on me. Shouting something to me.

I don't hesitate. I listen to my instincts: I run.

I turn, sprinting blindly into the forest, faster than any mortal. I feel a slight pang of guilt as the shouting fades into the distance.

Only…why can't I remember being attacked? I feel confused, groggy. My head throbs.

I'm not sure how long I've been running—maybe only a few minutes, or maybe many—when I reach a small clearing. I slow to a walk, though I keep my pace brisk. I have no idea how soon the others will come after me, if at all.

It hadn't been a conscious decision to run. But now that I'm here—wherever I am—I realize that instinct might have led me further astray than I'd intended.

I push through some thorny brush on the opposite side of the clearing, earning myself a few cuts, but I'm too impatient to care. I just need to orient myself and figure out where I am.

And then what? A small voice whispers. I ignore it. I'm not sure what my plan is at this point, or if I even really have a plan, but at least I'm doing something.

I'm still arguing with myself internally when I stop abruptly, suddenly faced with a stone wall.

Not a wall. A cliff face. A sheer, towering cliff that continues as far as the eye can see in either direction. A cliff so tall it blots out half the sky and leaves you feeling dizzy just from looking at it. Which means…

I turn, slowly. The trees tower above me, but through the dense greenery I see another cliff face, perhaps a mile away.

The Pass of Ends. The only way into Altheara from Alos.

But we'd been hours away, if not an entire day. How could we have traveled here so quickly?

We hadn't, I realize. We hadn't traveled here quickly at all. Which means it's not just a few minutes I can't remember. It's hours. Last night, and judging by the light of the sky, at least half of a day.

Had I collapsed? Again? Or perhaps the healing had exhausted me more than I'd realized; I was still unused to magic.

I hear a small *crack* from the forest behind me. I turn, but nothing is there. Probably just a small animal. Still, a chill goes up my spine. I need to hide, to gather myself and regroup. Plan.

I start to jog parallel to the cliff face, the wind picking up as I do. It's cold enough to make my skin sting, but I don't care. My eyes strain, watering from the wind, but after a few minutes I finally see what I'm looking for: a divot in the cliff face.

"Please, please, please," I mutter. Please let this be what I think it is.

The Pass of Ends is supposed to be littered with caves and hiding spaces, mostly burrows for the wild things that live out here. I duck around the outcropping, and I want to cry in relief when I see a cave entrance. I strain my senses, but I don't hear or smell anything. Slowly, I duck through the opening. The last thing I want is to surprise some unsuspecting beast in hibernation.

The pathway through the cave is narrow and winding. Every step I take is full of caution, but the passageway is short, and I quickly reach a chamber. It isn't huge, and there isn't much in it—just dirt and a few twigs—but it's empty. There's a hole directly in the middle of the ceiling, and a faint, watery light streams from it.

I can hear a slow trickle of water in the corner, and I turn, trying to orient myself. Despite being shielded from the wind, it's cold in here, and I grip my cloak tighter.

When had I put on my cloak? I don't remember wearing it before.

No sooner has the thought crossed my mind than a dark, piercing scent reaches me. Close, I realize. Too close. And in this cave, that can only mean one thing.

I spin, facing the cave's passageway, and there *it* is.

The mysterious scent I had kept picking up on; the potent aura of magic I had felt during my journey. Something that now dwarfs in comparison to the magic that radiates from what's standing before me. A creature with eyes as golden as mine are silver, burning bright even in the dim light of the cave.

"Well," the male says. "We meet at last."

20

My eyes flick over him, judging the threat. He's tall, even by Crafter standards, but what worries me more are the weapons strapped to his body. A sword strapped to his back. A dagger at his hip. The hilt of two more knives in each of his boots.

I'm sure there are more I can't see.

Rings line his fingers, and a tattoo peeks out from under his sleeve. From what I can see of his wrist, it's in a language I don't recognize—symbols in an ancient dialect.

Not mortal, clearly. The magic rippling from him is… powerful.

Too powerful.

He lifts a brow. "If you're thinking about running, I wouldn't recommend it. I would have you pinned before you'd made it two steps."

I can't bring myself to speak, feeling as though all the air has gone out of my lungs. The male leans against the wall of the chamber. His movements remind me of a panther, settling in to wait before a kill.

I open my mouth to ask the most basic of questions—*who are you*—but instead what comes out is: "Why?"

The male examines the walls of the cave, his expression bored. "Why what?"

My palms clench. "Why have you been following me?"

"Have I?" He still doesn't look at me.

"Yes," I say. "I recognize your scent."

This seems to pique his interest, but barely. "You can track scents?"

His question catches me off guard. "Of course. All Crafters can."

"No," he says. "They can't."

I switch topics. "Your eyes. They're…" *Impossible. Confusing.*

He crosses his arms. "I'm unable to read your mind, believe it or not. You might want to finish your sentences."

My shoulders tense. "You didn't answer my first question. Why are you following me?"

He still hasn't looked at me directly. "I can't tell you."

Slowly, I unclench my hands. I'm relatively certain he's not going to attack at this point. "What *can* you tell me?"

"I guess you'll find out, depending on what you ask."

"Fine." I take a deep breath, trying to quell my irritation. "What's your name?"

"Taleas."

I wait, but he doesn't say anything else. "Aren't you going to ask me who I am?"

"I know who you are."

"How did you know I was here?"

"I tracked your scent."

"But I thought—"

He holds up a hand, his head cocked towards the cave entrance. "We have about eight minutes before your entourage comes to find you," he says. "You might want to stop your sputtering and get to the point."

I stare at him, outraged. "You're the one who's been following *me*. I don't—"

"Seven and a half."

I throw up my hands. "Why don't *you* tell me what you think I should know?"

He sighs, irritated. "That's not really how this works."

As much as he won't tell me, he has to be here for a reason. I wrack my thoughts for a question, something useful. "What do you know about the lands across the wall?"

"I know plenty. You'll have to be more specific." I notice he seems to be purposefully avoiding looking at me. In fact, he's looking everywhere *but* me.

My hip is aching from where I fell on it earlier, but I ignore it. A question I hadn't even realized I wanted to know falls from my lips: "Is there any way to break an Oath?"

"No. And yes."

Source, I want to hit him. "Helpful."

He raises a brow but doesn't comment on my tone. "Theoretically…it's possible. But it's never been done. You'll be wasting your time."

"I don't have another choice." The ache in my hip is increasing. I reach toward it rub the soreness, trying to be subtle. Before I can, the pain disappears. I frown.

"You have another choice," Taleas says. "Your only choice, at this point. You cross the wall and carry on with your task."

My stomach drops. "How do you know about what I have to do?"

"I know things."

"Was there an announcement across the continent?" I gripe. "Does *everyone* know I'm meant to kill the prince of Altheara? I thought assassinations were meant to be secret, for Source's sake."

His face tenses, like he's irritated. Or trying not to laugh. "If there was an announcement, I didn't hear of it."

"If you know so much," I say, "then why won't you tell me how to break the Oath?"

He pulls a dagger from his side, and I stiffen, but he only examines the blade. "Because it would be useless. But…I suppose I can tell you one thing."

I wait, but he keeps his eyes on the dagger. "What?"

He looks up. "If you were desperate and foolish enough… there are records, in Altheara. Scrolls of magic. The kind that could be used to break an Oath."

My breath comes out in a rush. "In Altheara?"

A nod is the only confirmation I get.

"But…" I struggle to speak. "That's impossible. Althearan lands are mortal."

He sheaths the knife. "Impossible, yet true."

Does this mean I need to be prepared for magic to be used *against* me? I had never considered such a daunting possibility.

No. Althearan lands have no magic. The wall between our lands makes sure of that. But if somehow the scrolls were brought across the wall, to a land *with* magic, if somehow, they figured out how to wield it…what sort of destruction could they cause?

Or…what if I'm wrong? What if somehow the boundary wall has allowed magic to cross?

The world seems to tilt a bit. "Where are the records? What magic do they speak of? Do the Althearans know of it, or does it simply dwell in the land?"

Taleas frowns as he appraises me. "Stop breathing like that, or you'll faint. Haven't you had training?"

Actually, I think I'm closer to vomiting than fainting. I

brace my hand on the cave wall, swallowing back the bile in my throat. "Breathing techniques weren't mentioned."

He scowls. "Crafters. Absolutely useless. High Lady, and yet they've left you as little more than a powerless child."

"I am not a *child*." I look up long enough to glare at him, though I still feel sick. "And if you think we're so useless, maybe *you* should lead our training."

What a horrible thought. I'd pity anyone forced to spend time with him.

I can tell he's still monitoring my breathing, but a slow smile curves his lips. "I'm sure I could teach you all sorts of things."

The suggestion is clear, though it's equally as obvious he doesn't mean it.

"You called me a child a moment ago," I point out.

The smirk doesn't leave his face. "Perhaps I should have said child*ish*. Immature. Naïve."

"I know what childish means," I snap, jerking upright. "And I would never *train* with a male as repugnant as you."

The smirk disappears. His eyes narrow. "You wouldn't have the chance. If you survive what you're about to do, you'll have a war on your hands, for a kingdom I have no interest in." He crosses his arms. "We won't be seeing each other again."

I mirror his posture, crossing my own arms. "Good."

A muscle tics in his jaw. "Good."

We're staring at each other, neither of us friendly, but as I meet his gaze—his eyes really, truly meeting mine for the first time—his jaw tenses, just slightly, and he slips a ring from his finger. He flips it to me, and I catch it.

"A ring?" I say dubiously.

"There will be threats you'll encounter across the wall that you've never faced before. This ring is…special. It acts as a stabilizer for magic. Amongst other things."

I'm already wearing one enchanted ring against my will. I'm not inclined to accept another, no matter how desperate I am. "I've never heard of such a thing."

"I wouldn't expect you to," he says dismissively. "But I'd accept it, if I were you."

Hesitantly, I slip the ring on. It's large enough that it fits my thumb. "What would happen if it fell off?" I ask.

"Don't use it unless you need it," he says. "And then if you do…well, don't remove it."

I hold out my hand, watching the gold glint in the dim light. I feel…nothing. No glimmer of magic. Taleas looks bored, and I immediately feel like a fool, fluttering my hand like a courtier. I slip the ring off, putting it in my pocket.

"You can thank me any time now," he drawls.

I grit my teeth. "Thank you."

He doesn't seem to notice my flaring temper. "You know, that ring will only help you if you manage to survive."

"And you don't think I will?"

"I think that decision lies with you."

I roll my eyes. "Do you have any more words of encouragement, or can I leave now?"

He's examining his blade again. "I know you expect to fail."

"I have no intention of—"

"Don't you? Are you more afraid that you won't complete your task, or that you will?"

I have no answer, because truthfully, I am not sure.

"It was you, out in the forest," I say. "Wasn't it? After the Strin attacked me." I push the edge of my sweater up, exposing a strip of my abdomen. "How did you heal me? Those injuries were severe. I should be scarred. If not dead."

I know what I speak is truth. The thick scars that still linger on my back are proof: some wounds are too great for magic to heal. Even Crafter magic. But my abdomen is smooth. Not even a scratch.

He stares at the skin of my stomach, though his gaze is distant.

I drop my sweater. "Are you a Healer? Are you…a Crafter?"

We stare at each other for a moment, and the barest glimmer of amusement crosses his face. He cocks his head. "The Althearans are close. I suppose you have a choice to make, Lady Vyzrais."

Clearly, he doesn't plan to see what that choice is. He moves to leave.

"Wait," I say. "Taleas."

He jerks a little as I say his name. He turns to look at me.

"Do you…" I clear my throat. "Do *you* think I'll fail?"

I'm not sure why I'm asking him, letting my weakness show.

His face is as impassive as ever. "Be careful, Lady Vyzrais. You Crafters aren't the only ones who have chosen to meddle with things they shouldn't."

I open my mouth to ask another question, but a sharp breeze breaks through the cave, making the dirt swirl and I blink, turning away. When I open my eyes, he's gone. The air ripples with the scent of his magic—like fresh water and cedar and iron.

I feel strangely restless. Some part of me wants to run after him, demanding more answers. Or maybe some part of me just longs to give him a hard smack upside the head.

I close my eyes, pressing my palms to my eyelids. Some,

tiny, hidden part of me had always considered breaking the agreement with the Althearans. Taleas has forced me to confront that part. Am I truly willing to go along with my uncle's plot against the Althearans? All for the Crown of Alos? I'd always accepted it was a duty I had been born to, and it was what other people wanted for me. But do *I* want it?

My entire body rebels at the traitorous thought, even as another part of me contemplates leaving. I could go to one of the isles off the coast. I could make it to the eastern side of Alos and find a ship to take me. From there, I could even travel to the East Continent, though my very existence there would be considered a threat. It would be dangerous. I would have to build a new identity.

I stare down at the silver Oath ring on my finger. All of these wild ideas are useless. I'm tied to the agreement I made with my uncle. Which is precisely why he made me swear to such an Oath.

Except now I know that there *is* a way to break the Oath— potentially—except it still requires me crossing the wall. I would laugh at the irony, if any of this were a laughing matter.

I straighten and make my way to the cave's entrance. As I'm exiting, a horse emerges from the trees: Vhetta. Aslen is astride.

Her face is held tight, as if in pain. It occurs to me the last time I saw her, she was a few breaths away from a fatal injury. The fact that she's upright, let alone riding a horse, is a miracle.

I don't bother with any preamble. "Is anyone hurt?"

"Everyone is alive." She dismounts Vhetta, though I can tell she's gritting her teeth. She peers at the cave entrance. "You managed to find a hiding spot, I see."

I cross my arms. "And I see you managed to find me."

"It'll take more than some bird-monster to deter me."

"An *iikampi*," I correct. "I've only seen them in books."

"Yes, well, I think I'd prefer if they had stayed there."

I look at the direction she came from. "Where are the others?"

"They'll be here soon." She walks back to Vhetta, giving her a pat on the neck. The mare tosses her head; her eyes are still a bit wild. Not that I can blame her. If I were a horse, I wouldn't have stuck around this long.

"Is Arturon okay?" I ask. "All I remember is falling, and then—"

"He's fine. I told you; everyone is alive. That was nothing. Unexpected, maybe. It would have been fun, if I hadn't been trying not to rip my stitches the whole time. And if I hadn't had to deal with Thyo panicking about you running off. Not that I blame you. I'm glad you seem to be improving your survival instincts."

I notice her hand has subtly drifted to her abdomen, pressing on it, and I decide to stop asking questions. A minute later I hear hoofbeats, and Thyo appears, riding Odreya.

Arturon is tethered loosely to Odreya's saddle. Behind Thyo are Demelan and Gideon, also on their horses.

"Luze," Thyo says. He dismounts, striding over to me. I'm shocked when he reaches out, cupping my face in his hands. His eyes are alert even with the weariness behind them. "Are you hurt?"

I'm stunned by his touch. "I'm fine."

His face relaxes, relief washing over his features. His hands slide down to my shoulders. "Good. Good. I thought, when I saw you run away…" He trails off, shaking his head. "It doesn't matter now. You're safe, and that's what's important."

It's odd, how awake I feel after my encounter with Taleas. It's almost as if I see the very world slightly differently, as though something inside of me has shifted, just slightly. Which is perhaps why my mind has slowed, why I haven't broken free from Thyo's touch.

Taleas was right: I only have one choice. I have to continue on to Altheara. Perhaps I will find a way to break my Oath. Perhaps not.

Either way, as the prince's right hand, Thyo is only one thing: my enemy.

Which means I will have to play a game. A game I have resisted.

Until now.

So, I let him continue to touch me and I say, "I'm glad everyone is okay. It was all so disorienting…I ran without thinking."

He doesn't seem suspicious. "Anyone would have."

Behind him, Aslen rolls her eyes.

Carefully, I step away, breaking free from his touch. "We should go," I say. "Before we lose any more light."

The sight of him has reminded me of the hours I'd lost prior to the attack of the *iikampi*. I had thought I was simply dealing with fragile mortals. Now I am not so sure. I could have merely collapsed from using magic, my exhaustion getting the best of me. Or perhaps something else happened—perhaps something was done *to* me. I let none of this show on my face, however.

We organize and mount, riding to the gateway at the wall, only a few miles away. It's a massive archway chiseled into the stone, a soft, shimmery light fluttering through the opening. The magic looks similar enough to the boundary used to trap me in my exile to make my stomach lurch.

Thyo lets the others ride ahead. "Now isn't the time but… once we're in Altheara, there are things we should discuss,

Luze. Important things." He hesitates. "I want you to know I am glad for this agreement between our lands. I know the prince feels similarly. And I hope you will come to find yourself compatible with him, given time."

His words prick my unease. He almost sounds nervous.

"I agree," I say. "I am exactly where I need to be. For Alos."

"And for Altheara," he says. "What's ahead of us will be for the greater good of the entire continent."

I look back at the gateway. If only he knew.

My job is to be a spy and assassin. So far, I have been a damsel.

Alos is my home. This is where I belong. I was born to protect these lands, no matter the cost. Perhaps it is not the path I would have chosen, but it's my path, nonetheless. I twist the Oath ring on my finger, steeling myself.

If I'm not already a spy and an assassin, then I will have to become one.

And with that thought, I cross the wall into Altheara.

Shadow

21

I sit, dripping with sweat.

At least I'm outside. The only freedom I'm allowed, currently.

Of course, I'm not sure if I would really consider it freedom. After all, there are four armed guards carefully placed throughout the garden. I *think* their job is to be unnoticeable, but I can feel every one of them like a bug on my skin. I try to ignore them, focusing on the book in my hands.

I snap the book shut. It's useless.

I am trapped.

My misery had started as I'd crossed the wall. That had been three days ago.

As soon as I'd crossed the boundary, a hot, damp gust of air had hit me. Then, I'd seen the cascades of vines tumbling from trees, the fronds and palm leaves at every turn, the way everything was so *green*. In the distance a disturbingly tall tower made of black stone rose above the treeline.

Then had come the short journey to the Althearan capital, though it had felt like an eternity. The heat was bad enough, but the humidity? Unbearable.

The one bright spot—if it could be called that—was the vague interest I had felt for the Althearan architecture. It looked old—impressively so. The tower of shimmering black stone I'd seen was called Etalus. Desolate, an abandoned relic from the Old Kingdom, but still standing. I'd stared at it as we'd passed, trying to hide my awe. Its height was equal to anything I might have seen in Alos.

Then there had been the wall enclosing the Althearan capital, Ceneth.

Ceneth's wall had dulled in comparison to the wall bordering Alos and Altheara, but even I could admit it was impressive in its own right. Twelve towers were stationed around it.

Of course, it also made my gut twist to think about trying to escape that wall and those towers. Not as much as it made my gut twist to think of the treatment I had received upon officially arriving in Altheara…

And now, sitting in the garden, I stand abruptly, beginning to make my way toward the castle. I ignore the way my guards instantly meld into formation. Sometimes I pretend they're puppies, simply following me around to play. Perhaps if they were hounds under my control, I would feel regal, striding about the castle with my followers. Except we all know who these particular wolves are loyal to, and it isn't me.

I've just passed a section of bright purple orchids when I see a figure striding toward me. It's Aslen, and seeing as her eyes are fixed on me, there's no way to avoid her. I fold my arms, cupping the book in front of my chest as a kind of shield. "What?" I say, as she stops in front of me. "What do you want?"

"I've been sent to convey a message."

My spine stiffens. "I'm not going."

"You don't even know if that was the message."

I'm acutely aware of the eyes and ears behind me. "Was it?"

Now she looks annoyed. "If you would just—"

"No."

"Luze, why can't you—"

My temper flares, as it so often does these days. "I said *no*. If he wants to plead his case, he can talk to me himself. Something he hasn't deigned to do yet. So, my answer is no."

I don't wait for a response, sweeping past her.

I ignore my audience as I enter through the castle doors. This entrance, at least, is one of the less populated ones. It goes past the kitchens, rather than the main hall.

Instead, I'm only subjected to a few cold stares as I make my way through the castle halls. One female with pale brown eyes stares at me, her eyes narrowed as we pass by. I don't see her mouth move, but I hear a whisper that sounds more like a hiss. *Crafter.* I want to snort at the word. In these lands, the mere description of what I am is considered an insult.

Finally, I stop in front of the doors that mark my room, my four guards still in tow.

Two of them, Nikal and Vilena—the Twins, as I call them, because their looks and mannerisms are eerily similar—step forward to open the doors. Something I allow only because the last time I insisted on opening a door myself, it had resulted in such a fuss that Aslen had been summoned to come to me herself and explain, in a sour tone, why it was crucial I respected the rules of Althearan etiquette.

I enter the room, shutting the doors. My room is the one place I don't have to be accompanied. I breathe a sigh of relief.

Until I realize I'm not alone.

"This one is lovely," Iyanna says. She's rifling through the massive wardrobe in my room and pulls out a dress of deep blue. It looks like crystals have been sewn directly into the fabric.

I try not to sigh. In the past few days, I'd discovered that I do, in fact, have a love for fashion. I'd been deprived of beautiful things for so many years, and since arriving in Altheara I'd been presented with more pleasing gowns than I could count. However, there's only so much energy one can have for pretty dresses when your mind is on murder.

Iyanna glances over, noticing my lack of response. "Did you enjoy your time outdoors?"

"Certainly," I say. "I walked around the rose garden for the twelfth time."

If she notices the slight hint of sarcasm in my tone, she doesn't react. Iyanna had been assigned to me as a handmaiden upon my arrival. She wasn't hostile, but she wasn't exactly friendly, either.

As I sit, allowing Iyanna to begin working on my hair—an intricate updo requiring numerous pins—I allow myself to fume, as I so often have the past few days.

My determination to be strong, to be more than a damsel, had been spurred as I'd crossed the wall. Unfortunately, so had my misery.

Firstly: where was Prince Adriel? If I were betrothed to someone and they showed up in my kingdom after risking life and limb to arrive, I would think it might be slightly higher on my priority list to greet them. I hadn't even been summoned by the queen. It aggravated me more than I wanted to admit.

More frustrating than that, however, was the interaction I'd had with Thyo shortly after my arrival. He had walked me to my rooms. I'd wondered at the fact he hadn't had a servant do it, until we'd reached my room, and realized why he'd chosen to do this particular task himself.

"These are your living quarters," he'd told me, opening the door. He'd gestured to the four guards in the hall. "These are your guards. They will follow you at all times. If you attempt to evade them, it will be assumed you are attacking the peace of the kingdom and will be immediately imprisoned without trial. I'd suggest you don't allow yourself to be found in that position."

I'd stared at him, mouth gaping, but he wasn't done

"I have matters to attend to this week," he'd said. "But we need to talk. Soon."

"Why? So you can lecture me more about where I can and can't go?"

He had shifted, almost uneasily. "I'll send for you soon."

Except he hadn't. I hadn't seen him since then.

It was as though something had flipped inside of Thyo, as though some part had emerged that I hadn't even known existed. His cold, regal tone, the threat in his words—it was nothing like the Thyo who had held my face in my hands, relieved to find me unharmed from the *iikampi*. This Thyo was my enemy, through and through.

Once the door had shut behind him, I'd grabbed the thing nearest to me, which happened to be an ugly blue vase, and thrown it against the wall.

And now, days later...I stare at the small table the vase had been sitting on. It hadn't been replaced.

Which brought me to my main irritation: the dinner I was supposed to attend tonight. My engagement dinner. A welcoming dinner.

It didn't feel very welcoming.

Aslen had been the one to deliver the message that I was required to attend this dinner. I would meet Prince Adriel while I was there.

Except I had no interest in whatever spectacle the Althearans wanted to create by having me meet him for the first time at a public event. It increased my suspicion that the prince was a pompous pig. It made me angrier than I wanted to admit.

So, I had told Aslen I wouldn't be attending the dinner. If Prince Adriel wanted to introduce himself, he could make the trek across the castle to do so.

This had not been taken to kindly and had resulted in Aslen becoming a page of sorts, relaying messages back and forth, which had become increasingly hostile.

I frown at the thought, and Iyanna pauses.

"Did I hurt you?" She's currently twisting the last of my hairstyle into an intricate braid while I sit at the vanity.

"No," I say. I sound more forlorn than I want.

Our eyes meet in the mirror. I wonder if she'll comment, but she simply purses her lips and looks away.

About half an hour later, I'm seated on my small couch, still wearing the sparkling, cobalt-blue gown and reading the book, when the door to my room opens. I already know it's Aslen.

"What a surprise," I say without looking up. "Going to try to force me to go to this dinner?"

"Yes, actually," a voice says. I look up, startled.

It's Thyo.

I stand, tossing the book aside. "What do *you* want?"

"I'm here to escort you," he says.

I can't help it: I'm instantly annoyed. "You've ignored me for days. Why stop now?"

His jaw tightens. "I know I promised we'd talk. I just..." He trails off.

It irritates me. "Learn how to have a conversation, Thyo. Until then, you can leave."

I stride past him, moving to wrench the door open for him to exit, but a hand appears over my shoulder, pressing against the wood. I give the knob a tug. The door doesn't move.

I turn. "Really? You—"

The words die on my lips as I see how close he is.

"Why are you so stubborn?" he asks.

I glower at him. "I am not."

The frustration I've felt since arriving finally has an outlet. It gives me a grim sort of pleasure to watch him fight for patience.

Thyo places his other hand against the door, trapping me between his arms. "You will go to this dinner, Luze, so help me gods."

"Or what, Thyo? You'll do *what?*"

His face is only inches away. We stare at each other, neither of us relenting. I notice the half-moons under his eyes, the tiredness etching his face.

I reach up, shoving him. Hard. Hard enough so that even though he's braced against the door, he stumbles back a few steps.

"I'm not going to your stupid dinner," I snap.

His face is like thunder. "You are a—"

I don't get the chance to hear what I am, because there's a loud knock at the door.

I turn, wrenching it open. "What?"

Aslen stands on the other side, her hand still raised. Slowly, she lowers it, taking me in. "Demelan sent me to check on you. He thought it would be…prudent." She looks between me and Thyo. "I guess he wasn't wrong."

"There's nothing to check on," I say. "I'm not going to this dinner, and that is final."

Thyo speaks from behind me. "It is not final. You will go, or—"

I whirl towards him. "Threaten me, and I will rip out your entrails and shove them so far up your—"

A loud cough interrupts us. We both turn to Aslen.

"If I may," she says. "It doesn't seem as though either of you is getting very far with your conversation."

"If she would just—"

"—he's the one who—"

"Enough," she interrupts.

"You don't understand, Aslen," Thyo says, yanking a hand through his hair. "I haven't—she doesn't—"

She waves him off. "Thyo, everyone is expecting you. Go."

He doesn't move. I can tell part of him wants to keep standing here, arguing with me. Finally, he relents. He stalks past us both.

"I'll see you at dinner," he says to me.

"See you in the Abyss," I mutter. I glower at his retreating form, wishing I had something to throw.

Aslen just stands there, watching this with a bemused expression, like she's puzzling something out. Unlike me, she's wearing her usual outfit of pants and a jacket, only nicer. I wonder if she owns more than two outfits.

"I take it you two didn't have a very fruitful conversation," she says.

"That's one way of putting it." I yank at my skirts as we walk into the hall. I walk slowly. I don't want to encounter Thyo again before I have to.

"Your guards tell me you're awfully glum," she says.

"I'll be sure to be much perkier the next time I see them."

"Well, at least now you've talked to Thyo. I'm sure that cleared things up. Right?"

"Right," I say. "It was a very enlightening conversation. I feel so much better now."

We walk through the halls of the castle. My impression of it has remained the same: it's large, though not nearly as grand as something I would expect in Alos. The decorations are tasteful, but practical. Unlike Crafters, I have the sense that Althearans are less concerned with aesthetics and beauty, and more preoccupied with things like functionality and convenience. I have an inkling even the dresses I've received are not the norm for Altheara, and that I am being made to be a doll—a living representation of the frivolity and riches of Alos.

"I know you're mad at Thyo, but your situation could be worse," Aslen says.

"How?" I ask.

She shrugs. "You could have arrived in Altheara only to find that the prince was an ugly, miserable goat."

"And he still may be," I say. "I wouldn't know, would I?"

She frowns. "What—"

She's cut off by our arrival to the dining hall. No one is seated yet. Most are still milling around, chatting, with drinks in hand. I was right: none of the attire here is as opulent as mine. Which makes it all the more apparent when a silence falls over the room as I enter.

I feel anxiety welling in my stomach, but I lift my chin. A servant walks by with a tray of goblets, offering me one, and I take it. I take a small sip, nearly choking at the sour, fizzy taste.

Luckily, Gideon emerges from the crowd, walking over to me.

"Gideon," I say, relieved.

He inclines his head. "Lady Vyzrais."

He's more formal than I expect. Some people are still staring at me, though most have resumed their conversations. There's an uncomfortable level of tension in the air.

"What is this drink?" I ask him quietly "It tastes awful."

He laughs. "It's a kind of fermented drink. We use a plant to make it. I don't think you would have it in Alos."

I turn to Aslen to see her reaction. She's still standing behind me, a deep frown lining her face.

"I have to go," she says abruptly. "I'll be back."

I watch her retreat. "That was odd," I murmur. I take another small sip, noticing the slight sweetness makes it slightly more tolerable.

Gideon smiles slightly. "It's not unusual for Aslen. She doesn't care for manners."

"And what about other people?" I ask.

He raises a brow. "Such as?"

I try to keep my annoyance in check. "Will Prince Adriel be joining us?"

Surprise flashes across his face, followed by a deep discomfort. "You haven't spoken to him yet? I thought once we crossed the wall…but perhaps I was mistaken." He clears his throat.

I watch his discomfort uneasily. My intuition is telling me there's something I've missed that's obvious.

Gideon shifts a little. "Ah, well. It's been a busy week for all of us. I'm sure you will, er, meet everyone tonight. I'll introduce you to my husband at some point."

He points to a male across the room. He looks similar to Clydon—fair coloring, blue eyes—but he's shorter and rounder.

"I would like that," I say honestly. I haven't forgotten that Gideon is as much my enemy as anyone else here, but his quiet nature means I don't feel quite the same animosity. I take another sip of my drink, scanning the room.

The dinner hall is lavish, and large. Deep, dusky lavender skies are framed by large windows that overlook the castle grounds, though the candlelight reflecting off the glass prevents me from seeing much. Doorways to a large terrace are open, letting in the humid air. The climate here is different to Alos. It's much warmer and wetter, and all of the plants have large leaves, vines, and flowers.

"Luzeandra, darling!"

I look up as a female sweeps toward us.

"And Gideon, dear," she says. "You haven't come to see me all week. I began to think you'd forgotten about little old me."

Gideon smiles, bending down to kiss her cheek. "My apologies. There were matters I had to attend to."

The female glances at me. "Aren't you going to introduce me?"

Gideon clears his throat. "Of course. Lady Vyzrais, this is Lady Qvez. Thyo's aunt."

She smiles at me. "You can call me Hessa, dear. My, what a beauty you are." She studies me, staring at my eyes for a beat too long before she continues her perusal, scanning my body. I resist crossing my arms. "You will certainly make beautiful children with the prince," she says. "Of course, I've heard such terrible things about the ability of Alosians to bear children. That they're like mules. Practically infertile. You really ought to see Phaelina. She's a marvelous healer, knows things most people have forgotten."

I have absolutely no idea how to respond, but luckily, I'm saved from having to.

"I hate to interrupt," a smooth voice says, "but I'm eager to meet our new princess."

I look to my right, where a male has arrived. He's handsome, with silver-flecked hair, confident in a slightly arrogant way.

"Atemox Conrith," Hessa says disapprovingly. "You ought to wait for a formal introduction."

He raises a brow. "Did you?"

Her frown deepens. "Of course not. Why should I? I am the aunt of—"

"Lady Qvez, we should find your seat," Gideon interrupts. "Dinner will begin soon, and I believe Lady Nara wanted to speak with you."

Diverted, Hessa allows Gideon to lead her away. I watch them go with relief.

"Atemox Julian Conrith," the male says, reaching out a hand. "Though you're welcome to call me Conrith. Everyone aside from Lady Qvez does."

I'm struck by the casual nature of his handshake. His hand is cool and strong in mine.

"I'm Luze," I say. "Though everyone here seems to insist on calling me Lady Vyzrais."

"Ah, well, our people see etiquette as a sign of discipline. It probably seems strange compared to where you come from."

"I suppose," I say. I can't tell if his words are meant to be an insult or not.

Gideons words are still in my head, in the background. *I thought once we crossed the wall…*Once we'd crossed the wall—what?

It implies that Prince Adriel would have had something to say to me *before* crossing the wall. Perhaps Gideon was referencing the letters that had been sent to the council?

I'm distracted by a sound behind me—almost a huff—and

I turn. Aslen has returned and is looking at Conrith with a sour look on her face.

"Aslen Fereaux," Conrith says. "It's good to see you."

He's perfectly polite, and yet I sense an undercurrent to his tone.

Aslen crosses her arms. "Try to remember to keep your mouth closed when you chew, Conrith. I checked the seating arrangement, and I'm stuck sitting across from you. I don't particularly savor having to stare at your face as it is, let alone when I can see half-masticated food lolling around."

My eyes widen, but Conrith merely laughs, looking delighted.

"Come on." Aslen grabs my arm, pulling me away.

"That was a bit rude, don't you think?" I glance back. Conrith is still grinning, his eyes on Aslen.

"Not when it comes to him," she says flatly.

We arrive at the table. I read placard in front of us. *Lady Luzeandra Vyzrais, of Alos.* The one to the left of it reads, *Atemox Julian Conrith, Overseer of Hallin.*

"Where are you sitting?" I ask.

Aslen gestures towards a chair across the table, a spot down from me. Directly across from Conrith.

I start to sit down, but she stops me. "Not yet," she says. "Not until the queen arrives."

"Who's sitting there?" I ask pointing to the seat across from me.

"Thyo," she says.

"Then where will the prince sit?" There's only one other chair, seated at the head of the table. I'm assuming it's for the queen.

"I'm sure he'll find a spot," she says evasively.

Just like that, it clicks.

How could I have been so stupid?

A loud bell-gong sounds, but I barely hear it or notice everyone coming to stand by a seat at the long table.

The room goes quiet, and my heart begins to thump in my chest. Servants open the set of double doors marking the entrance in the dining hall. The queen enters the room.

And Thyo is escorting her.

Which is when my mind finishes putting the pieces together, and I know my flash of realization seconds earlier is true:

The reactions from the others when I'd asked about the prince.

The way Thyo had been avoiding me.

The little test of virtue in the forest, when Thyo had said he needed to know my character before crossing the wall.

The way there is only one seat across from me, the highest-ranking spot at this table.

Thyo isn't the prince's right hand.

Thyo *is* the prince.

22

I'm not sure what my expression is, but the queen is staring directly at me. I try not to flinch.

Her dress is a dark grey, contrasting with her black hair, which is free from the silver strands I've come to realize are common to mortals. Her irises are dark, like Thyo's.

Thyo releases her arm. The queen strides to stand at the head of the table, a beatific smile breaking across her face. Quietly, Thyo moves to stand at the chair across from me. He doesn't look at me. It doesn't matter: I am staring daggers at him.

"Welcome," Queen Seli says, loud enough to echo throughout the room. "We are honored to have you—our most trusted friends and allies—with us on this momentous night of celebration. We are here to welcome Lady Luzeandra Vyzrais to our lands"—here she gestures to me with her goblet—"while celebrating the engagement between her and our prince: Adriel Thysol Arronax, our future king. We are a court of few ceremonies, so I'll save any speeches for when our bellies are full." She raises the goblet in toast. "For now I simply say: *salum autum.*"

There's a loud echo of *salum autum* down the table and I mouth the words, but nothing audible comes out.

A servant pulls out the chair for the queen and she sits. After a moment, everyone else sits, too. We're served what looks like a small, roasted bird, the beak still intact. I stare down at it queasily.

"So." I look up. The queen is staring at me, her goblet in hand. "Luzeandra Vyzrais. We finally meet."

Those nearest to me seem to go quiet, though everyone stays focused on their food, trying to pretend not to eavesdrop. I'm at a loss for words. My mind is screaming at me to say something, but everything around me feels surreal, like I'm in a dream. *Thyo is the prince.*

"Luzeandra was still acclimating," Thyo says, saving me from responding. "Tonight was the first night she felt she could adequately greet our court. Our travel was long and tiresome."

Well, if that's the story we're going with.

Queen Seli casts her son a fond smile, before looking back at me. "Thyo told me you needed your rest, that I shouldn't summon you and that we would meet soon enough."

"Did he, now," I say tightly.

Seli doesn't seem to notice the tension. "Thysol is so thoughtful. You must know this, of course. The way he insisted on traveling to Alos himself! I worried, however. For all I knew—for all our advisors knew—he was lying in the forest, murdered by some Alosian."

"Yes," I say. "What a terrible thought. That your very own *prince* traveled all the way to Alos to fetch me, only to meet his end."

My grip on my fork has caused my knuckles to go white. Down the table, Aslen grimaces.

Seli frowns slightly, but before she can speak, Hessa, who's seated next to Aslen, speaks. "How horrible of an idea. Our precious Thyo, lost to those people."

Seli takes a sip from her goblet. "You never know, Hessa. I would trust a rabid dog before I would trust a Crafter." The queen laughs lightly, but I feel the tension around me. Next to me, Conrith is taking an overly-drawn out sip from his goblet.

"Nothing of the sort," Thyo says. "We merely had a few unexpected incidents."

"Really?" The queen says. "Were the Alosians too busy fawning over dresses and jewels to give you directions?"

Hessa laughs at this, as does the male to the left of Conrith. Aslen catches my eye. She shakes her head slightly.

I ignore her.

"Actually," I say, my voice slightly too loud, "for as much as *Prince Adriel* may have thought himself equipped to travel into Alos, he was ill-prepared for the dangers of our land."

I am still staring daggers at Thyo, my anger making me forget the façade I should be putting on. I only realize it when the table falls silent.

Seli recovers first. "Do tell," she says coolly. "I'm sure we are all intrigued by the thought that Alosians face any challenges at all."

I've dug myself too deep to get out. "We were almost felled by an Alosian boar. There was also an attack by a giant bird— one of the *iikampi*. And, of course, there was the Strin."

Distantly, I think I hear a fork drop.

"One of the Strin," Seli repeats. She turns to look at Thyo. "You didn't mention that to our advisors during our meeting."

Thyo twists his goblet between his fingers. "It was a short meeting."

"It's a miracle you all survived," Conrith says, his face serious. "Let alone returned with all limbs intact."

"Well," I say, about to mention Aslen's injury. Then I think better of it.

The queen notices my hesitation. "Were there any injuries?"

Hessa gasps. It seems to be a habit for her. "Oh, what a horrible idea. Seli, we shouldn't speak of such things. At dinner, no less."

Seli gives her an impatient look. I suspect Hessa is Thyo's aunt on his father's side; there's no chance these two females are related.

"There was one injury," Thyo says. "Aslen was badly injured while protecting us."

Next to me, Conrith goes still.

"She would have died," Thyo continues. "If not for Lady Vyzrais."

"Really?" Hessa says. She's openly staring at me. "How so?"

"With her skills, equal to that of any of our medica. Perhaps greater," Thyo says. "And with her magic. A kind of healing magic none of us in Altheara can fathom."

Really? First he lies to me, then ignores me, only to show up to dinner not as Thyo, but as Prince Adriel, and now *this*? I feel all the table's eyes on me, and my neck prickles uncomfortably.

"Impressive," Conrith says. He sounds like he means it. "And lucky. Huntress Fereaux would be sorely missed."

Aslen glares at him, as though his words had been an insult.

"I suppose luck is to be had all around," Seli says. "The gods seem to have blessed us recently. I have no doubt they ensured your safe return."

Her words rankle. Her tone is dismissive, as though this story is spectacularly uninteresting, but I *had* used magic to heal Aslen. I was certain some of it had been luck, but I was also certain the Althearan gods hadn't been involved.

The conversation switches to new topics, and I'm ignored for the next few courses. I don't mind. I merely sit quietly, simmering with anger toward Thyo. Finally, after the last course has been served, Queen Seli stands, holding her goblet.

"I'm sure all of you are aware of the importance of tonight, and what it signifies," she says. "Needless to say, we will soon see an abundance Altheara has never known before. This engagement between our prince and Lady Vyzrais will be a short one. Those of you here, in our inner court, have already been invited to witness the ceremony in a few weeks. We have hastened this alliance because with it comes opportunity. A chance at redemption for Alos. A chance for justice to win, in the end."

My gut feels sour. Her words are ones any Crafter might say—only in reverse.

"With this marriage will come the beginning of trade between our two kingdoms. Routes that will lead right into the heart of Alos. Routes that will provide new medicine and other commodities."

That can't be right. My uncle had said nothing of trade routes; why would he have agreed to something so precarious as allowing Althearans free reign in our lands?

If I fulfill my Oath, he will not have to fulfill his promise to trade, I realize. And if I do not fulfill my Oath, I will die, and he will find a way to weasel out of the trade then, too. The promise of a diplomatic marriage must not have been enough to convince the Althearans. The suggestion of trade would have been the only thing to truly entice them.

"And so," Seli says, "knowing the debt that will be paid with this alliance, I invite you all to treat Lady Vyzrais as you would any new guest: with an openness of mind, trusting that she will reveal her true character naturally. *Salum autum!*"

The responding roar is much less subdued than before. The energy becomes raucous.

Someone lightly puts a hand on my shoulder, and with a start, I realize Iyanna is behind me. She leans down, speaking quietly into my ear.

"It's time to leave," she says. "The night will become different, now. It's best if you return to your rooms."

I glance around, noticing that female in a pink gown is now practically sitting on Demelan's lap. Further down the table, two males are standing, comparing swords. As I watch, one of them lunges forward, demonstrating an attack, while still holding a full goblet in his hand.

Distantly, I hear myself speak. "I think that would be best."

I stand, glancing at Thyo, but he's speaking to Conrith and doesn't look at me. I have a sudden urge to throw my goblet at him. Or perhaps grab a sword from one of the males and stab him.

The thought jolts through me. I don't know why it didn't occur to me before.

Thyo glances up at me, his dark eyes meeting mine for just a moment before he looks away again.

Thyo is Prince Adriel.

Prince Adriel is the one I have to kill.

Which means I have to kill Thyo.

23

I'm RELATIVELY CERTAIN I've only been asleep for minutes when there's a bang on my door.

I sit up, my heart pounding. There's the sound of another fist on the door, followed by a voice. "Luze? Wake up."

Aslen.

I slump back into the pillows. "Go away."

The doorknob rattles. "The stupid key they gave me doesn't work."

I smile grimly, pleased at my luck. "Too bad," I call. "Guess you'll have to come back another time."

I hear her curse, and then the entire door rattles. "If you don't open this gods-damned door in the next ten seconds, I'm kicking it down."

I roll my eyes. There's no way she would actually—

There's an explosive *thud* and the sound of wood splintering.

"Stop!" I cry, scrambling out of bed. My foot gets tangled in the sheets as I try to hop towards the door. "Stop! I'll open it!"

There's a second thud, and I curse. I finally make it to the door, unlocking it and yanking it open. Aslen stands there, looking extremely satisfied with herself.

"Are you insane?" I say. "No, don't answer that. I already know you are. The question is, why is your insanity directed towards *me* right now?"

"Because," she says. "I've decided I'm done coddling you. You're in Altheara now. You need to be able to take care of yourself. Enough people want to kill you as it is. No more lounging around in silk nightgowns."

I cross my arms. I am, unfortunately, currently wearing a silk nightgown, so I don't even have a good retort. "Thyo didn't even respect this agreement enough to tell me who he really is, so why should I—"

She holds up a hand. "I don't want to hear it. That's between you and him."

"You lied to me too, you know," I say. It feels heavier to say than I want to admit. "It was just Thyo playing a part."

She crosses her arms. "I was under orders. Is it possible I thought the entire idea was stupid? Yes, but I thought that about the entire marriage agreement. I thought there was no chance any Alosian would be even remotely tolerable."

"And now?"

"Well, you're less awful than I expected," she says. "So what do I know?"

"Fine," I say. "Then just tell me this: if Thyo isn't the Hunter, who is?"

I had lain awake half the night wondering. I'm pretty sure I know, but Aslen's next words confirm it. "Isn't it obvious?" she says. "That would be me. Aslen Fereaux, Huntress of Altheara." She says the words mockingly. "Yet another reason why I don't want to discuss Thyo, seeing as my whole job is to protect and advise him."

"You didn't do a very good job of that this week," I mutter.

"Yes, well, he can be stubborn. He's not the only one." She looks at me pointedly.

How did this become about me? "Fine," I say. I step back to let the door shut. "Wait here. I need to get dressed."

"Two minutes," she calls through the door. "Or I'll start redesigning your door again."

I sigh loudly, hoping she can hear it.

I ready myself quickly. The fact that Aslen had been a part of Thyo's lie stings, but she was right: it had been his decision. As much as I want to hate her for it, I would have done the same if the roles were reversed.

Aslen is waiting in the hall when I emerge. My guards are nowhere in sight. Perhaps she's sent them off.

She gives me a quick once over. "Good. I was worried you might try wearing one of those horrible voluminous gowns."

I scowl. "My gowns are not *voluminous.*"

She acts as if I haven't spoken, simply striding off down the hall. Gritting my teeth, I follow her. It's quiet in the castle. Only the faintest pre-dawn light illuminates the windows, and we pass only a few servants.

Aslen leads me out of a side entrance of the castle, one I haven't used before. Following a winding gravel path, I realize we're heading to the south—the back of the castle, and everything that lies beyond.

I haven't exactly been allowed to explore freely, but after loitering by a few windows in the castle and exploring the grounds as much as I could, I'd put together a map in my head. I knew we were in the capital of Altheara, called Ceneth. There were other protectorates, but the road we'd taken in from Alos had led us straight here, and I'd seen none of them.

Ceneth was shaped like a circle, with the castle set in the center and a wall marking the perimeter. Looking above with a birds-eye view, to the north was the city center, where all the markets, business, and official buildings were. The gardens were to the west of the castle. The gardens were too exposed to make for a good escape route, so I'd already ruled it out. Leaving through the north—the city center—wouldn't be easy either. Which left me with two options: south, or east.

To the east, there were a collection of nondescript buildings. I'd only glimpsed them through a window. I had yet to figure out what they were used for.

Now I'll discover what lies to the south.

My hopes of any escape being through the south of Ceneth are quickly dashed when I see the long lines of buildings and enclosures that face us. Despite the early hour, this part of Ceneth is already vibrant with activity. I see chores being done, trainees exercising, and a few people who are sparring. They all look young.

Still, Aslen doesn't stop to peruse the surroundings. Students glance up at us as we pass, and they seem equally fascinated with the sight of Aslen as they are with me.

"Welcome to the Alcheaum," Aslen says. "Ceneth's training ground for the Galdrion. Our students live, eat, breathe and train here. Each protectorate has one, but Ceneth's is the largest, of course."

She leads me around a low building that looks like a set of barracks, until we reach a simple arena. It's lined with stone and little else. A table sits by with a collection of weapons. Beyond it, perhaps thirty feet away, is another training ring, but this one is filled with straw dummies…and people.

They're being led through a series of exercise with an instructor, but I can tell every single one of them notices our arrival. More than a few turn and stare.

"*Focus!*" the instructor bellows. He's short, with deep

wrinkles etched into his face. "Train your minds to ignore needless distraction! One second is all it takes the enemy!"

The trainees quickly look away.

Aslen points to a table full of weapons. "Take your pick. You won't know exactly what you're looking for, but—"

I spot one similar in shape to a Zashet. "I want that one."

She frowns. "That one has the shortest reach."

I shrug, reaching past her to grab it. "It doesn't look as heavy."

My words don't seem to please her, but they don't seem to surprise her, either.

"Well," she says. "If you want to impress an Althearan, you'll need to know your way around a weapon or two. Every Althearan begins training when they're a child, for hours every day. Which means it's nearly impossible for you to catch up. Even with me teaching you. And considering what we're starting with." She waves a hand at me, as if to summarize that my very existence does not, in fact, reflect that of a warrior. "Still. You at least need to learn how to defend yourself."

"You'd think my four highly trained guards tracking my every move would be enough of a defense," I say dryly.

"Do you see any guards right now?"

I look at her pointedly.

"That's not the same," she says. Behind Aslen, the instructor calls a foreign word—something that sounds like *ketsa*—and the trainees slash at their dummies.

"I don't want any guards at all," I say, irritated.

Aslen selects a weapon off the table. "Thyo isn't exactly the most easygoing of men, in case you hadn't noticed. He'll need time to adjust before he lets up on the guards."

Thyo, meaning Prince Adriel. Everything in me wants to

start ranting, but the source of my anger isn't here, and it won't do any good to yell at Aslen.

"Now," Aslen says, marching into the center of the training ring. "Let's start with one of the most basic techniques. In the Galdrion, we use our own words, but that'll just confuse you. In Alos, you'd probably call this a thrust."

She demonstrates, and even though I can tell she slows down the movement for me, it's quick and brutal. She gestures over to the other training ring. "It'll come up next in the sequence they're doing. Watch."

Sure enough, the instructor calls a new word—*rakaza?*— and in unison, the recruits thrust their swords at the dummies. I hear a smattering of thuds as the blades meet wood. One of them, a boy who looks to be about twelve, catches me staring. He glowers at me.

"See?" Aslen looks pleased as she surveys the younger students. "That's why I brought you here. So you could see what the training is like."

My desire to cut until my muscles ache, to fall into the rhythm and patterns of movement, is almost irresistible, but I hesitate. The more I can do to appear as less threatening, the better. Which is why I let my arm flop a bit as I copy the thrust Aslen demonstrated.

Aslen frowns. "What in the Abyss are you doing with your arm? You're moving like it's already been half cut off."

"I've never held a sword," I lie. "It's heavy."

The look on her face has me fighting back a laugh. "You handled that Alosian in Hatal when he tried to grab you. And I saw you hold a knife to Thyo's neck. I know you're not completely inept."

Her tone is a little too casual at that last part, and I

suddenly wonder if Aslen has noticed much more than she's let on.

"That male in Hatal was drunk," I say. "It barely took any effort. And Thyo… I think he let me win that fight. I think he found it entertaining."

She looks vaguely disgusted. "Probably. I don't know anyone who could best Thyo at that close of range."

We work for the next hour. Every time she corrects one thing, I force myself to mess up another. I even drop the sword once or twice for good measure. By the time we're done, Aslen has lost all of her patience.

The whole experience isn't terrible. Watching Aslen grind her teeth as she points out that a sword should not, in fact, be held with only three fingers is immensely entertaining.

Plus, I get to watch the other Galdrion train firsthand. My uncle would be thrilled, though all I've seen so far is that the Galdrion *alchea* are immensely disciplined. No wonder they become such highly trained warriors.

Aslen finally lets me stop to have a drink of water, which is when the class across from us ends. The boy who glared at me earlier lingers, sneaking glances at us. Well, sneaking glances at Aslen.

Aslen notices. "Liev," she calls. "Stop skulking around and come over."

He jogs over immediately, his expression morphing into what could only be called adoration.

"Huntress Fereaux," he says, a bit breathlessly. "If I can be of service, it would be an honor."

I'm surprised by the way her expression softens, just slightly. "You can let Aver know we're almost done here. And remind him to meet me at the Estuary with Thyo. Without you reminding him, he'll probably show up to the castle gardens."

Liev seems delighted with the informal way she's addressing him. "Of course. Shall I let the prince know, as well?"

"No. He'll remember. And he's in that meeting with Atemox Conrith, anyway."

My ears perk. More of this Atemox Conrith.

"And what about *her*?" Liev's whisper is less than subtle. "I saw her swinging that sword like it was a bouquet of flow—"

I hear a sound and turn just in time to see Aslen smack the back of his head.

"Ow!" he cries, clutching at his skull.

"You will treat Lady Vyzrais with respect," Aslen says sternly. "And more importantly, you'll remember not to gossip, especially when the person you gossip about is *right in front of you*. Now go."

Shooting her a wounded look, Liev lopes away, still rubbing the back of his head.

"Lovely," I say. "Violence against children. What an illustrative moment for me to witness."

"I barely touched him. And someone has to do it. Liev has ten sentences out of his mouth before he thinks about whether or not he should say them. He was right, not that I was going to tell him. You really do swing your sword like a bouquet of flowers. Very dainty. Very princessy. Very likely to get you killed on a battlefield."

I follow her as she starts to walk back to the castle. "Seeing as you failed to teach me anything useful, I find it unlikely I'll be on a battlefield anytime soon."

"I did not *fail*. I have a strategy. I merely have to implement it."

"What, teaching me to smack people upside the head like you did with Liev?"

"Maybe I should try smacking *you* upside the head."

Our bickering continues all the way back to the castle. We reach the doors to my room, and she leaves with only some brisk, parting words: "I'll be back in the morning. Find something useful to do in the meantime besides moping around."

I don't bother with a response. Still, her words stick with me. So, I exit my rooms after I eat breakfast, only to find two of my guards, Krenz and Oclas are stationed outside once more. I repress a sigh.

"Where would you like to go today, Lady Vyzrais?" Krenz asks. He seems to be the chosen spokesperson between him and Oclas; I've never heard Oclas utter a single word.

Since I've been here, I've learned there are four places no one cares if I visit: the library, the stables, the gardens, and my room.

The thought of going to the library makes me feel bored, and the gardens don't sound any better. The idea of sitting in my room makes me feel claustrophobic.

"The stables," I say. Maybe seeing Arturon will help this restless feeling.

We exit the castle from the southeastern side. I glance to the east as we walk, noticing that same series of low, nondescript buildings.

"Perhaps we could take the long way, so I might see more of the grounds." I try to sound casual.

In my peripheral, I see Krenz and Oclas glance at each other. "I suspect the eastern portion of the castle grounds would be of little interest to you, Lady Vyzrais," Krenz says.

"Is it part of the Alcheaum? I trained there with Huntress Fereaux, earlier."

Krenz pauses. "That region is for our medica and houses the Estuary."

The Estuary…the same place where Aslen had mentioned

Thyo and others would be having a meeting. I let the subject drop, even though my curiosity is piqued.

It isn't long before we reach the stables. The scent of hay and horses soothes me almost immediately. It's a large building, and there's no shortage of grooms and other stable workers. It strikes me again how efficient Althearans are. No wonder my uncle suspects they're preparing for war; they all act as if they're constantly preparing for battle.

I make my way down the stable aisle, scanning each stall to find Arturon's.

"Luze?"

Demelan has stepped out of a room to my left. Behind him, I see a wall of saddles. He glances at my guards. "I didn't expect to see you here," he says.

"I wanted to see Arturon," I say.

He looks surprised. "He's at the far end. I'll show you."

We walk together down the aisle, Krenz and Oclas trailing behind us. "I saw you at dinner," Demelan says. "You were surrounded by too many admirers for me to interrupt, however."

I snort. "I think the table decorations received more admiration than I did."

"You did well," he says lightly. "It was an honor to witness you hold your own against our court. Especially with all things considered."

We reach the last few stalls and I see Arturon. I unlatch the stall door, slipping inside. He's eating hay from a feeder in the corner, but he nickers as I approach. I rub a hand across the inky blackness of his neck, wondering why my chest feels so tight.

"Did you agree with his decision?" I ask suddenly.

I look up to see Demelan shifting uneasily. "With what decision?"

I look at him pointedly.

Demelan grimaces. "It was merely a safety precaution, Luze. Thyo doesn't trust anyone easily. He wanted to see for himself what you were like before he revealed who he was. It might have just, er, gone on a bit too long."

"That's one way of putting it," I mumble.

It's something about the slightly apologetic look on his face that calms me. Demelan does not seem to mind my anger. Perhaps even agrees with it.

"I think Arturon missed you," Demelan says, changing the subject. "The first two days he paced constantly. We turn them out to pasture to run and he would stand at the corner closest to the castle and stare at it. I've never seen anything like it. It's like he knew you were in there."

"Do you usually work in the stables?" I ask.

Demelan's grin fades a little. "Not really, but my father used to run these stables. I like to oversee whenever I can." He gestures to Arturon. "He'd like him. He always believed you couldn't pay too much for a horse that could think for itself."

"An interesting trait for a horse," I observe. "You'd think you'd want it to be obedient, above all else."

Demelan shakes his head. "Some less experienced horsemen might want that, but my father has always been of the opinion that the strongest partnerships are when the rider asks, and the horse chooses to say yes. A sword will cut wherever you point it, without question, even in battle. To ask a horse to do that is much more meaningful."

It's interesting to me that Demelan's entire demeanor changes when he's talking about horses. Some of the swagger leaves him—the chivalry, the debonair smiles—and the look in his eye changes to something softer.

It's only when Krenz and Oclas snap to attention, and

Demelan straightens from his casual posture that I realize something has changed.

Namely, that something now stands outside Arturon's stall.

I feel myself tense. "Prince Adriel."

Thyo nods to Krenz and Oclas. "Leave us. I'll escort Lady Vyzrais back to the castle."

I wonder if I should protest, but it seems pointless. Demelan gives me a slightly apologetic look before he departs.

It's quieter once the others are gone. Everyone else in the stables seems to be avoiding this end.

Thyo has stepped inside the stall, shutting the door behind him. He leans against it. "Arturon looks well," he says. "Perhaps the rest has been good for him."

"He'll get bored, eventually. It only takes so long before horses go crazy being kept in one place for so long."

"And yet, if we were to turn him loose, he would try to flee. It wouldn't be safe."

"Arturon is smart. He knows what's best for him."

"And yet, if he relies on only himself, he'll most likely end up all alone."

"Perhaps he's been lied to too many times, and he's grown tired of it. It's better to be alone than with people you can't trust."

Thyo cocks his head. "I thought we were talking about horses."

"We are." I cross my arms. "What do you want, anyway? You sent my guards off. You must have something you want to say to me."

"Were you looking for something in particular?" he asks.

"An apology might be a start. Not that I would believe anything you say, *Prince Adriel*."

I'm surprised at my inability to keep my hostility in check.

His expression doesn't change. "I was doing what I needed to keep my kingdom safe."

This infuriates me so much that I cross the stall, jabbing a finger into his chest. "It was nothing of the sort! Your petty tests of virtue were one thing. Even lying to me at the beginning might have been forgivable. You had so many chances to tell me the truth, Thyo. Instead, I was getting to know you believing you were nothing more than the prince's right hand. Not the prince himself!"

"Why does it matter?"

"It matters because I wouldn't have become—become—well, friends with you, if I had known!"

Friends is the wrong word, but I can't think of a better term.

"That's exactly why it needed to be that way," Thyo said. "Do you know what it's like, never knowing what people want from you, suspecting that they're only looking for something to gain? I wanted to know if I could trust you."

"And in the process, you did the opposite," I say. "I know exactly what it's like not to be able to trust people, Thyo. All you've done is proven yourself a coward." My finger jabs into his chest again.

His eyes darken. He reaches up, gripping my hand. "Do not call me a coward."

"Coward," I hiss.

Our gazes are locked, our bodies almost pressed together in the heat of the argument. As soon as I realize this, I jerk away.

"I want to go back to my rooms," I say.

Thyo closes his eyes, heaving a sigh.

"*Now*," I say, more insistently.

"I didn't find you to argue," he says, his eyes still closed.

"Then why did you?"

His eyes open. "You should know that I'm not in the habit of apologizing."

"Really? I never would have guessed."

"But," he says, "it has been mentioned to me that perhaps I ought to apologize."

"By whom?"

"Aslen."

"That's ironic."

"You have no idea," he mutters. I'm not sure he's even talking to me.

I cross my arms. "And are you planning on taking her advice?"

His jaw is tight. "I'm sorry," he says. "That I lied to you. Even though I believe in why I did it. It's not in my nature to be trusting, but…perhaps I should have handled things differently."

It's not the best apology I've ever heard, but by the expression on his face, I can tell even that was unpleasant for him.

"Aslen told me you began training with her," he says abruptly. "That you went to the Alcheaum today."

I'm taken aback by the change in subject. "And?"

"I found it confusing."

"Confusing," I repeat. "Why?"

"I thought it was strange." His words come haltingly. "I suppose I assumed you would ask me."

I almost want to laugh. "Ask you for what?"

He shifts. "For training, or for…anything. For help."

The desire to laugh is slowly turning to anger. "For *help*?"

"Are you going to keep repeating what I say, or answer the question?"

"Was there a question? I don't think I heard it."

"You and Gideon are friends. You're training with Aslen. Now you're going to the stables and spending time with Demelan."

"I still haven't heard the question."

"You've forgiven Aslen, even though she also lied about her identity and position," he says.

"That's different."

"Why?"

I don't have an answer.

He heaves a sigh. "I don't want to be forever at odds with you, Luze."

It doesn't matter if Thyo had betrayed my trust; I never should have given any in the first place. Hadn't Clydon always looked the same way, said the same kinds of things? And look how that had turned out.

"I don't want to fight with you either," I say, finally.

He hesitates. "Perhaps we could have a fresh start."

I'm slightly taken aback. "What do you mean?"

"A new beginning," he says. "We could leave all the lies behind us. We could honor the agreement between our lands and strive for more than just fragile peace. We could choose to trust each other, Luze."

His words surprise me. His eyes are steady and clear. I can tell he believes what he's saying, and that's the most frightening part of all.

I could lie. I could pretend to trust and be trustworthy. Isn't that what a spy or an assassin would do?

Thyo is offering me something right now that I do not want to accept for any number of reasons. I cannot trust him, and he should not trust me.

An image flickers into my head: the way Clydon had

pretended to be honorable. The way that I had believed him. The way that I had been used. Am I willing to become that?

"No," I say. "I can't."

And I walk away.

24

Another three days pass.

I'm still unsettled from my conversation with Thyo.

However, it drives me to pursue another option: I can try to find the scrolls Taleas mentioned and break my Oath.

One night, I attempt to sneak out of my room, but I'm caught almost immediately by Nikal standing guard by my door—one of the Twins—who gives me a thin smile as he accepts my excuse that I had run out of water.

My only other option was to escape my room via the balcony. The walls adjacent to me are made of smooth stone. I wasn't sure if I could traverse them. If I couldn't, it would be a long fall down. I decide to wait until I'm a bit more desperate before I attempt any escape that way.

I spend my mornings training with Aslen, frustrating us both. I make sure to act as inept as ever, even tripping over my sword once or twice, mostly using the time to try to learn what I can about the Galdrion.

To Aslen's credit, she merely grinds her teeth and gives me feedback about how to improve. She's relentless and stubborn, and I can tell it will take a long, long time before she admits failure.

On the fourth morning, when someone knocks at my door, I yank it open, expecting it to be Aslen

"Good morning," Thyo says. He steps in the room, shutting the door behind him.

I step back. I feel intensely awkward at the sight of him, considering our last conversation.

"I'd like you to join me today," he says.

I'm instantly on guard. "For what?"

"I have more meetings. They're beginning to feel rather endless, in fact. I'd like you to attend one of them with me."

I wonder what his motives are. "That's all? You want me to just…sit in a meeting?"

He nods.

Okay, then. "Why?"

"Get ready. Iyanna will guide you there," he says, ignoring my question.

So much for his speeches and apologies. The urge to argue nearly overpowers the intense desire I have to go to the meeting, but I resist.

Iyanna arrives shortly after he leaves, and I'm unable to entertain even her bland attempts at conversation. My mind is racing, wondering what kind of meeting I'll attend and why Thyo wants me there.

Iyanna walks with me after I finish getting ready. She takes me to a section of the castle I haven't been to before on the eastern side. She leads me to a set of double doors, which are open. Inside, I can already see a few people milling around, though fewer than I would expect. I quickly realize this room is adjacent to top floor of the east wing, the only part of the castle I haven't visited. The east wing is marked by a set of massive doors, however, and this meeting room seems much smaller.

A large table is situated in the center, and it's covered in papers. Mostly maps and diagrams, from what I can see.

A flash of auburn hair catches my eye. Aslen stands at the table, perusing a scroll. She looks up as I enter. "There you are. Thyo told me you were coming."

There are three other people in the room, gathered in a cluster by a window. They're examining a map together. Two are males I don't recognize, but one of them is Conrith. He looks up. When he sees me, he looks pleasantly surprised. He comes over, giving me a slight bow. "The guest of honor. How are you finding Altheara since I last saw you, Lady Vyzrais? Joyous, I hope."

I wonder, not for the first time, if he's mocking, or actually sincere. Judging by Aslen's expression, she seems to think the former.

"I visited the stables," I say, purposefully giving him the most boring answer possible. "They're quite large."

"And did you encounter Vhetta, Aslen's mount?" Conrith inquires.

"I didn't," I say, wondering why he's asking me about Aslen's horse. "But I've met her before. She's…nice."

"Indeed." I can hear barely repressed laughter in his voice. "They're a well-suited pair. Vhetta is a fine mount, shadowed only by the caliber of her rider."

I glance at Aslen, startled, but I can tell by her face she already knows where this is going.

"After all, Huntress Fereaux, your talents are legendary," Conrith continues. "Your grace and stealth, your swordsmanship, your talents with a bow—"

"Go to the Abyss, Conrith," Aslen snaps. She stalks away, joining the others by the window.

Conrith stares after her with an expression that can only be called affectionate. His face clears when he catches me looking at him. He clears his throat.

"So," I say, thinking it wise to change the subject. "What position do you hold in the Galdrion?"

"I oversee Hallin," he says. "One of our southern protectorates."

I file away this information. "What is Hallin like?"

Conrith makes a small expression of distaste, there and gone. "I'm not sure how I would describe Hallin. Someone who had been born there might find it charming, in its own way. The same could be said for all twelve of the protectorates, I suppose. And Ceneth."

"And you were born in…"

"Dolaon," he says. "It's one of the eastern protectorates, by the sea. It's how I first met Aslen. In fact, I was there the day she—" He cuts off abruptly, clearing his throat. "The day I met her, that is."

I can tell there's more to the story, but before I can ask anything else, Thyo enters the room. Everyone straightens, and the air in the room suddenly feels much more formal.

Thyo doesn't engage in any theatrics. He gestures to the table. "Let's begin, shall we?"

Aslen sits on Thyo's right, and I sit next to her. Conrith is on Thyo's left, with the two other males seated consecutively after him.

"Adolex Roseh," Thyo says. "Any updates?"

One of the two males I don't know speaks. "We have what I believe will be the final list. All but two have responded. As we expected."

I examine the map in front of me. *Viser Mountains,* it reads. The map shows detailed drawings of what looks like a mountain range, with various routes marked through it.

"What about Kemerel?" Thyo asks. "Aver, an update?"

Kemerel…where have I heard that before?

The second male—he must be Aver—speaks. "They've agreed. With limitations."

Conrith leans forward. "What limitations?"

"They want to come directly to Hallin," Roseh says. "Or, as they see it, meet us halfway. They don't see any of the protectorates as truly being within the kingdom."

"There's a massive stretch of beach on the south side of the mountains," Aslen says. "Why wouldn't they want us to come to them? Then they can stay on their fancy war-ships."

Kemerel. I remember now: an island off the coast of the East Continent. Kemerel was said to be fiercely independent and under no one's rule, known for their sea warriors and nautical warfare.

Aver shrugs. "You know them. Paranoid lot. Afraid we're going to attempt to sink their ships, I suppose."

"It doesn't matter," Thyo says. "We'll agree to it."

Conrith and Aslen both look at Thyo with expressions that range from skepticism to annoyance.

Aslen taps her fingers on the table restlessly. "Thyo, be wise. Kemerel is an untested ally. They all are. And they aren't known for being mild-mannered."

"No one has ever traded with them, that we know of," Conrith adds. "Not in recent history, at least."

"Exactly." Thyo looks at them both with a cool gaze. "Altheara will be the first. And in order for us to have that privilege—and that advantage—we'll need to make certain allowances."

"I don't like it," Aslen says.

"I agree," Conrith adds.

Aslen frowns at Conrith before she continues, "We'll be

initiating trade with the north at the same time. Do you really want to deal with Alos and all of those trade routes while you give Kemerel free rein to come marching onto our land? It's like letting your enemies come in both the front and back door."

Conrith glances at me and clears his throat. "I'm not sure I agree with all of your points, Huntress—"

"So make one of your own."

"—but I agree with most of them," Conrith finishes. "Roseh, Aver, any thoughts?"

"I reside in Ceneth full time, as you know," Aver says. "You and Roseh are much better equipped to discuss how this may affect Hallin, Conrith."

Roseh rubs his chin. "Strategically, I have my reservations. Politically, however, there are certain factors we may not be considering, and matters in which I am outranked. As are even you, Atemox Conrith."

I notice he doesn't mention Aslen. I study the map in front of me again. The Viser Mountains must border the southern edge of Altheara along the coast. Which means all of these drawings show ways in and out.

"What do you think, Luze?"

It takes me a moment to realize Thyo has spoken to me. I look up to see them all staring. "What?"

"I'd like your opinion," Thyo says. "On allowing Kemerel to come directly into Hallin for trade."

I see Roseh and Aver glance at each other. "Perhaps Lady Vyzrais might need further education before she can truly understand what you're asking her," Aver says. "As it is, I'm not sure her opinion is relevant here."

His tone suggests that he can't possibly imagine a world where my opinion would be relevant.

Thyo doesn't even look at him. "Her opinion is important to me, Aver. But if you feel as though it would be a waste of your valuable time, you're free to leave."

Aver's jaw tightens, but he doesn't move. I stare at Thyo in surprise. Why does he care what I think? I feel an unexpected flicker of warmth that I try to ignore. "I suppose it would become clear on the consequences of a failed alliance, and how dire your need is for whatever you're getting from them," I say slowly.

"Go on," Thyo says.

What was it Clydon had said all those years ago? *You know little of ruling, Luze.* It's true, except…I had spent eleven years alone with nothing to do but read and think.

I clear my throat. "I would use Keracleas's formula for a risk analysis. She's a historian from the East Continent. She examined the politics and strategies of the Thousand Year War in her books. Have you outlined various routes, their strengths and weaknesses, the costs and benefits?" I tap the map in front of me. "The Karkinthian pass would be a wise choice. The narrowness of the route, the bridging, all of it means a difficult, slower approach, which will be far easier to control if you're allowing people onto your lands."

Aslen is grinning. "You heard her. Roseh, Aver, have you used Keracleas's formula? Or analyzed different routes?"

"Lady Vyzrais is right," Conrith says. "We'll need some of our strategists to outline a plan before we agree. We can't make a final decision until we've outlined every potential scenario."

Thyo nods. "Do as Lady Vyzrais says. Have it done by tomorrow."

Roseh and Aver stand. They seem eager to leave.

Aslen and Conrith are slower. They both still look amused. It strikes me what a deadly pair they would make if they got along.

"Go to the medica without me," Thyo tells them. "I'll be there shortly."

They both leave, a wide berth between them. Aslen shuts the doors as she goes.

"So," Thyo says. He gestures to the table and all of the papers. "What did you think?"

"Why did you invite me to join, anyway?" I ask. "After our last conversation, this isn't what I expected."

He looks away. "I shouldn't have said what I did the last time we saw each other."

I hesitate. "That's not what I meant. I just don't understand why you invited me. Why not just lock me away somewhere at this point?"

"Is that what you think of me?" he asks. "That I'm that kind of person?"

"Maybe," I say honestly. "I don't know."

"Perhaps I like you."

"You barely know me."

"I know you," he says. "Perhaps more than you think."

I don't know how to respond. "Well, thank you for inviting me."

Thyo looks slightly bemused.

I sigh. "I guess you're not used to me being nice to you."

"I suppose not," he says. "But you're welcome to continue."

"Don't push your luck."

He cocks his head. "Perhaps I could compliment you, instead."

I cross my arms. "That isn't necessary."

"There are the things I first saw, of course," he says. "I'm sure you remember one of them. When I first saw your eyes."

My cheeks feel warm. "You mean when you stared at me like you'd just seen a sea creature?"

He tries not to smile and fails. "But most of all, I remember our very first argument. How you insisted you would walk, and I would ride, because as a frail Althearan man, there was no way I could possibly survive the trek."

"You probably wouldn't have," I interject. "In retrospect, I should have let you walk."

"I did save your life, if you'll remember. When the boar tried to kill you."

"Only because you managed a lucky shot." I pause. "How did you know to kill it by sending your knife through its eye, by the way? You never told me."

Thyo's smile fades. "I didn't. It was luck, as you said."

I study him. "Interesting, that you got so lucky."

He stands. "The others will be waiting."

"I'll go, too," I say, trying to hide my eagerness.

"There's no need for you to bother with joining." He looks tired. "Meetings with the medica are never particularly enlightening. I avoid them when I can."

"Still," I push. "I wouldn't mind going." If only so I can finally explore the eastern portion of Ceneth. Not that he needs to know that.

His expression has smoothed. "I'm sure you have better things to do."

It's a dismissal, and I feel the warmth evaporating between us. I hadn't even realized it was there until now. Thyo sending me away has only served to remind me that whatever joy I'd taken from having my opinion heard, whether or not I was even in the room, was still under someone else's power.

What I wouldn't give to be the one with power.

25

I'M TRUDGING BACK to my rooms when it occurs to me that I have no guards with me. I halt in the middle of a random hallway, weighing my options.

"I'm sure you have better things to do," I mutter, echoing Thyo's words. "Right, like stare at the walls of my ceiling?"

Impulsively, I decide to ignore Thyo's dismissal and follow the others to the medica.

It's a long, slightly confusing walk. The grounds of the castle take a while for me to navigate, especially as I try to choose the route with the fewest people. As I navigate around one particularly massive hedge, I finally spot the collection of stone buildings that make up the medica. Each of them is built long and low, except for one that seems to be in the center of the collection and has a steeple. The buildings are arranged like a horseshoe, with the steepled building at the apex. In the center is a courtyard, where a large tree with long vinelike branches is situated.

I approach cautiously, but no one seems to notice me. It reminds me of the Galdrion training grounds. Everyone here seems to have a task they're assigned to. One female carries a basket of herbs, walking briskly as she crosses the courtyard. A male is carrying a stack of parchment as he enters the tall, steepled building. Two guards are stationed outside. I feel certain that tall building, situated in such a position of prominence, must be the Estuary.

I resume walking, sticking to the outskirts of the courtyard as I head toward the Estuary. One female glances at me as we cross paths, but she seems in a rush, carrying what looks like a stack of linens, and doesn't look back.

I'm about halfway to the Estuary when I see two people sitting on a bench underneath the tree in the center of the courtyard. One of them is a male. The other person is Iyanna.

They have a book between them. It's too far for me to decipher, but I see what look like formulas scrawled on the page.

"The ratio is what's most important," Iyanna is saying to the male. "Without the proper balance of elements—"

She glances up as she speaks, and too late, I realize I shouldn't have stopped. Her normally composed expression flickers with shock.

She snaps the book shut immediately, standing up. "What are you doing here?"

She sounds furious.

I'm so taken aback by her radical change in demeanor it takes me a beat too long to respond. "I'm attending a meeting. With Aslen."

Her grip on the book begins to make it look like a weapon. "Aslen isn't with you."

"She has a meeting with the prince. And Conrith." I gesture towards the Estuary. "I'm going to join, and—"

She shocks me when she grabs my wrist, pulling me back the way I came. "You can't be here."

Her grip is surprisingly strong, but I pull my arm free

easily. "I have every right to be here. As I said, Aslen is meeting Prince Adriel in the—"

"Estuary," Iyanna finishes. "Yes, I know. They arrived long before you did. Why don't I go and check with them, and see what they say about you joining their meeting? Or see what they have to say about you being on these grounds at all, for that matter."

I try not to grimace. Mother of the Abyss, she's called my bluff, and she knows it.

"Very well," I say finally. "I suppose I'll visit another time when I'm escorted by Huntress Fereaux. Or the prince."

Iyanna's features have carefully slipped back into their usual bland, composed expression. "Certainly, Lady Vyzrais. For now, I recommend you return to the castle."

Despite her now-calm demeanor, Iyanna stands resolutely, and I have a feeling she's going to watch me all the way across the courtyard. Sure enough, I look back once I've almost exited the medica, and she's still standing there, watching.

Cursing my failed attempt, I head back to the castle. If only I had kept my head down, if only I hadn't stopped…

I won't make the same mistake twice. Now more than ever, I'm certain something is being hidden in the medica.

⸙

Yet again, I steel myself and enter the dining hall.

It's lit similarly to the first night I was here, but everything else is much less formal. There are no decorations lining the table, and there are only about fifty people, compared to the hundred or so from last time. I notice the queen's chair at the head of the table is empty, and I feel a wash of relief.

Thyo is the first to spot me, and surprise crosses his face.

I see several scowls and a few quiet mutters from the rest of the table. I make my way to the end. As soon as I sit, chatter gradually fills the air once more.

"You decided to join us," Thyo says. I hear the question within the statement.

I try to look airy. "I suppose I got tired of eating in my rooms."

I'm not entirely sure why I'm here. I keep telling myself it's because I've realized the more I spend time with the Althearans, the more I'll learn. It could also be because every time I'm locked away in my room, I begin to feel claustrophobic, like I'm trapped in exile once more.

I'm served a bowl of soup the color of a fig. I eat a spoonful, expecting it to be sweet, but it's surprisingly savory.

Aslen is seated next to Thyo, and, unfortunately, Hessa is next to her. She leans forward. "Have you seen Phaelina yet, Lady Vyzrais?"

I frown. "Phaelina?"

"One of our medica," she explains. "She's very good at aiding with fertility. Gods know you will need it, being an Alosian."

Next to me, Demelan coughs, and it sounds suspiciously like a laugh. Gideon is sitting next to him, pointedly keeping his eyes on his food. And next to him is a blonde male who I remember is his husband—Cyrian. I glance at Thyo, who looks pained.

Hessa makes a tsking sound. "There's time to tour Altheara later, darling. Why, if I had ever gotten married—"

"Poor bloke," Demelan says under his breath. I'm not sure I'm meant to hear. He blushes when I raise an eyebrow at him.

"—and there are such beautiful records in the Estuary, as it is—"

This catches my attention. "What?"

Hessa stops, obviously surprised at being interrupted. Or perhaps that I'm interested enough to ask a question. "Oh, yes. Our oldest records are kept in the Estuary. Anything of great importance lies within it."

I force myself to keep my expression unaffected, but inside, my heart is pounding.

Hessa is still talking. "Why, I once had a terrible issue with sores between my toes—"

"It's mostly just dust," Aslen says, interrupting Hessa. She's buttering a bread roll. "I'm not sure who would choose to spend any time in the Estuary, unless it was one of these two." She nods at Cyrian and Gideon. "Even thinking about all those records makes me want to sneeze."

Hessa gives her a dark look for interrupting, but I speak before Hessa can respond. "Perhaps your training practices are lacking, Huntress. I've never heard you mention anything about this record-room. It sounds enthralling." I smile at Hessa, who looks bolstered by my comment.

"Aslen is right," Gideon says. "Or, rather, she's almost right. Very few people are allowed into the Estuary. Particularly to where the records are kept."

Aslen gives me an insolent look. "And maybe once you stop tripping over your own two feet every time you hold a sword, I'll consider you ready to expand your training."

"Aslen, please," Thyo says tiredly.

"It does seem like a gap in knowledge to not know about the Estuary," Cyrian observes. "One that Aslen might have had more forethought to include while teaching Lady Vyzrais."

He smiles at me, and even though we haven't been formally introduced, I feel a familiarity with him.

"You know," Demelan says, "Lady Vyzrais *is* an Alosian. Crafters are powerful. Maybe Aslen is afraid."

I tense, but Aslen merely throws a chunk of bread at him.

Hessa huffs. "Just because this is a small dinner does not mean we should allow decorum to dissolve. If you'll excuse me."

She plucks her goblet from the table, moving down to the far end.

"I suppose we should consider apologizing," Gideon says.

Aslen pours more drink into her goblet. "Don't bother. She likes when we're rude. It gives her something to think about."

"Aslen," Thyo says. "That is my aunt, you know."

She toasts him. "And aren't we glad you're not nearly as pompous as her. Only about half."

"Or maybe just a bit more than half," Demelan says.

Aslen grins devilishly. "It's all for show, after all. Even Prince Adriel likes to break the rules when he gets the chance."

Thyo shakes his head exasperatedly, his expression alight with humor. My stomach flutters a little.

"Aslen is one to talk," I say. "You should have seen her the first day of my training. She almost broke down my door. I had no idea she was so eager to spend time with me. It was rather cute, actually."

Actually, it had been mildly terrifying, but my comment is worth it just to see the look on Aslen's face right now.

Demelan laughs so hard his drink comes out of his nose. Cyrian hands him a cloth.

Gideon shakes his head. "You're brave, Lady Vyzrais. Make sure to lock your doors tonight. Not that it would help."

"Lock your balcony doors, too," Cyrian says. "Aslen is known for scaling the walls every now and then."

"That was one time," Aslen says.

"Two, actually," Thyo interjects. "If you include that prank with the water bucket."

She sniffs. "I wouldn't call that a prank, so much as a necessary revenge."

Demelan leans on the table. "So, Luze…it seems the rumors are true and Aslen *is* training you. I wouldn't have believed it. You seem to be alive and with all limbs intact."

He winks at Aslen, and she narrows her eyes at him. "Careful, Demelan."

"Aslen hasn't seriously harmed me yet," I say. "Though she did smack a small child upside the head my first day of training."

"Which one?" Cyrian asks.

"Liev," I tell him.

Demelan laughs. "Of course it was Liev. He's been in love with Aslen since the day he laid eyes on her."

Aslen reaches across the table as if to hit him, but he dodges her. I notice a few looks sent our way from further down the table, but most quickly look away.

"He is a child, Demelan," Aslen says.

"So? Even young boys can fall in love. Many times, in fact. I did, as a boy. Just because we're not allowed to—"

"Yes, yes, we all know," Aslen says brusquely.

Not allowed to…what? Is it just me, or has she cut him off because she looks uncomfortable?

The slow grin spreading across Demelan's face tells me he's caught it, too.

"So," he says. He leans back a bit, as though settling in. "Aslen. How is Conrith?"

She shoots him a look so dark, anyone else would shrink away. Demelan doesn't even flinch.

"He's been his usual self," Aslen says. "Arrogant. Full of inane comments. Twice as pretentious as Hessa could ever be."

I can tell Demelan isn't done yet. "He certainly is a handsome fellow."

"Then perhaps you should court him," Aslen says, her tone icy.

Cyrian is watching the two of them and looks vaguely nonplussed. Gideon simply looks resigned.

Demelan pretends to mull it over. "I've found I prefer the company of women. Perhaps Gideon or Cyrian might take a shine to him."

"If not for the fact that both are married, not the least to each other," Thyo says, exasperated. "Really, Demelan."

Demelan takes a sip of his drink, toasting to Gideon and Cyrian. "And may they have a long, prosperous marriage. If only Aslen and I could find such happiness. At least you've found your bride, Thyo."

There's an awkward pause. I don't look at Thyo. "I'm sure Aslen could find a husband in a heartbeat," I say. "If she so desired."

Aslen glares at me, as though I've insulted her.

"Certainly," Cyrian says. "Huntress Fereaux is of high rank. Any member of our Galdrion would be honored to accept her hand for that alone."

"Which is why Aslen has turned down not one, not two, but *three* suitors," Demelan says gleefully. "Ah, I miss those days. To watch the young hopeful pups dashed to shame by the Huntress herself. Perhaps Conrith will be next."

I see Aslen's hand gliding toward her hip, where she would normally have a knife, and I eye her speculatively. I wouldn't put it past her to stab Demelan if it came to it. Somewhere non-lethal, but painful.

Gideon lets out a cough. Once, then twice. I wonder if he's trying to tell Demelan to be quiet.

"If Conrith asked for my hand in marriage I would shoot an arrow through his eyeball," Aslen says. "Which he is aware of. He would be a fool otherwise."

Demelan snorts but this time, stays silent.

We're interrupted by a male who comes up from the other end of the table to chat with Thyo. Thyo greets him with familiarity. He stands, and they step aside to discuss something. I can't hear what it is over the rest of the table's chatter.

Aslen pushes back from the table, not bothering to say goodbye to any of us. I watch her leave, wondering if she's actually offended.

"Don't worry," Demelan says, catching the direction of my gaze. "Aslen doesn't like to talk about her personal life."

"She also doesn't appreciate idle gossip," Cyrian adds. "Which is why she and Demelan make a terrible combination."

Demelan makes a sound of protest.

Gideon pours more drink. "When it comes down to it, Aslen is as honorable as any one of us."

"That isn't the word I would use for some of the pranks she's pulled," Demelan says grumpily. "I wish the marriage addendum weren't law. Then Thyo could be kind and ship her off to one of the protectorates whenever she gets out of hand."

This catches my attention. "What marriage addendum?"

All three of them fall silent and I catch a few glances exchanged.

Gideon is the one to speak. "It's just an old law. Thyo has been coronized, of course. But he can't actually fulfill the role of king until he's married."

I glance at Thyo, but he's still deep in conversation. "It doesn't matter who he marries? Only that he does marry?"

"There have always been pressures from advisors to marry someone that would create a political advantage," Demelan says. "But…yes."

"What about me?" I ask. "Once we're married, what rule will I have?"

"You would have to be coronized to have any true power," Gideon says. "I'm sure Thyo intends to do so after the marriage.

There is an awkward beat. I can tell Gideon doesn't necessarily believe what he's saying. Thyo may merely keep me as a pawn, a bride who gives him power but does not truly have her own.

Thyo returns. "What did I miss?"

Demelan clears his throat, looking uncomfortable. Before anyone can respond, a female approaches our end of the table. She looks like the other Althearan women I've seen: modest dress, slightly weathered looking, with an air of confidence that can only come from having trained in the Galdrion.

She curtsies to Thyo, then turns to me. "Lady Vyzrais, my name is Elowin Auster. I wanted to introduce myself and invite you to join me for tea. I have tea in the gardens most days, with a small group of ladies within the inner court. You would be welcome."

I'm taken aback by her invitation, but I force myself to smile. "That's very kind of you," I say.

She gives me another smile and curtsy. Her gaze lingers on Thyo before she leaves.

Demelan nudges me. "A bit of teatime can't hurt, eh?"

"I'd rather spend time in the stables, actually," I say.

For once, Demelan doesn't joke. He just sighs. "I as well."

"Lady Auster is worth getting to know," Thyo says. "She's well-connected. And she happens to be well-educated on the Althearan court. She could offer guidance."

I'm a little taken aback by his speech, and the obvious admiration on his face as he talks about her. I immediately want to slap myself. It's none of my business who Thyo may be interested in.

"You're beginning to build up quite the list of activities," Demelan says teasingly. "Before you know it, you'll be hosting balls and planning your own teatime with other ladies."

I'm close to making a sarcastic comment when I notice Thyo's expression. I take a long sip of my drink, suddenly regretting coming to this dinner. He looks so…optimistic.

I don't want to think about all the reasons why he shouldn't be.

26

I BEGIN TO have a tight knot of anxiety in my stomach as more days pass.

I hadn't realized how difficult it would be to remain objective. I had expected to arrive here and be treated abysmally. Certainly, I've noticed the hostile stares at dinner and when I walk through the halls, but enough people have been warily welcoming to me that I've begun to feel the stirrings of guilt for what I have to do.

Worst of all is the fact that now every time I see Thyo, I imagine murdering him. How would I do it? A blade to the heart? Poison in his drink?

The silver Oath ring seems to tighten on my finger and my desire to break into the Estuary becomes stronger than ever.

I wake up especially tired one morning. Aslen bangs on my door as usual. I dress grumpily, walking with her to the Galdrion's training area. We pass by the usual motley mix of *alchea* doing their chores. Except Aslen follows a slightly different path this time, and we pass by a training area I haven't seen before.

At first, I think it's instructors sparring with each other;

then I realize these students are just older that I've seen so far, though still young.

And lethal.

The way they spar is deadly. One female only looks to be about sixteen. Sweat drips from her face as she wields her sword against her opponent, who happens to be much bigger, a male with sandy colored hair. Both of them look as though they might think nothing of it if they accidentally disemboweled the other. If I didn't know better, I might say they were Crafters. The speed, the strength, the brutality behind each cut…

I try not to shudder. Thank the Source they have no magic. If they did, they would be equally as dangerous as any Alosian warrior.

"We're going to be doing things a bit differently today," Aslen says, leading me on.

I'm about to ask her what she's talking about when we round the corner and come upon the usual training area. The smaller arena is empty, as usual, and the one adjacent to it is filled with some of the younger students training in a class, also as usual.

What isn't usual is how Thyo happens to be standing next to the weapons table.

I crash to a halt. "Absolutely not."

Aslen gives me a withering look. "Don't be a coward. It's just Thyo."

"I'm not—I can't—"

I can't think of a rational excuse for why I don't want to see him right now.

Aslen pokes me in the back. "Stop wasting time."

I force myself to walk over to where he's waiting.

"Good morning," he says. I notice the half-moons under

his eyes seem more pronounced again. He must be terrible at sleeping properly.

"Good morning." I try not to let my tension show. I don't think it works.

"I thought I should check in on your training," he says. "Despite it being Aslen's idea, I thought it might be good to have multiple people tutor you."

"I'm not sure that's wise," I say. "I've only been training with Aslen for a short while. I wouldn't want to, er, interrupt her process."

Aslen gives me a look but doesn't say anything.

"Aslen, give us a minute," Thyo says.

She shrugs, clearly disinterested, and walks away. I notice her barking at a student who seems to be engaged only half-heartedly in their lesson.

Thyo studies me for so long, I begin to bristle. "What?" I ask.

"I want to understand," he says. "I see you start to relax, to open up and then it's like something switches and you become guarded. Your wall goes up again."

"I don't have a wall."

"You know, you are my fiancée," he says. "Technically. In case you'd forgotten."

I squirm uneasily. Him using that word—fiancée—makes everything feel a little too real. "You could have anyone you wanted," I blurt. "Anyone, and you would be king instantaneously. Gideon and the others told me that you've already been coronized. Why not one of your own? An Althearan. Someone who fits in. Like Elowin Auster. Is it really just for the trade that you chose me?"

Now he looks confused. "Elowin? Why would I marry her?"

I shouldn't have brought this up. "Just forget it."

He looks a little bemused. "Are you jealous of Elowin?"

"No." I keep my eyes on the weapons table. Now more than ever, I want him to leave. And then I want to hit things. With a sword. Hard.

I hear the smallest of sighs, that nearly inaudible, irritated exhale I've heard from him more than once. "Luze, if there's something you want to know, just ask."

I fiddle with the handle of an ax. "There's nothing I want to know."

And why would I? After my conversation with Hessa at dinner, I'm certain the scrolls I'm looking for—if they really do exist—will be in the Estuary. With any luck, I'll break into it soon, break my Oath, and leave Altheara.

Of course, then I'd have to explain to my uncle why I broke our agreement, and I'll be sent back to exile.

So, back to my original plan: murder Thyo.

Thyo's hand comes up, barely touching my chin, to lift my face.

"You seem rather angry to be someone who's about to wield a blade," he says lightly.

I jerk my chin away. "Is this a joke to you?"

He raises a brow. "Not in the slightest. I'm merely trying to get to know you."

"Well, don't."

We stare at each other, and I'm not sure what would happen next, except Aslen interrupts us.

"You're beginning to cause a scene," she says. "The recruits are getting distracted. They seem unsure if you're about to have a duel or a passionate embrace."

I look over. The recruits don't *seem* distracted. Their instructor—the same male I always see teaching them—is bellowing as loudly as ever.

"Eyes up!" he barks. "Drills on footwork mean you use your feet, not your eyes. Unless you want the back of your neck open and exposed for the enemy to behead you. Would any of you like a beheading? I should think not. Barnable, what did I just say? Look where your feet are. *Look*, you fool. Except you don't need to, because your eyes are already down, *exactly where they shouldn't be—*"

I glance at Thyo to see his reaction, but he only seems amused. Something glimmers in his eyes, and then he calls, "Gregori, there's someone I'd like you to meet."

I stare at Thyo in disbelief, but he doesn't seem to notice.

The instructor yells another order to his charges, and then he heads our way. "Thysol," he says. They clasp each other's forearms. "Come to check on the *alchea*? I've got the young ones out on the obstacle course today, but I can call them back."

"No need," Thyo says. "I just wanted you to meet Luze. I have a feeling Aslen never got around to introductions."

Aslen rolls her eyes behind his back.

The male—Gregori, I suppose—studies me for a moment, his eyes slightly narrowed. "This is the Alosian twit with the sparkly eyes?"

I stiffen at the insult, but Thyo only raises a brow. "Careful, Gregori. She can be more murderous than she looks. Especially when it comes to insults about her lands."

Gregori snorts. "Perhaps if she had been born a male. The rumor is they teach those Crafter females next to nothing."

I straighten. Gregori is an inch or two shorter than me, and it makes me feel better to be taller. "For a land that seems intent on mocking its neighboring kingdom at every turn, you certainly act rather all-knowing about the customs of our land."

I notice a few of the *alchea* swiveling their heads towards us, trying to eavesdrop without being caught.

A sly look comes over Gregori's face. "Far be it for me to deny you the chance to prove me wrong, Princess. Take your pick." He sweeps his arm towards the weapons table.

I'm not sure I've heard correctly. "What?"

"Go on," he says. "Choose your weapon, and you can show me how little I know of Alos and its ideas about training females."

I glance at Thyo, wondering if he's going to step in and intervene, but he stays quiet.

It's a bad idea but… "Fine," I say sweetly. "We'll see if Aslen has taught me anything useful."

Aslen scoffs. "My teaching is legendary. It's my pupil that lacks ability."

I stalk over to the table, finding my usual sword.

"Interesting choice," Gregori comments. "Rather short and light. That weapon is usually chosen by the children."

I smile innocently. "I suppose such a choice can only be expected from a weak, inexperienced Alosian female."

Almost all of the *alchea* closest to us have stopped their drills completely, staring at us. A few of the younger ones have their mouths hanging open.

Gregori's eyes narrow. He turns back to the students. "You," he barks at one of the *alchea*. She's young, maybe fourteen, with dark blonde hair. "In the sparring arena with the princess. Now."

The girl looks mildly terrified, though I suspect it has to do more with Gregori than me. I give her a small smile and her face goes stone cold, as though I've mortally offended her. I step into the marked, pitted dirt, feeling slightly foolish. She's barely a young woman, after all.

"Rules," Gregori says. "One, no removing of eyeballs. Our medica haven't figured out how to reattach them. Two, no purposefully fatal wounds. Three, slices and dices are fine, but stab your opponent, and you'll lose a point. And no amputations, of course."

I stare at him, wondering if he can possibly be serious.

Thyo clears his throat. "Gregori, I think both Luzeandra and I would prefer if she weren't stabbed at all. Points notwithstanding."

Gregori gives Thyo a stern look. "She's meant to be the queen of these lands one day, yes? Then I would hope she's smart enough to at least attempt to do things our way, rather than whatever frivolous notion of training Crafters practice."

My grip tightens. Deep down, I know I should care little what this male thinks of me, but my stubborn side aches to wipe the smirk off of Gregori's face, overriding the logic that tells me I should continue to hide any ability with a sword, that I should simply forfeit and let them believe me to be weak and useless.

"How does one of us win?" I ask.

Gregori snorts. "You don't die. Force your opponent to the ground for more than ten seconds, and we consider it a kill."

"And if one of us decides to forfeit?"

He gives me a disgusted look. "Would you forfeit in battle?"

I roll my shoulders. "Let's get on with it, then."

The girl has been watching me silently, and at my words, her eyes become intent, focused. Source help me.

"On guard," Gregori calls. I stand loosely, unused to their drills, and I hear a few snickers. "And—*exelec!*"

Apparently, this is a call to fight because the girl comes swinging.

Luckily, my instincts don't completely fail me, and I raise my sword in time. The movement is slightly awkward—I haven't done this properly in a while, and the sword is less balanced than my Zashet—but I block her cut, nonetheless.

I notice the force of my block makes the girl stumble slightly. My kind is stronger than her. Much, much stronger. And faster. Even if my training has been less, I have an advantage.

I step back, considering this newfound idea.

"Now, now," Gregori says, sounding bored. "Let's not play with our food before we eat it."

I'm not sure which one of us he considers the food in this scenario.

A resolute look crosses the girl's face, and she approaches again, feinting a few times. I match her movements, my body settling into a natural rhythm, Gregori and Thyo and the onlookers fading away.

She cuts low, and I try to move away, but the tip of her sword catches me, and slices a short, shallow cut into the skin of my thigh. I gasp, more from surprise than pain.

Her expression doesn't change; apparently, sparring with actual injury isn't new to her.

We circle each other. It's mostly her feinting and me blocking, trying to ignore the stinging of my thigh.

The girl lunges, and I know the movement is real this time. I see my opening. I block her cut, our swords crossing, and I twist, bringing her blade closer to me, locked behind the grip of my own.

"You're very good," I tell her.

Her eyes are wide, startled by my strength, and she looks confused. "Why—"

I shove her away, using the flat of my sword to send a solid *whack* across her ribs—it even makes a sound—and she gasps in pain, which is when I use the flat of my foot to kick behind her ankles, sending her crashing to the dirt.

I stand over her, my sword carefully pointed inches from her throat.

"*Achelec,*" Gregori calls. He looks annoyed. "Off guard."

I pull my sword away from the girl, reaching out my hand instead. Slowly, she takes it.

"What's your name?" I ask, pulling her to her feet.

"Kahri," she says. Her eyes flick to Gregori, then back to me. "You fight well."

"So do you."

"Enough chattering," Gregori snaps. "Now that you're warmed up, princess, I suppose we ought to test you."

Kahri leaves the ring, giving me a slightly sympathetic look.

"That wasn't a test?" I ask.

Gregori shrugs. "I know toddlers who could fight like that."

My temper flares. "What now? Are you going to hide behind another child or fight me yourself?"

There's a collective gasp from the watching *alchea.*

Gregori smiles. "Perhaps another day, princess. I had a much better candidate in mind. Thysol, would you do the honors?"

Thyo no longer looks amused. "What?"

"Surely you've already rolled with her?" Gregori says. "This can't be the first time."

"Watch yourself, Gregori." Thyo's voice has gone cool.

"It isn't the first time," I say. The anger from our fight earlier hasn't faded, and it seems to be flaring right now. "Thyo and I have *rolled.*"

Thyo narrows his eyes at me. "If you'll recall, I had you pinned within seconds."

I spin my sword in a lazy circle, and his eyes track the movement. "Actually, I remember it being a moment of desperation for you. If *you'll* recall, pinning me to the ground was the only way you could make me speak to you."

A few nervous titters sound around us. Aslen is watching me, her face tight.

Gregori slaps Thyo on the back. "It's settled. Into the arena, Thysol."

Thyo gives him a withering look, and I try not to laugh. He suddenly looks less like a prince and much more like a disgruntled boy. Still, he goes to the table of weapons, quickly selecting a sword.

It's dark and heavy-looking, with a reach that measures at least half a foot beyond mine. I shift uneasily.

"Well, darling," Thyo says, stepping across the stones that line the training area. "Shall we?"

I narrow my eyes. "Certainly, dearest."

"On guard," Gregori calls. "Same rules apply. No intentional fatalities. No eyeballs."

"As if I'm going to intentionally stab her in the eye," Thyo mutters.

I smile innocently. "Of course not. My eyes are much too pretty. Yours, on the other hand…"

He narrows his eyes at me, but Gregori calls *exelec* and Thyo immediately transforms.

Suddenly, it's not Thyo I'm looking at. Instead, it's a male who looks lethal.

I grip my sword, wondering how on earth I'm going to fight him. Unlike Kahri, I know Thyo is trained. Clydon's lessons suddenly seem like child's play.

I feint, and Thyo matches my movement easily. Too easily.

"Don't hold back," I say, trying to buy time. "I wouldn't want to win unfairly."

A slow smile crosses his face. "And yet, you have more than one advantage."

I narrow my eyes. We're circling each other, our movements like a dance. "What advantage?"

"For one, you're right: you do have very pretty eyes," Thyo says. "It's distracting, trying to spar with someone so beautiful."

I feel the disgust on my face. "You cannot be serious."

I cut overhead, trying to surprise him, but he blocks me easily. "I'm entirely serious."

I strike, and he parries. "What's my other advantage?"

He lunges, moving faster than I can imagine, and I block him, but I'm unsteady, and he twists behind me, his arm wrapped around my body, and his sword at my throat.

His lips are at my ear. "Your other advantage is that I would happily let you win, if only it meant we could be alone, and I could see another type of sword in your hand entirely."

I gasp, outraged. "You—You are—" I try to find a bad enough word. "You are a—"

I give up on words and use my elbow to jab him in the gut. Hard.

I hear a choking sound and I dive away, grabbing my sword in the process, before coming up to face him. I can tell his words were meant to distract me, throw me off-balance, but there's actual heat in his gaze, a look of intense desire that causes a flush to spread across my skin.

No, no, *no*. I banish the sensation away.

"Well," he says, his breath still tight. "Not what I had in mind, but it'll do. For now."

I scowl at him. "Pig."

He attacks again, and I dodge his cut, rolling under his blade and missing it by inches. I'm up on my feet again instantly, but he's right there, and I barely raise my sword in time.

I curse internally as the force of his sword makes our weapons ring. Being stuck out in the Barren Forest, I had so rarely trained with anything *alive*. Even with Clydon, it had only been a single opponent. I never had the opportunity to practice against multiple people, to find a fluidity in my fighting, whereas Thyo…Thyo makes it look like an art.

I dart away, creating some distance, and he lets me, his eyes tracking my every movement. He edges to the left slightly, and I stay on my toes, watching him carefully.

"Get on with it, already," Aslen barks. "This is a duel, not teatime."

I hear laughs from the watching students.

I'm never going to win this on skills alone. What do I have that Thyo doesn't?

Magic, obviously. But that's no use here.

I suspect I might be a hair stronger than Thyo, though barely, but I'm fast. Faster than he is, and all of my senses are heightened compared to his.

Thyo has been watching me as I've been scrutinizing him, and his look of amusement fades to one of concentration.

"Plotting, are we?" he says casually. This time he moves to the right, and I sidestep away.

"Not at all." I twist the sword, wincing as I feel an ache in my wrist where he had twisted the blade away.

Thyo notices. His brows tighten in consternation. "Are you—"

Which is the only chance I need.

I slice at him, fast, faster than I've moved in the midst of a swordfight, and I see his eyes widen in surprise.

A memory wells up. One that had never disappeared; one that would always be bittersweet:

"There are no moments in battle. Your enemies will not allow you time to catch your breath or build your strength, Luze."

"What enemies, Clydon? I'm alone. There's no one out here but me."

"I'm here."

A wave of anger and grief pour through me unexpectedly, and I strike overhead. Thyo barely catches it in time. The block of my sword catches with the edge of his sword, and using all of the strength in my body, I twist down and around.

His sword clatters to the ground.

I feel shock in the silence around me.

Especially once I realize Thyo is bleeding.

"Oh, Source." I throw my sword to the ground, rushing to him. It's a spot along his rib cage. I had cut through his shirt and into the flesh. I place my hands gently on his ribcage, horrified. "Source, Thyo, I'm so sorry, I didn't mean—"

He places a hand on mine. "Luze, relax. This is barely a scratch."

The sight of the blood sends a wave of dizziness through me. I force away the images that threaten to overwhelm me, the images of another time with my family's blood on my hands.

My voice has gone up in pitch. "I didn't mean to, I swear. I wasn't trying to hurt you. I didn't—"

Aslen interrupts my rambling, handing me a cloth. "Calm down. Don't just let him bleed."

I hadn't even noticed her come over. I lift the rag she's given me—it's surprisingly clean—and press it gently to his cut. As I do, some of the blood from his cut touches my hand, and I jerk away.

Something is wrong.

His blood is repellant. I feel like I've just touched oil slick. Not because of how it physically feels; it looks like any other blood. But there's…something else. Something thick and dark that clings to me.

"Luze." Thyo is watching me worriedly. "It's fine. Truly. I've had much worse." He takes the rag from me gently, pressing it on his wound. "See? I've almost stopped bleeding."

I can feel an iciness to my fingers where his blood is, a small humming. It undulates. Like…

Distantly, I hear Gregori barking at his students to go back to their drills. I stand shakily. "You should go to the medica. You might need stitches."

Aslen makes a sound of agreement. "She could be right, Thyo. And I for one will not be stitching you up."

He makes a face at her. "That's the best news I've heard all week. Don't forget, I saw your attempts at embroidery as a child, Aslen."

The noise fades as they bicker. I can barely keep my knees straight, can barely keep myself upright. The blood on my fingers still hums with darkness.

I know it. I can feel it.

No. I must be wrong. I'm mistaken.

Unless Taleas had been right. He had hinted at it, but I had been too blind to see, too stuck in my beliefs, in everything I'd always been taught.

It's impossible. Unless…

No. The Althearan lands don't have magic.

But Thyo does.

27

That night, I escape.

Dinner the other night had given me an idea. The stories they had told about Aslen scaling the walls of the castle means there's a way to do it.

About ten feet to the right of my balcony was a column. I'd dismissed it before because it was too far from my balcony to be able to reach. Theoretically, if you were able to reach it, the way down wouldn't be too challenging. The column was designed with divots, which held plants. As long as you didn't mind squashing a plant or two, they would make excellent footholds.

Then again, this all relied on me being able to actually get to the column. Something I had studied carefully, looking for each nook and cranny I could fit finger-and-toe tips into. So late at night, I take off my shoes and after a quick scan of the courtyard, drop them off my balcony. The noise isn't thunderous, but it's loud enough that it would draw attention if someone was nearby. I wait, but no one comes.

Trying not to hold my breath, I ease one leg over the

balcony, then the other. I refuse to look down. If I do, I won't be able to release my grip on the balcony railing.

I have a hard enough time as it is. The walls are made with a smooth stone. They are, however, joined in flat pieces that have small cracks. They're thin, but it's just enough of a ledge for my fingers and toes to grip onto. Barely.

Sending out a prayer to the Source, I dig my fingers into the stone, finally stepping off the balcony. My fingers begin to hurt almost immediately and my feet ache.

I count my breaths, taking a step each time. Tiny, fine movements across the thin ledge.

I've memorized every step. I count them off in my head. *One. Two. Three. Four...*

By the tenth step, I'm halfway there.

I can feel the texture of the granulated stone under my fingers. I hope I don't accidentally pull one from the wall and go crashing to the floor with it.

Ten steps later, and I reach the column. I want to gasp with relief when my hand clutches one of the divots. I have to be careful, but I've done the worst part.

It only takes me a few minutes to carefully shimmy down the column, and then my feet touch the ground. I dart to my shoes, yanking them on.

I quickly lose myself in a maze of hedges. I keep my pace quick, not daring to hope that this will be easier than I expected. I see the steeple of the Estuary right before I hear voices. Many of them.

I angle myself to look between a few of the small buildings. There's a mass of people in the courtyard of the medica.

"Perhaps the addition of the etherwood is unnecessary." A female with a long black braid is speaking. "We could omit it."

This sets off a riot of chattering, which seems to be people agreeing and arguing in equal amounts. There must be at least thirty people gathered.

I walk a bit further, still keeping myself hidden behind the shrubbery and buildings. I reach the last building before the Estuary. There's an open, exposed gap between the two.

I hover at the corner of the building, weighing my options, when a glint of glass catches my eye. There's a window on the side of the Estuary. It's large enough to climb through, but high, set deeply in the stone. And unless my eyes are deceiving me…it's slightly ajar.

To get closer, I'm going to have to cross a patch of open ground that provides no cover. My only shield is darkness, and even that is interrupted by the torchlight framing the entire courtyard.

Holding my breath, calling back every bit of stealth I can muster, I dart across, reaching the back wall of the Estuary. I press myself flat, quietly exhaling. I can feel the ridges of the stones under my hands. The texture is much rougher and more uneven than the stone inside the castle. I'll be able to climb up to the window, as long as I'm careful. The only risk is being spotted.

Slowly, I ease myself around the corner. I can see a glimpse of the group in the courtyard, still arguing. At least they're distracted. One of them looks up, staring at the Estuary. I freeze, wondering if I've been spotted, but after a moment, he turns back to the group.

Praying no one comes around the corner, I keep myself as close to the side of the Estuary as possible and begin my climb.

It's slow work. Sweat begins to drip down my temple, and my palms grow sweaty, making my grip on the stone slick.

Finally, I reach the ledge of the window. I want to gasp with relief as my hands hook over the edge and I pull myself up. The room beyond the window is mostly dark. There's only a fireplace, and the flames are low. I wonder why it's lit at all. It's warm here, even at night.

I pull my knees up. The floor is clear beneath me, and it isn't so far that I'll hurt myself. I think. I peer around the room one last time before I do, making sure it's empty, and with a quick breath I drop down, landing on my toes. My feet sting from the impact, but otherwise it's as graceful an entrance as I could have hoped.

The room is large, with a cot, a table and chairs, and a massive, open cabinet that lines one wall, its shelves filled with various bottles and jars. It looks like a treatment room.

I'm here, in the Estuary. I could be only steps away from finding whatever secrets Altheara holds.

I carefully slip out of the room. I'm worried I might encounter someone, but perhaps I'm lucky there's a meeting outside. It's eerily quiet in here. I look at the row of doors lining the hall, wondering which one might be the records room. Where would all-important records be?

I head down the hall, praying that my hunch is correct. I near what I think is the entrance, and dimly, I can hear the chatter of voices beyond from the group outside. I slow, peeking around the corner. No one is in the entryway. I quickly walk down the hall, looking for anything that might give me a clue.

I round another corner, and just when I think I'm going to have to risk doubling back and opening doors one by one, I see a set of arched doors at the end of the hall. A circular pattern of swirling lines decorates the wood.

My pulse quickening, I hurry towards it. I'm overly eager, and I grab one of the handles, pulling on it. It doesn't move. Which is when I glance down and see the heavy metal lock chaining the door handles together.

I curse. It's not a simple, dainty lock. No, this lock looks as though it could withstand even the likes of Aslen. I want to pound my fists against the wood, but instead I force myself to take a deep breath. Think, I tell myself. What could I use to break it?

There had been tools in that treatment room. Perhaps I can find something to pick the lock or break through it.

Grimacing at the fact that I'm so close and yet so far, I head back to the room I'd entered through, cursing my luck. The more I traipse around, the more likely I am to get caught.

I've just re-entered the treatment room from earlier and I'm about to rush to the cabinets to look for something to break the lock when a chill runs up my spine.

"My, you Crafters have certainly gotten sneaky over the years."

I freeze.

I hear a *tsk*ing sound. "Come, girl, don't be a child. Just because you don't look at me doesn't mean I'm not here. Nor that I cannot see you."

I turn, slowly. By the fireplace in a chair sits a female who looks impossibly old.

"I—I didn't—"

She makes that clucking sound again. "Don't be frightened. You did well. I've been waiting for you."

I stare at her, at the eyes shining out from the deep grooves in her face. Eyes that seem alight with humor. My mind races. Had my guards somehow alerted the castle and the rest of Ceneth to my disappearance? Had they realized I wasn't in my room? Was everyone already looking for me? Had this been a trap?

"Quiet," she snaps. "You think too much. It's like a hive of wasps buzzing. Incorrigible."

My mind goes blank. And then: "You can read minds?"

"No," she says. "But they can."

She lifts her hand, lit by the flames of the fire, and I see, just barely, something twisting around her hand. Something dark and smoky, there and gone.

I step back, bumping into the line of shelves behind me. "What was that?"

"I'm disappointed," she says. "I'd hoped your father might have reached you and explained more to you. A futile hope, it seems."

"I have no father," I say.

I have *a* father; just not one I know of. The Crown always has multiple consorts, to increase the chance of pregnancy. I had never met any of my mother's. I had never cared. Saelis, my tutor, had been father enough.

She sighs. "As I said. I was so looking forward to our conversation, but now…"

I force myself to focus, even as I wonder if I'm dreaming. "You knew my mother's consorts? How?"

She grins. Two of her teeth are missing, but the other ones gleam sharp and white. "I knew only one. I took little interest in the ones that weren't fruitful. I was only interested in you, you see."

I shift a little. "I don't understand."

"And how can you?" She shifts in her chair. "For as much as you crave knowledge, you seem to be spectacularly afraid of the truth, Lady Vyzrais."

I cross my arms. "You're wrong."

"Am I?" She gives me a shrewd look. "Then why haven't the memories returned?"

I suck in a sharp breath.

Her face creases into a grin. "You thought you'd kept that well-hidden, didn't you? So much has been ripped from you, and you've repaired so little."

"It doesn't matter," I say. "What's done is done."

"You only think that because you are afraid to regain what you've lost," she says. She gestures to the wall behind me. "Some of those might do the trick if you were so inclined."

I turn to look at the bottles and jars behind me. I spot one I recognize. *Namaris rose.* I had seen that exact herb in the apothecary in Hatal. I scan the labels of several others. *Silverweed. Etherwood.* I don't recognize all of them, but some of them…

"Those are Alosian herbs there," I say. "How do you have them?"

"Plants can be grown anywhere, girl. All you need is a seed and a hand suited for nature."

"But these can't possibly have the same qualities," I argue. "After all, our land is full of—"

"Magic? Yes, it is. That wall sees to it. The same as it saw to leeching almost every drop from the earth of Altheara. Like building a dam. Except that dam has a crack. Your wall is imperfect, you see. And so, through luck or fate, we are able to grow crops with just enough magic to feed them."

This information should be shocking, but I feel strangely calm. I look at the bottles again, picking one up to turn it in my hands. I look back, a sense of intuition pricking me. "Are you Phaelina?"

She laughs. "Not dull-witted, I'm glad to see."

"I'm Luzeandra Vyzrais," I say. I'm fairly certain that somehow, she already knows who I am.

"Where do you believe magic comes from, Lady Vyzrais?" she asks.

"The Source," I say, puzzled by this change in topic.

"Yes. And why do you believe Crafters can channel the power that flows from the Source?"

I open my mouth, then close it, realizing I don't have an answer.

Phaelina doesn't seem to expect one. "Magic flows throughout this realm. It happens to be strongest on this continent because of the current location of the Source. It would flow freely, if not for the wall. Magic always seeks a conduit; it dislikes being contained."

"You're saying magic looks for those that can channel it," I say slowly.

She seems pleased with my response. "Precisely. It filled the bodies of the Othos, more than any other creature we know of. It filled the bodies of the Wytches, to some extent. It's drawn to Crafters, who have channeled it so exquisitely for so many years."

I'm becoming frustrated. "I don't understand why you're telling me this."

"Think," she says, her tone becoming sharp. "No mortal can channel magic. It can make them a bit faster, a bit stronger, keener in the senses and sharper in the mind. It's the reason you could use magic to heal a mortal, same as anyone else. Mortals have enough spirit to accept magic, you see. But they do not have the strength of spirit to wield it. It would burn them up; make them go insane. Any mortal who attempts to absorb and channel magic would do so on a dying breath. No, for magic to be channeled, you must be born to it. You must be a being with the strength of spirit to withstand whatever it is you create."

I slowly digest her words, noticing how carefully she's chosen them, noticing how she seems to be trying to tell me something without saying it directly.

The horrible truth is beginning to dawn on me. "It's not only mortals in Altheara, is it?"

Her eyes are bright and clear despite her age. "Ah, there it is.

The spark of intelligence your mother was known for. I'm glad to see she passed it on."

I flinch. "How did you know her?"

"It's a long, long story," she says. "I'm the one who gave her that pendant, in fact. Though it was always meant to be yours."

My hand floats up to my blood pendant, the one I always wear. "It was?"

Her eyes glitter in the firelight. "That pendant is the result of a deal that was made. A deal that I was involved in when it was brokered. An agreement involving you, in fact."

"What deal?"

She clucks her tongue. "None of that. You have far too many things to think of right now."

She's right. My head is spinning.

"My advice," she says, rising from the chair, "is to stop being so afraid. Only you command yourself, Lady Vyzrais."

I don't want Phaelina to leave—I have so many questions, so many things I don't understand—but she gives me a knowing look, one that has me staying quiet.

When she leaves the room, I stand for what feels like an eternity but is only minutes.

I take a slow breath, trying to gather myself. I'm not sure of exactly how much time has passed, but I can't risk anyone going into my rooms to check on me, only to find that I'm not there. It won't be tonight that I break through the door. I don't have enough time. I take another breath. I almost can't stand to walk away when I'm so close, but...

I'm not ready to leave Altheara, either. Not yet. There are too many mysteries I want to untangle. For now, the scrolls will have to wait.

28

Before I leave, I impulsively grab one of the tonic bottles on the shelves, called *Fire Blend*. I slip it into my jacket pocket. Just as I'm turning away, another label catches my eye.

I stop, staring at it. If anyone finds me in possession of this particular herb…

I take it anyway. Putting the second bottle into my jacket, I carry a chair to the window. I can just reach the ledge if I stand on the chair, and though my fingers struggle for purchase, I manage to pull myself up.

I glance around once I'm situated on the ledge. The group in the courtyard is still arguing, their voices loud, and hopefully, distracted. I don't see anyone else in sight. I slide down a bit and let myself drop.

The way back feels faster, but not fast enough. All I can think about is what I will say if I am caught, if I have to explain myself to Krenz and Oclas, and if—

I round the corner of a hedge at a near run and with an *oomph* my body slams into someone else's.

I gasp, trying to straighten myself, wondering what excuse I'll give—perhaps it's only a random servant who won't recognize me—when the dim light of the grounds casts itself over the person's face. Source curse me, it's Thyo.

"Luze?" He looks confused. He glances past me, as if looking for others. "What are you doing out here?"

I can't think of an excuse, so I say, "What are *you* doing out here?"

"I was summoned to the medica," he says. "Phaelina asked for me."

That dratted hag. She had probably planned for me to get caught. So much for her wise words and knowing looks; she was as Althearan as the rest of them.

"You never answered my question," Thyo says. His confusion has melted into suspicion. "What are you doing out here?"

This is bad, and even worse if he finds out I broke into the Estuary, let alone discovers the bottles in my pocket. Yet despite the circumstances, I feel annoyed. "You can walk freely. Why can't I? Why can't I simply stroll around outside at night if I want?"

He watches me, unsmiling. "Is that what you were doing? Going for a stroll?"

"Yes." I cross my arms. "I don't need my every move watched. It's insulting. And you know, it's awfully—"

I stop speaking abruptly as he reaches out, his hand clamping onto my wrist.

I stare at him, confused. "What are you doing?"

I feel it, then. A sickening sensation of something crawling up my skin, strangely familiar. I yank my arm away, hard, and this time Thyo lets go. I swipe a hand over my skin, shuddering, but the feeling is gone.

"You saw Phaelina," Thyo says. I gape at him. His skin is paler than before, the circles under his eyes pronounced. "Let's go," he says. He grabs my wrist again, but I don't feel that same crawling sensation.

"Hey!" I protest. I try to pull my arm again, but he's got an iron grip on it, and the element of surprise. I stumble slightly, but he doesn't slow.

"She told me I was a fool," Thyo says. I don't even think he's speaking to me. "I suppose she was right."

"Who?"

He doesn't respond, continuing to haul me along with him. I think about fighting him off—I'm sure I'm strong enough to get away, if I really wanted—but what would be the point?

We're almost to one of the main entrances to the castle when I clear my throat. "I can't go in the normal way. Not to my room, at least. My guards will know I left."

He looks at me. "How did you get out?"

I chew on my lip a little. "I may have gone over the balcony."

"You jumped?" He looks disbelieving.

"No." There's no point in hiding it. "I figured out how to climb down."

He uses his free hand to pinch the bridge of his nose, fighting for patience. Without saying anything, he tugs me along to a different entrance.

We only encounter two servants. Both of them widen their eyes, quickly stepping aside as we pass. I try not to grimace. Even more witnesses. Lovely.

It doesn't take me long to realize we're not going to my room. I guess he's not going to make me climb back up the walls of the castle.

He leads me toward a western portion of the castle I haven't explored very much, until finally, he comes to a door.

It's unlocked and unguarded. He opens it. "Inside," he says. His tone is clipped.

He's still displeased, and on top of it, he looks tired, but I also see the challenge in his eyes. So, I square my shoulders and enter the room.

As soon as I enter the room, I see why it isn't guarded. This room reminds me of barracks. There's almost nothing inside of it, aside from furniture. No decorations, no sentimental trinkets. It doesn't look as though the bed gets used very often, either. The linens are tucked in tightly with not even a wrinkle.

He points at the bed. "Sit."

I sit.

Thyo drags a chair over, sitting in front of me.

"Now," he says. "What were you really doing out there?"

My chin juts up. "I told you already. I was going for a walk."

He leans back in the chair. "Luze, I lead the Galdrion. I rule these lands in all but name. My mother has not ceded the throne to me because I am not married, but she has allowed me to run this kingdom for years. Which means," he says, now leaning forward, "if you lie to me again, I will be forced to assume the worst. I will have no qualms about shutting you away in one of our prisons. They're rarely used, but I can guarantee you won't like it."

My throat feels tight. "You wouldn't."

"Try me."

He's bluffing, I think. I had been caught in a compromising situation, to be sure. But he doesn't *really* know where I was, what I was doing, or why.

"How did you know I saw Phaelina?" I ask. Because clearly, there's no hiding that. He'd said it aloud; he knows.

His gaze narrows. "Do you know why I brought you here, to my room?"

His room? *This* is his room? It looks fit for a soldier, not a prince.

"Because I'm offering you a chance," he says, not waiting for a response. "If anyone else found out about you sneaking around, particularly near the medica, there would be nothing I could do. If my mother found out…well, she's not known for her mercy."

I picture Queen Seli's face. He's probably right. She wouldn't take pity on me.

"Which is why I'm giving you a chance to explain yourself," he says. "Now."

A million excuses fly through me. I can't tell him about the scrolls, or my Oath.

"I know there's something you're hiding about the medica," I say abruptly.

Thyo looks surprised. I can tell this isn't where he expected the conversation to go.

"I kept noticing how secretive everyone seemed to be about the medica," I continue. "Including you."

"So you went to there." It isn't a question. "To the Estuary?"

I clear my throat. "And there may or may not have been a window that was left open, so I just happened to take advantage of the opportunity. Since it presented itself."

He studies me. I can't read his expression.

Finally, I speak. "So, are you going to lock me away?"

My sarcasm fails to hide the nervousness I feel.

He doesn't answer my question. "Phaelina told me this would happen. She had certain instincts about your character, even before you arrived."

My eyes narrow. "Perhaps you should have listened to Phaelina."

"Perhaps," he says. "But our kingdom has only kept itself alive by virtue of the fact that we've managed so many well-guarded secrets. It's in our nature."

There's a beat of silence.

"You touched me and knew I'd seen Phaelina," I continue. "How?"

He smiles, but it's grim. "You already know, don't you? She said something."

"She didn't. Not really. I know that you have…something. When you bled, after we fought, I felt something. I sensed some kind of…magic." I have to force the word out. "But I don't know what, or why, or how. I don't even understand how it's possible."

We've come to a crossroads. One of us has to make a choice. I already know too much. I can tell he's realized this, too.

My heart pounds. Will he truly try to lock me away? If he does…I will be forced to kill him, right here and now.

"How much do you know of our history?" he asks.

"Little," I say, trying not to look tense. "Only what I learned in Alos. The books I read were mostly about the war."

"Then you don't truly know about the Galdrion," he says. "It was during the Thousand Year War. Althearans were dying rapidly. We were going to become extinct. Wiped away, forever. Until a man named Galdrius came up with an idea. He was an adviser to the king at that time. He wanted to find a way for mortals to have access to magic. Galdrius urged the king to have soldiers attempt to capture Crafters. He wanted to experiment."

I feel queasy at the word *experiment*. We both know what it means.

"He forced Crafters to perform magic on mortals, to attempt to heal them, or infuse them with power. After some time, he realized mortals could absorb magic, to some extent. Just an edge. Enough to make going into battle more than a suicide. But it still wasn't enough. There was no way to capture and contain enough Crafters to force them to help us. Galdrius knew the war between our kingdoms was overwrought with prejudice and that no one would willingly join, either, but there were other lands he might turn to. The East Continent, for one, but they wanted nothing to do with us. Then there were the Isles. Galdrius traveled to them. He went to one isle in particular. One that legend said was cast in shadow."

I suddenly have a very, very bad feeling. "The isle of the Wytches."

"Yes. Galdrius recruited the Wytches to the cause. Perhaps some were moved by Galdrius's pleas for help. But some of them were wrathful. They didn't care what they were fighting for, but they were happy to, as long as they joined a battle."

"They came to Altheara." My voice is nearly inaudible.

"Some did," Thyo says. "And those that did helped Galdrius. They taught him everything they knew."

"And then they left?"

"Some," Thyo says. "Some found that they preferred living in these lands. Galdrius's wife was one of them."

I still. What he's saying—

"She wasn't the only one," Thyo says. "Other Wytches found mortals to fall in love with. Some simply married because they sought power. Some—the more powerful ones— were especially twisted by the shadow magic they had. I'm sure you know the origins of that story."

I nod wordlessly.

"It saved Altheara," Thyo says. "And slowly, Wytch blood was infused into some of our lineages."

I study him, the way he's watching me, his jaw set.

"And you," I say. "What are you?"

We both know what I'm asking.

"Half," he says softly. "I'm half-Wytch."

29

"That's impossible." I stand, unable to sit. "Wytches died out. Even if some blood remains, it's diluted. How can you be half?"

"They haven't died out," he says. "They're hidden. No one can reach their isle unless the Wytches wish it. They are few in number, and isolated. But they haven't died out. And if the need arose…they would join us."

"How?" I press. "How do you know?"

"Because my father married one."

I'm rooted to the spot. "You mean…your mother…"

I stare at him, trying to connect all of the pieces. A chill runs through me as I realize the implication. Queen Seli is a Wytch. A full one.

And then, again: Thyo is half-Wytch.

Thyo is merely watching me as what I'm sure are a hundred different emotions play across my face.

"What can you do?" I finally ask. It's best if I stick to logic, to knowledge.

He rubs his palms together. "Little. I'm too limited. I'm only half-Wytch, and I grew up in lands where there's no magic contained within the earth. Being in Alos was…extraordinary. That's the most I've ever used my power."

Something occurs to me. "The night the Strin attacked, Aslen yelled something. She said something about you shielding us. Is that what she meant?"

"Yes," he says. "The shadows are…fickle. But they always protect the user. If the user dies, the shadows within them die."

I wonder if he's lying, but his eyes are clear. "Have you ever used them on me?"

He hesitates. "There's something about you…something that repels the shadows. It isn't easy to surpass. I've never encountered it before."

"But you were able to touch me minutes ago and know I'd seen Phaelina." I shudder at the memory of that crawling sensation.

"I think you're weaker here. Even so, just that single touch drained me."

I mull this over. He doesn't seem to know about the bottles I stole, thank the Source.

"Touching me hurts you?" I ask.

He smiles slightly. "Not when it's like this." He reaches out, grazing my arm. "But if I try to use the shadows, then yes. It's an imperfect ability and limited, even without you blocking me. Phaelina has told me of those who don't require physical contact to glean knowledge, but I have to be touching the person."

I feel a bit squeamish. "The shadows talk to you? As though they're alive?"

"Something like that. It's not exact. And the shadows don't fear me. I'm not powerful enough, and I don't have enough control. They offer more than just information; they offer opinions. Which means any knowledge is vague and inexact, and more than a little frustrating. And it exhausts me if I use it too much."

"Why?" I ask.

"I'm not like you," he says. "Wytches were never created to have this kind of power, and even if we were, Altheara doesn't have the same kind of magic as Alos. Being here…I have nothing to pull from aside from myself. It's exhausting."

I think of my conversation with Phaelina. "Then why create all of the herbal formulas? Why do you grow Alosian herbs?"

"Everyone in the Galdrion takes them," he says. "They give them sharper reflexes, better strength; they're less likely to succumb to illness. For those of us with Wytch blood, what we take can give us more power."

"Then why trade with Alos?" I ask. "You're already growing what you need."

"I told you there was an illness that spread through the protectorates years ago," he says. "An illness that could have been stopped, if only we'd had enough medicines. Instead, we didn't have enough. We had to choose. *I* had to help choose. Tell me, Luze, how do you decide who within your kingdom should live, and who should die?" He stares at nothing. I see a glimmer of pain in his eyes. "My father died from it. He refused to take any medicine. He didn't want to take even a single dose away from his people."

"I'm sorry," I say quietly.

Any trace of magic discovered in Altheara by an Alosian would mean war. And not simply war, but war with the intent to decimate, to stamp out any chance of magic in Altheara. They would hunt down every last person with Wytch blood.

And Thyo…he would be first on their list.

My chest feels tight. If I return to Alos, as is my plan, if I tell anyone about this secret, I will be sentencing Altheara to death. People like my uncle would stop at nothing to eradicate Altheara if they knew of this.

And yet…there's a reason the council would want to attack Altheara. If there's a conflict between our lands again, Alos may be at a disadvantage without this knowledge.

I stare down at my hands again. "I don't know what to say."

"You have a choice. One you'll need to make soon."

My head snaps up. "What?"

"You know what the cost of this knowledge would be," Thyo says. "I can't ever let you return to Alos knowing any of this. If you attempt to leave, I will have to act accordingly."

A small chill runs up my spine. "Are you threatening me?"

"No," he says. "But there are certain precautions our medica have been able to provide, that I would need to utilize."

I'm tired of how coy he's being. "Just come out with it already."

"It would wipe your memory away," he says bluntly. "It's an anesthetic tonic, but given in a powerful dose, it creates an amnesiac effect."

My hand drifts up to my head, as though that will somehow protect it. "It would wipe away all of my memory since coming to Altheara?"

"No. It can only work for so many days. At most, a week. Which is why I'll need you to make a choice by then."

I stand abruptly, the chair crashing to the floor with a bang. "If you come near me with that tonic I will kill you."

I'm breathing hard. He can't possibly know why the suggestion of tampering with my memories has triggered such a strong reaction, but I don't care.

"I hope I don't have to," he says.

"I could lie," I point out.

He holds out a hand, as though offering it. "Which is why I'll need more than your word, once you decide."

I hold back my grimace. Right. His shadows will tell him if I'm lying.

I cross my arms, and he lets his hand fall. "I just need to know one more thing, then."

"Of course," he says. "There are no more secrets to guard. Whatever you want to know, I'll tell you."

I take a breath. "Tell me the truth: have you ever used your magic on me to do more than gain answers? To affect me in some way?"

I hadn't forgotten that night in the forest during our journey when I had lost time. Had that been Thyo?

Thyo exhales, looking away. "My power is under control because of the remedies I take, because of people like Phaelina who have guided me, but I'm always at risk of losing control. It means there's always a part of me…" He closes his eyes, and I'm startled to hear the shudder of a breath that comes out. "There's always a part of me that *wants* to lose control. I told you that I've never felt anything like when I was in Alos. I tried to explain to you, the shadow element, and your lands…it was intoxicating. I made mistakes."

He hasn't answered my question. Not really.

My throat feels tight. "It was the night Aslen was attacked, wasn't it? I thought perhaps the magic I had used to save Aslen had done something to me. It was you."

I see a flicker of regret. "After what happened between us in the forest, and then when I failed to protect you from the Strin…I thought you might leave us and return to Alos. The shadows were so insistent. It's a voice in your head, and you think it's your own voice, Luze. I knew if you left there would never be another chance. The shadow magic I used on you isn't pleasant, but it doesn't have any lasting effects, I promise you. It's simply like sleeping. Like taking a very long, deep nap."

Even though I'd thought I had known, his words still make me recoil. "Have you used it on me since then?"

"No." He shakes his head vehemently. "I haven't used my magic since we crossed the wall. I couldn't, even if I wanted to. I was telling you the truth: something about you blocks the shadows. I think after the Strin attack you were weakened, and it made it easier."

"And you wanted that badly to stop me from leaving?" I ask. "This is all because you want medicines? Surely there could have been an easier way of creating a trade agreement, Thyo. Why do you want this so badly? Why have you fought so hard? It doesn't make any sense."

He's quiet for a long moment. "Because," he says haltingly. "Because of something I was told many years ago."

I feel a trickle of dread. "What?"

"You've met Phaelina," he says. "She can sense things. And yet, that's only a fraction of the power that can exist with Wytches when it comes to knowing the unknown. There was an old companion of Phaelina's. A very old, very powerful Wytch, known as a Seer. She visited our lands when I was sixteen. She told me that Altheara was doomed to be extinguished forever. Mortals would encounter an endless sleep—death. She said that my only hope was a Crafter who would come to our lands. That this Crafter would have a reason to come to Altheara, and it would change Altheara's future irrevocably. That she would be the only thing that would save our people."

A chill runs down my spine. "I'm not some girl from a prophecy who's destined to save your lands. This Seer could have been lying, anyway."

"My shadows told me enough to know she wasn't lying," Thyo says.

I rub my hand over my forehead. I'm not sure I even believe in such a thing as prophecies. And even if I did, I can't possibly be the person this Seer meant. I'm not anyone's savior.

"What else is it you want to know?" he asks. "Whatever it is, I'll tell you."

"No more secrets," I say. "Promise me. Swear there is nothing else you're hiding."

His gaze is steady as he says, "I swear. I promise you that there will be no more secrets between us."

It's only words, and yet I feel myself relax slightly.

"What else?" Thyo says. "What else do you need?"

"I want to be free of my guards," I say. "I can't decide whether or not I can have a life in Altheara when I constantly feel as though I am a prisoner, Thyo."

He nods slowly. "Fine."

I'm surprised he's acquiesced so easily. I bite my lip. "And I need time. I just need…time."

I can't tell him why, of course. He's revealed his secrets, but I've said nothing of mine. How will this change things? *Does* it change things?

"Luze, I will need to know, beyond a doubt, that you never intend to return to Alos, that you will never share what you know with them," he says. "I can give you a week. And then… you can decide."

I wonder what lengths he will go to in order to ensure I never leave.

"Fine," I say. "One week."

When he offers his hand, I accept it.

And our deal is made.

30

Iyanna arrives the next morning and announces the queen has requested me.

"In her parlor," she says. "I'll walk with you."

We ascend to the fourth level of the castle, walking down a long, empty hall, before we pass a large tapestry with a lion on it. Next to it is a set of double doors, with a guard standing out front.

"You can enter," Iyanna says. "She's expecting you."

I open the door, feeling nervous. The timing feels too coincidental.

Queen Seli is sitting on a small, mauve couch, drinking a cup of tea. She looks up as I enter. I haven't seen her since the dinner she attended, but I'm struck by the sharp lines of her face, the cool, steely look in her eyes. A look that I now know comes not only from her personality, but from her birthright. I'm torn between trepidation and awe. In front of me is a real, live Wytch; a being I thought only currently existed in history and myth.

"Lady Vyzrais." She gestures to the couch across from her. "Please sit."

I glance around the room as I do. It's surprisingly dainty compared to the rest of the castle, the furnishings more luxurious than anything else I've seen.

"Well," Seli says, once I'm settled. "I think we both know why I requested you to come see me."

I swallow. "I suppose."

She pours a cup of tea for me. "I sense that underneath the veneer of politeness, of modesty, of manners—all the things that make women more boring—you're actually a very forthright person, Luzeandra. I sense that because I am much the same. I, too, appreciate being given the truth. Secrets have a way of festering. So let us agree to not trifle with one another."

I straighten, tensing slightly. "What do you want to know?"

"My son told you about me." It isn't a question. "About his lineage, and, as a result, mine."

"Yes." I don't deny it. "He told me you're not from Altheara."

Seli sits back, her posture casual. "That I'm from the Wytch isle, you mean." She studies me, her gaze sharp. "You seem to be handling the news rather well. Unexpected. I would have suspected at least one bout of hysteria."

I try to control my reaction by picking up my teacup. "Because you assume all Crafters to be fraught with whims of emotion?"

"Because you are in a foreign land and have just had many of your core beliefs shattered," she says. "This has been a closely guarded secret for many years. Accepting the idea of Wytch blood infused into lineages hundreds of years ago is one thing. Learning that Wytches still exist is quite another."

"Do they?" I put my tea back down. "Do they really exist?"

"They do," she says.

"And you left?" I ask cautiously.

"I was sixteen when I left my home," she says. "Rather young for a Wytch to be without her coven, but I was powerful. I knew living there would never be enough for me. I eventually intended to travel to the East Continent, before I met Thyo's father."

I digest this knowledge. "And he didn't mind? That you're a Wytch?"

Her jaw tightens. "I am only a Wytch in name. I lost any shred of power when I gave birth to Thysol. It almost killed me. I am little more than a mere mortal now."

"You've never gotten it back?"

"Never." Her face is carefully set, but I see a flicker of emotion in her eyes. "Granted, Jonis—Thyo's father—was relieved. I come from a powerful bloodline. It can be difficult for mortal men to fully grasp what it means to love a powerful woman."

"Thyo said his power is weak," I say. "Because he's only half-Wytch."

She purses her lips. "Once shadow claims you—by birthright or any other way—you have little choice in the matter. And shadow is…unpredictable. It will control you, if given the chance."

I wonder why she sounds as though she's warning me, even with her impassive expression.

"It seems odd to me that Crafters still believe Wytches no longer exist," I say.

"Is it?" she asks. "With the way our lands are cut off from one another? You know, only small animals can cross the gateway between our lands. When Alos and Altheara require communication, they use a hawk to send a letter. Before Thyo contacted your council announcing his ascension to the throne, a hawk had not crossed in nearly fifty years."

I pause. "I see your point."

"Well," she says. "That was all I wanted to say to you. It seems my son takes this agreement more seriously than I expected and I must now do the same."

I'm not sure how to interpret her words, but she stands, and I recognize my cue to leave. As I walk to the door, I notice a glass case, lined with a variety of objects. One of them is an unusual, twisted sphere.

"Some of my treasures," Seli says, noticing my focus. "That particular trinket is said to model the Orb of Thesalla."

I lean forward, peering at the sculpture. "The Orb of Thesalla?"

"It's an ancient tale," Seli says. "Rarely spoken of anymore, and probably untrue. According to the legend, Thesalla—Goddess of the Source—created an orb, from which all other Gods were born. A way to channel the Source, you see. Unfortunately, it became lost after many, many millennia, but some Wytches still hope it can be found."

I examine the gently curving lines of the glass orb in Seli's case. "Why would anyone want it? What would it do?"

"Anything the holder should desire. Wytches, however, would use it to cure themselves of shadow. A bit foolishly, I might add. If the Orb ever existed, it's surely at the bottom of some sea by now."

I try not to shudder. What must it be like to have a power so terrible you would want to be rid of it, forever?

I straighten. "Thank you for your time, Queen Seli."

Her gaze is as cool as ever. "One final note, Lady Vyzrais. I hope you understand the extreme generosity my son is offering you and treat it accordingly. I hope you are wise with what you have learned."

I'm not sure how to respond to that, so I simply nod, and I leave, wondering why I feel as though I was just both warned and threatened.

꙳

One day passes, then two. I can't decide what to do.

The best plan is to go to the Estuary again, break into the scroll room, take what I need, and leave Altheara, with all my memories intact and full of knowledge to deliver to the council. Including either breaking my Oath or killing Thyo.

Except every time I think about doing it, I hesitate. Once I commit that act, there will be no turning back. Just for a brief, fantastical moment, I entertain telling Thyo about my Oath. Would he help me?

No. Even if he took some small mercy on me, none of these other Althearans would allow it. I would probably be assassinated in my prison cell.

Aslen hasn't come to get me for training, nor responded to the notes I've sent her. I don't know why. But it leaves me without many distractions. I'm sitting in a chair by my vanity, mostly staring off into space, when there's a light knock on my door, and Iyanna enters.

"Oh," she says when she sees me. "Good. I was hoping I would find you here." She goes to the settee closest to me, sitting. "Your wedding is in two weeks, Lady Vyzrais. Most of the details have been accounted for, but I assumed it was time for us to discuss some of the more pertinent aspects of the plans. I have seamstresses working on a dress, but if you'd prefer to look at the sketches, or see the dress in person, we can visit any time you'd like."

The idea of a wedding with Thyo sounds so impossible right now, it's laughable. "Whatever you think is best, Iyanna."

"Of course. I'll show you the final result with enough time for modifications." She stands, pulling something out of her dress pocket and setting it on the vanity in front of me.

It's a small, dark bottle. "What is that?"

Her expression is calm and cool, as always. "A birth tonic. More accurately, to prevent a birth. Do you know what a contraceptive tonic does?"

I open my mouth, then close it. I'm not sure how to answer.

"For laying with a man," she says, not waiting for a response. "I would hope someone explained this to you many years ago."

I cross my arms. "I know how children are made, Iyanna."

"Children are but one facet of sharing a bed," Iyanna says. "I would also remind you that no one in this castle, let alone this kingdom, would take kindly to you trying to prevent a pregnancy. However, I find it's best to care little for the opinions of others when it comes to your own body and your own choices. If you should require a contraceptive tonic at any time, you may ask me."

I'm so taken aback by this conversation, I don't know what to say. "Isn't that a bit disloyal? You are an Althearan, after all."

She pauses, just a moment of indecision. "I am your handmaid, Lady Vyzrais. No one else's. I am loyal to Altheara…but as an accord of my position, I am also loyal to you."

It occurs to me that no one had ever confronted me about my first visit to the Estuary, when I had been caught by Iyanna. Had she kept it a secret?

"How did you become a handmaid, Iyanna?" I ask. "Why not join the Galdrion? I thought all Althearans had to."

"They do," she says. "And then they are evaluated, and some are sent out to be other things—servants, or inventors, or some other occupation outside of the Galdrion."

I feel uncomfortable; perhaps it had been too personal of a question. "I see. So that's what you did?"

She seems conflicted, as though she is debating something

"My story is very particular," she says finally. "I was ill, as a child. No one knew what was wrong with me. My parents are high-ranking in the Galdrion, in a protectorate called Venech. They hid my sickness. I had seizures, you see. I would have never been allowed into the Galdrion." She says this without any emotion. "Hiding my illness was nearly impossible. But I was determined to make my parents proud. I thought if I forced myself, that if I tried hard enough, I would somehow be cured."

My voice is quiet. "How did you hide it?"

"Herbs and tonics," she says. "I studied endlessly to find the right combinations. They helped but couldn't cure me. It only gave me time to hide my condition. I was always in trouble for poor attendance, of course, but my secret was hidden. And then…" She trails off. "An illness spread throughout the protectorates, killing thousands within weeks. I fell ill, and it made everything worse. I began to seize constantly. It was a miracle I had survived, and yet, I could no longer hide."

"So, you left?" I ask tentatively.

Her face tightens. "I would have died before I dishonored my parents. The Galdrion is everything to Altheara, and it is everything to my parents. I would have rather not existed than to know the shame they felt at my failure. No, I was discharged from the Galdrion. They were furious that I had hidden my illness, even though I had begun studying herbs and tonics all those years prior and had learned how to prevent the worst of it. I no longer seized. I still don't, as long as I take the correct formula, but they would make no allowances."

My throat is tight with empathy. "I'm sorry, Iyanna."

Her expression is as composed as ever. "Perhaps. I find I'm better suited to the medica. And still…" I see the smallest hint of longing. "I will never learn beyond the bounds of medicine Altheara has to offer."

"And your parents?" I ask quietly.

"My parents will never approve," she says. "They chose to love a dream more than their own child."

I had judged her too harshly—had disliked that perfectly composed veneer, the way she held herself so stiffly. Now I know what lies beneath it. "Thank you for telling me all of this," I say. "Truly."

"We'll know each other for quite some time, Lady Vyzrais. I suppose it's wise we become better acquainted." She grabs the bottle, slipping it into her pocket once more. It's not exactly a smile that crosses her face, but it's something close.

Once she leaves, I continue sitting in the vanity chair, this time a bit dazed. I am feeling more and more unsettled by my time in Altheara.

My conversation with Iyanna has reminded me of the herbs I stole from the Estuary. I'd gotten lucky that Thyo had only known I had seen Phaelina and little else. He hadn't seemed to know about the two bottles of tonic I had hidden in my jacket pocket.

Looking for a distraction from the uncomfortable feelings I'm having, I go to the couch, where I have the tonics wrapped and stuffed under the cushions. I pull one out, ignoring the other.

Fire Blend. I wonder what it's intended to do. It's meant for a mortal, of course. I have no idea what the effects would be if I drank it.

I bite my lip, wondering if I should try some. Before I can overthink it, I open the bottle and take a tiny sip.

It tastes wretched, like spoiled food mixed with ashes. I cough, barely swallowing even the sip. Do they have to drink this entire bottle? On a regular basis? How horrible.

Trying not to gag, I go pour myself a cup of water, waiting

to feel something. True Alosian herbs begin to work almost instantly, but these won't be as potent. Perhaps they won't even affect me.

After a few minutes, I feel nothing

Thirty minutes later, I'm still waiting.

One hour later, I've decided the formula doesn't work.

Now I just feel grumpy. I hadn't realized I'd been excited, half-hoping it would trigger the feeling of magic within me.

Muttering, I pace my rooms, intent on finding another distraction. I feel energized by my annoyance, almost reckless. Eventually, I rip my bedroom door open, unable to stay inside any longer. I'll pace around the gardens if that's what I have to do.

Only, when I open my door, there are no guards, and I remember Thyo's promise to remove them.

Elated at the thought, I take off down the hall. The only part of the castle I haven't visited is the east wing, so I head in that direction. I get lost and have to backtrack a few times, finally asking one of the servants I encounter which direction to go.

Eventually, I arrive at the meeting room I'd attended once before. Two guards are outside. I don't recognize either of them. I think about continuing on, but I stop. I gesture to the doors. "Is the prince in there?"

They glance at each other. "One moment, Lady Vyzrais," one of them says.

She knocks and enters the room. Only moments later, she emerges again. "You may go in."

Thyo stands as soon as I enter. "Luze? Is something wrong?"

Now that I'm here, I feel awkward, confused by my impulsivity. No one else is in the room, and there are papers spread out in front of him. Clearly, he's busy.

"No. I just…I wanted to see you." I go to stand by the table, staring down at the papers. "Are you still working on trade routes with Kemerel?"

"Yes." He rubs a hand across his brow. "No one can agree on which route is best."

"What resource do you want from them, anyway?"

He leans against the table next to me. "A mineral."

"A mineral? Really?"

"It's rare. It grows along their coastline. It has…certain properties. Properties which could be useful to us. It's called vaerium."

"Vaerium," I echo. "I've never heard of it."

"Most haven't. Especially on this continent."

"What does it do?" I ask.

He shifts some papers. "You're awfully inquisitive today."

"I'm just trying to learn more about you."

His brows rise. "About me?"

I push off the table, facing him. "Is that so strange?"

A small line forms between his brows. "You seem upset. Did something happen?"

His tone is gentle and to my horror, I feel a wave of emotion.

I should leave, I decide. Coming here was a mistake. I step away, about to make my excuses, but before I can, Thyo speaks again.

"You're doing it again," he says. "The thing you always do."

"What?"

He tilts his head. "You want to run. I can see it all over your face."

I narrow my eyes. "I have no idea what you're talking about."

His expression grows serious. "Luze, I need to ask. Is there someone else? Someone you left behind in Alos?"

My mouth feels dry. "No. There's no one else."

There wasn't. Not really. I certainly wasn't ever going to go back to Clydon. Never mind that it still made my chest ache to think of him. Or that I regularly contemplated the ways I would harm him when I returned to Alos.

"Then what is it?" Thyo asks.

It's that I'm so confused that every day I want to curse the Source for being in this situation.

"It's that I like you, and I don't think I should." The words burst from me. I'm feeling more and more wound up. "I want to stop feeling like I know you, only to realize you're still a stranger."

"What would you like to know?" he asks.

"Anything!" I throw up my hands. "Anything. Just so I stop feeling like I know you, only to realize you're still a stranger."

"In the Galdrion, we're kept celibate."

I blink. Once, twice. "What?"

"It's one of our laws." He meets my eyes. "And strictly enforced. Although some manage to get away with their various liaisons, as you can imagine. It's to ensure we won't be distracted from our duty. Especially with the risk of producing a child."

This is not where I expected him to go.

"But you're the prince," I say. "Surely, you could…"

"Not really. I'm under more scrutiny than anyone else."

"So, that night out in the forest, when we…"

He crosses his arms. "I'm not exactly versed in the art of courting."

"You're not terrible at it," I say, thinking out loud.

"What a glowing compliment."

I cross my arms, mirroring him. "Well, all of the lying didn't help."

"It's different here," he says. "I don't know if you entirely understand. In Alos…I haven't felt that free. I can never lose control here. It's heavier here, somehow. Or in Ceneth, at least. The only time I can breathe is when I'm traveling in another protectorate."

It's eerily familiar to how I had felt as a child. Except my mother had tucked me away in an attempt to prevent that burden for me, at least temporarily. I think of Queen Seli, with her cold air. She doesn't seem like the nurturing type. And with Thyo's father dead…I suddenly wonder if he's ever had anyone who's protected him.

"I understand," I say.

Something between us calms.

I clear my throat. "So, you really haven't been with anyone?"

His smile is wry. "Not until I'm married. Unless I want to ruin the good name of the Galdrion, defy our advisors, and become known as the rogue prince with no respect for the rules."

I can tell he's only half-joking.

"Are you allowed to do anything before you're married?" I ask.

"It's discouraged, but most do. I was no exception in my adolescence. I didn't want my first time kissing a woman to be on my wedding day, as it was."

How could he not have already stolen someone's heart, found someone he wanted to be with? Surely there was a long, long line of those that would have pursued him? His handsome face, the intensity that sometimes darkens his eyes…

The amusement in Thyo's face slides away, and I suddenly realize I've been staring at him.

I'm surprised at the level of heat that washes through my

body. I take a breath. "You've thought about it, then. With us. You must have, even when you were going back and forth about the treaty. Even before you'd met me."

"I would treat any woman—especially my wife—with care," Thyo says simply. "And I hoped that eventually, I would feel love. As would she. But it was all fictional. All a fantasy. Until I met you. The way that you were so fierce, and yet so cold. Like fire and ice. It was intoxicating."

For some reason, his description disturbs me. I don't know what to say back, either. When I think of Thyo, I think of shadows: dark and impenetrable, there one second and gone the next, something always lurking under the surface, even if I never know exactly what.

I feel slightly awkward, but not exactly displeased, either. "I'm sure you know I find you handsome," I say.

He seems more amused than flattered. "Do you?"

I look away, picking at my nail. "You must know you're attractive."

"No," he says. "But there were those times out in the forest where I thought, if only just for a moment, that you wanted me."

The words hang between us. My face feels hot.

"I did," I say. "But I didn't know who you were, at the time. Choosing you would have been a betrayal. And then once I'd found out you'd lied about who you were…"

I trail off. We both know how that story ends.

"I suppose I have another regret to add to my list, then," he says.

I huff. "This isn't a joke, Thyo."

"I didn't say it was. I thought about breaking the rules that night, out in the forest. I've thought about it since then. What you would feel like."

I'm not entirely sure how to describe the sound that comes out of my mouth. "Really," I manage.

This is wrong, some small part of my mind says. We shouldn't be talking about this. Not when my skin feels like it's on fire, for reasons that I don't want it to be.

I risk looking at him. He's watching me, his arms still tightly crossed, as though holding himself back, but I can't mistake the look in his eyes.

"I've had years of never taking anyone to bed, Luze," he says. "Of waiting for the person I could be with. And then I met you. Regardless of what you might think, I'm not as controlled as I seem to be."

I stare at him, speechless and overwhelmed by the sensations in my body. The air grows thick in the quiet. Hesitantly, Thyo reaches out, cupping my cheek. His thumb brushes the corner of my mouth.

This is a mistake. I know that. I know I have to leave Altheara. Getting any closer to Thyo is unwise.

Except my hands have somehow found their way to the front of his shirt, pressing against his chest, my breath unsteady. "I want you to—I need—"

I don't know what I need. Whatever is happening inside my body is foreign and overwhelming and I almost don't care.

Thyo seems to know better than I do, because he pauses, just slightly—enough time for me to pull back if I want—and then he cups my face in his hands, pressing his lips to mine.

I press into him, my hands sliding down to the hem of his shirt, fingertips grazing the muscles I feel there, something desperate urging me on.

Thyo seems to have a need of his own, his hands sliding to my waist. He grips my hips, turning me and lifting me with ease, setting me on the table. I feel giddy with energy flaming across my skin as he stands between my legs, his right hand gripping my calf before sliding up to my knee.

Which is when the door opens.

I let out a screech, shoving Thyo away.

"—the analysis of the Karkinthian Route," Conrith is saying as he enters the room. "Contrary to what you seem to think, I *can* actually find a book on my own."

"If you could find it, then you would have," Aslen says.

Cyrian and Gideon both follow behind her, each holding a stack of books. Demelan is there too, and for some reason he's holding a knife in his hand, spinning it.

They all stop short when they see me. I push myself from the table.

A slow grin crosses Demelan's face. "Well, well. It's good to see you, Luze."

I glance at Thyo, hoping he'll say something. I gesture toward the table. "We were just looking at maps."

This seems to bemuse Cyrian, who frowns as though my being on the table is a highly impractical way to examine maps.

"I apologize," Conrith says, though he looks completely unfazed. "We should have knocked."

"We don't have time for social calls," Aslen says. She brushes past us, throwing herself into a chair. She doesn't look at me. "We need to get back to work."

"Did you find what you were looking for in the library?" Thyo asks.

Demelan sits across from Aslen, still grinning. He twists the handle of the knife in his hand. The metal has an unusual green tint to it.

Gideon, to his credit, seems to have decided to simply ignore the entire situation. He places his stack of books on the table. "We did, but—"

"We're not sure investigating Karkinthian is in our best interest," Conrith finishes.

Aslen still isn't looking at any of us.

I've retreated away, my back bumping into a massive statue situated in the corner of the room. It looks like something vaguely from another age, or another land. Thyo watches my retreat, glancing between me and the others. I can tell he wants to say something, but not with the others present.

I should just go. But I feel rooted to the spot, still unsure of what, exactly, just happened, and why my lips are still tingling.

"I am in no way agreeing with Atemox Conrith," Aslen says, "but I don't think the Karkinthian route is our first choice."

Conrith gives her a sour look. "That is the exact definition of agreement, Huntress Fereaux."

"I said first choice," Aslen retorts. "You said, *in our best interest.* Those are entirely separate things."

"Arguing semantics is a waste of time," Cyrian says.

I lean a little on the base of the statue. I'm beginning to feel unwell. My heart is racing faster and faster, and I blink, noticing how sharp my vision is. My entire body feels hot, and I wonder if I'm sweating. I wipe my hand across my brow but it's dry, as are my palms, which are now beginning to burn.

"We've already agreed it's the safest, most difficult-to-invade route," Thyo interrupts. "As Luze pointed out in the meeting with Roseh and Aver, and she was right."

My body feels hot and cold, my skin crawling unbearably. I feel like my chest is going to explode. My hand grips the base of the statue, my nails biting into the marble. All of this from one kiss?

"It may be too much of a risk," Gideon says. "If they find the Fithian Pass and divert, it would be problematic."

Oh, I finally realize. Oh, no. The way I'm feeling isn't from that kiss.

"We've ruled it out," Conrith says. "It's too much of a gamble."

"Maybe *you* ruled it out," Aslen says, "but I don't believe the rest of us had that discussion. Not that I think we should spend any more time discussing the Karkinthian route, but it's amazing to me how you can be so conceited."

Demelan tosses the knife onto the table. "Aslen, give it a rest."

She and Conrith both ignore him.

"I may be conceited, but at least I'm not unreasonably stubborn and mulish," Conrith says.

"I don't think we should—" Cyrian tries to interject.

"You are the most ill-brained man—"

"—and you are an infuriatingly obtuse woman—"

"—as arrogant as any Crafter, maybe even *worse*—"

"—at least I'm not as idiotic as one, unlike you—"

"Shut up! Just *shut up!*"

My voice breaks through the argument, shocking us all. My skin is on fire. *Everything* is on fire.

Thyo steps toward me. "Luze—"

The ground below us lets out an unearthly groan, the floor vibrating, as though it will rupture. Books fall off the shelves and glass rattles; the ceiling makes a terrible keening sound as though it's being split. The ground underneath rumbles and rolls, throwing me off balance. I cling to the statue, but there's a massive *crack* as it explodes, followed by an almighty crash as it shatters to the floor.

It's over in a minute and then silence falls. Dust fills the room. I blink away the grit. Thyo is halfway to me, his hands gripped onto a chair, as though he'd grabbed it for balance.

Demelan is on the floor, coughing. Gideon had pulled Cyrian under the table. Conrith had yanked Aslen away, and his hands are still on her. She shoves him away. She coughs. "What in the Abyss…"

Guards have rushed into the room. Thyo brushes them off.

Conrith grimaces as he pushes himself upright. "That hasn't happened here in a while. I can't say I appreciate the reminder. Dratted, unstable lands."

"Luze?" Thyo comes to my side, putting a hand on me. "Are you hurt?"

I stare down at my hands. I expect to see something. Blood, maybe. But there's nothing.

"No," I say. "No, I…"

Words fails me. I suddenly feel as though I may be sick.

Thyo doesn't seem to notice. "It was just an earthshock," he says, his tone still worried. "I should have warned you when you first arrived. They aren't uncommon in this region."

Demelan is staring at the statue, now in hundreds of pieces on the floor. "She got lucky. That could have crushed her."

Something tells me it wasn't luck.

I tuck my hands behind my back. Both are trembling. "I'm fine. It just frightened me, that's all. I'll just…return to my rooms."

It's an abrupt exit, but I can't stand there even one second longer. I don't give anyone a chance to say anything before I flee.

It's only seconds after I get to my room that I vomit, making it to the bathing chamber just in time. I lay on the cool floor, wishing my heart would slow and my skin would cool. I close my eyes, but that only makes the awful spinning in my head worse, and my eyes fly open again.

I hold my hands up to my face, staring at them. Something

feels wrong, and I'm suddenly afraid I'm going to die. Every speck of my skin is crawling, and it feels as though someone has reached inside of my belly and is yanking on each of my organs in turn.

The tonic. It has to be the tonic. *Fire Blend.* Well, now I know what it does. Whatever is in that concoction, it clearly wasn't designed for me.

Yet, it means those concoctions the Althearans are designing *do* work.

With that last nightmarish thought, I sleep fitfully, with my head on the cold floor and my body still burning.

31

Something bright and shimmering pierces through the darkness.

It's masked by the fog surrounding me on all sides, but the warm glow beckons me closer.

"Hello?" I call. I reach out a hand, watching how my skin becomes cast in an eerie bronzed glow. I squeeze my eyes shut, dimly registering that I'm dreaming or having a vision, but this feels so real.

I open my eyes, but a murky haze still surrounds me. "I can't see anything with all of this fog," I complain.

A cool, pine-scented breeze rushes past, and the fog seems to curl away from it, forming a tunnel in front of me. I follow the path laid ahead of me, and as I step through the hole in the fog, it's like falling into a new world.

I'm in a forest. Birds sing quietly, and I hear the sound of water distantly, though it's different than what I'm used to—almost a roar, or a crash. There's a slight breeze here, and I smell the tang of salt.

Where the normalcy ends, however, is with the trees. Every one of them is crooked, curling into spirals, the top of the tree twisting around and around until it sits in the center. One tree in particular catches my eye. A golden light emanates from it.

The tree itself isn't the most spectacular—it's rather small, and dry-looking—and it's one that spirals into itself. In the center sits a light.

Not a light. An orb of some sort, with shimmering tendrils that caress the tree, as though the two are gently bound. I walk closer, reaching up, stopping just short of touching the light. I expect it to feel hot, but even with the few inches between my fingers at the light, it feels only pleasantly warm.

Hello, Gifted One.

I scream, yanking my hand away and tripping back. I look around, but no one is here.

I feel, rather than hear, a hum that seems like a laugh. *You have nothing to fear from me, child.*

My gaze snaps back to the orb, realizing: the voice is coming from the light.

"Who are you?" My voice comes out squeaky.

I feel a bit stupid talking to what looks like a large glowing ball, but this is my dream, after all.

I am the voice of All. The Daughter of Creation, the Brother of Time, the Child of Fate, and the One of Life.

Well, then.

I clear my throat. "I'm Luze."

I feel the voice laugh again. *I know who you are, Luzeandra Vyzrais.*

I strain my ears this time, trying to discern if the voice is male or female, but I can't tell. It seems to emanate from the earth and from the sky, from inside my head and from the orb itself, as though it's everywhere, all at once.

I try to think of something to say, since the voice seems to be waiting. "Where am I?"

The place of my birth, though this is no longer my home.

"And where is home, exactly?"

My home is where free will and fate meet.

"What does that mean?"

You'll find out, soon enough. When the time comes, you'll know you have found your home. But first, you must trust.

"Trust in what?"

I feel the voice smile. *Trust in your choices.*

I pause. "I don't understand."

It matters not. All choices can lead to the same fate.

"I know little of fate or prophecy," I say, "but I'm sure that can't be true. If it were, why wouldn't people simply sit around, letting their destiny find them?"

Consider sailing the seas, the voice says. *You may wait an hour, a day, a week, and each choice will change your path and what you experience while traversing it. One day, perhaps, you encounter a sea creature. Perhaps if you had waited and left the next day, there would be no sea creature, but a sea-storm would befall you. Still, you will reach the other side if it is destined. If something is fated for you, you will reach the far shore.*

"What if you never leave?" I ask. "What if you just stand there, staring at the sea, but you never actually sail?"

The voice is quiet for so long I wonder if it's disappeared. *I have seen infinite lives unfold since the time of creation, Luzeandra. The unhappiest beings are the ones that stand at the shore, not realizing that no choice at all is still a choice.*

The words put a lump in my throat. "Sometimes we don't get a choice. Sometimes our choices are made for us."

Circumstances may be forced upon us, the voice corrects. *The decisions you make are what define the story you live. Even your exile, when you felt as though you were trapped beyond hope, you never were. Fate simply plucked the thread of destiny you needed to walk.*

I feel my face flush. "You're saying that I suffered for all those years on purpose? That it was my fault?"

Fault? No. But was there a reason? Yes. We are not responsible for what is done to us, Luzeandra. But we are responsible for what comes after.

The voice sounds a little stern now, and I cross my arms, feeling defensive. "You're wrong."

It is not wrong. It is simply a choice. You will compel yourself to standing at the shore, believing that you do not deserve anything beyond where you stand. Worse, you will deprive the world of what you can offer, simply because you are too caught amidst your belief that you are flawed, incompetent, and unworthy. This will be important for you to remember one day, Luzeandra. You are only beginning your journey.

I open my mouth, wanting to protest, or perhaps scream, but the voice speaks quickly, almost like it knows our time is up.

For now, a token of knowledge: do not disregard the importance of offering a place where one has not been found. A gift bestowed is a gift returned. Remember this.

My brows pinch. "What—"

The voice cuts me off. *Your choices will come to you as they must, Luzeandra. Trust in their timing. What belongs to you must return and so it shall. Press your palm upon the tree.*

I hesitate, wondering if I should just pinch myself and try to wake up. Instead, I press my palm to the spiraling trunk of the tree.

Nothing happens. I wait, annoyed. "Why—"

My world is turned upside down once more, as though

I'm falling down a very long hole while spinning, and images flash past:

Riding my first pony, an overly plump beast who would try to bite me as soon as my back was turned, but who carried me on my first gallop through an open meadow, the wind whipping my hair and making my eyes water, even as I cling on, feeling freer than I ever have…

Zassa and I pulling out an old trunk full of scarves and clothes and jewelry, dressing ourselves in costumes and smearing our faces with little pots full of creamy, colorful concoctions. I don't notice the time pass by, only that Zassa and I keep ending up on the floor, wheezing from laughter at our antics…

My mother, sitting next to me as I curl into her side. She's teaching me to read. Not the old dialects that Saelis tries to drill into my mind; this book is fun and slightly wicked, with daring characters and romance and adventure…

Saelis, presenting me with a black, fluffy kitten, its paws tipped with white. The kitten curls into my chest to sleep as soon as I hold her. Saelis is gruff, but he tells me he found the kitten during his travels and that she needs a home. Your studies have gone well recently, he tells me. You deserve a gift…

The memories slow, becoming creeping and bright, surrounding me with a distant feeling of dread.

It's days before my tenth birthday, and I hide in the library, eavesdropping on my mother and Saelis. Something is wrong with me, something to do with my magic…

I flee in despair, running from the manor house all the way to the border. I will force the magic from myself if I have to. I will claim my gifts, or I will die trying.

I try to force the magic to emerge, and I want to scream as nothing happens. Tears begin to fall down my cheeks. I stare up at the stars sparkling in the sky, and pray to the Source, even as I sob.

The memory becomes blotchy, like water-stained painting.

There is a warm glow—pure joy—and the face of a male smiling at me, his voice kind, and a white-hot light fills my vision, fills the forest, as though a star itself has fallen from the sky and imploded—

And then comes the nightmare:

"Run," the male tells me. "Run straight to your mother. I cannot protect you, Luzeandra."

I run, my lungs burning. At least five Strin are behind me, cleaving through where I have broken the Wards.

I have a head start, only a minute, but it's enough to warn the guards. One of them shelters me, takes me into the uppermost tower with my mother and sister, while the other assemble and call for help. My mother wants to fight; she argues with the guards. It delays us.

The first to fall are my mother's guards.

Then, the servants.

Finally: My mother, arms outstretched, trying to reach me. A ripping, tearing sound. Crimson blood pouring across a stone floor.

The memory disappears, becomes blank. All I see next is the terrible vision: my mother and sister, dead on the floor. The Strin are gone.

I am punished. I scream as the Healer presses her palms to my eyes, the way that she rips away the memories of that night, and so much more

There is darkness.

I survive.

And then—

A small flicker.

The light is small inside of me. It has become only a small candle, only an ember I can feel in my chest. It offers me something.

Hope.

32

When I wake my mouth tastes sour and my head pounds.

Nothing else feels normal.

I feel…different. As though something has shifted. I'm not sure what.

My head continues to throb painfully. Slowly, I get up, pouring myself a cup of water. As I take my first sip, I realize how thirsty I am, and as I cautiously drink the entire cup, the pain in my head begins to ease.

I rub a hand over my brow. I go to my balcony doors, pulling them open. I can see only the faintest hint of pre-dawn light. I go back to my bed, sitting down.

That strange dream I'd had…

The details are already blurry. I press my hands to my eyes, trying to remember. Something about giving someone a gift, I think. The memories are clearer than the dream.

My hand rubs the skin at my chest. It feels terribly painful and sore. Underneath that…something warm. Something that threatens to crack the castle of ice I have built within myself.

I leave my room, quietly moving through the castle and

winding through the grounds, until I reach the medica, and finally, the Estuary.

I encounter guards, stationed in front of the entrance. One of them steps forward as I approach. "Can I help you?" he asks.

"I need to see Phaelina," I say. "I'm Luzeandra Vyzrais."

He and the other guard glance at each other. They recognize my name, clearly. "I'm sorry, Lady Vyzrais. The Estuary is strictly guarded. We would need orders from the prince to allow you in."

My hands twitch. I can still feel a small current of magic. "Then go talk to him. In the meantime, I need to see Phaelina."

He sizes me up, straightening a bit. "As I said, Lady Vyzrais—"

A burst of wind rushes past us, surprisingly cold despite the usual warmth of Altheara. I feel a groan in the earth beneath my feet. Both the guards' eyes widen.

"What's going on?"

I turn. Aslen is standing at the foot of the Estuary. She takes the stairs two at a time, coming up quickly.

The guard looks uncomfortable, if not a bit frightened. "Huntress Fereaux, I was explaining the rules of the Estuary to Lady Vyzrais, and telling her that without proper orders, I cannot—"

"It's fine, Zand." She cuts him off. "I'll escort her myself."

He and his partner step aside. They both seem relieved Aslen has taken over.

We walk into the Estuary, and she cuts me a look. "What's wrong with you? You seem…different."

"It's amazing you noticed. Considering you've been ignoring me for days." My voice is flat, but I'm more disinterested than anything; a squabble with Aslen is the least of my concerns.

I head down the hall purposefully; I know where I'm going this time.

Aslen's hand closes over the handle before I can turn it.

"You lied," she says. "About not being trained. As soon as I saw you with Kahri, I suspected, but I thought maybe it was just luck, or strength. Then when I saw you with Thyo…I knew. Why were you acting like you knew nothing, that you were terrible with weapons, all that time?"

"You're the one who insisted on training me," I say. "I never asked for it."

"You made me look like a fool!" she snaps.

Underneath her anger, there is a glimpse of something else: vulnerability. Perhaps Aslen had not offered to train me out of duty—but friendship?

A small—very small—wave of guilt twists in my gut. "I lied for the same reasons you've lied," I say quietly. "I simply made the same choice."

"And what choice would that be?"

"To protect myself. And I won't apologize for that." I twist the knob under her hand and enter the room.

Phaelina is there, sitting in the same chair by the fireplace. I had known she would be. I'm not sure if it's luck or intuition, but it doesn't surprise me that I've found her so easily.

What's unexpected is the fact that Thyo sits across from her. I stop short, and Aslen bumps into my back.

Thyo stands. "Luze?

"Thyo?" I say, surprised.

Thyo looks past me. "Aslen?"

"Phaelina," Aslen says, her tone exasperated. "Now that we've said everyone's name, can we get to the point of things? I for one have a lot to say."

I cut her a look. "You always have a lot to say."

Phaelina is watching all of us with a dry expression. "I am an old woman, children. If you're going to stand around and squabble like siblings, I ought to go take a nap."

"Aslen isn't my sister," I say. I point at Thyo. "And *he* is definitely not my brother."

Wind rattles against the glass of the window unnaturally. Whatever's left of the tonic is still working, clearly.

Phaelina cackles. "You'll need to learn to sleep well at night, Thysol. You're going to need plenty of energy with this one. Then again, a temperament like hers means you might enjoy not sleeping."

Aslen makes a sound of disgust.

I step forward, keeping my eyes on Phaelina. "You were right. The memories came back. Some of them, at least."

"What are you talking about?" Aslen asks.

Phaelina studies me. "You used a tonic, I presume?"

I nod.

"Unexpected," she says. "I thought it would take you much longer to do something so reckless."

Thyo's face is tight. "You used one of the Galdrion's tonics? Why?"

I hesitate. I'm not sure how much I should share. I had come to see Phaelina, not Thyo. But something about my experience with that dream, with the memories that still swim in my mind, makes me feel reckless. Or maybe it's the power I can still feel tingling in my hands—something larger than any single element. Something that I do not understand, that frightens me.

Something I crave.

"Oh, hoho," Phaelina says. "That was you?"

Aslen stalks over to stand next to Thyo. "What was?"

"I caused the earthshock," I say. "And that statue that, um, broke."

"Exploded," Thyo corrects. "That's impossible. That much magic…you shouldn't have that much magic here, even with the tonic. How much did you take? More than one bottle?"

Phaelina watches me. She looks delighted.

Again, I hesitate. "I had a sip."

Something in Thyo's eyes that makes me think back to my conversation with Seli. What had she said? *It can be difficult for mortal men to fully grasp what it means to love a powerful woman.*

"It made me terribly ill," I say quickly. "And it's already fading."

It's true. The power is slowing dissolving. All that's left is the slightest sensation in my fingertips.

Phaelina doesn't seem concerned. "You had to have pulled from yourself, as anyone else would in these lands, but with your lineage, my sense is that you would adjust, given time."

Aslen gives her a sharp look. "Given time? As in, what, if she continued taking it?"

"She would be powerful," Thyo says. "Extremely powerful."

There's an undertone to his words I don't understand.

Phaelina is surveying me. She seems gentler, somehow. "But that's not truly what you came here for, is it?"

Here it is. The moment where I've reached a crossroads. "It brought back the memories I had lost," I say. I'm only speaking to Phaelina now. I'm unable to resist speaking, as though the memories have awakened something in me that cannot be forced back in.

Phaelina sits back, her lips pursed. "I see."

"I don't," Aslen says. "Can someone explain what in the Abyss is going on?"

I can feel the pressure building in my head and my lips, the urge to spill my secrets. This isn't the same as revealing my Oath. Not even close. Perhaps it is even wise to reveal my history. Perhaps it will make everything easier when I do what must be done—when I betray them all.

"The Healers of Alos are powerful," I say. "Powerful enough to meddle with any mind they choose. They ripped memories from me when I was a child. The memory of a specific night, and any memory touched by joy. By warmth or happiness. They did it to punish me."

"But why?" Aslen asks. "Why would do they do something like that?"

I keep my eyes on Thyo. The intensity of his eyes, the darkness of the iris blending into the pupil. The way he watches me, steadily, unafraid. The way I know that steadiness will change to something like doubt, after I've said my next words.

And still, I say, "Because I murdered my family."

33

Aslen is the first to speak. "You did *what?*"

I don't miss the way she hovers in front of Thyo just slightly, as though protecting him.

"It was a mistake," I say. The words feel stuck, and I force them out. "It was eleven years ago. I ripped the Ward—the boundary that keeps our provinces safe. And then there were so many of them."

"Them?" Thyo asks.

"The Strin. I've never seen so many together. Five. Impossible to kill. I ran. Straight to my mother. To my sister. Even knowing what I knew. I led them straight to my home, to my family. I was selfish."

I press my palms to my temples, wishing I had a way to cleanse my mind, to erase all the things I don't want to see.

"It wasn't your fault." Thyo's voice is quiet. "You were a child."

"I was ten." My skin feels cold. "I knew better."

"Ten is still a child."

"Is it? Your Galdrion begin training when they're nine."

"It's different," he says.

"It's no different!" The glass rattles faintly again. It's good the tonic has already left my system, or I think the room would have shattered by now.

Aslen's hand drifts to the dagger housed on her hip, her expression wary.

My chest feels tight, but I manage to speak. "I'm fine."

She looks at my hands, which are clenched. "Then why are you bleeding?"

I think at first that it's a metaphor. Then I realize my palms are stinging. I look down. My nails have bitten through the skin. "My hands," I say distantly. "There's blood. On my hands."

"Thyo, do something," Aslen mutters. "I think she's losing it."

"Quiet, Huntress." Phaelina's voice is sharp. "Thysol—this matter is for you. We will leave you."

I almost don't notice Aslen's protests, the way she finally relents and help Phaelina from her chair, both of them leaving the room. It's only distantly I realize Thyo is guiding me to a low cot, helping me sit. He disappears, and when he comes back into my line of vision, he's holding something white. I try to focus. Bandages.

Quickly, efficiently, he wraps both my hands. It stings a bit as he does. I wince.

"I'm sorry," he says. "These are soaked in a formula to prevent any infection. It will only burn for a second."

He's right. The pain is already fading.

"There was someone else."

I don't even realize I've spoken until Thyo's hands still.

A small part of my mind screams *shut up.* Yet, I feel as though I've begun to purge a poison that cannot be contained any longer.

My voice is nearly inaudible. "I was punished after. It wasn't just memories. They took me away from my home. It was so cold in my exile. I remember thinking nothing else really mattered except the sun. That if I could just be somewhere with grass and trees with leaves, if I could just sit in the sunlight for even an hour, I would never complain again."

All I can see as I speak is that impenetrable wall of shimmery light trapping me in the Barren Forest. I feel my throat tighten, even as I know I'm no longer there.

I focus on Thyo, on the way his lips move as he says, "How did you survive it?"

"Clydon." I shiver. "He wasn't supposed to, but he visited me. He gave me gifts. He was the only thing warm in my life. I thought he loved me. I thought I was in love with him."

Thyo still kneels in front of me. "Were you?"

Was I? Had I ever been? Up until Maeven had told me of his betrayal, I would have said yes.

"I don't think you can love someone when it's based on lies," I say. "He left me. Not physically, maybe. But he abandoned me in every way that mattered. He has a wife and child. I found out when we were in Hatal."

"I'm sorry," Thyo says.

"Clydon is nothing in comparison to everything I lost." I stare off, not really seeing. "I spent so many years reliving the same nightmares over and over. After I took that tonic I saw things I had forgotten. And now that I have regained some of the memories I lost—the good things, the things I missed—I wonder what else I have lost."

"I understand," he says quietly.

How can he? It hardly makes sense to me. "I'm tired. I want to rest." It isn't a lie. Even my bones feel fatigued.

"I can help you to the castle," he says, starting to stand.

It surprises us both when I reach out, grasping his arm with my bandaged hand. "No. I want to stay here." It feels safer here, for some reason.

"Of course," Thyo says. "You can stay here as long as you like."

My eyelids are heavy, but I push my next words out. "Don't leave me."

He settles onto the edge of the cot as I lie back. "I won't."

"Stay," I try to insist, but I think all that comes out is a garbled breath.

As I slip into a dreamless sleep, I imagine him speak one last time. Just one word, spoken softly.

"Always," he says.

34

I'm not sure how long it's been when I wake up. I'm merely aware that I feel warm. I blink my eyes open, realized that the fabric I feel beneath my hand is not from bedcovers, but from a shirt. Thyo's shirt. My head is on his chest.

His breath remains steady. I can't see, but I think he's still asleep. Slowly, I ease away, sitting up.

He's softer in sleep. Younger, almost. I have the urge to reach over and brush his hair back from his face. Instead, I clutch my hand to my chest, confused about what, exactly, I'm feeling.

Everything comes flooding back to me. The way I had stormed into the Estuary, the way I had made my confession.

I bury my face into my hands. What had I been thinking?

Except…Thyo had stayed with me when I had asked. I'm not sure what that means.

Carefully, I climb off of the cot without waking him. He must be a deep sleeper once he's finally unconscious.

I have no idea what time it is, only that it's dark outside. I manage to get back to the castle without incident, slipping into my room and crawling into bed. My body is still tired, but my mind is whirling. All I can think about is my head on Thyo's chest, what it had felt like to wake up next to him. There is something inside of me now that flinches at the idea of leaving Altheara.

And that is absurd. I am still bound to my Oath, and I can never tell anyone here the truth. Not even Thyo.

When Iyanna quietly taps on my door with breakfast, I'm already sitting up, my arms curled around my knees as I try to simply breathe and not think about the future or the decisions I know I have to make.

Iyanna gives me a note from Aslen instructing—no, ordering—me to meet her at the Alcheaum where we normally train.

I leave my rooms and meet her, noticing that she's carrying a hefty bag over her shoulder.

"We're back to training, then?" I ask.

"If you're up for it."

"I suppose I am," I say slowly.

Our relationship is almost like siblings—except with an undercurrent of distrust I know will never fade. I haven't forgotten about our spat, the way she's ignored me for days. Then again, she isn't one for apologies and emotional conversations. Perhaps this is her way of repairing our rift.

I'm in a bad mood," she says. "So we're doing something new today."

That *something new* ends up being a massive obstacle course. Apparently, the entire course forms a circle, one that involves a lot of running, but she takes us to a portion of it that's more isolated. The wall of Ceneth is only a few hundred feet away. I stare at it, feeling a mix of both unease and desire. This wall, a smaller version of the one that borders the boundary between Alos and Altheara, marks the decision I have to make: to stay or to leave.

"Conrith left," she says abruptly, pulling me from my thoughts. "In the dead of the night, like a criminal. I mean, we're right in the middle of this Abyss-destined trade route planning, but apparently, he needed to go back to Hallin. To 'prepare the protectorate'. What, is he going to build signposts for the Kemerels?"

I decide to keep quiet.

"What do I care, anyways?" she says. "I don't. Care, I mean."

I pause. "That's good."

"We should train," she says abruptly. "I want to hit things."

She drops her supplies at the base of a tree, which is right by an obstacle involving a massive log. She opens the bag. "Things to throw, things to hit with…" She shakes the bag, which makes a clanking sound. "Whatever you want."

I'm still in a quiet, tired mood, but I see a small set of throwing knives, and I grab them, feeling a small spurt of excitement. They're carefully sheathed. I pull one free. I twist the knife, noticing the fine craftsmanship.

"Galdriel iron," Aslen says. "It's difficult to forge. It doesn't react well to the air when it's heated. But if you have a blacksmith who knows what they're doing, that blade will be impossibly sharp and will last forever."

"It's beautiful," I say. "And nicely balanced."

"If you want me to teach you how to throw it, I can show you—"

I throw the knife and it embeds itself in the log obstacle.

"—or you can do that," Aslen finishes. She gives me a terse look. "I guess I shouldn't be surprised, after the way you fought with Thyo. I haven't forgiven you for that, by the way. Gregori gave me an earful."

I go to pull the knife out of the log. "I learned how to

throw knives when I was exiled. I used to practice for hours. It was all I had to do."

She falls quiet.

I don't want to talk about my exile, and I don't want Aslen to pity me. "I bet," I say slowly, "that I might even be better at it than you."

She cracks her knuckles. "I'd be more than happy to prove you wrong."

"Deal." I point to a tree about fifty feet away. "Three in a row. Cleanest hits win."

"Child's play," she says. She points to another tree. "That one."

I size it up. "That has to be at least eighty feet away."

"Exactly. Scared?"

"What, of a tree?"

She takes a knife to the tree, marching over there and carving an X into the trunk. "X marks the spot."

I roll my eyes. "Obviously."

She walks back. "You want to go first?"

"By all means." I give her a mocking bow. "Ladies first."

She snorts, but grabs a knife, balancing it in her hand.

She's good. Very, very, good. The first two are almost parallel to each other, right in the center. The third wobbles slightly, landing to the right of the X. She grimaces.

"Not too bad," I say.

"I'd like to see you do better," she says, stalking over to yank the knives out.

When she comes back, she slaps a knife in my hand. "Go on."

As soon as I hold the knife, something inside of me settles. This, I know how to do. It lands, quivering, dead center.

"Lucky shot," Aslen says.

She looks a little bit less pleased when the second one lands right next to the first. Or when the third one lands next to them both.

I can't resist gloating, just a bit. "Still think it's luck?"

She waves a hand. "It's only because you're Alosian. You can see better, that's all."

"It's probably because I'm stronger," I say, my face smooth. "Perhaps you should try some strengthening exercises."

Considering Aslen's arms ripple with muscles, my comment is ludicrous, but it works: she's instantly annoyed. "You're a fool if you think you're stronger than me."

"I guess we'll never know."

She flexes her hand. "Or we could have an arm-wrestling match."

I glance around. No one is in sight. Which is why I crack a grin and say, "Fine by me."

We go to the log obstacle, which is just about the same height as a tall table, both of us getting situated.

"On the count of three," Aslen says. "One, two, *three.*"

I'm overly confident that we'll be at least somewhat matched, but as soon as she calls *three* I realize I'm doomed. I grimace, straining every bit of muscle I have, but it doesn't take long before my hand slams down into the log.

I pull my hand away, wincing. "No fair. It must be the tonics you take."

Aslen grins, flexing her arm. "Not in the slightest. I don't take tonics. This is all natural."

I put my arm on the log again. "Again."

She clasps my hand. "One, two—"

It's a dirty trick, but I start before she says *three,* pulling my full weight into it. She makes a sound of indignation. With both hands, I send her arm crashing into the log.

"I win!" I hop onto the log, throwing my fist into the air. "Oh, sweet, sweet victory—"

"You cheated!" she says, outraged.

I grin down at her. "Don't be a sore loser."

She climbs up onto the log next to me, pushing me. "Get down. This isn't a podium."

I shove her back. "*You* get down."

She reaches to shove me back and I raise my hands to defend myself, both of us vaguely slapping at each other. She whacks me in the elbow, hard, and I let out a squawk of indignation, lifting my foot to kick her, which causes both of us to lose our balance. We both hit the dirt, hard.

"Idiot," Aslen snaps, wheezing slightly.

"*I'm* the idiot?"

"You're the one who kicked me, how stupid can you be—"

"You're the one who tried to pull me down from the log!"

She reaches over to shove me, and I slap her away. She's just grabbed my arm, trying to stop me, when two people come into view. Both are jogging. One of them is Demelan, and the other is the advisor, Roseh. Both of them are shirtless.

Aslen and I freeze. I blink the dust out of my eyes.

Demelan stops short, taking in the scene. "It's not every day my fantasy of finding two women wrestling each other is fulfilled, but I can't say it's an unwelcome surprise."

Aslen releases me, untangling herself. My arm throbs painfully as blood rushes back. I'm certain it's going to bruise.

She sits up. "We weren't wrestling."

He glances at the log obstacle. "Did you fall?"

Despite his amusement, he's studying her carefully, his eyes roving over her face and body. Checking for injuries, I realize.

Aslen scowls. "Of course not. I was *pushed.*"

"I did not push you," I say indignantly.

"Right, you just kicked me like a cow—"

"Really? A cow? That's what you're going with?"

Roseh and Demelan are both staring at us, vaguely nonplussed.

I push myself to my feet, realizing I'm still on the ground. Aslen does the same.

"What are you doing out here, anyways?" she asks, annoyed.

He raises his brows. "Just a run." He glances at Roseh. "Though I don't think either of us expected the additional entertainment. What are you doing all the way out here?"

"Avoiding people," Aslen says. "Which you've now ruined. And really, Demelan, don't you own a shirt?"

"It is hot outside," I point out. Personally, I don't have a problem with them being shirtless. Both of them are exquisitely well-developed. It must be a result of their training.

Roseh seems the least comfortable out of all of us. "It's only warm in Ceneth," Roseh says. He clears his throat. "And a few of the other protectorates. Hallin, for example, is much cooler."

"Well, you don't see me running around half-naked, no matter where I am," Aslen says. "I have this little thing called dignity."

"That's not what it looked like a minute ago," Demelan says dryly.

Aslen cuts him a look.

"We were having a training session," I say, trying to restore some stateliness to the situation. "We just became, um, distracted."

Demelan looks as though he doesn't particularly believe this, but he accepts it graciously enough. "Well, we ought to keep going. Roseh?"

"Right behind you," Roseh says.

Demelan gives us a cheery goodbye, and Aslen and I watch as they cross the log obstacle, disappearing into the trees as they round the curve.

I only speak once Demelan is a safe distance away. "He really does care for you, you know. Even if he jokes."

Aslen gives me a startled look. "Demelan? Don't be ridiculous."

Part of me wonders if I'm wrong, if perhaps I misread the look on his face, but I don't think so.

"I just didn't realize how protective he is," I say. "It was all over his face."

She rolls her eyes. "You hallucinated, then."

I shrug. "Suit yourself. But all I'm saying is, if one day he confesses his undying love—"

She starts to come after me and I burst out laughing, darting away.

"You are incorrigible," Aslen says. "If I didn't owe you for saving me from that Strin, I would be throwing a knife at you right now."

My smile fades. "You don't owe me anything." I start to collect all of the weapons, which are strewn everywhere.

"When you're queen of Altheara, don't think it changes anything," Aslen says. "I don't care if you rule the kingdom, I'll still knock you on your ass."

"Good to know."

We start to walk back. "So are we ever going to talk about what happened yesterday?" Aslen says.

My humor slides away. "No."

"Well, I'm going to. I'm in charge of taking care of Thyo, you know. And after what I heard yesterday, I'm a little concerned."

I tense. "Concerned about what?"

"About your kingdom," she says. "If what you said is true—and I didn't even hear the full story—I want to know what makes Alosians so comfortable with exiling a child."

Her words shock me. Mainly, that she is not suspicious *of* me, and that she is worried *for* me.

"I murdered my family," I say. "Isn't that enough?"

She heaves a sigh. "You led some monsters to your family by running away when you were scared. I don't think that's quite the same thing."

"I knew better. Perhaps, if my mother had been anyone else…but it wasn't only my mother I killed. I killed our Crown. I killed my sister, the only other heir." My words catch. "I denied the people of Alos a ruler they could trust."

She hesitates again. "You know, Luze…I'm not exactly an expert on family. My own family hated me. But I don't blame myself for that, mostly because I left them before they could convince me it was my fault. I wonder if you've been told a story so many times, you've come to believe it's true."

"Maybe," I say, unconvinced, though everything about what she's just said surprises me.

"Thyo told me, you know." She shifts the bag over her shoulder. "About what you discovered, and how he's given you a week to decide whether to stay or leave."

I can't tell her it's so much more complex than that. "He wants me to agree to never return to Alos."

"Is that a problem?"

"I'm a Crafter," I say. "For all that might have happened, Alos is my home."

"Your home," she repeats flatly. "You mean the home full of the people who blamed you for an accident, locked you away in a frozen forest as a child, and then sent you away to a new kingdom? I don't think they want you, Luze."

I suck in a sharp breath, and her expression changes.

"I didn't mean that," she says. "Well, I did, but it came out wrong."

"You're right," I say. "They didn't want me."

Her surprise is apparent, and we both fall silent on the way back to the castle. I lose myself in thought, mulling over her words and what lies ahead of me.

I can follow my uncle's plan. I can kill Thyo and return to Alos. Altheara will become an even greater enemy to Alos—to me—than it already is, though weakened. It would be the simplest path. My whole soul rebels at the idea.

I can simply refuse to fulfill my Oath, even if I never figure out a way to destroy my Oath ring. Of course, then I'll die, so I'm not particularly keen on that option.

If it exists, I could find the way to destroy my Oath and leave Altheara. This option is perhaps the least logical of all. If I leave Altheara I will have no loyalty from them; nothing will change. They will still be my enemy. But if I break my Oath and return to Alos alone, my uncle will have no reason to let me ascend the Crown, either. I could fight it, but with the council on his side… No. I might have to flee the continent entirely, without either kingdom's loyalty to protect me.

Or, the last option, the one that fills me with equal parts terror and joy, the one that will risk the most… I can find a way to destroy my Oath and remain in Altheara. Thyo will have to know, however. I will have to tell him about the promise I made to kill him. A lifetime of shame and despair make every fiber of my being shy away from the idea. And yet…

Perhaps all Alos holds for me is dark memories and a war between rulers. I will have to give up so much if I go back. I will have to give up handling weapons, even. I will have to give up the friendships I've made in Altheara, even as much as I want to deny the idea of a friendship with an Althearan. Even people like Phaelina, who, even as little as I know her, has already offered so much wisdom. I have no one like that that I trust in Alos anymore.

Maybe I've been holding on to a dream that doesn't exist.

35

When I send a note to Thyo asking him to meet me at the stables, I'm strangely nervous. I wonder if he'll ignore it. Part of me is hoping he does.

He doesn't. He's there before me, waiting by Arturon's stall.

He smiles when he sees me. "Hello."

I clear my throat. "Hi."

His hand reaches out, brushing a piece of hair back from my face. Warmth fills me even as I want to step away, out of reach.

"I wondered if you might want to go on a ride with me," I say in a rush. "I thought perhaps we could ride into the city center. I haven't seen it yet."

He looks surprised, but his whole being seems to lighten. "I would like that."

I fidget. "I mean, only if you have time. I know you have all of those meetings, and—"

"Luze." He cuts me off. "You are my priority right now."

I try to ignore the low swooping in my belly.

We tack up, and when he meets me out front of the stables, he's leading a horse that isn't Odreya.

"Is Odreya okay?" I ask.

He tightens the girth. "She is. But she's getting a bit on in years, and this filly—Glori—needs the experience." He pulls the stirrups down, checking the length. "She's only three, and she comes from the same stallion as Vhetta. Aslen's mare, if you remember."

"I remember," I mutter, leading Arturon over to a mounting block.

Our ride starts out quiet, at first. I wonder if I should be making conversation. Maybe Thyo feels equally as awkward as I do, considering the last time we were together, we were asleep in a cot.

The filly he's riding, Glori, seems content only if she's half walking, half prancing. I'm certain she could bolt off in a heartbeat. Still, Thyo seems relatively calm riding her, his contact with the bit light.

"You handle her well," I comment. "I thought Demelan was the horsemaster of the group."

"He is," Thyo says. He scratches Glori's neck, and she snorts, her gait calming, just slightly. "He's been working with her. She's come a long way. She used to bolt as soon as anyone mounted her."

I don't remark that she still seems close to it. "Will she be okay in the city?"

He smiles. "I guess we'll know once we're in the market. If she takes off, crashing through the stalls, we'll have our answer."

I give Arturon a scratch on his withers, suddenly grateful for his placid pace.

The further we get from the castle, the less organized things seem to become, especially as we approach the heart of the city. Everything in Altheara is built to seem so formidable. It lacks grace—none of the designs are particularly delicate—but it makes up for it in size. All of the streets have a militant feel.

"What's the city used for?" I ask. "Is it only the Galdrion, or…"

"Galdrion and civilians," he says.

"So you train everyone, and then what, kick some people out and they become civilians?" Like Iyanna, I think, but I don't say it.

He shakes his head. "It's more complicated than that. Everyone serves at least a few years. Most people who have some other passion—in business, or invention, or whatever it is—are perfectly happy to have been trained in the Galdrion before departing to pursue a different kind of apprenticeship."

We reach the edge of a market. Buildings line the street on either side. People come and go. It's similar to the castle in that everyone looks as though they have a purpose. Yet it feels slightly more relaxed here. I see more people greeting one another, stopping to chat.

Thyo stops Glori, dismounting. He gestures to a tie post. "We can leave them here."

I dismount. "Afraid of Glori trampling some innocent bystander?"

He makes a small face at me, and I laugh.

We tie them and luckily, Glori seems much more sociable than her half-sister, Vhetta. She immediately has her nose on Arturon's withers, nuzzling him. Arturon, for his part, quickly settles in, his eyelids already drooping.

Thyo and I press into the market. It's busy enough that I have to be careful not to bump into others. The air is full of scents of fresh cooked food; I smell sizzling meats and warm bread and something tart, like lemons. I notice a few unfriendly looks sent my way, quickly modified as soon as the person realizes who I'm with. Even if it weren't for my height, for my looks that indicate I am a Crafter, my eyes are too unnatural to escape notice.

I'd encountered animosity at the castle, but I hadn't interacted with enough people to truly understand how Althearans might feel about my presence, and the hostility surprises me, even as expected as it should be. It reminds me there will be more than one obstacle to overcome if I remain in Altheara.

We pass by other stalls. One catches my eye. It's full of bracelets and other jewelry. I step forward, peering at the bracelets. They're wooden, each of them with a thin, single charm adhered.

The vendor looks slightly nervous as we stand there. She bows deeply to Thyo. "Prince Adriel."

I pick up one bracelet in particular, which has a small, silver pearl attached to it. "This is beautiful."

The vendor looks delighted by my compliment. "That pearl was sourced directly from the shores of our Venech. I plucked it from the oyster myself."

I put it down, slightly regretful. "It's lovely."

Thyo's hand stops me from placing the bracelet back on the table. Instead, he undoes the clasp of the bracelet, sliding it over my wrist and closing it once more.

He pulls something from his pocket. "Here," he says to the vendor, passing her a handful of coins. He pays her in Althearan currency, rather than gold or silver, so I'm not sure how much it is. Judging by the vendor's wide eyes, it's plenty.

"Oh, you're too kind," she says. "But really, you must take it for free, I insist—"

Thyo holds a palm up in refusal. "Please. It's my pleasure."

She continues to gush as we leave. I hold my wrist out, admiring the pearl glinting in the sunlight. "Thank you," I tell him. I suddenly feel shy. "It's beautiful."

"You wear that necklace all the time," he says, gesturing to the blood pendant around my neck. "Something from Alos. And now you have something from Altheara."

I look away, my cheeks warm.

We melt back into the crowd. "Is Venech another protectorate?" I ask.

"It's next to Dolaon," Thyo says. "One of the most lucrative protectorates, not the least due to how much fishing is done there. It's a popular placement request for members of the Galdrion. The weather is certainly favored amongst everyone."

"I'd like to visit," I say.

He pauses, just conspicuously enough for me to notice. "I had planned on taking you there after the wedding. Once everything with the trade routes is settled, of course."

After the wedding. My stomach lurches.

Someone jostles me, hard, and I'm almost swept away. I reach out instinctively, clutching Thyo's hand. He looks down, surprised, but his fingers intertwine with mine.

And then…I don't let go.

I try to keep my face calm, even as my heartbeat quickens.

"May I show you something?" Thyo asks.

"Yes," I say, slightly taken aback.

He tugs me along, still holding my hand, and goes to a stall where he purchases a bag of roasted nuts. He manages to do it while still holding my hand. Now that he has me in his grasp, he doesn't seem to want to let go.

He leads me further down the market, towards a large building with pillars. The entrance is massive, with a large, marbled ceiling, but it seems mostly empty. Confused, I follow him as he leads me to a set of stairs. We take them, going up one, two, three, four flights, until he leads me down a hall, to yet another small staircase. At the top is a door. He opens it…

…and we step out onto a rooftop.

I blink, the sun stinging my eyes a little. Once they adjust, I walk to the edge, finally pulling my hand free. There's a small wall along the sides so I don't have to fear falling over the edge. Still, I'm careful as I peer down.

It's a bird's-eye view. Scanning the horizon, I realize that I can see most of Ceneth from here, all the way to the castle, and even beyond.

I turn back to Thyo. "This is amazing. I can see the entire capitol from here."

He walks over to me. "My father used to take me here. Whenever I needed a break, he said, though I suspect it was when *he* needed a break."

I look at the bag he's still holding. "And the food?"

"Ah." He smiles. "These provided endless hours of entertainment."

He opens the bag, pulling out a small, roasted nut, and squinting across the rooftop, he throws it.

It lands on the opposite rooftop soundlessly.

"Really?" I ask, amused. "That rooftop is huge."

He grins. "But what you don't see is that small stain, which is what I was aiming for. My throw is impeccable."

I narrow my eyes. I actually do see the mark he's pointed out. "Let me try."

He hands me a nut. I feel a bit foolish, but I line up my arm, tossing the nut.

It falls short, landing in the street below. My eyes widen as I lean over the edge. "Oh, Source. I hope I didn't hit someone."

"It's the risk of the warrior's journey," Thyo says solemnly.

I roll my eyes. "Give me another one."

And so, for some time—I'm not sure how much, because I lose track of it—we throw, each challenging each other to various marks. A flowerpot on a balcony, a doorway, a decorative statue.

I find myself laughing. I feel lighter than I have in a long time.

At one point, Thyo stands behind me, trying to help me throw. So much for my skills with throwing knives; throwing food apparently requires a completely different set of abilities.

I can feel his breath in my hair as he says, "Now don't just use your shoulder, use your wrist—"

The nut still falls short. "See," I complain. "It's not me, it's—"

I stop short as I turn and he's right there.

"It's what?" he asks, his brow raised.

I swallow. "Nothing. It's just a silly game, anyway."

The sun is setting behind him, casting him in a warm glow. I notice that the half-moons that normally rest under his eyes have all but disappeared. For once, he looks rested.

I hesitate and then I reach out, my fingers trailing the space along his cheekbone. He stills, watching me carefully.

"You look well," I say. "Sometimes...I don't know. Sometimes you look so tired."

He smiles. "I had no idea you cared so much for my well-being."

I huff, pulling my hand away. "I don't. I'm just saying, you could probably use a better sleep schedule, maybe skip a meeting or two. That's all."

He catches my hand. "No, don't ruin the moment. It was such a nice one, too."

I make a face. "About to accuse me of wanting to run again?"

"No," he says. "Actually, all I can think about right now is how beautiful you are."

I look down, though I don't move. "Do you only want me because of the prophecy you believe in, Thyo?"

I hadn't realized how much the thought is weighing on me until I say it aloud.

"No," he says. "In fact, I've realized the only reason I believe in the prophecy is because what the Seer said has come true. Partially, at least."

I search his gaze. "What do you mean?"

"She told me I would fall in love with this Crafter," Thyo says. "That it would be impossible for me not to, even if I tried. She was right."

I go very, very still. "What are you saying?"

"That I love you," he says.

I have no words.

"I never wanted the Seer's words to be true," Thyo says. "I fought it. I didn't want to give up control. And if I had to, well, I wasn't going to fall in love with the person who held the fate of Altheara in their hands, regardless of what the Seer told me. And then there you were. You, intelligent and strong and beautiful. You, always with your guard up, always ready to run. You've made it impossible for me to love you, and impossible for me to not love you. And now, if you leave Altheara, it will be the greatest regret of my life. Not because of trade or medicines or peace agreements, but because I will regret losing you."

This—all of it—is too much. I want to flee.

"I'm not the person you think I am, Thyo," I say. "I never have been. I told you what happened, what I've done."

And there's so much more I haven't told him.

"I don't care," he says. "I don't believe it was your fault."

I pull away. "Then that makes you a fool."

"I've seen your goodness, Luze," he says. "You could argue we've already been through more than most people getting to know one another. I know who you are."

I laugh without humor. "I'm not sure nearly getting killed together counts."

"It does to me. We may not know everything about each other, but I know your heart, Luze. I saw what you did for Aslen."

"How do you see me, Thyo?" I ask. "As some kind of savior?"

"I see you as you are," he says simply. "And...I love you."

I am frozen, torn between wanting to leave and wanting to stay.

He steps toward me, slowly. He reaches out, gentle coaxing my chin up. "Why does that make you afraid?"

"I can't be fixed, Thyo." I need him to understand this. "I don't think I can even fix myself."

He's steady, his eyes serious. "Perhaps you don't need to be fixed, Luze. And even if you do...perhaps I could love you, all the same."

When he kisses me, it's slow and sweet. It's a balm, soothing and mending.

He leans his brow to mine. His scent surrounds me, that dark, smoky aura that has begun to feel familiar and comforting.

"I don't know how to do this," I whisper. "I don't know how to trust I have a place here, in Altheara."

"How can I prove to you that you do?" he asks.

I speak carefully. I tell him my idea.

And he says yes.

36

I feel trepidation over my decision. The next day, I begin to wonder if I have made a mistake. If I have set myself down a path I cannot reverse.

I unroll the scroll that marks my decision. I had gotten a formal copy of it. I trace my hand over the signatures there. Mine. Thyo's. Phaelina, as a witness and advisor to formalize the document, who could apparently do such things.

Iyanna knocks, and I quickly re-roll the parchment, adding it to a bag I have stowed away. "Come in," I call.

She enters, carrying a lunch tray. "The queen has requested to see you. I'll have your lunch here for you when you return, however."

My pulse quickens. I wonder what the queen knows.

I go to the parlor I'd met Queen Seli in last time. She's reading a document when I arrive, one hand carefully tracing her lips as she peruses it.

"Queen Seli." I hesitate by the doorway. "You wanted to see me?"

She waves to a chair. "Please sit."

I sit, crossing and re-crossing my ankles.

She sits back, adjusting her skirts. "I am planning a trip to several of the protectorates. I'd like for you to join me."

This is unexpected. "For how long?"

"A few weeks, perhaps," she says. "After the wedding ceremony, of course."

"That seems like quite a long time," I say slowly. "How soon would we leave?"

"A few days after the ceremony, at most." She sets her tea down. "It may seem sudden, but this trip has been planned for quite some time."

I don't want to outright refuse, but the idea of traveling with the queen alone sounds less than appealing.

"I'll speak with Thyo about the trip to the protectorates," I say. "I'm sure he'll take no issue with it, since it's your idea, but I'd like to speak with him first."

An expression crosses the queen's face, but it's gone too quickly for me to read. She stands. "Of course. It's a wise decision to go, Luzeandra. You'll see."

I stand, assuming we're finished, when the queen speaks again.

"One more thing, before you depart," she says. "Phaelina mentioned to me that you've taken an interest in the work at the Estuary."

I shift, wondering if a reprimand is coming. "I have."

"We have records," she says. "Records that are—shall I say—far more potent in nature than what is contained in the library." The queen surveys me. "I would like to offer you the chance to access the knowledge contained within the Estuary."

"That's very generous, Queen Seli," I say, surprised. It seems almost too good to be true.

Seli rises, going to a small wooden chest and opening it. She retrieves a thick, complicated-looking key. She hands it to me. I accept it, noticing the intricate craftsmanship of the design.

"I've informed our medica and the guards that you are to be allowed access to the Estuary," Seli says. "And Luzeandra, in return for this favor, if you come across anything interesting, please do bring it to me."

"Anything interesting," I repeat. "Such as?"

She waves a hand. "Only the gods know. I'm far too busy to go and look through those scrolls myself, you see. It's an idle request, Luzeandra. Don't think too much of it."

It's a bit of an odd request, but harmless. "If I find anything, I'll be sure to bring it to you," I say.

I sense our meeting has come to an end, and I leave.

⁂

I go to find Thyo, finding him where he usually is—the meeting room he spends too much time in.

The guards let me in wordlessly, used to me by now, and Thyo is there, situated in a chair, poring over papers in front of him. He looks up as I enter.

"You're back," he says. I walk over to him, and he pulls me next to him, dragging the chair so it's flush with his. I'm surprised by the level of quick, easy affection we've attained so quickly.

I settle into the crook of his arm, glancing at the papers he's perusing. "More work?"

"More ideas for a trade routes," he says. "One of our leaders from Tellas wants a coastal route implemented."

"For Kemerel?"

He hesitates. "For Alos, actually. We're finishing the final drafts to send to your council. Some were already agreed upon, of course, but this is a modification. It would allow Altheara to access Alos by sea."

It falls quiet for a moment, and then I say, "I went to see your mother."

"Did you?" He sounds distracted, still examining the paper in his hand.

"Actually, she requested to see me." I clear my throat. "About a trip to the Althearan protectorates."

He looks up. "When?"

I keep my eyes on the papers. "She said we would leave immediately after the ceremony. I'm surprised she didn't mention it to you."

His body feels stiff next to mine. "I knew a trip was planned. Eventually. But after the ceremony is too soon." I feel his body relax. "It doesn't matter. You're not going."

It irks me, his phrasing: *You're not going.* As though it's a command.

Now *I* feel stiff. "A trip to the protectorates isn't an unwise idea. Your mother is right that I've seen very little of Altheara."

"I suppose," he says. "But the trade routes are my priority right now. I can't leave until they're settled."

I look at the papers in front of him. Every single province of Alos is carefully outlined, and Almaru—home of the Alosian court—is marked with a star. Complex, seemingly random lines are drawn across the map, connecting Alos to Altheara. "Thyo, I've barely even looked at these trade routes with Alos. I'm more familiar with the trade you have planned for Kemerel, which is absurd."

He seems unconcerned. "These routes have already been agreed on, as I said. There's little for you to do."

I pull away, getting to my feet. "Yes, but I'm saying I *want* to know about these trade routes."

He keeps writing, still distracted, even as he says, "You're upset. Is this because of the trip to the protectorates?"

"If I want to go on a trip of the protectorates, I'll go," I say. "This isn't about that."

He sighs, putting his pen down. "If I let you go on the trip, will you be happy?"

I stare at him. *Let* me?

"I won't be commanded, Thyo," I say slowly. "Not by you. Not by anyone. Not anymore."

He rubs a hand across his forehead. "I'm sorry. I'm not commanding you. I should have chosen my words more carefully."

Slowly, I relax and settle in next to him once more. "Can't you find a time to rest?"

"I could," he says tiredly. He presses his hands to his eyes. "If I wanted to let one-thousand-and-one things go undone, that is."

Instinctively, I reach out, brushing my hand across his temple, and he leans into the touch. There's something charged between us.

"Just because we made certain commitments, it doesn't mean that I own you, Luze," he says quietly. "I merely hope you will see things as I've seen them. I want to make sure you know that."

"I know," I say.

There's only one thing left between us. That thing is why I hold myself back: I haven't told him about the Oath. Part of me—a foolish part—still hopes that perhaps I can avoid telling him, somehow. But I will have to, for everything to work.

Thyo reaches out, smoothing the lines on my forehead. "What are you thinking?"

"Can't you just use your shadows?" I ask, a bit bitingly.

Thyo raises his brows. "Not when I'm this exhausted. I would rather you chose to tell me, anyway."

I can't. I don't know how. I look back at the maps. "How did you become so good at all of this? At ruling Altheara?"

"I wasn't, at first," he says. "Everyone was petrified of me when I first entered the Galdrion. Even the instructors. They were afraid of a breach of etiquette, of offending my mother, offending me…And that fear would have been to my detriment. You learn very little when people are terrified of criticizing you."

"What changed?" I ask.

"Aslen," he says. "She picked up a sword and challenged me to a duel. She said that everyone was going to lie to me, and tell me I was better than I was, and I would believe them. She told me I would never be any good with a sword if I didn't train with someone who didn't care about hurting me. And then followed Gideon, who was the only boy she could stand to be around. Probably because he wasn't secretly in love with her or threatened by her skills. And then after Gideon came Demelan. Aslen used to be afraid of horses, you see. Demelan noticed and helped her. He wasn't terrified of her or threatened by her. He might have been secretly in love with her—Demelan has a tendency toward infatuation—but if he was, he kept it well-enough hidden so that they could tolerate one another until eventually, they became friends."

"And then Gideon married Cyrian," I say. "So now you have all of them."

He smiles. "And you have all of them, too."

Not the way he did. But one day, perhaps. If they are able to forgive me.

"It's good," I say. "That you have so many people you can rely on."

He rubs my arm. "And you don't?"

I rub my arms, struck by a feeling of loss. "No. My sister would have been someone I trusted, I think. Perhaps my tutor, Saelis. Everyone else in my life always wanted something from me."

"That sounds lonely," he says.

I trace one of the lines on the map in front of me. "It's worse to be betrayed than to be alone."

Thyo is quiet for a long moment. "When my father died, I felt completely alone for the first time. His death made me feel powerless."

I touch his hand. "I'm sorry."

He stares off, unseeing. His grip on my hand is tight. "After all he had raised me to be, I failed when it mattered most."

"You didn't fail," I say. "There was nothing you could have done. You can't blame yourself."

"I don't," he says. "Not anymore."

"Good," I say.

Neither of us moves. There it is again—a thick tension between us.

Oh, for Source's sake. Someone has to do *something*.

I'm tired of waiting. I impulsively I pull Thyo towards me, pressing my lips to his. He grips me tightly, pulling me by the waist, hooking my knee over his hip until I'm straddling him. Apparently, he was holding himself back as much as I was. A feeling of frisson envelops me, almost like my magic, but different.

His lips are still on mine, and then he presses his lips onto the edge of my jaw.

"I suppose this chair has benefits, compared to the table." My words come out as gasp.

"Maybe." Slowly, he makes his way down my neck, tracing my collarbone with his lips. "I think I'd like to try both."

Thyo reaches under the hem of my blouse, tugging it over my head. I wear only a thin, cropped undershirt, and Thyo's hands graze my waist through the silk.

"Wait," I say, pulling away from him, and standing up.

He looks like he wants to argue but before he can speak, I turn my back to him. Quickly, I dart to the door, twisting the lock. I won't be intruded on again.

"I need to show you something," I say. "Just to prepare you. I don't want to shock you." I hesitate. What if he reacts badly?

"Luze?" I hear the underlying wariness in his voice.

My hair is loose, hanging down my back, but I sweep it over my shoulder, and I hear Thyo's slight intake of breath. I'm still wearing my silk undershirt, but my scars are dark enough to be visible through the sheer fabric.

Before I can think too long, I grasp the hem, pulling the shirt over my head.

This time, Thyo is silent. I hear him rise.

"What are these?" he says from behind me.

I shiver, though I'm not cold. "The worst of my scars."

His voice has gone dark, but he sounds eerily calm. "From when you were attacked?"

I don't turn. "They tried to heal the skin the best they could. Even Crafter magic has its limits."

I noticed he hasn't touched my back, and I'm grateful.

"Luze." His voice is quiet. "Luze, look at me."

I turn, slowly. My hair hangs over my chest, covering me, but I still feel uncomfortably exposed.

Thyo looks at me intently. "I hope you know your scars don't make you any less beautiful."

I grimace. "My scars are ugly, Thyo. You don't need to lie to me."

He leans down, kissing my jaw. "Your scars are part of you, and since I love you, that means I love your scars. Though perhaps not how you got them." He takes a shaky breath. "That you were even able to survive—"

"We don't need to discuss it," I murmur. I reach out, tugging at the edge of his shirt, and he lets me remove it, helping me pull it over his head. An involuntary smile crosses my face at the sight of his bare chest. I trace a finger over his skin. "You know, Thysol, you happen to be very pretty yourself."

He laughs against my lips, easily lifting me and this time, setting me on the table. "I'm glad someone can finally appreciate it."

I pull him over me. He's careful, his weight barely pressing against me. I grip him tightly, pulling his body closer to mine.

Thyo bends down, pressing his lips down to the center of my chest, right below the hollow of my throat.

"Like stardust," Thyo murmurs, his mouth trailing down my body. "Starlight."

"Such poetry for a prince," I say, somewhat teasingly, but it comes out breathless.

Thyo pauses, his lips hovering above my navel. I feel edgy, restless, wanting his mouth to continue its descent. Hunger fills his gaze, but still, he doesn't move. "We will only go as far as you want to," he says, his eyes intent. "If there's any moment—if I hurt you, or if you don't want something, or if I do something wrong—you need to tell me."

"I will," I promise. "But Thyo?"

He looks at me cautiously. "Yes?"

I swallow. "If there's something *you* don't want, or something you don't like, just tell me. We only have to go as far as you want to, after all, so please don't—"

He laughs, rising over me to seal my mouth in a kiss. "I love you," he murmurs.

His words cause a glow to burst in my chest.

It doesn't take long before we're pressed to each other, our skin completely bare, and I sigh at the sensation. I've never felt anything like it. There's something here that never was with Clydon—warmth, affection. Laughter, perhaps.

But when Thyo's hands skim my hips, when his hands tangle in my hair, I don't think of Clydon. I don't think of anything at all, really. My mind is quiet, and it feels…

Divine.

Perhaps there's more than one kind of magic in this world.

37

Afterwards, Thyo and I go to my room and don't leave for three days.

A sort of serenity falls over me. Whenever there's a knock at the door, Thyo is the one to get up, and he steps outside the door, closing it, so all I can hear are muffled voices. Sometimes he returns with rolled papers.

Mostly, I think he does it so I don't feel obligated to put on clothes. Instead, with the door shut, I mostly just lay strewn out across the bed, wrapped in sheets. I know he's putting aside many obligations. I don't think either one of us cares.

Iyanna comes once, part of our normal routine, but I send her away with a note for Aslen. I don't want her to come hunt me down, after all.

Occasionally, usually for a few hours every day, Thyo works in the sitting room. He pores over papers he's brought. I find that I like the alone time. I read books or pull on a robe and go sit on the balcony. Sometimes, I simply nap.

I wake up on the third morning, curled into Thyo's side. His breathing is slow and steady, and I hold still, enjoying the peace of the moment.

There's a loud knock at the door, and Thyo stirs, groaning.

"What in the Gods—" He curses. "They're relentless."

I smile. "Stay. I'll get it."

I rise, pulling on a robe, and drawing the bedroom door closed behind me. I open the sitting room door, fully expecting to see a servant there with a tray of food, but instead, it's Aslen.

"Amazing," she says. "You haven't fallen into a coma or been mysteriously eaten by a wild beast. I was beginning to wonder."

"You can't possibly be here for training," I say. "I sent a note with Iyanna days ago. I'm taking time off. A vacation. I'm not sure if you've heard that word before, but it's—"

"Yes, yes, I know," she says testily. "And I'm happy for your happiness, even if it now means I'm alone with only my sword for company, but unfortunately, there are things Thyo can't avoid any longer. Since I've been told he's sequestered away in here, I've come to deliver the message."

"Fine," I say, miffed that the bubble of peace surrounding me for the past three days has finally been interrupted. "I'll tell him."

"I mean it," she calls, as I shut the door. "Luze, so help me, you'd better tell—"

I go back to the bed, climbing under the covers. Thyo pulls me closer, hooking my leg over his hip as he starts to tug on the knot I'd used to tie the robe.

I laugh, grabbing his hands. "I'm under strict orders to send you away."

"I don't want to," he grumbles. He buries his face into my neck, and I feel goosebumps on my skin. "I want to stay here. With you."

I'm tempted to ignore Aslen's request—Thyo is now

trailing kisses down my arm, pushing the sleeve of the robe away—but I sit up. "I think she meant it. Honestly, the fact that she didn't break down the door was an improvement for her."

Thyo flops back, still looking disgruntled. "I've changed my mind. I have no interest in ruling Altheara. Someone else can do it."

I smile. "But who else could possibly keep Aslen under rein?"

He stands, and I watch as he dresses. "No one, including me, could keep Aslen under rein." He turns, seeing me watching him, and his eyes darken. "If you keep looking at me like that, I won't be able to leave this room."

I grin, cupping my chin in my palm. "My apologies. I wouldn't want to keep you from your duties, after all."

He looks highly reluctant to leave. "I told my mother the travel to the other protectorates will have to wait until I can go with you."

"Meaning, we won't be parted."

"Exactly," he says. He comes over to kiss me, a slow kiss that has me pulling his shirt.

He stands, straightening it. "I'll be back as soon as I can manage it. And Luze…there are things we still need to discuss. Once I return."

Worry pierces me. "What sort of things? Something bad?"

"Of course not," he says smoothly. He bends, placing a kiss on my brow. "We'll talk about it later."

I decide to go to the medica after he leaves. I pull the key Seli gave me from a small bag I have packed that contains other precious things: Taleas's ring, a scroll, and the two tonics I stole from the Estuary.

The guards recognize me when I reach the Estuary.

"Lady Vyzrais," one of them says. He steps aside, pulling the door open. "You may enter."

"Thank you," I tell him.

I go left, down the hall that I remember from the night I'd broke into the Estuary. All that moves is the light from the oil lamps affixed to the wall, flickering dimly.

I reach the arched doors marking the records room. I take out the key, fumbling with it a bit as I try to figure out how to insert it into the lock. Finally, I hear a loud *click,* and the lock pops free. I glance around me, vaguely uneasy, before shaking it off and pulling the door open.

It's enormous. At least, compared to what I'd expected.

In front of me, beyond the doors, is a small platform, with a spiraling staircase that leads down. The room beyond is made of stone, and I dimly see thousands of shelves, the light from the hall only barely illuminating the room. I can't see much more than shapes and outlines, due to how dark it is. I squint, noticing a few small oil lamps on the floor, and a bowl filled with small, thin sticks, presumably to light it.

I grab the lamp and one of the sticks, going back to one of the lit lamps in the hall, using it to light the lamp I hold.

I hurry back, eager to enter the scroll room now that I'll be able to see. I grab a few more of the lighting sticks and light a second lamp, hoping there are more downstairs. I make my way down the staircase, carefully balancing both lamps. All of these scrolls—all of those records. I can't believe it's this easy.

I snort at the thought. It hadn't been easy. Not at all. It's ironic, actually, that after everything, I'd simply been handed a key to the scroll room.

As I reach the foot of the stairs, I realize I still haven't actually found anything yet, and to do so is going to be difficult. All of the scrolls are bound carefully. As I wander through, lighting more lamps that are carefully situated throughout the room, I can see by the texture of the rolled scrolls that some look newer, and some look ancient, as though a simple breeze might cause the material to dissolve.

I sigh, then sneeze at the dust. This is going to take a while.

Picking a section at random, I pull a scroll off one section of shelves. Delicately, I unroll it.

The storage of most stone fruit and root-plant must be…

Nope. I give the scroll a quick scan to make sure, but the entire paper is about winter planning for foods.

I grab another scroll, quickly realizing that this particular shelf seems to be about food, specifically winter. I start to go through the shelves, one-by-one, pulling scrolls at random. Some are about equipment for the Galdrion. Six shelves are devoted entirely to weapons. I spend far too long going through twelve shelves before realizing that each of them focuses on the twelve protectorates. The next shelf is on Ceneth.

Starting to become a bit weary, I go to the next row, again drawing a record at random and unwrapping the scroll. The next shelf is about some isle with beings called Blood-Singers, which I quickly ignore, putting the scroll back. The next few cubbies are also about various isles.

Rows and rows later, I'm ready to give up. I walk around the shelves, looking for something that will give me any clue, any sign.

I spot a cubby that, oddly, houses a chest, rather than the scrolls being loose. I grab it, pulling it off the shelf, brushing dust off the top.

The lid doesn't open immediately, and I realize there's a latch. Inspecting, I brush my thumb across the center.

"Ow!" I yank my thumb away. Something sharp has cut

me. I look at my thumb, at the bead of blood that forms there. Blood has gotten on the latch, too.

I go to wipe it off, sure some Althearan will hunt me down if they find out I've been bleeding over their precious records, when the latch suddenly clicks and the chest opens.

Cautiously, I open the lid. The inside, as I'd suspected, is full of scrolls. I pull one out carefully. The paper is so fragile, it looks as though my very touch might turn the scroll to dust.

The Writings of Galdrius

Scroll 52, Recorded in this 506th Year of the War.

I ponder that so few know the truth of this war. What the war seems to be about—magic and territory and control—seem such easy, simple things to fight over. Why the war started is another thing entirely. I worry that too few will know the truth, that this war began due to an ill-fated love.

The Thousand Year War. It must be. I keep reading.

I am not old enough to remember, but I am told there was a time when the Othos, the Crafters, the Wytches, and the mortals all coexisted on this continent. The Othos in the north, the Crafters in the middle, and the mortals in the south. The Wytches moved between their isle and the mortal lands. The ruler of the Othos had shrouded the northern lands in magic and mist, and it was impenetrable. The Crafters attempted to follow suit, but this was before the wall, so a young Wytch—her name was never noted—was able to travel to Crafter lands, to see if she could learn their magic and perhaps share some of her own. She dreamt of a world undivided. She met a young male Crafter who seemed to share her vision, and they fell in love.

I stare at the faded ink on the scroll. This is unheard of. A Wytch had fallen in love with a Crafter?

My love, my wife, who tells me her ancestor was that young Wytch, has told me all of this. The male Crafter betrayed the young Wytch, you see. The male Crafter was intrigued by the shadow element; Crafters only have access to the four earthly elements. He believed if Crafters were able to attain more elements—including shadow, which is perhaps one of the deadliest—they would be unstoppable. The Crafter population was greater than the Othos, they lived longer than the mortals, and were more powerful than the Wytches. With shadow, Crafters could claim the entire continent as their own, and eventually conquer the isles, perhaps looking as far as the East.

I think of Clydon and my uncle, Eskar. Two males that I can easily envision as the young male Crafter, intent on conquering lands, accepting the price of betrayal and greed.

The male Crafter was unsuccessful, and he had left a broken heart in his wake. Perhaps foolishly, she killed his true love—a Crafter female he was joined to. This did not go unnoticed. The mortals were blamed. Thus, beginning the war. The young Wytch vowed that for as long as she lived, her very life would be a curse upon Crafters. I suppose selfishly, I am glad that things happened as they did. For through this terrible trouble and strife, I have met my love, my wife, a Wytch with immense power, who has shown me how to save Altheara.

The scroll ends. I simply sit, staring at it for a long moment. Then, all in a rush, I start grabbing scrolls, quickly reading through them.

So many are devoted to Galdrius's wife, the Wytch he had married. He never names her. He talks about the formation of the Galdrion, about the Orders—First, Second, Third, Fourth—how each one is given a name, how each one has a different strength. How the discipline with which they are trained forms them into warriors, but the herbs the Wytches grow make them formidable. How the Wytches form new weapons, how one Wytch senses a mine full of iron—potent, durable iron—and leads the Althearan people to harvest it.

The Writings of Galdrius

Scroll 107, Recorded in this 511th Year of the War.

Rumor abounds that the High Lady of Alos has given birth. A baby girl—the new heir. They have named her Emrisa.

I stop here with a flash of recognition. My mother was named Emrisa.

Already, those I have sent to gather information tell me this child is powerful, perhaps one of the rare Crafters to have three elements.

Reading about her birth somehow hurts worse than thinking about her death.

I fear she will change the course of this war. That if not her, her children, or her children's children. Their lives seem endless. I feel wearier by the day. I am unsure if it is my age—I have recently reached my fiftieth year—or perhaps simply the endless battle.

My love tells me that I am being absurd, that fifty years is nothing. She's right, and yet, my life with her is far too short. Her power unnerves me. She tells me that I am being foolish about this, too. Perhaps she's right.

I have thought again how I despair that we will never have children together. She tells me that it's simply the cost of her power, that children cannot be borne from her. She tells me to have a child would be a great sacrifice, anyway. She asks if I have begun to grow unhappy. I tell her my only source of unhappiness is that we will not have lifetimes together. That we will not have a life without war together.

Alas. My ramblings have no place in these records. They are the sentiments of a man who simply wishes for peace.

I skip to another, later scroll.

The Writings of Galdrius

Scroll 198, Recorded in this 521st Year of the War.

She has done it.

She has discovered a magic so powerful, so potent, it will win the war.

It will take years to accumulate what she needs. But the future is now certain.

We—

The scroll is ripped. I trace my fingers along the jagged edge. Digging through, I look for other ripped scrolls, finding one.

__The Writings of Galdrius__
__Scroll 192, Recorded in this 520th Year of the War.__
*I am unsure of if we should purse this particular course
of magic. The language is something from another land.
I trust her, and yet—*

Hmm. Not a match. The scrolls are from two different dates, each torn independently. Who knows why they're ripped. They're so old, it could have happened by accident at some point.

__The Writings of Galdrius__
__Scroll 204, Recorded in this 522nd Year of the War.__
I am tied to her as I never was before.
She asked it of me, and I agreed without second thought.
I have made my Oath.

I suck in a sharp breath, my heart beginning to pound. How is it possible that here, in the midst of Galdrius's writings, I have found a reference to Oaths? Does this mean the answer to breaking one lies within these scrolls?

Galdrius goes on to explain that the Oath he has made to his wife is to temper her magic, that he has allowed some of the shadow magic to creep into his being. It happened after his wife, the Wytch, had accidentally killed someone in a fit of rage.

I feel slightly sick. Can the shadow power truly cause such violence? Was it just because Galdrius's wife was so powerful?

__The Writings of Galdrius__
__Scroll 311, Recorded in this 534th Year of the War.__

I have begun to grow weak.

My wife's power has extended my lifespan. I am grateful for it. I feel stronger, despite my age. And yet, underneath that, I feel something is wrong.

My wife gives me herbs to heal me, and yet, they do not work. Perhaps it is simply my time. This war is endless, as it is. I will not live to see peace. I may as well slip away, Sehenna welcoming me into the dark bosom of the Abyss.

The further I get into the scrolls the worse Galdrius seems to become. He complains of headache, nausea, even waking places and not knowing where he's been.

My wife has become obsessed with the Heir to Alos, the young Emrisa. I do not know why she cares so much for what is merely a child. The girl is grown now, well into her twenty-third year. But to me, an ill, old man, she seems as much a child as the young alchea we train, those small, frightened children who we must shape to face war. There is a man who guards the young heir. My wife insists that it is he who must be targeted. She seems obsessed with the male, almost as much as the girl.

Another scroll…

I have found out that my wife does not lack the ability to have children. She has chosen it.

I found out by mistake. I had mixed up our tonics. I had taken it and had strange symptoms. The young medica had been so wide-eyed and afraid when I had gone to her with the near-empty bottle. She had examined it, telling me that I had mistakenly taken a contraceptive tonic. She continued to apologize profusely, probably due to the rage she saw in my face.

I thought perhaps it was a mere mistake. Until my wife had become ill with a mysterious headache and pains. She had drunk my tonic. Which means…

I cannot bear the thought. I tell myself I am too suspicious. And yet…I have begun to notice I feel stronger without the tonic she gives me.

Why has my wife lied all these years? Why had she simply not told me she had not wanted children? I confront her. She tells me it is because having children will rip her power away from her. That a Seer on the Wytch Isle told her so.

I think of the Oath I had made to her. I had vowed to siphon the excess of her power, to be a vessel when she thought she might go mad. I had, within my Oath, promised that I would never betray my wife, that I would always stand faithfully by her side.

She tells me that I am weak, fragile. That I have swallowed much worse. That I had looked away when she had captured Crafters, when she had tortured them, experimented on them to see what magic she could yield, what power she could invent. But this magic she has discovered will not merely end the war. It will end our humanity.

As mortals, what else do we have? I must break my Oath. If I betray her, I will die. But if I break my Oath… Then I can stop her. For the sake of peace.

My hands are trembling so fiercely I almost can't continue

reading the scrolls, but I manage to keep looking through them, until:

The Writings of Galdrius

Scroll 352, Recorded in this 538th Year of the War.

I have sought out the Seer from the Wytch Isle, and she has told me how to break my Oath. The magic of my Oath was formed in Alos, she tells me. And so, to Alos I must go.

"Magic must be broken where it was created," she says. "Especially this magic."

She tells me how. She says that to break an Oath, you must weaken to the point of death. You spirit must be so close to the Abyss, your body near the endless sleep that awaits you, that the magic of the Oath no longer recognizes your ties to this realm. It is not easy, she tells me. Oaths are not meant to be broken. They are not meant to be shattered and ruined.

I ask her if people have died breaking Oaths. She tells me they have, that as a mortal, I am more likely than most to pass while trying to undo what has been done. I am not afraid. If my time has come, so it shall. I will be dead either way.

The scroll ends.

38

I tell myself to breathe. A breath in. A breath out. Taleas would approve.

There is…so much.

Too much.

I don't know how to absorb it all.

My mind feels oddly still. I would expect it to be racing, but it feels as though it has overflowed and now that it can hold no more, it has gone quiet.

This is the answer on how to break my Oath: I have to die. Or almost die.

I have learned to love Altheara. Not all of it. Just parts. The efficiency of everyone here, the way the Galdrion were so disciplined, in a way I now understand so much more. Galdrius had mentioned children *shaped for war*. Altheara had learned a perseverance I don't know if Alos could ever truly understand.

Yet Alos is my home, and I love it, too. There are people who have harmed me who reside there, but that is precisely why I cannot abandon my homeland, leaving the kingdom to become corrupt and polluted.

I haven't taken any tonic, but I feel a tingling in my palms.

I sense the faintest ripple of my magic. I know without a doubt that this is right. I know exactly what I want.

Am I brave enough to risk everything to have it?

⚘

I wait for Thyo in my rooms, unable to sit due to my restlessness.

Someone knocks, and I all but leap up.

I'm filled with disappointment when I realize it's Iyanna.

"I have a note for you," she says. "From the queen."

I accept the paper from her. "Has she requested me?"

"No," she says. "She simply asked me to pass it on."

I unfold the paper. It says:

Luzeandra—

I have been informed you visited the Estuary today. Did you find anything of interest? I so would be curious. Please do let me know.

The door opens again, and this time it's Thyo. Iyanna quickly excuses herself.

I toss the note aside, Seli's words already forgotten. "You're back."

Thyo looks weary but pleased to see me. "I was gone for longer than I expected."

He kisses me, and I linger. His fingers brush against my waist, and it takes effort, but I pull myself away.

"We need to discuss something," I say.

He reaches out, his fingers brushing across my temple. "Anything."

"You won't like it," I say.

Those words aren't enough. They won't prepare him. But what will?

"I doubt that anything you tell me could change my opinion of you very much," Thyo says.

"You don't understand—the things I haven't told you, the things I have to tell you—" My words are tripping over one another as they rush out, as I fight the urge to simply close my mouth. It would be easier in some ways if I simply continued to lie. If this were Clydon in front of me, I would have.

But Thyo is not Clydon. And I did not love Clydon the way I love Thyo. Even as that thought terrifies me.

I take a breath, looking down at the floor, steadying myself. "I want to go back to Alos."

He goes still.

I look up. "Before you say anything, there's more."

He seems to find his voice. "More?"

"I made an agreement after I was exiled," I say.

"An agreement." His tone is indecipherable.

A knot forms in my chest—how can I make him see? How can I explain? "It was the only way I could be free. The only chance to escape." My voice borders on desperate.

He's still frozen. "What kind of agreement?"

I hold out my right hand, where the silver Oath rings glints. "I made an Oath."

His voice is quiet. "An oath to do what?"

Once I utter these words, I cannot take them back.

"To betray you." I cannot use the full word—*murder*.

It isn't enough for him. "Betray me how?"

"You know how." My voice is nearly inaudible.

He goes to one of my balcony doors and looks out.

"I need you to say it," he says. His tone—it's utterly unreadable. It somehow feels worse than if he were raging.

"Say what?"

"Say the words." He still doesn't look me. "I need you to say what exactly you agreed to before coming to Altheara."

"I never meant—" I start.

"*Say it.*"

I swallow. Hard. "I made an Oath to kill you."

He blows out a breath, hard and fast. His hand runs through his hair, that habit that I've already stored away in that part of my mind that holds all of the things I know about him.

"You have to understand—"

"Stop," he says. "Just…stop. I need a moment. You owe me that, Luze."

Minutes pass. It feels like hours.

Finally, he turns. "You showed me that ring as though it meant something, as though this agreement you made was binding."

I grip my hands together to stop their shaking. "An Oath binds you to the promise you make. Your very own Galdrius made one. He writes of it, in his scrolls."

He's momentarily distracted. "Galdrius's scrolls are gone. No one has ever found them."

I'm sure I know what I read. But now isn't the time. "It's a promise bound by magic, Thyo. If you don't fulfill an Oath, it kills you."

He watches me, unmoving. "What are you saying?"

"I would die," I say. "If I leave my Oath unfulfilled, it will kill me."

"And what will you do?" Thyo asks. His posture is rigid.

I quickly realize what he's really asking, and my words trip over themselves once more. "Thyo, I would never—I can't—I don't want to kill you."

He lets out a bitter laugh. "That's good to know."

"I mean it." This much is true—I do not want to kill him.

I never have. That fact calms me slightly. "Maybe in the beginning I considered it. But there's too much between us. Even if…even if you hate me now."

He shakes his head, looking away. "I don't hate you."

"You don't?" My voice is quiet.

"No," he says. "It might be easier if I did."

"I've thought the same thing before," I say. "But Thyo, I have a plan."

His wariness is apparent. "A plan that doesn't involve either of us dying?"

"Yes."

He crosses his arms. "You might have led with that, Luze."

I sit on the couch. The worst is not over, but he hasn't called for guards to come imprison me. That fact alone gives me hope. "It will be difficult. Extremely so."

He sits across from me. "What is it?"

"I have a way to break my Oath." I fiddle with the ring on my finger. "It requires me to return to Alos. The magic has to be broken where it was created."

Distrust crosses his face. "You want to return to Alos and have me believe that you will return? That you won't betray me? You could be making all of this up, Luze. Perhaps there is no Oath."

His doubt stings. "If you don't trust me, give me the anesthetic you told me about. The one that erases memories. Erase this whole week, if you must." I take a breath. "You know what was done to me, the way my memories were tampered with. You know what it would cost me. But for you, I would take that tonic willingly."

I can tell I've surprised him. "Is that what you want?"

"No." I lean forward, clasping my hands. "It's not what I want at all. I have an idea, Thyo. Breaking my Oath meant I could never return to Alos; keeping it means betraying you. But if you trust me and let me break my Oath, we can take back Alos from my uncle and all of the people he's corrupted into following him. We can have Alos *and* Altheara. Together."

I don't think I've ever seen him look so shocked. He rises, beginning to pace. I let him, allowing my words to sink in.

"Our lands could truly be at peace," I continue. "I could rule in the north. You in the south. But together."

Something shifts in him, but it's there and gone so quickly I can't pinpoint what it is.

"We would be separated?" he asks.

I smile slightly. "Not all the time. I'm sure we would need to travel back and forth. But I have much to repair in Alos. I will need to be with my people until I know our future is secure."

"But how do you intend to destroy the wall?" he asks.

This time, I'm the one who's surprised. "You want to destroy the wall?"

His dark eyes are intense. "There can only be one ruler, Luze. We will have to truly become one kingdom, for unity."

I frown. "What are you saying?"

"Alos cannot be allowed to hoard magic any longer," he says. "Crafters will have to learn to respect the authority of Altheara."

I make a small sound, something between a breath and a laugh. "You make it seem as though Alos will no longer exist. That the entire continent will be under Altheara's rule."

He's silent for a beat too long.

I stand abruptly. "No, Thyo. When I speak of uniting the lands, I intend to do so peacefully. Perhaps Alos requires change, but so does Altheara."

His brows rise. "What change would you have in Altheara?"

I look at him incredulously. "You have children training as though death will arrive at any minute, Thyo. You treat your people as though they are weapons."

"Because of your kingdom and the threat they pose," he says. "You think that will end just because you decide to unite the continent?"

"I won't force my people send their children off to be trained as war heroes," I retort.

He laughs bitterly. "Look at us, having this conversation. You think our kingdoms won't feel the same? If I give up the strength of Altheara by not enforcing us as the ruler of the continent, if I allow the Galdrion to diminish, who will protect my people?"

"And if you try to undo everything that makes Alos what it is, they will rebel," I say. "We are a land of law and tradition. They won't listen to you."

"No," he says. "But they'll listen to you."

"Am I a pawn?" I ask slowly. "Is this what your plan was?"

His tone is level. "I could ask you the same."

"If it were my plan to betray you, why would I have told you of my Oath?" My voice is steady. "I want us to rule together, Thyo. But I won't force my people into military servitude, and I will not destroy the wall. Not until I know Alos is safe."

"Then little will change," he says.

Frustration leaks into my tone. "Why do you insist on behaving as though there will be war? You cannot always force change with a fist, Thyo."

"Why do you think we act as if we are fighting for survival?" he asks. "Because of your people. When the sickness spread in our lands—"

"Enough of this sickness!" I snap. "People become ill,

Thyo. Kingdoms suffer. Do you think Alos has never experienced terror or plague?"

"And you survive it easily." His voice is getting loud. "With all of your magic and healers and riches."

I am just as loud. "We cannot help that we are more powerful than mortals!"

He shakes his head. "It all comes back to this, doesn't it? Even the unwillingness to be tied to something as mundane as *man* or *woman*. Your kind see themselves as superior to Althearans, to any other beings. And it will be your downfall."

"*Your kind?*" I repeat. "Lest you forget, I am a Crafter. When you speak of my people, you speak of me."

"I see that now," he says. "I thought you were different, but perhaps you're exactly the same as your uncle and all the others who betrayed you. You were willing to kill me and destroy an entire kingdom just to save yourself from an exile, after all."

I jerk, my face stinging as though he has slapped me. A heavy silence falls over the room.

He steps toward me. "I shouldn't have—"

"Get out." My voice is cold.

He pauses, and then he leaves without another word, the door slamming behind him. I collapse onto the couch once more, pressing my hands to my face. This is not the end. Everything I wanted depended on this conversation, but there is another path I have planned. One without Thyo. One that may break my heart.

Unless I can find another way.

39

I SPEND HOURS pacing the room, and when night falls, tossing and turning. I am equal parts afraid and furious.

I don't hear from Thyo. I spend the morning restlessly wandering my room, replaying our argument over and over in my head. Where had I gone wrong? How had our conversation started so well and turned ugly so quickly?

I can't bear the spinning thoughts in my head after a few hours. I leave my rooms, wondering if I'll find my guards reinstated, but none are outside my door.

I wander down one of the empty halls of the castle, my worries nagging at me. Where will Thyo and I go from here?

I have only one option. An option I had planned for. A plan that I do not want to enact, but one that I must, if Thyo cannot see reason and we cannot compromise.

The thought of it sickens me. I had had hope, only for it to be dashed to pieces within minutes. I had been filled with so much joy. Shouldn't I know better by now? Look how everything in my life has turned out: my exile, Clydon's betrayal, the loss of my family, even my weak, unstable magic…

Whatever star I was born under, it was cursed.

With only these unpleasant thoughts for company, I find myself in front of the large doors of the library. It's a large space with multiple levels and towering ceilings. Everything gleams free of dust. It's surprisingly quiet; I see only one or two people on the main floor. I take the stairs to the second floor, looking for an isolated corner, when I come across Gideon, seated at a table.

"Luze," he says. He puts his book aside. "Were you looking for something?"

"Not really," I say. "Just looking, I suppose. Why are you here?"

"Cyrian." He yawns. "He prefers to work in the early hours of the morning while it's still quiet."

"Where is he?" I ask.

"He just went to get us tea," he says. He gestures for me to sit, and I do. "He says he can't focus in the morning without it. It's a good thing his work predominantly takes place in books. Otherwise, he might be out there with a sword in one hand and a cup of tea in the other."

His tone is exasperated, but the expression on his face is pure affection.

"Gideon, why did you marry Cyrian?" I ask abruptly.

He pauses. "Do you mean, what made me want to marry him?"

"Maybe." I pick at the peeling title on the book in front of me. "I mean, how did you know? Really, truly, know that it was right?"

I can feel his eyes on me. "I'm not sure something like that can be explained."

"Of course," I say, suddenly uncomfortable. "I shouldn't have asked." My argument with Thyo has left me edgy and restless. I am being too free with my emotions, too obvious with my questions.

"It wasn't one thing," Gideon says, surprising me. "It took time."

"But what if you don't have time? What then?"

"You should know, Luze, that Thyo is protective of Altheara. And yet, he's now protective of you, as well. Balancing the duty you have as a leader with the love you have for someone isn't easy."

I stare off at the shelves of books. "Sometimes it seems impossible."

"Not impossible," he says. "Cyrian is one of our strategists, and he has taught me this: if one plan fails, another takes its place. There are always answers."

"That requires having enough freedom to make choices," I say, almost to myself.

His lips purse. "Even some of the greatest leaders in this realm often had very few good choices, if any. Many required the willingness to make large sacrifices. Have you ever done something for someone else, even if it required sacrifice on your part?" he asks.

This question strikes too close to my home. "Hasn't everyone?"

"Not necessarily." He gestures to the walls of books. "Read any book in here. Plenty are filled with stories of those who refused to give, even slightly."

"That can be just as harmful as living a life intended only to please others," I point out.

"Exactly," he says. "In matters of negotiation and trade, the most skilled diplomats can make it seem as though they are sacrificing a great deal to get what they want—when in fact they never will. And sometimes, that sacrifice will be true—but the outcome is worth it."

I sit back, digesting his words. "What an exhausting way to live. Never knowing how much you can trust someone, even if they give you your word."

He smiles slightly. "Exactly. I don't think anyone in these history books would argue that ruling is not lonely."

Before I can respond, Cyrian returns, carrying two cups of tea. "Oh," he says, the teacups wobbling slightly. "Luze. If I'd known you would be joining us, I would have brought more tea."

"It's okay," I say. "Thank you, Cyrian."

Cyrian puts the teacups down, starting to push one toward Gideon, when he stops. He frowns. "Wait. I can't remember which one I added honey to."

"The one you carried in your left hand," Gideon says. He glances at me wryly. "He told me once that it was because he was less likely to drop it."

I'm strangely touched by the thought. "To make sure he never drops yours?"

"No," Cyrian says. "To make sure I never drop mine. I'm the one who drinks it with honey."

I laugh, and Gideon smiles. He reaches out, brushing a blonde curl back from Cyrian's forehead. "So selfless."

Cyrian's cheeks flush pink when Gideon touches him. They look at each other, and there's so much between them, I start to feel like an interloper.

I clear my throat. "I should go. Aslen's probably hunting me down for training by now."

Cyrian glances at me. "You're welcome to stay, if you'd like."

Gideon's arm has slid across Cyrian's shoulders. It's a casual movement, except I see his fingertips trailing across his arm. Cyrian's cheeks flush pinker.

I stand. "Really, I have things I have to do. I'll come back another time."

After I leave, I don't go to find Aslen. I'm no longer listless.

My conversation with Gideon has helped me see what I need to do. I only have one path forward.

So, I send a note to Thyo, requesting he visit me that night.

Then, I prepare myself.

§

I pour two goblets of wine, my hands shaking slightly. An empty tonic bottle, one I had stolen from the Estuary all those nights ago, sits on the table next to the goblets. I grab the empty bottle, tucking it away in a bag I have hidden on the far side of the room.

There's a light knock on the door, and Thyo enters.

I straighten. "Hello."

He looks more wary than I would have expected. Almost regretful. "I was glad to receive your note," he says.

I sit on the couch. I am wearing a dress, this one a soft dove grey. "Will you sit with me?"

He crosses the room, settling on the couch next to me. "I should begin by apologizing. Whatever happened to you, it was not chosen freely. What I said was unforgivable."

I reach out, brushing my fingers across his hand. "No. It wasn't." He seems to understand the insinuation, that I have forgiven him. "I want to stay in Altheara," I say.

He is cautious. "You do?"

"But I have to break my Oath. You know this, Thyo."

"I do," he says. He glances toward the wine goblets but doesn't take one. "Is this meant to be a negotiation?"

"I suppose," I say. "Although I'd rather think of us as partners than opponents."

"I feel the same," he says.

I take a breath. "Good. Then what do you need to trust me, Thyo?"

"I want to know that when you leave Alos to break your Oath, you will return. I want to go with you."

"You want to accompany me as some sort of guard?"

"Not a guard," he says. "As your husband. I want us to make these agreements and to seal them with marriage. I take such an agreement seriously, Luze. You know what marriage will mean."

I do. Not just the significance of it in any land, but especially in Alos: if I am married to the Althearan prince and he remains alive, I can never be Crown. Not unless we take Alos together. Not unless Thyo is by my side. Alos will not accept a Crown who is wed to the enemy, who cannot produce children with a fellow Crafter.

If we marry and Thyo is alive, I can never leave him.

"Why not wait for the ceremony?" I ask.

"Because I want it to be something you choose," he says. "Something just between us."

There is a long beat.

"Yes," I say.

His eyes widen. "Yes?"

I smile "I'll marry you. Just us. Us and…" I trail off. "Who can marry us?"

A beatific smile has broken his face. "Phaelina."

Of course. I lean forward, pressing my lips to his. "Then let's go. Tonight."

His lips are warm on mine, his hand tangling in my hair, but he pulls back slightly. "Then you agree? We will go to Alos together?"

"Yes," I say. "Come with me. But Thyo, I am not ready to destroy the wall." I hesitate. "I am willing to consider some of the proposals you've made. Perhaps Alos needs more discipline; perhaps you need more guarantees of Altheara's safety. I am willing to cede to some of what you have suggested. All I ask is that we do not act rashly."

He pulls back slightly. "I understand, Luze. Truly, I do. But I feel you cannot see your kingdom clearly. It worries me."

I try not to look at the wine, still sitting in front of us.

I take a deep breath. "I need you to promise you will not act rashly. That I can trust you."

His expression is clear. "I only want what is best for both of our kingdoms, Luze. I always have, and I always will. Change will be required. You know this."

Panic begins to swirl in my veins; he cannot see reason. I feel a creeping sense of foreboding. I had had a brief flash of hope, that I could reconcile everything, that I could save us from the nightmarish fate I had always feared…

"Change will be required, and I know this. But I fear you do not know Alos as I do, Thyo." I lift my chin. "I have lived in Altheara; you have barely been in Alos. The ideas you may have about my people may not be true. We cannot make decisions based on history. If we do, we will simply end up in another war."

He is quiet for a long, long moment. My heart is pounding. I am glad he is not close enough to feel it.

"I take none of this lightly, Luze," he says slowly. "I want what is fair for both of our kingdoms. I promise you, we will only do what is needed to ensure the best future for the continent. And we will do it together."

I hold his gaze. "You swear to me you will not take any actions unless we both agree to it?"

He nods. "I swear. Any decision we make, we will take together."

I exhale. The relief makes me shaky. "Thank you. That was the only assurance I needed."

He glances at the wine goblets. "Should we celebrate with a toast?"

I smile, pressing a finger to his lips. "Soon. I intend to celebrate with you in a number of ways. But I meant what I said. Let us go to Phaelina. She can be our witness. I want to be joined to you, Thyo. In all ways."

His eyes are intense, and he leans in to kiss me again, his lips lingering. He presses his forehead, and we sit like that for minutes, maybe hours. I don't know. I am so relieved I am nearly dizzy. Slowly, my pulse slows.

Finally, he presses another kiss to me. He smiles, cupping my chin in his hand. "I need the rings," he says.

I laugh, forcing it only slightly. "I had no idea you were quite so eager to marry me."

"You have no idea." He is almost devout as he looks at me. I glance away, my cheeks warming.

"I don't want to waste another minute," he says. "I'll go fetch the rings and return for you. We'll wake Phaelina if we have to."

He leaves, promising to return soon. The joy in his eyes makes my heart bloom.

While he's gone, I gather the wine goblets, taking them to the bathing chamber.

Then I dump the wine I had poisoned with Blackvine down the drain.

40

My life steadies.

In the days that follow my revelation to Thyo, I am cocooned in what I think must be bliss—everything feels perfect.

Or almost perfect. Something is still nagging at me. I pore over my thoughts—everything that has been said and done—trying to reassure myself that the uneasiness I still feel is because of the trials ahead of me.

Days pass. I wake most mornings with Thyo, cocooned in warmth. I can't resist staring at the iron ring on my finger. I take it off, slipping it in my pocket before I leave my rooms. No one else can know. Not yet.

I return to my mornings training with Aslen. After training, I usually go to the stables and spend time with Arturon. Demelan is there sometimes. He usually seems glad to see me. I don't know how much he knows, or what Thyo has told him, but we mostly talk about horses, anyway. Demelan becomes softer, quieter, as he runs his hands down their legs, explaining anatomy and movement to me, how to keep my horse safe and well on even the most treacherous roads.

After training and spending time at the stables, I usually go to the library and spend time researching. I've started expanding what I read. Occasionally, Cyrian or Gideon is there. I feel a tentative friendship begin to form. Cyrian takes the time to help me find books or explain things to me, even in the midst of his own work—philosophy, political matters on the other lands, more history.

Thyo usually finds me in the library, and then we walk to the gardens together. I'm not sure why we go there. Maybe because it's quiet and neutral territory. We can talk without being overheard. Mostly, we discuss how to break my Oath— where I will need to travel to; how far into Alos is enough. How to ensure I survive. I can see he hates the fact that I'll have to risk my life for this, and yet, what other choice do we have?

We decide we'll have to go after the public wedding ceremony, which is only in a few days.

We speak of lighter things, too. Sometimes we just sit in the garden as the sun sets, my head on Thyo's shoulder. There is something strong and solid between us now—something inextricable.

So why am I still so afraid? Is it because I finally have something to lose?

Perhaps it is the guilt of what I had almost done weighing on me. The way I had poisoned Thyo's wine with Blackvine…

I tell myself it was merely a precaution, that I wouldn't have been able to go through with it. I tell myself this now that everything has steadied.

But I know it is a lie.

I wake early the next morning when Thyo brushes a kiss to my cheek. I do not rise for a while, staring at the black iron ring on my finger instead. The ring that Thyo had placed himself, with Phaelina as our witness. The ring that was still a secret.

I slip it off and put it in the satchel where I keep important things.

Iyanna brings breakfast, and when Aslen doesn't arrive for training—unusual, but I'm sure she's just busy—I decide to go to the gardens, taking a book with me. Perhaps walking outside will ease this restless feeling I have inside. I cannot escape the feeling in my gut that something is pulling me away from here. Pulling me north. Toward Alos. It's my desire to break my Oath, to have the worst over with.

The castle gardens are beautiful. The plants are different from anything in Alos. Most bloom with flowers, and although it's humid, it's a cooler day than usual The soft breeze soothes me, helps me think.

I sit down on a stone bench, looking at the landscape. A flash of movement catches my eye. A hawk has settled on a branch nearby. It watches me, its eyes unerringly intelligent.

I had been so foolish, believing that Thyo could not see reason, that we could not compromise. My plan had almost slipped from my fingers, but I had managed to save it.

I close my eyes, the sun shining on my face. Peace. Perhaps I can find peace again.

Once I break my Oath, I will feel better. I'm sure of it.

Later, I pass a few hours reading a history book on the Thousand Year War, still trying to find mention of any special magic used during the war, like what Galdrius had mentioned in his scrolls. So far, I've found nothing.

I return to my rooms after a while. I lock the door, pulling a small chest out from under my bed, hidden behind the skirts.

I had brought the chest containing Galdrius's scrolls with me from the Estuary. I was sure it was forbidden, but frankly, I wanted them within easy reach.

I pore over them again. There are a few at the bottom I must have missed before. These scrolls date further back, long before Galdrius had decided to break his Oath.

I skim one of them.

Regarding the lands of the far-off East Continent, Kemerel is prominently known as—

The name catches my eye. Kemerel…the place Thyo has formed a trade agreement with.

Kemerel is perhaps best known for the prophecy that states a key between gates will unlock their land, and the lands of this realm. This legend is ancient, and yet the sea-warriors still believe it will come to pass.

I roll my eyes. First Thyo's Seer prophecy, now this one. I've come across far too many prophecies for my liking. I continue reading.

Kemerel, with its sea-washed shores, is said to house a material of great value. This mineral is hewn into the caves and cliffsides of their shores, a bright blue-green color that catches the eye almost immediately. This mineral is said to have extraordinary powers, a gift left behind from the Old Days, before the reach of other magical creatures. It's said this gift was left as a defense for mortals, for this mineral contains the capacity to kill any magical creature instantly, with only a single cut. It can also be used to pierce anything enchanted, strangling the magic within and killing its power.

The scroll is torn, as so many of them are. I flip over the scroll, but there's nothing on the back. Why had Galdrius been researching Kemerel?

Thyo and I had talked about Kemerel once. What had he said?

"What resource do you want from them, anyway?"

"A mineral."

"A mineral? Really?"

"It's rare. It grows along their coastline. It has…certain proper-ties. Properties which could be useful to us. It's called vaerium."

There are plenty of creatures with magic. Not just Crafters. The Wytches, for instance. And the entirety of the East Continent, which is just as powerful as the West.

I try to shove aside my doubts, but they linger.

I wander through the castle, wondering where Thyo is. Perhaps trapped in one of his endless meetings.

Eventually, I reach the small meeting room I've been to before. The same room where I'd caused the earthshock; the same room where Thyo and I had been together for the first time. My cheeks warm at the thought.

When I open the doors, the room is empty. Further down the hall are a set of massive double doors that mark the eastern wing. Whatever is behind those doors is the only part of the castle I haven't explored yet. I stride over, pulling on the handle, but the door doesn't budge.

"Lady Vyzrais."

I jump slightly, trying not to look guilty. It's Iyanna.

"I've been looking for you," she says. "Your dress is finalized. You'll need to try it on, to see if the final measurements fit."

I glance back at the doors to the east wing. "Now isn't a good time."

"It won't take long," she says. "The seamstress knows to expect you."

I bite my lip. "Is she in the castle?"

Her face is smooth. "She's located in the city center. It's only a short ride. Or walk, if you prefer."

"I can't right now." I try not to look suspicious.

"We really do need to check the fitting," she presses.

"I, um, promised Aslen I would meet her for training," I invent. "She'll be wondering where I am."

She hesitates, almost as if she might argue. She must care deeply about this dress. "Very well," she says. "But I will need you to come with me soon. I'd prefer we didn't leave alterations until the last minute."

"Right," I say quickly. "Well, I'm just going to…" I gesture down the hall, walking away. I stop after a minute, glancing back to see her disappear around the opposite corner.

I wait for a moment before going back to the locked door. I'm about to tug on it when the door is pulled open from the other side.

It's Demelan. "Luze," he says. He sounds shocked—almost agitated at my presence. It's unusual for him.

"Is Thyo in there?" I ask, trying to peer around him. "I need to speak with him."

Demelan glances back into the room, his face tight. "Now isn't a good time. You're not supposed to be here. This meeting is for the Galdrion only."

That comment stings. I had thought Demelan and I, along with the others, had been building some semblance of trust.

The hurt makes me angry, and that makes me impulsive. In the split second he turns away, I shove past him, darting into the room.

"Luze—" Demelan says, trying to stop me, but I evade him.

The space is huge. There are hundreds, if not thousands of papers in this room—maps, diagrams, drawings, formulas, scrolls. It's endless. A massive table is situated in the center, and at least thirty people are gathered around it. Some of them are talking, pointing to a paper in front of them; others are working independently.

I maneuver around Demelan, getting closer to the table. There is an assortment of weapons on the table, all with a green-blue tint, as though made from a sea-colored stone.

Unease pricks through me. This room feels as though it is the epicenter for something.

I spot a bright auburn braid halfway down the table, and I quickly realize I know people in this room.

Aslen. Cyrian and Gideon, poring over something together. Aver and Roseh, even.

Thyo.

They're all so intensely focused, no one seems to have noticed me. I look at the paper on the edge of the table, closest to me, feeling a jolt of surprise when I realize it's a map of Alos. It's similar to the map I've seen of the planned trade routes between Alos and Altheara.

Except this one has symbols. There are markings of war ships and spots labeled as "vulnerable".

My mind freezes and then restarts as I try to interpret the symbols. I stare at the spots on the map that are marked with symbols I recognize as units of soldiers. Armies of different sizes, organized in different areas—at points of entrance in Alos.

Hatal is drawn in detail. According to this map, it will be the first place to be invaded.

My mind flashes to the manor house. To my home. The only remnant of my mother, of Zassa, even if it merely stands as a memory.

I can't move or speak. This can't be real. Those symbols…

"*No.*"

I don't realize the word has ripped out of me until the room goes silent.

"Luze," Thyo says, his voice filled with alarm.

"You promised," I say. Everything tunnels. It's only Thyo I see. "You *promised.*"

He steps toward me, slowly. "Just calm down."

"Do not tell me to *calm down.*" I am rooted to the spot. "These are plans for war," I say. "Aren't they?"

Aver rises from his chair. "Prince Adriel, should I escort—"

My fist clenches. "If you touch me, I will kill you."

Aver falters.

Everything inside of me is too still. Too calm. Unnaturally calm.

"Luze," Thyo says again. "Let's talk in private. We can discuss this."

I look at the weapons strewn on the table, at the blue-green tint to the metal.

"You promised," I repeat. Everything begins to sort, becoming clear. "The vaerium…all those plans for trade…but Kemerel is far. To already have these weapons, to be initiating trade— you've been planning this for years. Haven't you?"

I wonder if I've ever known any of them at all.

What I do know: Altheara has plotted this long before I came here. *Thyo* had plotted.

"I didn't lie to you," Thyo says. He steps toward me, quickly, and I step back, just as quickly. He stops. "Nothing has happened yet, Luze. I told you any decision we made, we would make together."

"But this is what you intend, isn't it? You're simply waiting for me to come around to the idea of war? Or you have some other plan in place, something that will make me want to overthrow Alos?"

I am met with silence. I know I'm right.

I swallow back my revulsion as it occurs to me: I had helped them. I had sat there and discussed the best trade routes from

Kemerel. I helped in a part of planning this war, all without knowing it.

Thyo is silent, simply watching me. His eyes are dark with the shadows I had thought I could ignore.

"Perhaps we should go somewhere more private," Demelan says.

"You've plotted the perfect war," I say to Thyo, my voice soft. "You had all the pieces in place, and I was merely a pawn you could use to help decimate Alos."

"That's not true," he says. "We don't intend to—"

"Stop!" I press my fingers to my temples. "If you wanted peace, you would not have wanted the vaerium."

I wonder how he had learned about vaerium. Perhaps a scroll, like I had. Except his reaction had not been one of trepidation; it had been one of relief, perhaps even of excitement.

"The vaerium is merely a safeguard," Gideon says. "We want to do this peacefully, Luze."

Every part of me feels like it's splitting in half.

"There will be no peace," I say. "Alos will not merely surrender to Altheara." My mouth twists on the word *Altheara*.

"Luze, calm down," Thyo says. "You don't understand everything. Not yet. Not fully."

I laugh, the sound slightly hysterical, my rage simmering, a flush of energy working its way through me. I hear a creak in the floors, almost a groan. "What don't I understand? Do you intend war or not? Have you intended war, all along?"

Demelan's grip on his sword has changed. Slowly, Gideon rises from his chair.

"Why even make the agreement?" I ask. "Why have me come to these lands if all you intend is war?"

"We always hoped for the chance of an alliance," Cyrian says. "You should know that, Luze."

I can tell by his face Cyrian believes this. It's laughable.

My uncle had been right. I hadn't been sent on some hare-brained mission. The Althearans were as evil as Eskar had predicted. I feel a giddy, almost hysterical sort of appreciation for my uncle, as conniving and paranoid as he is.

"There's nothing more to discuss," I say, my tone level.

Aslen steps toward me. "Luze—"

Thyo raises a hand, cutting her off. His eyes have never left me. "This conversation should not be had here. Aver and Roseh will escort Luze back to her rooms. And I will go with them."

Aver stands and tries to grab my arm. I snatch it away. I am frozen, but not *that* frozen. "I will disembowel you before I let you touch me."

He doesn't try to grab me again.

I don't look at any of them as I leave. None of them matter anymore.

The walk to my rooms feels interminable. Thyo enters with me. "Fetch four guards," he tells Roseh. "Her balcony will need to be guarded, too."

Roseh keeps an impassive expression. Aver looks smug, even entertained. I should have taken the opportunity to hit him when I had the chance.

Thyo closes the door behind us, locking it. "I couldn't explain," Thyo says. "Not out there. Not with all of them. Not when I owe you an explanation."

"I don't care."

I feel cold inside, but this is a chosen coldness—I do not want to care, and so I will not.

"Just allow me to explain," he says.

Nothing he can say could make this better.

"There's nothing to say," I say. "Do what you will. Lock me

away. As long as I never have to look upon your face again, I will be glad."

His voice is low. "You have hidden so much, and yet you are unwilling to forgive the same?"

Despite myself, I choke a bit at his words. "Forgive? You already speak of forgiveness?"

"You made an Oath," he says. "You told me yourself, that your plan was to betray me."

Rage flies through me. "Do *not* compare my Oath to this, Thyo. I fought against it. I never wanted to be the kind of person who would murder for their own kingdom's gain."

"And I have not committed any crimes either," Thyo says. "We are not at war, Luze. Everything you saw—all of it—is mere papers. Nothing has been enacted."

Yet. I can hear it, even if he doesn't say it.

"All of those trade routes, the marriage agreement, everything between us—was it all a lie?"

He is silent.

"*Tell me!*" My voice cuts through the room.

"At first we thought you could be used to bargain," he says. "That Alos would stop at nothing to get you back, if threatened. Until you'd revealed to me not only the extent of your exile, but the crime for which you had been punished, and I realized you were not as valuable to Alos as we'd believed."

Despite everything, those last words lance straight through me, making me lose my breath. "And then?"

"And then I realized I could turn you to our side," he says. "That you could become a powerful ally. I meant everything I told you, Luze. I love you. I want to rule this continent with you. I forgave you for your mistakes; can you not forgive me for mine?"

I look at him, at the surety of his expression. It frightens me, this feeling I have, that suddenly I have begun doubting myself, wondering if I'm the one being unreasonable.

"Are you willing to end these plans?" I ask. "To agree to not start a war with Alos?"

"Alos cannot be allowed to continue on as it has," he says. "Your people cannot change; they know only greed and privilege."

"All because Alos refused you aid?" I ask. "That mistake is enough for war?"

"Do you know what the letter I received from your council said when I requested aid?" he asks. "When I asked simply for medicines, medicines that would have cost nothing to your people?"

I have a sinking feeling in my gut.

"Your council said the lives of mortals were beneath their interest," Thyo says. "I watched my father's dying breath while holding that letter. Your kingdom hoards a power that is not theirs to claim. I will never watch people I love die like that again, Luze, knowing that I could have done something differently. I failed my people. I failed my father."

"You didn't fail," I say. "There was nothing you could have done. You can't blame yourself."

He looks at me incredulously. "Blame *myself*? I don't blame myself, Luze. I blame Alos."

I should have known—how had I not seen it, this hatred and resentment he has for Alos?

"You will rip all peace from this continent," I say.

"I do not want peace," he says. "My people barely survived the Thousand Year War. The reason we survive now is through fear that drives us to force children to join the Galdrion, to spend hours training. Fear that forces us to ingest herbs, to stockpile weapons that may be our only hope of protection. If that were not enough, you know of the prophecy I told you. I have to live with that knowledge, every day, Luze. That at any point, Altheara could be eradicated."

"This is insane, Thyo, that you live by this prophecy—"

"And I will die by it, if I must," he says.

I throw my hands up. "That Seer may have lied, Thyo! How many innocents will you kill, all to prevent the vague proclamations of some woman? Alos may never commit another war. There are a thousand possibilities, and yet you choose this one."

He is shaking his head as though unwilling to hear me. "You yourself told me you wanted to rule one land, that we could rule Altheara and Alos. Together."

I begin to pace. "Not by killing my people! Thyo, unless you massacre Alos, they will retaliate. Your fears will come true. The very choices you're making might cause this so-called prophecy to manifest. There are other paths."

"Can you be so naïve to think that everyone is as just as you are, that everyone believes in a world that can be good and fair? You forget the violence of your own kind. War is the only way. You were right—we can rule. We can unite our lands. But it will require sacrifice."

I am stunned by his words. I don't know if he's wrong. Maybe I am naïve. Maybe I am foolish. Maybe my idea to unite our lands peacefully had been a frivolous notion. But is war better?

"Nothing I can say will change your mind," I say. "Will it?"

"Nothing has changed between us, Luze," he says, not answering. "Not really."

I step back. "I cannot support this, Thyo. I cannot be with someone who wants this. I won't be a part of unnecessary bloodshed. Perhaps there isn't another way to unite our lands. I don't know. But I won't agree to this, either."

He won't release me, I realize. He can't. He can't let me go. For so many reasons.

"You're going to lock me away, aren't you?" I ask. My voice is soft.

"I don't want to," he says. "That would not be my choice. Nothing I've said or done has been a lie, Luze. My choice would be for you to be by my side. For you to know, truly, and deeply, that I care for you, and for you to understand why this is the only way."

We've come to it. The crux of what this revelation will mean. "And if I don't?"

"You cannot return to Alos," he says. "Beyond that…you will have choices to make. We both will."

He hasn't threatened me. Not yet. I wonder if he could use shadows to bend me to his will. I have a vision of myself with blank eyes on a battlefield, slaughtering people. He wouldn't do that. Would he?

"I do love you," he says. "Please. Please understand."

This quiet plea cuts through me. I know he loves me. But love isn't always enough.

He reaches for me. "Luze—"

I step out of reach. "I need to think," I say. "The least you can offer me is time, Thyo."

This pleading scares me more than anger or threats ever could. I need him to leave, because I am afraid if he doesn't, I will give in.

I don't think he'll leave, but there's a rap on the door. Thyo goes to answer it, wrenching the door open. "What?"

I hear quiet murmurs outside, and then two guards I recognize as Nikal and Vilena step into the room. While the door is open, I can see Krenz and Oclas in the hall beyond.

"Nikal and Vilena will be stationed on your balcony," Thyo

says. "Krenz and Oclas will be outside. It will be this way until…
decisions have been made."

And with a last look of regret, he leaves.

◈

Hours pass. Night falls.

I ignore the watchful eye of my guards.

I go to my bathing chambers to wash up, to change into the
same clothes I'd traveled to Altheara in. It makes me feel better
to be in my riding breeches, my jacket pressed against my body.
I pull the bag with my precious items free from its hiding spot.
It doesn't matter if the guards see. The contents are hidden, and
I need what's inside close by. I pull out Taleas's ring from the
bag, slipping it into my pocket for reassurance.

Then I wait.

My best opportunity will come when I am transported
somewhere—to another room in the castle, to wherever they
might take me.

I'm not sure what time it is when the door opens. I expect
to see Thyo again, but instead, it's Aslen.

She clears her throat. "Hello."

I ignore her.

She looks at Nikal and Vilena, standing by my balcony
doors. "You can wait outside. I need to speak with her."

"We're under orders from the prince not to leave her alone,"
Nikal says.

"And now that I'm here, she won't be." Her tone brooks no
argument.

They look sulky, but they leave.

She comes to stand across from me. I don't look at her.

"Fine," she says. "You don't want excuses or apologies. I wouldn't either. But I'm here for a reason."

I finally look at her. "Then tell me or get out."

Her jaw is tight. "You don't know everything about me. You don't know about where I'm from. I thought we would have time, but…well. I'm not from here, Luze. My people… they wanted me to do things. I refused. I was used to teach a lesson and then left for dead in the sea. I'm only alive because the Althearans took me in. They allowed me a place on these lands; they allowed me the opportunity to escape."

I wonder if this is a trick. "What does this have to do with anything?"

"It matters because, by blood, I am not an Althearan," she says. "I am loyal to them, but I wasn't always. I know what it's like to be between lands, to not know who you can trust, to have your heart in one place and your mind in another. I know what it's like to be betrayed. I know what it's like to be alone."

"This is some kind of plot to convince me to side with Altheara, isn't it?" I ask. "A lovely speech or two about how I should overcome the betrayal, realize it's all for the best, forgive and forget?"

"No," she says. "Thyo doesn't know I'm here."

"Then what do you want, Aslen?" I ask tiredly.

"You saved my life with the Strin," she says. "Where I come from, that means something. Beyond even what it would mean to you, or to an Althearan. I can give you a chance. A chance for freedom. The same chance I was given. Freedom is a life, symbolically. I owe you that."

"Meaning?" I ask.

Her eyes are bright. "I'm here to help you escape."

41

THE PLAN IS simple, and terrifying.

And I have no time to question it.

She lays it out for me, and then she pauses.

"You have a choice to make," Aslen says. "This will be it. Forever. There will be no turning back. And you have to decide now. We'll only get this chance once."

I yank my bag over my head, glancing at the balcony. "How soon—"

A massive *boom* rocks the castle.

The answer to *how soon*, is, apparently, *right now.*

"Go!" She shoves me toward the balcony.

I hear people screaming and running. Only a moment later, another explosion goes off.

I climb over the balcony railing, digging my fingers into the crevices of the wall like I have once before. I just manage to make it to the column, my fingers gripping into one of the divots, when another *boom* shakes the walls. I keep my focus on the column, climbing down carefully, even as I rush. I land on the ground and someone crashes into me as she runs past.

I narrowly avoid someone else as they sprint by. No one will look twice at me right now.

I make it all the way across the castle grounds, around and through all of the hedges, all the way to the Galdrion training course, the same one Aslen and I had trained at—that day seems like ages ago—without being detected.

I wait for what feels like hours. Finally, I hear a sound and Aslen emerges from the dark, holding the reins for Vhetta and Arturon in each hand.

"Sorry," she says. "There was a delay at the stables."

I manage a short nod. The border wall of Ceneth is only a few hundred feet away from us. I tie my bag to Arturon's saddle and make a move to mount him, but Aslen stops me.

"Don't get on," she says. "Not yet."

We walk our horses closer to the wall. Just as we're about to break through the treeline, Aslen stops.

"Listen carefully," she says. "We're almost at a shift change for the guards who oversee the borders of Ceneth. Once we hear the strike of a bell from the tower to our west, we'll only have a minute or two to cross through without being seen. No longer. And that's if we're lucky."

"Will they be on foot?"

"On horseback," she says. "Which is why we won't have long."

My heartbeat quickens. "So as soon as we hear the strike…"

Her face is grim. "We go."

We wait for what feels like an hour, neither of us talking. Actually, I think it's no more than a few minutes, but the time seems to drag on painfully.

Finally, there's a loud *gong* of a bell to our left, and Aslen motions for us to move.

"Quickly," she hisses. She goes ahead of me, Vhetta skittering a bit and tossing her tail.

I yank Arturon forward, and we follow Aslen, though it's difficult to see in the darkness.

The boundary wall surrounding Ceneth is made of stone, and I'm wondering how we'll cross it when I hear a scrabbling sound, like the crunching of rock, and I see the hole in the wall. It's tiny compared to the wall, about six feet tall and four feet across.

I squeeze myself through, hoping Arturon will fit. He ducks his head, following me calmly, and I send out a prayer of gratitude to the Source for having an intelligent horse.

Meanwhile, in front of us, Vhetta and Aslen have stopped, both frozen. Vhetta's ears are pricked, her head turned to the right.

Towards the tower to the east, from which a guard is coming.

"Move," Aslen hisses. "Now!"

She yanks Vhetta forward, and I do the same, both of us running, and the horses breaking into a trot.

We go crashing into the forest on the other side. There's a slope to it, almost like a ditch, and I trip, almost falling except for my grip on the reins. I hear the sound of hoofbeats on the path behind us.

Aslen gestures wildly towards a hedge of brush, and I pull Arturon towards it.

We stand behind the brush, and I want to gasp for air, but I hold myself still, hardly daring to breath.

The hoofbeats have gotten closer, perhaps twenty feet away from us. "Whoa," a voice says. "Easy." I hear the sound of a horse skittering a bit, as though it's shied.

Through the brush I see the glow of a lantern. Aslen and I

stare at each other, both of our eyes wide. Sweat trickles down the side of my face.

Finally, the rider moves on, and the sound of hooves fades in the distance.

Aslen's face breaks into a grin. "Wasn't that fun?"

She seems to have forgotten why we're here, or what we're doing. I merely look at her, and the smile slides off her face.

I lead Arturon over to a fallen log, using it to mount. "We need to go."

She mounts, and I follow her as she and Vhetta head deeper into the forest.

"You're sure you know where you're going?" I keep my voice quiet.

"I could travel this path blind and in the dark," she says.

"We are in the dark," I point out.

"Exactly. We'll be fine. I'll take you to the last tower on our side before Alos. After that, the roads are barely patrolled."

My gut clenches as I think of everything I still have ahead of me.

We travel for most of the night, and my body grows tired, but my eyes are alert.

Aslen informs me that there are little-to-no predators in these parts, so we don't have to worry about being attacked. "It's only once you get past the last tower that there are predators again," she says. "Including the occasional Strin, if they cross the boundary."

At some point I notice the sky beginning to lighten. Eventually, Aslen leads us out of the forest, and after a mile or so I realize we've been traveling parallel to a road all this time.

"We should be safe traveling on the road from now on," she says. "I doubt anyone will be out this far."

I'm reassured by her knowledge of the Galdrion and their systems.

The sun has become only the barest tint of orange on the horizon when she pulls Vhetta to a stop.

"There," she says, pointing ahead of us. "The last tower. Etalus."

I look up, seeing the massive, looming black tower, perhaps a mile away.

"This is where I stop," Aslen says. "I'll be going back into the woods as a precaution. Keep following the path. A river runs right below Etalus. Use it. Then keep moving."

I meet her eyes. She's calm, but I see a hint of trepidation there, and so much more.

"Thank you," I say. Despite her betrayal, I want to leave this small peace between us. She had lied—but she had also helped me.

Her face tightens. "I am sorry. Please remember that when…"

She doesn't finish her sentence. She turns Vhetta around, disappearing in the trees.

It doesn't take me long to reach Etalus. I shiver as I approach the tower. The base is crumbling slightly, but the rest of the structure looks intact. It's made of sleek black stone.

"Only a minute," I say to Arturon, stroking his neck. "We'll just use the river and go."

I dismount, leading Arturon down a rocky path that leads to the river below. It's wide, and the water rushes by furiously. Even from the shore, I can tell it's deep.

I let Arturon drink, and I splash water on my face, trying to wake myself up. I lead Arturon back up the path to the main road, looking for something I can use to mount, when I spot a cloaked figure seated on a dark grey horse. Alarm rings through me.

"Luzeandra," the figure says. A hand reaches up, pulling down the hood of the cloak.

Iyanna. She dismounts, the movement smooth. "You're far from the castle. And yet, I feel that my venture outside of the capitol was more planned than yours was."

I shift nervously. "Perhaps."

"You weren't what I expected," she says. "And for that, I'm sorry."

She reaches into her pocket, pulling out a handful of something. She cups it in her hand, her lips gently pursed. There's the sound of sand shifting, and I see whatever is in her hand, carried by the wind, showering me in a dark mist.

I yank Arturon away, certain the time has come to flee, but whatever the wind carries has reached me, and I blink. I'm suddenly on the ground, Iyanna standing over me, and then I'm swimming in a dream.

<h1 style="text-align: center;">42</h1>

THE SOUND OF water rushing past fills my ears, blocking everything else out. Something cold presses into my back, chilling my skin.

My eyes blink open. The ceiling above me ripples. I squint. Not ripples; it's the reflection of water, casting greenish-blue waves on the black stone. The sound of water drips nearby.

Disoriented, I try to sit up, which is when I realize: I can't. Metal cuffs chain me to the stone table I'm on. My breath quickens, coming too rapidly, and my head spins.

"Calm down," a voice says.

I look to my left and Iyanna is there, leaning against the far wall.

"Iyanna," I croak. Despite all of the water, my throat feels dry. "What—"

"I can't let you go," she says, cutting me off. "So don't ask."

"Why?" I yank at my wrists, but the cuffs barely move, aside from cutting into my skin. "Why can't you let me go?"

"Because she's following orders," another voice says, this one ringing out sharp and clear.

I turn my head again. There, in the arched stone entrance to the chamber, stands Queen Seli.

My first reaction is one of relief.

"Please," I say to Seli. "Iyanna brought me here. I don't know what—"

Seli sweeps into the room, and I stop talking. I think about her words—*following orders*—and my skin prickles with fear.

My head is spinning. "But why—you're Thyo's mother—"

"Your sputtering will have to wait," Seli says. "We have other matters to attend to first." She holds her hand out towards Iyanna, palm up. "The tonic, please."

Iyanna steps forward, placing a small bottle in Seli's hand. I don't see a label, but it looks like the same bottled tonics used by the medica.

I yank at the metal cuffs desperately, but they barely move. Seli approaches my head, her expression blank, and pries open my mouth, pouring the bottle into my mouth before forcing my mouth closed and plugging my nose. My body's panic at lack of breath finally wins, and I choke down the liquid. Seli makes a sound of approval, tossing the bottle aside.

I turn my head to the side, retching, but nothing comes up.

Seli makes a tsking sound. "Even if you managed to vomit, it wouldn't help."

I cough, still retching. "What was that?"

"Preparation," she says simply.

I look between her and Iyanna, fear making my heart pound. "For what?"

Seli doesn't get a chance to respond, because a sharp pain rips through my abdomen, making my vision go white.

I twist my legs up, trying to curl them into my chest. It must be whatever she just gave me.

Seli watches me unsympathetically. "It shouldn't last more than a few hours." She motions to Iyanna. "I'll have Iyanna come back to check on you in a bit."

"Wait—" I choke out, but they leave the room, and I am alone.

Time seems to pass in starts and stops, sometimes agonizingly slow, and other times, the time between the episodes of scalding, tearing pain is short.

I breathe through my teeth, closing my eyes against the pain, but its nearly unbearable. It feels as though I'm being stabbed in the gut, over and over.

I'm not sure how much time passes, but eventually, the pain eases slightly. I doze off, awakening to a light slap on the cheek.

I jerk my head away. Iyanna is standing there.

"I apologize for hitting you," she says. "You wouldn't wake. It was that or a bucket of cold water." Her face is impassive. "She'll be coming to see you in a bit. I would prepare myself, if I were you."

"Iyanna," I say, my voice hoarse, "Where's Arturon?"

"With my horse," she says. She rubs her forearm. "If it makes you feel better, he bit me."

I smile a little, my eyes burning. "Good."

"He's an intelligent animal," Iyanna says. "And protective. I wonder if there's something about Alosian horses."

I squeeze my eyes shut, praying that somehow Arturon will escape and be discovered. No one knows I'm here. My absence is surely known to more than just Aslen now, but everyone will think I've crossed the wall when they can't find me. Including Aslen.

"How long have I been here?" I ask.

"Just a few hours. Perhaps half of a day."

I stare up at the ceiling. "Why?"

"I'll let Seli tell you," Iyanna says. "It is her story, after all. Mine is much simpler. I help the queen because of what she offers me. But I am not loyal to Altheara. I am loyal only to myself."

"Because of what they did to you?" Another stabbing pain hits me, a remnant of the tonic, and I wince, twisting. "Because they removed you from the Galdrion?"

"Because I wanted more for myself," she says. "I always have."

My twisting has pressed something small and hard into my skin. Taleas's ring in my pocket, I realize. I try not to let my expression change, keeping my face contorted as if in pain. Slowly, I maneuver my hip as close to my hand as possible, trying to grab the ring.

"I was so ashamed of who I was," Iyanna continues, almost to herself. "Seli was the first person who noticed my skill in the medica. She taught me to think for myself, to understand that I didn't have to be a part of the Galdrion to be worthy."

"And worthy you are," a voice says.

I flinch. Queen Seli has returned.

Seli approaches, perching on the edge of the stone table. "You've caused me a certain amount of trouble, Luzeandra. If Iyanna hadn't alerted me that you had been escorted by all those guards from that dreaded war room, I never would have known something was amiss. I never would have known to have her waiting for you. Certainly not after your grand escape. How *did* you manage so many explosions?"

My head is foggy. Before—I had seen Iyanna before I had entered the eastern wing, before everything had fallen apart. She must have waited until I'd emerged, hiding nearby.

Seli waves a hand. "I suppose that's of little importance. I have you now. And I need you to tell me what was written on those lovely scrolls of Galdrius's."

I'm having trouble focusing. "What?"

"I knew you would find them," she says. "Galdrius was a fool, but he knew to enchant his records. I've been in that scroll room hundreds of times, and they never appear. They have never appeared to *anyone,* in fact. I realized years ago that he had enchanted them so they could only be discovered by a Crafter, believing that any Crafter that made it into Altheara must have a purpose. Such a duplicitous man."

My only thought is to lie. "I don't know what you're talking about."

Seli slaps me, hard and fast.

"Do not lie," she says, in the same conversational tone as before. "You will not like the result it produces."

My cheek stings. "What do you want with those scrolls? There's nothing important on them. They're journal entries."

She scowls. "They are much, much more than that, Luzeandra. *I* was the one who had given Galdrius all of his ideas. He simply claimed them as his own, desperate to be seen as a leader, as someone worthy. There is a spell I want. He would have recorded it. I know it."

An image of the ripped scrolls comes to my mind. "Some of them are ripped," I say quickly. "I never saw a spell."

She watches me carefully. "You look as though you're telling the truth, and yet…" She leans forward, pressing the tips of her nails to my skull. "I warn you, this may hurt."

Her nails dig into my flesh, and then a sharp bolt of pain strikes through my eyes. I scream, unable to help it, not when my very mind feels as though it's being shredded—

And then it's over.

"Hmm." Seli sounds displeased. "You aren't lying. What a disappointment."

I notice her hands are shaking as she leans away, her face pale.

"I thought you didn't have magic," I say. My breath comes in gasps. "You said when you gave birth, it was ripped away."

"It was," she says. "Mostly. Iyanna, with her brilliant mind, managed to concoct a tonic especially for me. It draws from the imprint of power I once had. I have always been an exceptionally powerful Wytch." Pride fills her voice.

"Why do this?" I ask. "What about Thyo?"

"My son is the greatest disappointment of my long, long life. But then, that marriage agreement, when I realized it was *you*—it was though a gift had been delivered straight from Ahmela herself. You are special, Luzeandra. You, too, have been betrayed, have been shunned and banished in ways that no one truly understands when they have not experienced it. It makes you different."

My only thought is to keep her talking. "Who betrayed you?"

She settles back. "I am not a normal Wytch, Luzeandra. I have made sacrifices. Sacrifices which even my fellow Wytches could not tolerate."

I'm not sure I imagine the glint of madness that's in her eyes.

"Seli is not my full name," the queen says. "Here, it is Artseli. Think hard, Luzeandra. I was the first amongst Wytches to have shadow magic. Do you understand what that means?"

"Artseli," I repeat. "I don't—" I stop short. Somehow, my mind works fast enough, noticing the similarity of the letters, the clues that Seli has given through her words. My blood runs cold. "Ilestra," I say.

Artseli. Ilestra. The same word, merely reversed.

Seli laughs delightedly. "Isn't it horrendously banal? If only my kind hadn't vowed that I must always be marked by my name, that the truth of who I was could never truly be hidden. I have lived by so many variations over the years. All of them ghastly, of course."

"It's impossible," I say. "Ilestra was before the time of the Crafters."

"Little good it did me," she says. "I should never have allowed your kind to form."

Words get stuck in my throat. "You would be old. Impossibly old."

"I am," she says. "Though many of those years were spent in long spells of shadow-sleep to preserve myself. I think I look rather well, don't you?"

"It was you who stole shadow," I say. "From the Othos. From Cariel."

"That beast of a male had it coming," she snaps, suddenly annoyed. "You have no idea what those Othos are like. Why, the bite marks I witnessed on my sister—" She stops short, taking a breath. "They didn't deserve their power. After I stole shadow magic from the Othos, I returned to the Wytch Isle. And did they greet me with pride? No. They shunned me. They felt the shadow creeping in, and they hated it. They hated *me.* I had made a choice I should not have, they said, and it affected them all. I was an outcast. For hundreds of years, I was in misery."

She exhales, her voice calming. "Finally, I traveled back to the west. I traveled to Alos. There, I met a male Crafter. He made me promises. And then he betrayed me." She stares at the walls, at the light glittering on the black stone. "He tried to take the shadow power from me. He was unsuccessful. I killed someone close to him, the female he truly loved. It did not go unnoticed. The mortals were blamed. And thus, the war began."

She adjusts her skirts, as though we are at tea, and this is simple conversation. "I was too weak then. So, I spent my time learning. I traveled to isles, to continents far and wide. I learned how to expand my life. Death is required," she adds, seeing my expression. "I must kill someone and steal their lifespan. Even then, I have to be careful. I began to grow weary of having been alive for so long. And then I met Galdrius. Galdrius accepted me. All of me. I think some part of me truly cared for him. I had a place, once again. And then he, too, betrayed me. He broke his Oath. Not that it mattered; I killed him anyway." She sighs. "I waited for so long. I went back into hiding, traveling to a far, lonely isle where I lived amongst mortals and pretended to be one of them. I met Thyo's father, Jonis, the King of Altheara, and he took me for his bride, believing me to be only a young Wytch."

"And you had Thyo." I'm compelled by her story despite the circumstances.

"An accident. And what a disappointment he has been. He is so adamantly loyal to Altheara." She stares off, distantly. "Let us not linger on such things, however." She gives me a small pat, rising. "Let us begin, instead."

She walks away, and I crane my neck to see her opening a small chest on a table.

"Begin what?" I ask. Fear courses through my veins. Uselessly, I yank at the cuffs locking me in place.

Seli pulls a small knife from the chest. "The extraction, of course."

My heart begins to pound wildly. "Extraction?"

She pulls a small knife out from the chest. "There's a chance you'll faint and won't even feel me taking the magic. Although that's unlikely. It's a rather excruciating process."

I pull at my chains again. My wrists feel raw and bruised beneath the cuffs. "You want to take my magic?"

"Of course," Seli says. "Haven't you been listening? You happen to have a particularly potent form of magic that I would like. With it, I can find what I seek."

"I have no magic," I insist.

Seli almost looks sympathetic. "The fact that you believe that is the very reason we are here."

I'm finding it difficult to breath, my eyes on the knife still in her hand. "What—"

Without warning, Seli reaches over, slicing a deep cut down the length of my wrist.

I scream against the pain, a wave of heat crashing over me and my head spins dizzily. Blood pours from the cut.

Seli examines the cut, her expression clinical. "You know, you're losing little, Luzeandra. Living through war is tedious, believe me. And even if not for war…you would have never been a true queen of Altheara. Thyo would never coronize you. He loves Altheara too much to give you that kind of power. In fact, I could argue that I'm saving you from an idle fate as little more than a doll-queen. We both know you would be crushed by being so impotent, so helpless—nothing more than a pretty, powerless lady on a throne."

Dimly, distantly, it concerns me that Seli, despite her insanity, seems to understand something about me that no one else has ever recognized—that I am not content to merely sit aside, sacrificing power for comfort. This thought doesn't last long, however. The blood loss is making me lightheaded. "You're right," I gasp. "If Thyo truly loved me and trusted me, he would have promised to give me equal power. So why not let me go? Clearly, I am not important."

It hurts to acknowledge this, even if I'm only saying it for her benefit.

Seli nods, as though I've made a good point. "Your death with serve another purpose, however. Thyo may not trust you, but he cares for you as much as he is capable of caring for anyone. Grief makes people reckless. Once your body is discovered, Thysol will be only too happy to invade Alos. He will be filled with bloodlust. It will be chaos.

"But why?" I ask. "Why would you want war?"

Her eyes are distant. "A male hides in Alos, too cowardly to leave the safety of the nest he's built. With a war, he'll be unable to hide from me any longer."

"One male?" I try to keep conscious. "You would start a war over *one* male?"

"No," she says. "His death will merely be an added prize. War will help me explore the continent freely while I look for what I seek. I will cross into Alos as soon as you are dead, in fact."

Dark spots fill my vision. "What are you seeking?"

Her eyes seem to glow. "The Orb of Thesalla."

"But the Orb is lost," I argue. "Even you said—"

Seli reaches across me, slicing open my wrist on the other side. The pain clogs my throat, making me too weak to scream.

Seli moves down to my feet. "Save your strength, Luzeandra, and do not worry about my plans. Try to hold on a bit longer. I'm not quite ready for you to die yet."

Zassa, I think. And my mother. If nothing else, I cling to the hope that I will see them soon.

Seli yanks off my shoe. "Now, I'm not sure how deep this

needs to be, but I say we practice caution, hmm?" She presses the tip of the knife to my foot.

I know how much this is going to hurt, not just this cut, but the magic Seli is going to pull from me. I suck in a breath, praying to the Source, to the Gods, to anything—

"Wait," Iyanna says.

The knife hovers over my foot. "What?'

Iyanna steps forward, allowing some of the blood from my wrist to dampen her finger, examining it in the pale light. "Something is different. Her blood is too stable."

"And why would such a thing occur despite your preparations?" Seli asks. Her voice is dangerously cold.

"I don't know," Iyanna says. "Perhaps it's an aspect of her constitution."

Taleas's ring. While Seli had been telling her story, I had managed to slip his ring onto my finger. I can feel it now, the warmth emanating from it, strengthening me. Still, I'm near passing out.

"Well," Seli says. Her tone is back to the lightness is had before, which is somehow more frightening. "I so had hoped to be done with this soon. My incompetent son may actually demonstrate a backbone and attempt to search for her."

"He'll think she crossed the wall," Iyanna says. "Do not rush this, Queen Seli. You will regret it."

I hear a clatter that sounds as though Seli has tossed the knife.

"Fine," she says. "Tell me when she *is* ready." She exhales. "I'm impatient, Iyanna. I don't like feeling weak. I hope, for your sake, that you are correct about all of this."

Iyanna doesn't hesitate. "I am."

I hear footsteps, what I think is Seli retreating. I feel Iyanna's presence hovering over me.

"It would take much more for you to die," she says. "Just so you know. The tonic she gave you is what's making you feel so much worse."

I force my eyes open. "Why are you helping her?"

"I told you," she says. "I care nothing for Altheara. I care for my own future."

I'm beginning to shiver. "And what will you get by helping her?"

"She will reward me," Iyanna says. "Once she has what she wants. She is going to take me with her once she leaves Altheara."

"How do you know she isn't using you?"

"She isn't." An edge enters her voice.

I sense something—a chance, an opportunity. "What is it you want, Iyanna? Truly?"

She's still examining my cuts with a clinical expression, but she looks up, meeting my gaze. "I want to be respected," she says. "I want to study with the greatest medica of the world, to learn more about medicine than anyone ever has."

I keep my eyes on hers. "Seli can't offer you that."

Her expression flattens. "She can, and she will. Why do you think I'm loyal to her?"

This is my only chance. "She can't, Iyanna. She intends for there to be war. Do you think there will be a time of peace to study medicine in the midst of that? Do you think Altheara won't want you, their most skilled medica, alongside them, treating their wounded? Seli does not care about you. She will leave you as small and as insignificant as before."

Iyanna is quiet for a long time. "I will wait if I have to. She will help me achieve what I want."

A memory comes to me: the words I had been told in that

strange dream, with the crooked trees in the forest, and that voice emanating from the golden light.

Do not disregard the importance of offering a hand where one is needed, of offering a place where one has not been found.

Perhaps it was meaningless. And yet…

I take a breath. "Seli can't offer you what you truly want," I say. "But I can. I can offer you a place in Alos. Toluz, our coastal province, is known for our Healers, known for the power of the medicine they practice there. I could give you a space there, to train."

"They will not accept me," Iyanna says. "A mortal, training with them?"

"They will accept you because I say so." Pain has made my voice sharp. "They will accept you because I am Crown, and my word will be law."

I can feel Iyanna wavering. I hardly dare to breathe.

Finally, she exhales. "You can certainly make a convincing speech. But my decision is made. I am afraid, Lady Vyzrais, that this is happening, whether you like it or not. I do apologize, you know. I think we might have grown to be friends, if not for this."

Her words are a crushing blow. I am overcome with exhaustion. It had been my last hope that Iyanna might have helped me. Without it, I have nothing.

That sickening thought is all I cling to as I slip into unconsciousness.

43

I AM NOT sure how long it has been when I'm awoken again.

"She's weak." It's Iyanna's voice. "You can begin."

"Excellent." Seli sounds pleased. "You have been most helpful, Iyanna. I knew I was correct in choosing you all those years ago. You would make an excellent Wytch if you had the power for it."

"We'll need to leave quickly," Iyanna says. "Once it's done. Will your magic be strong enough to rip through the barrier?"

"Oh, Iyanna." Seli's voice sounds regretful. "Can't you see what a disaster that would be? No, you'll need to stay behind and explain my absence."

Iyanna pauses. "But I thought I was accompanying you. So that I could leave Altheara. Perhaps travel to the east."

"And you will," Seli says. "It may take me some time, but eventually, you will be free to go wherever you wish."

"When?" Iyanna asks. "When do you expect I will be able to leave Altheara?"

I feel a chill enter the air—a feeling of tension in the chamber.

"You are under my orders," Seli says. "I alone hold the key

to your future. Have you forgotten? When the time comes, you will leave Altheara, and not a moment before then."

I can feel the tension, even in my weakened state. I can hear something rattling; perhaps she's choosing another blade.

I feel Seli's hand clamp around my ankle, holding it down as the prick of a blade touches the bottom, and I suck in a breath—

"Wait."

The sharpness disappears. "What now, Iyanna?" Seli's voice is chilling, all the airiness from it gone. "I am tired of these theatrics."

"I need to check her blood once more," Iyanna says. "To be sure."

I feel her hand, the touch gentle, as she twists my arm.

And then something clinks, so softly I don't think anyone but me could have heard it.

The cuff on my right arm. It's become unlocked.

I am immobile, hardly daring to breath.

I feel her touch again, and then my right arm is free. The cuffs still rest on both wrists, but they're fragile feeling. As soon as I pull on them, they'll open.

"Well?" Seli sounds irate. "May I continue?"

Iyanna's hands press on my face. "I need to see if she's truly unconscious."

She hovers over me, her fingertips lightly pushing my eyelids open. She blocks any view of Seli. I blink. The blood loss is addling my mind. I'm lost in a haze of confusion. She says nothing, but she grips my arm tightly, staring at me. I understand the message.

Get ready.

Iyanna pulls a small bag from her pocket, smashing it to the ground.

Black mist explodes, filling the chamber within seconds. It's nearly impossible to see.

"Iyanna!" Seli bellows. "Iyanna, what is this insanity—"

I feel a hand touch me, and I gasp, pulling away uselessly, afraid it's the queen.

"Move!" Iyanna yanks me off the table. I can see nothing, but Iyanna pulls me along, and I follow her blindly. She pulls me up one flight of stairs, then another, and all of my focus goes towards staying on my feet and not falling. I push myself forward, even as everything tilts sickeningly.

We burst outside of the tower, the sun outside blinding me, but Iyanna yanks me along, both of us stumbling to where two horses are tied.

I cling to Arturon's sadly, and Iyanna is suddenly there, shoving me up.

"Get on!" she snaps. "We have to go, *now.*"

My wrists have begun to bleed again, the blood smearing everywhere, but I pull myself over the saddle, weakly grasping the reins.

I almost can't believe this is happening; blood loss has addled me. I wonder if I'm dreaming. My heart seems to be thumping unevenly, and I can barely stay upright. Iyanna curses.

"You've lost too much blood," she says. "I can't treat you here. We need to cross the wall. Your lands will help heal you."

We wheel the horses away, riding up the riverbank, across the bridge, passing Etalus. Terror grips me; the queen must be only moments behind us.

I hear a slamming sound behind me; I'm sure she's emerged, but I don't look back. We gallop into the woods, toward Alos, and behind us, I hear a scream, a scream that shatters the earth and makes it shake. It pierces my ears; I've never heard such a scream, a scream of pure rage.

In return, there is a deep, bellowing roar that seems to come from everywhere and nowhere, a roar that makes me feel as though my eardrums have burst.

I know that sound. But it's impossible.

I know what that sound means…but even if I believe it, even if I believe Seli has somehow summoned them—

We cannot stop. Spots fill my vision, and I grit my teeth. I can't faint. Not now.

We're somewhere in the middle of the woods—I don't recognize where—when Iyanna reaches out, grabbing Arturon's reins. I have so little control, I don't resist. We come to a stop.

She looks me dead in the eye. "My betrayal means I have broken my ties with Seli permanently. I hope it was not in vain. Do you promise to adhere to your earlier words? To provide me with a home in Alos, a place to train with your Healers?"

I wonder what she would do if I said no; would she simply leave me for dead? Alert Seli to our presence and beg for forgiveness?

"You will have a place in Alos for as long as I live," I say. "I swear on it."

"Then take this." She pulls something from the pack attached to her saddle, tossing it at me. I catch it. It's a shirt. "Rip it in half," she instructs. "Wrap it around your wrists."

I do as she says. My work isn't perfect, but it seems to stop the flow.

"You're lucky she didn't cut one of your bleeding points," Iyanna says. "You would have been dead long ago."

"Lucky," I repeat. I'm exhausted, barely holding myself up in the saddle. "I don't feel very lucky."

"You're alive, aren't you?" Her voice is flat.

We continue riding, only stopping once for her to pluck

some mushrooms she spots growing at the base of a tree. Iyanna studies them for a moment, before handing two to me. She tells me to eat them.

"Mortal medicine. Not very powerful, but they'll help keep you alive," she says. "For now."

I shove them in my mouth. I feel little, at first, but after a few minutes my head clears slightly.

We ride for another mile. The sun is fading quickly, and it's quiet. Eerily quiet.

"That sound," I say. "I heard her scream, and then…"

Iyanna keeps her eyes trained ahead. "She can summon the Strin. She told me once. She calls them through the barrier, at times. To inflame the hatred toward Alos."

I don't know how to react to this information. I have so little left in me. "What if we encounter them?"

She says nothing, her expression grim.

"She can't control them beyond summoning, can she?" I ask. "If she directs them, somehow…"

Her words are bleak. "She used to. I no longer know if she has enough power. If we come across them, it won't matter either way."

As if in response to her words, she pushes her horse forward again. We ride hard. White foam begins to form a sheen on Arturon's neck.

Brief flickers of light dance in my vision, and I blink, wondering if I'm near fainting again, but I realize it isn't a hallucination: something glimmers ahead of us through the trees.

"The wall," Iyanna says. "We've reached it."

Relief blooms through me. We're about to emerge from the treeline when I realize we are not alone. Iyanna yanks her horse to a halt, as do I.

There are people, in front of the wall, all of them on horseback.

They're far, but I would be a fool not to recognize them.

Thyo. Aslen. Demelan. Gideon.

They seem to be in the midst of an argument. I focus my senses, trying to listen.

"You can't cross the wall," Aslen is saying. She has a hold of Thyo's horse's reins, as though holding them both back. "If you drink any more tonic, if you try to rip the barrier—"

"It would be a task fit for a suicide," Gideon says. "You know this, Thyo. You cannot simply go running into their lands. Even if you make it to Luze, you have no idea what will happen. They could capture you, kill you."

"Perhaps she's still in Altheara," Demelan says, his face unusually grave. "And if not…what's done is done."

"I don't care." Thyo is staring at the wall, at the shimmering archway, which so resemble the boundary of my exile. It ripples like silk, shielding any view from beyond. "I never should have left her alone. I should have explained, made her understand."

I see Iyanna glance over at me in my periphery. My hands grip the reins too tightly.

We can't cross until they're gone. We have no weapons. Our only chance is of outrunning them, but I don't want to attempt that. Not yet.

Iyanna's voice is nearly inaudible. "The Strin." I glance around, alarmed; has she spotted something? "A distraction," she murmurs.

I stare at her. A distraction? For us, or for the others? Is she suggesting we simply hide and wait for the Strin to attack them? The idea borders on barbaric.

"I can feel she's close," Thyo says. He's still staring at the wall. He looks half-mad. Aslen had mentioned a tonic; I wonder how much he's taken, how much of his shadows are overwhelming him right now. "If she crossed, it would have been only recently. I can find her. I can bring her back."

"Thyo, let her go," Aslen says. "You saw her face. She will never agree to this war, and you will never agree to end it. She will warn her people. Our priority now needs to be acting quickly before Alos can prepare."

"You don't understand," he says. "Without her—"

He freezes.

Demelan's hand goes to his sword. "What is it?"

Thyo turns in his saddle, staring into the woods. He can't see us. Can he?

"Luze," he murmurs.

A chill runs down my spine.

Gideon glances around, as does Demelan.

"She's not here," Aslen says, her voice tight. "She crossed the wall. It's what any sane person would do."

I look at Iyanna. Her jaw is set, her shoulders tight.

"When the opportunity is there, we run," I whisper. Slowly, I push Arturon forward, out of the woods.

"*Luze!*"

Thyo has spotted me. He sends his horse forward to us. I gather up my reins, ready wheel Arturon and run. My heart pounds.

"Luze," he says again. He sounds frantic. His eyes are darker than usual, as though the pupil has swallowed the iris. "You're still here."

Every muscle in my body feels stiff. "I'm leaving, Thyo."

"Please," he says. "Let us discuss this."

"There's nothing more to say. If I have to fight you, I will."

I look past him. The others look astonished to see me, Aslen most of all.

There is a restless, almost uneasy quality to him, and I wonder again what kind of tonic he has taken. "You cannot simply leave. We discussed this. You agreed, when I told you of the secrets Altheara holds."

"That was before I knew you were planning war," I say.

He stills, and the change to stillness is so surprising, I flinch. "Your arms. You've been cut. What happened to you?"

Aslen has trotted her horse over to us. "What are you doing here?" She sounds angry.

I hear the double meaning—she can't speak freely, but she's not merely asking on Thyo's behalf. She's asking why I'm not long gone, not after the opportunity she gave me.

It isn't my place to try to protect them—any of them—anymore. But I can't leave without telling Thyo of his mother, of her plans. She has helped fuel this war, after all. I have to leave but if I am honest, if I take these precious few moments to explain, perhaps I can prevent this war.

"Your mother did this, Thyo," I say. I hold my wrists out. "She tried to take my magic for herself. This war suits her purposes. This war isn't necessary. You need to be more worried about what lingers in your kingdom, rather than anything across the wall. Your mother is dangerous."

Thyo looks at me like I'm insane. "My mother would never do such a thing, and even if she wanted to, she couldn't. She lost her power when I was born."

I am exhausted and confused; I don't know how to find the right words to convince him.

"It's true," Iyanna says. "You need to beware. All of you. Don't be fools."

I cut her a look. I don't think Iyanna has room to sound so righteous, but I don't correct her.

Thyo shakes his head. "None of this makes any sense. But it isn't important. Not right now. Luze, come back with us. You can tell me more of this story. You can explain. Just stay in Altheara. I was wrong before. Just—please. Don't leave."

His voice is desperate. *I was wrong before.* I stare at him, conflicted. Does he mean he won't attack Alos? Iyanna is silent next to me. The others are watching. Demelan has his hand on his sword; Aslen's mouth is pressed thin. Everyone seems to hold their breath.

"I return with you, and then what?" I ask.

His eyes seem to clear, just slightly. "I believe in the prophecy, Luze. You will save us. I believe in you. You are everything the Seer promised, and more. I love you."

I search Thyo's face. I had believed I deserved my exile. The loneliness of that existence, of living with that shame, had given me a desire to be loved above all else. I had broken myself into pieces for Clydon expecting him to do the same. All it had taken was the grasp of his hand, and I had lost myself. Have I done the same with Thyo?

The question is not whether I should trust Thyo. The question is whether I can trust myself. Perhaps the desire to be loved will always be my fatal flaw. Thyo wants me. But what do I want?

I take a breath. I look up at him, certainty settling over me even in the midst of this chaos.

"I'm sorry," I say. "Love isn't enough for me. Not anymore."

My heart breaks.

And then the Strin rip through the wall.

44

The scene in front of me suddenly dissolves into madness.

It happens so fast—one Strin. Then two.

It's my nightmares come to life.

Iyanna has wheeled her horse away as it tries to bolt. Underneath me, Arturon shies, yanking at the reins.

Demelan, Gideon, and Aslen all react immediately, drawing their weapons, shouting.

Thyo is the only one who doesn't, who reaches out, his hand outstretched, grasping Arturon's reins. "Wait—"

There's a bone rattling hiss, the sound of Aslen's arrow singing through the air, steel clashing from Demelan's blade—

The Strin are in a frenzy, and they will not be able to hold them off.

"Luze!" Iyanna is shouting at me. "*Now!*"

I try to kick Arturon away—he's already trying to run—but Thyo doesn't release the reins.

"Promise me," he says, his voice desperate. "Luze—"

What does he want me to promise? Arturon tries to bolt, his body going one way, and mine going the other. For a terrifying second, my foot gets caught in the stirrup, and I wonder if I will be dragged, but it falls free. My back hits the earth with a hard thud.

All in a blur, I see Thyo dismounting, the commotion behind him, that sickening, rattling sound of the Strin, the sound of Thyo drawing his sword. He unsheathes a dagger from his hip, tossing it to the ground next to me.

"Take it," he says to me. "Use it and—"

His words are cut off as Gideon yells—in pain, in anger, in fear, I don't know.

I push myself to my feet, groping for the dagger. Iyanna is suddenly there, still on her horse, trying to drag me along as everything spins around me. I hear an ear-piercing cry, as Aslen screams Demelan's name. He's on the ground, unmoving, and I don't know why, I don't know what's happened—

I hear an inhuman scream, this one more familiar, the sound of a horse in pain. I stumble, pulling myself away from Iyanna as I look around frantically, spotting Arturon trying to bolt as one of the Strin attacks him.

"No!" I scream, running toward him, gripping the dagger in my hand. "*No!*"

Arturon has fallen to the ground, squealing, and I hear the rattling hiss of the Strin as it opens its mouth, it's teeth glistening.

"*No!*" I scream again, my throat raw, and it catches the attention of the Strin. It rises, distracted, and Arturon struggles to his feet, running away.

There's a screech behind me, and I turn to see Thyo fighting the other Strin, his movements quicker and more fluid than I've ever seen. He slashes at its belly, creating a deep gash, rolling out of the way before it can return the favor.

Aslen is injured. Blood pours from her arm as she draws another arrow, her face contorted in pain. Gideon drags

Demelan, trying to get him out of the way. Blood pours from Demelan, from—somewhere. Everywhere. I can't tell. There's too much blood.

The Strin behind me screams, and there's the sound of bones breaking, followed by a ripping, tearing sound and a horrible stench.

I turn. The Strin is ripped apart, perhaps enough to kill it. I don't know how; Thyo has done something, used his shadow magic, maybe, but the other Strin, the one that has been approaching still comes for me, and if I don't move, I will die. I raise my dagger, ready to fight or to run to the wall. Ready to survive.

Which is when a third Strin rips through the barrier.

Someone grabs me, yanking me away. Thyo.

"Go," he shouts. "You have to go, there's too many—"

The third Strin is already upon us. Thyo shoves me aside, and I roll out of the way as his sword comes up to fight it, when I feel a claw against my back, a disgusting, rattling breath in my ear.

It's the other Strin, the one with ripped limbs; it hasn't died, it's merely weakened. I clench the dagger in my hand, determined to finish it, at the same time Thyo looks up, seeing me there, the Strin's claw poised to slice my throat. I hear Iyanna screaming something, distracting the Strin to Thyo's back, and then I stab, stab with all my might into the chest of the first Strin, the weakened one, because I know I can kill it—

Except Thyo has thrown himself in front of me, his sword arcing, decapitating the Strin, but the force behind my movement is too strong to stop. I feel the small, sickening catch of his ribs as my blade slides through his side and into his heart.

Into Thyo.

Another scream wrenches from me, unnaturally loud.

Thyo is frozen, his sword still gripping in his hands, the Strin's head falling to the earth, and then he, too, drops to the earth. My hands are still on the dagger, and it slides out as he falls. Blood pours from him.

"No, no, no, no, *no*—"

I scramble to the ground, tossing the dagger aside. I have to undo this, somehow, I have to, *I have to*—

I summon everything I have, every drop of magic. The bindings on my wrists slip, and I begin bleeding once more, but all I feel is the blood, no magic. I want to scream and scream and scream because I am too weak, and we're too far from the wall. I am fragile from what Seli has done to me, and whatever I do, it will not be enough. I can't let him die, not like this, not when so much between us has been broken and rebroken, so much unfinished.

I feel the undulation of shadow mingling with the blood that continues to pour into my hands.

"Luze," Thyo says, his lips barely forming the words.

Please, I pray. *Someone, anyone, anything. The Source, the gods, the Abyss. Anything.*

I feel the whisper of the shadows on my hands as they're coated in his blood, as my blood mingles with his. I lean closer, desperately trying to pour something into him, to take back what I have done.

Thyo shudders. Blood coats his lips, his skin deathly pale.

"No!" The word wrenches from me. "You will *not* die on me!"

I can hear and feel the chaos around me, as though I am in the eye of a storm. Gideon yelling something; an arrow singing past as Aslen lets it fly. Iyanna, a sword ringing from her hands. The Strin, that horrible screech, that horrible sound of bones breaking as they move.

"Luze," Thyo says again, trying to speak.

"I'm here." I grip the blood-soaked fabric of his shirt. "I'm here."

"I'm sorry," he breathes.

My eyes burn. "You're going to be okay, Thyo."

"I would have stopped the war," he murmurs. "For you."

Tears run down my face. "I'm going to fix you," I say shakily. "I will, Thyo."

He tries to shake his head, the movement barely decipherable. "Go." His lips form the words again. *Go.*

I notice a haze surrounding us, a visible dark mist, and I realize it's his shadows; it's the first time I've witnessed them fully formed.

He's trying to shield us. Shield me, with the precious last few seconds he has.

"I love you," I say. I don't know if it's true, but it's the only thing I have left to give him. "I love you. Just stay with me."

I hear it—just the barest breath of a word as he looks up at me.

Go.

I feel his heart still under my hand, and the blood stops flowing. His eyes stare straight up into the night sky. The only light in them is the reflection of the stars that shine above.

"Luze." Iyanna is there, yanking on my arm. Distantly, I notice the panic in her tone. "Luze, we have to leave."

Thyo is dead, and I have killed him.

I killed him.

I killed him.

I realize I'm speaking aloud as Iyanna drags me to the horses. There's a scream, unnaturally heart wrenching. Aslen, on the other side of the clearing, still fighting, using a sword, but now she's frozen, staring at Thyo.

"Gods," she says. "Gods, no, *Thyo*—"

I can't hear anything else aside from the blood rushing in my ears, from Iyanna physically hooking my foot into the stirrup and shoving me up, my leg swinging over Arturon automatically. My fingers are numb, but they clutch the reins.

"Now!" Iyanna is yelling. "Go, now!"

Her words are too similar to Thyo. It spurs something in me. We take off, pushing the horses into a gallop. Something is wrong with Arturon's gait; he's injured, but terror pushes him on, just as it does me. My body is moving of its own accord; my mind still sits on the earthen floor, feeling Thyo bleed out under my hands.

The Strin don't pursue us. No one pursues us. There's no one left. The others will be dead soon if they aren't already.

The boundary parts for us like silk. We ride through.

We are in Alos. The thought hits me. We are back in my kingdom. We are back in my home.

Every fissure of my body screams to turn around, to go back.

45

EVENTUALLY WE STOP to give the horses a break. Neither Iyanna nor I speak.

We stop by the stream that runs through this part of the Barren Forest. The wounds on my wrists have begun to heal, now that I am back in a land of magic. I plunge my hands into the water, washing the dried blood off my skin. Mine, and Thyo's. I'm grateful for the way the cold burns, waking me up. When I pull my hands from the creek, my silver ring, my Oath ring, slips and slides. Slowly, I pull it off. It sits in my palm, simple and innocuous.

I throw it into the rushing water.

I know what its removal means. I had completed my Oath. I had infiltrated Altheara. I had learned about the Galdrion, about the Wytches and magic that made them powerful.

And I had killed their prince.

I let out a gasp, folding over. I wonder if I will throw up, but nothing comes out.

"I killed him," I say. It's no more than a breath.

Iyanna is beside me at the stream. "He made the choice

to put himself between you and the Strin, in the path of your blow. It was his own fault."

I don't respond, though a feeling of hatred rises through me.

"It was an accident," she says. "And he was never going to let you go. Not really. You were his fiancée, and Prince Adriel never took kindly to losing what he considered his possession. He won't come after you now."

"He wasn't my fiancé." I stare at the snow lightly coating the earth. "He was my husband."

I think it's the first time I've ever seen her look shocked. "Your…husband? But the wedding ceremony never happened. That…that would mean…"

"We didn't want to wait for the ceremony." I feel an ache in my chest. "It was his idea. A small ceremony. Just for us."

She digests this information. "It doesn't matter. With Thyo dead, you have no ties to Altheara."

If only she knew. "I was coronized," I say.

Iyanna looks stunned. "That's impossible."

I stand, walking over to the bag still hooked onto Arturon's saddle. I pull out the scroll I have kept safeguarded in there. "Read it, if you must."

I hand it to her, and she unrolls it, scanning the document. Finally, she looks up. "But then this means…"

"That as soon as we married, I became queen of Altheara." I feel nothing as I say this. I'm simply numb.

"How?" Iyanna asks. "Why would Thyo agree to such a thing?"

"Because he loved me." I stare off into the forest. "Before I came here, I made an Oath to kill Thyo. I intended to break it, but if I couldn't, I needed a way to ensure my safety. Alos has been corrupted by my uncle. I wanted the Galdrion to fight by my side to reclaim my Crown. If Thyo had not agreed, or if I could not break my Oath…I would have made his death look like an accident. With Thyo's signature on that coronization, with the trust I had gained from the others, I would have remained queen. The Galdrion would have been mine to control."

Iyanna watches me warily. I sense her unease. What I have described are the actions of someone cold-hearted. A killer. A spy. An assassin.

"Just now, with the Strin," she says slowly. "When you stabbed Thyo. Was that—"

"An accident," I say. "I never meant for that to happen."

I'm not sure if she believes me.

The coronization had happened the same day as the one Thyo and I had spent on the rooftop, when he had told me he loved me. I knew I had a chance, then. A chance to take advantage of his trust.

I stare down at my remaining rings. The silver Oath ring is gone, but my gold ring from Taleas is there. On my ring finger, a Galdriel iron ring, black as shadow, remains—a symbol of my union to Thyo.

I don't tell Iyanna a truth: that I had loved Thyo and wanted it to be real.

When I had knelt in the snow the day my uncle deposited me in the Barren Forest, I had vowed that if I ever escaped my exile, I would do everything I could to gain power, to never be a victim again. That vow has led me here.

I have experienced too many betrayals, but I would have taken back Alos with Thyo. Until I had seen his plans for war, and known that we could love each other, but we would never be able to trust one another.

I had fallen in love with Thyo. That was my weakness. But I had protected myself. That was my strength.

Iyanna speaks again. "Queen Seli's rule would have passed on to Thyo as soon as he married. And if Thyo is dead, then rightfully, you are queen. You have to claim your rule."

I don't meet her eyes. "It doesn't matter now."

Not yet. But it will.

"A queen of two kingdoms," Iyanna says. "That's what you intend, isn't it?"

I ignore her. I go to Arturon, mounting him. "We need to go." I take a breath, feeling the beginnings of magic swirl over my skin. I had left Alos thinking I had no power, but now there's almost too much, even in my weakened state.

Iyanna doesn't argue, and we ride on.

Magic continues to undulate around me. It burns hot and cold, as though exploring my body and finding its place. I shiver at the way the magic trails down my spine. Every part of my body feels awake. It's as though I can feel beyond the reach of my own skin, further into the depths of the forest.

I can feel the creatures and beasts that lurk as Iyanna and I ride on. I feel them still in fear as they sense me, and my power. At the power that stretches far beyond me, returning only to whisper secrets. The creatures are afraid of me and the power that now shrouds me. A power tenfold of that which Thyo ever commanded, a power expanded by what I am and my birthright.

Thyo has died. He is really, truly dead. And I know this, with certainty, because somehow, in some way, I have taken something from him. I have taken a power that was never mine but was given to me through blood.

A power that I can feel settling into my bones, into my very soul.

After

I RIDE THROUGH the forest, both away and towards everything I wish I could outrun.

Grief and terror still pull at me, but underneath it my skin hums. A dark mist surrounds me, threading through my fingers, encircling my wrists.

I shake my hands, willing the shadows away, but they only cling tighter, winding through my veins, above and within my skin.

I have power.

They whisper to me, and I understand: they have been given to me, through violence and darkness, and now they crave my essence. They are alive, and they cling to me, craving me.

Craving my power.

My power feeds the darkness, but instead of simply claiming it, the darkness returns to me, grazing across my skin in what feels like a stroke of affection. I don't resist it.

I have power.

The power of shadow.

It's…intoxicating.

I welcome the shadows home.

Acknowledgements

First, to my parents—thank you for reading more drafts of this book than any two people reasonably should. Your patience, encouragement, and endurance in the face of version 37 (and 38, and 39…) are superhuman.

To my brilliant beta readers—Catherine, Whitney, and Alex—thank you for your kindness, your thoughtful notes, and your uncanny ability to spot plot holes I tried very hard to ignore. You made this story better.

To the therapists who helped me navigate the darker corners where the roots of this story came from—thank you for being as unflinching with me as I tried to be with Luze's journey. Your guidance helped bring this story to light.

To my dog, Azrael, and two cats, Bellatrix and Cleopatra—thank you for being my late-night writing companions, foot warmers, and snack managers. Your quiet presence (and occasional keyboard interference) kept me grounded.

Finally, to you—the reader—thank you for choosing this book and giving it your time and attention. If you made it to this page, I already like you a lot. Your support means the world to me.

LAYLA RAZ HANSON wrote her first book at eight years old—an illustrated epic about a runaway hamster that set off her desire to be an author. Many years and one Theatre degree from UC San Diego later, she's proud to be publishing her debut fantasy novel, this time with fewer rodents and—hopefully— better grammar. She's taught writing for over a decade while simultaneously pursuing a career in the medical field, and is deeply passionate about stories that mix adventure, emotion, and characters who make you feel seen. When she's not writing, you'll find her hanging out with her Husky-Malamute and two black cats, rewatching *The Mummy (1999)* or wandering through bookstores she probably shouldn't be left alone in.

*One of the best ways to support authors is by leaving
a review. I'd be honored if you would leave a review
for A Craft of Starlight via the link below.*

- Layla

https://www.amazon.com/author/laylarazhanson